David Lawson Johnstone

In the Land of the Golden Plume

A tale of Adventure

David Lawson Johnstone

In the Land of the Golden Plume
A tale of Adventure

ISBN/EAN: 9783337023928

Printed in Europe, USA, Canada, Australia, Japan

Cover: Foto ©Andreas Hilbeck / pixelio.de

More available books at **www.hansebooks.com**

IN THE

LAND OF THE GOLDEN PLUME

A TALE OF ADVENTURE

BY

DAVID LAWSON JOHNSTONE

AUTHOR OF 'THE PARADISE OF THE NORTH;' 'RICHARD TREGELLAS;
'THE MOUNTAIN KINGDOM;' ETC.

WITH SIX ILLUSTRATIONS
BY
W. S. STACEY

W. & R. CHAMBERS, LIMITED
LONDON AND EDINBURGH
1894

Edinburgh:
Printed by W. & R. Chambers, Limited.

CONTENTS.

LIST OF ILLUSTRATIONS.

IN THE LAND OF THE GOLDEN PLUME.

CHAPTER I.

PROLOGUE—FIVE YEARS BEFORE.

IT is now several years since the natives around Hamilton Gap, North Queensland, made the last attempt to frighten their white supplanters. In those days there were two homesteads at Hamilton, which, lying at the base of a range of scrub-covered mountains, nearly two hundred miles up country, was (and, for that matter, still is) the outpost of civilisation in that direction. The principal run included the low ground on both banks of the Hamilton River, and belonged to a settler named Maitland; the other, greater in extent, but not so valuable, comprising as it did the slopes of the hills, to Mr Dennison. Little Ruth Maitland could remember the time —it was before the date of her father's misfortune—when there were but five white people in the district, of whom she was the youngest, but not the least important. Then came Mr Dennison, followed in a year from Sydney by his two boys, Walter and Frank: the first playfellows she had known. For three years they had grown up together, sharing in each other's lessons and scrapes, mastering the queer dialect of the tame blackboys (natives), and listening together to their stories of the customs and exploits of their forefathers before the coming of the English, and their warnings of what their wild brethren might still do if the intruders neglected the smallest precaution. It was not long before these warnings were justified by the event.

Although Walter Dennison, the eldest of the three, was not more than eleven when the incident happened which begins this story, he is not likely to forget it while he lives. It was his first excursion with his father into the mountains, whither Mr Dennison was in the habit of exploring in search of gold. Two of their own blacks were with them, and they were returning after three days' delightful but unsuccessful journeying—delightful to Walter, notwithstanding the absence of adventures with the bushmen such as his imagination had led him to expect. Just as dusk had fallen, the little party of four arrived at a point within sight of home, and drew up to breathe their horses before beginning the descent into the plain. Suddenly Walter, who had dropped behind with one of the natives, was startled by a loud shout from his father.

'Here, Walter! Jimmy! Quick!'

Hurriedly they galloped up, to find Mr Dennison gazing eagerly in the direction of home.

'Look, boy!' he cried, pointing with his hand. 'What do you see? There—straight in front!'

Walter's eyes had already sought the spot, and made out a luminous appearance in the sky. An exclamation of dismay escaped from him: it could mean only one thing.

'Oh! the house is on fire, sir!'

'It looks like it, but'——

Here one of the blacks said something in his own language to his companion. Mr Dennison caught a single word, but it was enough to rouse a vague feeling of apprehension. He turned sharply upon the speaker.

'What! Blackboys?'

The black nodded.

'You're sure?'

'Yohi' (yes).

'And we've four miles to cover,' said Mr Dennison, as if to himself. 'On, then!' No more; but Walter happened to catch a glimpse of his father's face, and saw that it was white and stern-set.

If the instinct of the black was right, it was no time for lingering. So, Mr Dennison leading, they raced madly down-hill, escaping as by miracle a hundred dangers; and as they rode Walter thought of Frank, a year younger than himself, at the mercy perhaps of the wild, degraded, treacherous abor-igines from the bush. The tribes around Hamilton had never taken kindly to the white man. They had shown this several times by slaughtering the sheep and cattle, and, more than once, by cowardly attacks upon one or other of the shepherds. Attempts had been made to conciliate them; they had met them all with treachery. But for their whole-some dread of firearms, they would doubtless have attacked the settlement itself long ago. And Walter, as he remem-bered stories of their cruelty to Englishmen who had fallen into their hands in other parts of Queensland, shuddered to think of poor Frank's probable fate. And the rest? There were two white men on the run—Brunton, his father's overs-man, and a shepherd called Thomson. The boy had been left in charge of Brunton and several tame blacks of whose fidelity there could be no doubt; for the tame black, on the strength of a pair of shortened trousers and a few words of broken English, has the utmost contempt for his more savage fellows. There was one gleam of hope: the Maitlands' homestead was within a mile, on the other side of the river.

One mile—two miles—and the steepest and most dangerous part of the way had been traversed without mishap. Now and again, through the trees, they saw the gleam of the fire as they dashed along—Mr Dennison first, Walter close behind, the blacks at his heels. Then they emerged from the bush: in another minute they would pass the hut of the shepherd, Thomson.

'Stop!'

Walter pulled up by his father's side.

'We must see if Thomson is safe, Walter—if he is here,' said Mr Dennison.

The little cabin was just visible, looming blacker against the black of the night. As they approached the doorway, Mr Dennison called out softly. There was no answer. Then they noticed that the door was open—next moment, that a form as of a man was stretched across the threshold. Walter, scarcely realising, pressed forward.

'Is it'——

'Ah!' cried his father, quickly. Then, as he dismounted. 'Halt—no farther, Walter! Wait here.'

He took his father's bridle, and waited—watching him as he drew near, stooped over the body, and finally knelt down beside it and gently turned it over. Then he heard his summons:

'Come here, Walter!'

In a second he was off his horse and beside his father. And this is what he saw in the dim light: poor Thomson lying in his own doorway, his revolver by his side, his clothes saturated with blood from half-a-dozen ugly spear-wounds. The boy turned sick as he looked, and for a moment could grasp no more.

A touch of his father's hand on his shoulder recalled him to realities.

'Oh! is he dead?' he asked.

'Hours ago.   Poor Thomson!'

In a whisper.   'By the blacks?'

'By the blacks.   And foully murdered—see! the wounds are mostly behind.'

'And—and Frank?'

Mr Dennison did not reply, but went and picked up the dead man's revolver.   It still contained five charges: only one had been spent.

'Here, Walter—you may have to use it soon enough,' said Mr Dennison, in a hard tone.   Then he motioned to the boy to take poor Thomson's feet, and together they stumbled with the corpse into the hut and laid it on the bed. It was the least and, at the moment, the utmost they could do.

Outside, meanwhile, the two tame blackboys had been peering about in the manner of their race; and now a cry from Jimmy, the more intelligent of the pair, told Mr Dennison that the man had made a discovery.   Running out, followed by Walter, he perceived him standing over the dead body of a native, in whose heart Thomson's bullet had found its billet.   Walter scarcely glanced at it.

'And Frank?' he repeated, plucking at his father's sleeve. There was room in his head for but the one thought.

'Frank ! . . One instant first. Then '——

Turning to the blacks, he addressed them in their broken dialect. They knew of the murder of the shepherd: he told them of the probable danger of those at the homestead, and that themselves were about to venture into the thick of the fighting. Could he depend upon them to help him against the enemy ?

The answer was prompt.

'Me fight—me white man blackboy !' cried Jimmy, flourishing the dead native's spear.

'Yohi—me fight too !' cried his companion.

Then Mr Dennison, convinced by their tone of their sincerity, gave the word to continue the journey. Not more than four or five minutes had been spent at the hut, but the little party, haunted by the fear of what might await them, spurred on faster and yet faster. Fortunately there was now a well-defined track, familiar both to the horses and their riders ; and they had also the reflection of the fire, flickering behind the rampart of trees which surrounded the house, to guide and hasten them, if that were possible, on their way. The bush was strangely silent. Strain their ears as they might, Walter and his father could distinguish no sound but the drum of their animals' hoofs and the panting of the blacks behind. This until they were within half a mile of their destination ; and then, ringing out sharp and clear in the stillness, came the report of a couple of shots fired in quick succession. For the first time for half an hour they breathed freely : at the least, the besieged were still holding out.

'Thank God !' muttered Mr Dennison.

'Again !' cried Walter, as another volley rang out.

Five minutes later they drew up at the border of the

fringe of trees surrounding the homestead, dismounted, and waited while Mr Dennison crept forward to reconnoitre. He was back before the blacks had finished hobbling the horses.

'They have only fired the outhouse yet; the house itself seems all right,' he reported.

'Are there many?'

'A good few, I think. They haven't heard us, so we must take them in flank and try a surprise. Don't fire until I do; then, as quickly as you can. And shout, make a noise —you, Jimmy, Tommy, as well. Do you understand?'

'Yes.'

'Then come.'

With that he led the way through the wood in a transverse direction, so as to get well in front of the house without being seen by the enemy. Walter and the blacks, imitating his caution, trod closely in his footsteps. The main buildings stood in the middle of a great clearing, marked out by the boundary-line of trees, and were enclosed by a low paling-fence; and outside the fence were the yards for penning the sheep, and the outhouse which the savages had fired. Although it was now burning low, it still threw a strong light across the space between it and the house—thus giving the defenders, concealed in the shadow of the veranda, an immense advantage over the assailants. But evidently the latter, strong as they were in numbers, dared not attempt to carry the place by storm.

Walter had time to notice this as he crept round, and to notice also the group of forty or fifty natives gathered just beyond gunshot of the homestead. At last his father stopped. He had reached a spot in a direct line with the blazing hut, which was between him and the house, and much nearer to

the wood than to the latter. Not until then did the boy
understand the bold game they must play for success.

Mr Dennison held up his hand. 'Are you ready, Walter?'
he asked.

'Yes.'

'Do as I do, then. And mind! don't break cover until
you see me doing it.'

Next moment the struggle had begun. Mr Dennison
fired; Walter, pointing his revolver at the group of blacks,
did likewise; and Jimmy and the other native, unwilling to
be mere spectators, contributed a most unearthly and awe-
inspiring howl. Then, without waiting to see the result,
Mr Dennison and Walter changed their position and again
fired, rapidly but carefully; and did so—Jimmy and Tommy
materially aiding to deceive—until it must have seemed to
the surprised savages that a large party lay concealed in the
wood. The issue was hardly doubtful for an instant. Those
in the house, hearing the welcome shots, responded with a
volley and a loud cheer. Taken by surprise, and conceiving
themselves caught between two fires, the besiegers hesitated
only a minute before they turned tail and fled,* followed by
parting shots from Walter and his father as they scurried
across the clearing to gain the shelter of the wood. It was a
complete rout.

Mr Dennison and Walter, leaving the friendly blacks to
see after their dead and wounded kinsmen, hastened towards
the house. 'It's us, Brunton—Walter and I,' shouted the
former, heedless of grammar. 'Are you all safe?'

* It should be repeated that the aboriginal inhabitants of Queensland,
members of one of the most degraded of human races, had an almost
superstitious dread of firearms. To this fact many a settler has owed his
life.

The oversman appeared on the veranda steps. 'Ay, barring poor Thomson, Mr Dennison,' he answered.

'And Frank?'

'Here I am, father!' cried that young warrior, showing his flushed and eager face—and not forgetting, even in his excitement, to display a revolver with all the pride of one who has just used it to some purpose.

Another defender now came forward in the person of Sam Price, one of Mr Maitland's men from across the river, who had been sent by his master to help, and had managed to get into the house without the knowledge of the enemy. By him and the rest, including the half-dozen faithful natives, Mr Dennison's opportune arrival was warmly hailed. Brunton's story was soon told. The trouble, it appeared, originated the day after his employer's departure, when he had occasion to whip one of the blackboys—a lazy and evil-disposed rascal who had lately been taken on—for some slight act of theft. The man disappeared; but as this was quite a common effect of punishment, no more was thought of the matter. On the afternoon of that day, however, one of the other blacks appeared with the astounding intelligence that a large force of 'wild men' were in the vicinity, and had already speared Thomson. He had been a witness of the murder, had seen that the fugitive was of the party, and in great fear had run all the way to the homestead to give the alarm. Brunton's precautions were speedily taken. First he had sent a native to warn the Maitlands, whence he was to go on to Baronga, the nearest station of the black police,* twenty-five miles through the bush. Then the horses were stabled, and everybody was withdrawn into the house. When at last the

* The black police, an efficient body of mounted natives, recruited from different tribes, and officered by white men.

bushmen appeared, they were received so warmly that they made really no serious attempt to attack the homestead; and thereafter the defenders succeeded in keeping them at a safe distance by firing upon them as soon as they ventured within gunshot. In this they were assisted after dark by the light of the burning hut.

Jimmy now came in with the information that the bushmen had left five of their number behind them—all dead, he added significantly. Then the report of a distant shot was heard.

'They have attacked the Maitlands!' cried Mr Dennison. 'Quick! we must ride over to their help!'

'What if it's a trick?' asked Brunton, who was a cautious man.

'A trick! It isn't likely. And even if it is, there's poor Maitland to consider.' For Mr Maitland, you must know, had lately lost the use of his legs owing to an attack of paralysis: a misfortune which, little as he complained of it, rendered the prompt help of his neighbours all the more necessary. Brunton saw this, and changed his ground.

'And the lads?'

'They must come with us. Yes: take your rifles and revolvers. Are yours reloaded, boys? Mind and keep close to me. Ah! there are the horses. Are you ready? Now!'

Of the exciting events of the next half-hour the boys retain but a confused recollection: the swift ride down to the river, the faithful blacks following on foot—the fording of the water—the sight of the Maitlands' homestead in flames—the quick retreat of the cowardly bushmen on their approach, chased to cover by Brunton and Price—ending with the rescue of the Maitlands from the house, to which the natives, adding experience to cunning, had managed in some manner to set fire. They were not a minute too soon, for at least half of the building was blazing merrily. As the Dennisons galloped up, leaving it to Brunton and Price to prevent a return of the routed enemy, two of Maitland's men burst out with little Ruth.

'Just in time, sir!' cried one of them, gently seating the girl on the ground. 'We'd about given up hope when we heard your shots; guessed we had only the choice of being roasted or speared.'

'And Mr Maitland?'

'Waiting his turn, sir. Insisted that the missie should be taken first.'

Dismounting, Mr Dennison turned to his sons. 'I trust her to you, boys,' he said. 'I am going inside for Mr Maitland.'

Crossing the clearing with the two men, he plunged into the burning house; and Walter, as he watched the flames running along the veranda and up the walls until they licked the roof, wondered if he would ever reappear. Frank had no such doubts.

'Don't be afraid, Ruth,' he was saying with his bravest air to the little girl. 'You're all right now. Look! I've got a revolver.'

But Ruth, notwithstanding her implicit faith in Frank, refused to be comforted until presently her father was carried out, chair and all, by Mr Dennison and one of the men, the other following with the strong-box. Little else was saved except the firearms and some clothing, and these only at considerable risk.

'I'm sorry for your books, Maitland,' said Mr Dennison. 'It won't be easy to replace them.'

'I'm thankful we've saved our lives—or, rather, that you've saved them for us, my friend,' replied the other. 'I must say it's more than I expected at one time.—Ah! there goes the roof!'

Fiercely blazed the dry timber of the house, and each of the little group had his own thoughts as he stood there in the reflection waiting for the end. Mr Dennison recalled his first visit to the cosy homestead four years before, when, wearied and worn-out by a twelvemonth's 'prospecting' in the mountains, unsuccessful, deserted by his companions, he had lighted by chance upon the place, and discovered in its master a cultured gentleman and a friend. He had set out after his wife's death in search of gold, leaving his children in good hands at Sydney; and, unlucky and disheartened, he had closed readily with Maitland's proposal that he should take up a vacant run near him. Did he regret it? Well, for three years he had had the boys beside him—for Maitland, after his illness, had offered to undertake their education, and he, observing his friend's success with Ruth, had gratefully accepted—and that was something. But now and again the old fits of restlessness, the desire to wander, had attacked and in some cases, more particularly of late, almost overcome him. Could he resist them much longer?—So he deliberated, while meantime his neighbour was a grim witness of the destruction of his home.

Presently Brunton and Price rode up, bringing the news that the bushmen were in full retreat towards the mountains, tracked by several of the faithful blacks. Nothing more could be done, they said, until the arrival of the black police.

'Except make yourselves comfortable with me for the present,' said Mr Dennison.

'For an indefinite time, I 'm afraid.'

'Oh! I don't know,' put in Brunton. 'We 'll soon run up a new homestead for you, Mr Maitland, and take good care not to give the blackboys another chance. Trust the troopers for that.'

The troopers arrived next morning, and, to do them justice, did not belie the oversman's confidence. Accompanied by Mr Dennison and two of the men, they set out immediately to punish the savages for Thomson's murder and their other misdeeds. The track to the mountains was marked out by the carcasses of sheep and cattle wantonly butchered. On the second day the tribe was surprised in camp, and—to cut short a long story—received such a lesson that the survivors never afterwards ventured near the settlement of Hamilton Gap.

A week afterwards, when the detachment of police had returned to Baronga, Mr Dennison and his guest were seated in the veranda discussing the future. Maitland made some remark about the rebuilding of his house.

'Is it necessary?' asked Mr Dennison. 'The fact is, Maitland, I was just about to ask you to stay here for good. Wait a minute! What would you say if I told you that I had determined to go on the tramp again, and wanted to ask you to do me a favour? There's the run, but Brunton can manage that as well as myself. As for the boys, I thought that if you didn't mind they might stay here under your eyes—I should like nothing better. In that case, of course,' he added, 'there would be no necessity to build another house.'

Maitland thought for a minute or two. 'You mean to make a long journey, then?' he said.

'To New Guinea, no less.'

'New Guinea!'

'Yes. To tell the truth, Maitland, I have the fit very badly this time. You know the reason. I've told you already of the promise I made to my poor father just before he died. I've been trying to fulfil it ever since—it's twelve years ago now—and I'm as far from success as ever. I seem to have no luck in this country, and so I mean to try if I have any better in another.'

'And why have you chosen New Guinea?'

'Well, I hardly know. I have always had an interest in it, I think. For one thing, it's a new and unexplored country, lying just at our door, inviting us to walk in ; for another, by all accounts there's gold in it. And, somehow, I have a presentiment that my luck will change. I might have gone long ago if it hadn't been for—well, for various things.'

Maitland nodded. He understood and appreciated his friend's delicacy in not referring to his misfortune.

'Now there's a favourable opportunity,' Dennison went on. 'The bushmen are disposed of for the next ten years at least, and the Gap's safe for the first time. And the boys are growing up to be of use.'

Maitland smiled. 'In a word, your mind is made up?' he said.

'Yes.'

'Then you must have your way, I suppose. I'm not surprised, for I've been expecting this for the last year.' He held out his hand. 'I won't say I'm glad, but I wish you luck with all my heart!'

'And you agree to my proposal?' asked Maitland, when they had shaken hands.

'I'll do more, old fellow. With Brunton's help I'll do

the best I can to manage your run along with my own.
When do you leave ?'

'In about a fortnight.'

He left sixteen days later.

.   .   .   .   .

Five years passed, and the wanderer did not return. They
heard from him once, about two years after his departure,
when he had visited the coast to prepare for a new journey
into the interior; and in the letter he had warned them
not to be anxious if a long time elapsed without news
of him. Anxious they were, however; and it was to relieve
their anxiety that Captain Barkham came to Hamilton Gap,
in the manner I have now to relate.

CHAPTER II.

'BUSHED' IN NORTH QUEENSLAND.

MORNING in North Queensland. In the middle of the bush a few acres of scrub had been cleared, the ground planted with various tropical fruits and vegetables, a house and a few rude huts erected, and the result was Baronga, the capital of a district as large as an English county. As yet the population consisted only of a lieutenant of the native troopers and a dozen men, with their wives and several children. Here it was that Captain Barkham, on his way from Cooktown to Hamilton Gap, had spent the night as the lieutenant's guest; and, having breakfasted, was now getting ready to resume his journey.

'How far by the road, did you say?' he asked.

'Close on forty miles. But it's roundabout.'

'And by the bush?'

'Not more than twenty-five.'

Captain Barkham considered. 'The Bingi may be trusted, you think?'

'The blackboy? I don't see why he shouldn't. You may depend upon it he'll play straight until he gets his money.'

'Then I guess I'll take the bush, lieutenant. This

cruising about on horseback don't exactly suit me—too much of it, at least—and so the sooner I get to Hamilton Gap the better I'll be pleased. If the horse is ready?' ——

The black face of a native corporal appeared in the doorway.

'Horse out, Joe?' inquired the lieutenant.

'Yohi.'

'Stonewall ready to start?'

'Sleepum very fast. Me kick um?'

The lieutenant nodded, knowing well that no gentler method was like to prove effectual, and with a grin of expectation his subordinate departed. A savage enjoys nothing more than to kick another savage.

The lieutenant and his guest followed him into the open air, where the whole population had turned out to witness the start, so seldom was it that Baronga had a white visitor. The captain mounted with some difficulty, being more familiar with the deck of a ship than the back of a horse, however quiet; and the troopers, faithful to discipline, refrained from smiling on seeing that their commander's face was solemn. Then Corporal Joe, having succeeded in rousing Stonewall, drove him forward with the butt-end of a carbine gently applied. Captain Barkham looked at the man rather doubtfully: he was undersized, as dirty and evil-looking as any of his fellows, and clad only in a loin-cloth. Perhaps he suffered by contrast with the trim policemen, in their uniforms of blue faced with red.

The lieutenant noticed the glance.

'Oh! don't judge the poor fellow by his looks,' he said, laughing. 'I daresay he's all right. All the same'—in a lower tone—'it may be wise to keep your hand on your revolver. They're curious cattle these half-wild beggars.'

'He knows his orders?'

The lieutenant repeated them to Stonewall, who nodded indifferently in response.

'And in case of accident,' the captain went on, 'I'm to head almost direct west, bearing latterly a little to the south?'

'Just a point.—Right?'

The captain seated himself squarely on his steed. 'Right!' he answered.

'Good-bye. Give my regards to Maitland and the boys.'

'Good-bye!'

Touching up his horse, he followed the guide, who looked neither to the right nor to the left, into the bush. The lieutenant watched them until they were out of sight, smiling a little at the rigid, awkward seat of the seaman : whereupon, emboldened by his example, the entire population showed its teeth in a general grin of amusement, and was happy.

For three hours or so Captain Barkham continued his journey through the bush without misadventure. Not an incident broke the monotony. The sky was without a cloud, but the heat was not oppressive to a man habituated to a tropical climate, and there was sufficient shade to make gratitude possible. The captain, being by nature unobservant, saw little of the beauty of the scene—trees festooned with vines, gorgeous orchids growing wild in the scrub, gigantic ferns of divers varieties, and here and there a little glade carpeted with the sweetest grass. Even to the parrots chattering in the tree-tops, or the groups of kangaroos and wallabies which fled at his approach, he paid little attention. He was thinking of his schooner lying in Cooktown harbour, and wishing with all his heart that his mission was successfully accomplished and he at sea again. For, truth to tell, the worthy captain was not at all comfortable in the saddle. Like most sailors, he was a timid rider, though, indeed, the horse was extremely docile ; the route was of the roughest ; and, above all, he was oppressed by a feeling of profound solitude. He had tried conversation with the black, but the result was not encouraging.

' Hey, Bingi—Stonewall—whatever you 're called—how far now, eh ?'

' Eh ?—yup—yup—worru !'

' Hamilton, stoopid—how far ?'

The black stared, wriggled his body, and politely returned the same answer.

'Don't you understand plain English, ebony-face ? Here ! Ham-il-ton '—pronouncing the words very slowly and distinctly—'Mister Maitland—how long to go yet ? Three hours, eh ?'

Stonewall rubbed his stomach reflectively. 'Yup—yup— bodgeree—wotsee ?' he inquired.

'Then you don't understand English ?'

'Yup—yup '——

The captain groaned. 'That will do,' he interrupted, and with sorrow gave up the attempt.

Grinning, the black went on. Paths and landmarks there were none—nothing but the flat, unending bush—but Stonewall found his way with the unerring instinct of his race. His movements were most erratic. Generally he kept well in front, throwing an occasional glance over his shoulder to see that his charge was safe. Sometimes he would stop to examine a gum-tree for fresh traces of the opossum, or with wonderful dexterity clear away the undergrowth in the horse's path with a few blows of his tomahawk : all in an agile manner pleasant to witness.

Captain Barkham's misfortunes began immediately after lunch, which was partaken of at noon by the side of a little spring.   Although he shared with Stonewall the modest repast of sandwiches made up by his kind-hearted host of Baronga, the savage did not appear to be satisfied, for he resumed his search for a tender 'possum to eat as dessert.   For a little, while he smoked a pipe, the captain lay on his back and watched him as he flitted from tree to tree and carefully inspected the trunks.   At last he came upon one on which some of the scratches were fresher than others, and of the kind made by the animal when ascending rather than when descending—good evidence to the initiated that an opossum was concealed above.   Half-turning, he shouted something.

'Eh?   What's that?' asked the captain.

'Potsum, missa!   Shs!' he answered, and began to climb the tree.

The captain, no wiser than before, got up.   As it happened, he was ready to go; and, being anxious to reach his destination, he saw no reason for putting off time while his guide, as he imagined, amused himself.   So, having mounted, he hallocd to the black to come down.   Stonewall continued to ascend.   He was twenty feet above the ground, and, whether he understood the captain or not, was evidently in no mind to give up his quest.   Barkham repeated the order: Stonewall replied with some gibberish, but did not obey.   For the captain, who was accustomed to prompt obedience, this was too much, especially from a naked savage.   If words were ineffectual, he must try the effect of a threat.   He drew his revolver.

'You've half a minute,' he said, pointing it at the fellow, 'and if you ain't down then'—a significant click ended the sentence.

'Here, come back!   Come back, I say!'

Poor Stonewall may not have comprehended the speech, but the mere sight of the firearm was quite enough to drive all thoughts of the opossum, and much else, from his head. With a look of mortal dread on his countenance, he slid down the smooth trunk. The captain smiled to himself at the success of his ruse—and then, a moment later, the smile died away. For the black, apparently believing in the captain's sincerity, had no sooner touched ground than he had taken care to put the tree between him and the revolver, and was now to be seen making off into the bush. The threat had been just a little too effectual.

'Hey, there! Where on earth are you going?' cried Barkham.

Stonewall ran on.

'Here, come back! Come back, I say!'

Still the black ran on. Then, in desperation, the captain fired into the air. He hardly knew what he did, but assuredly it was the worst thing he could have done. Stonewall was already half-mad with terror: the report confirmed him in his suspicions, and completed the work begun by the sight of the pistol. In a minute he was out of view amongst the trees.

Gradually Barkham recovered, and faced the situation in which, through ignorance of native peculiarities, he had placed himself. Pursuit was hopeless. His guide had, beyond doubt, disappeared for good. And there he was in the heart of the bush, with only a general idea of the direction to his destination, and less notion of the distance. If he had not been a man of courage, with confidence in himself, he might well have been dismayed by the prospect. What he did was, mentally, to shake himself together. For, guide or no guide, there was no alternative but to go through with it, and that as speedily as possible.

His first step, after having come to this determination, was to shape his route by the aid of the sun, and set out towards the west. It was not long before he missed the help of his late companion, whose knowledge or instinct had led him to choose the more open parts of the bush. Being without either the knowledge or the instinct, the captain found himself plunging deeper and deeper into dense scrub, and that, too, when there was no tomahawk to clear a way for him. Progress was slow in the extreme, and became more difficult with every step; the feeling of solitude, heavy enough in the forenoon, burdened him now with tenfold force; and for the first hour the traveller needed all his doggedness and all his courage to keep his heart from sinking. Then there was a change—for the worse. The ground began to fall and the vegetation to vary, and quite suddenly the captain was made aware by the bogging of his horse that he had reached marshy ground.

'Guess I must get out of this,' he said to himself, as the animal floundered about.

It was no easy matter, however; and a wide circuit had to be made, and various small streams crossed, before dry ground was regained. Half an hour was spent in the effort, but it was to some advantage, for now there was less and thinner undergrowth.

The captain pulled rein to deliberate.

'Seems to me we're in a big mess, lad,' he confessed to the patient horse. 'Better have taken the road, forty miles and all, eh? As to what's to be done—— But stop!' slapping his leg with vigour as an idea struck him. 'The very thing! Curious, now, I never thought of that before.

Yes: I'll give you your head, my beauty; you should know the run of these parts better than me, and we'll see if we can't do without that blessed nigger after all. So on you go!'

For a time the plan seemed to work well. The horse, finding the reins loosened, walked on—leisurely, indeed, but apparently in the right direction. For the second time the captain congratulated himself on his idea, and for the second time somewhat prematurely. The animal jogged on just as far as it suited its own purposes. Coming at last to a little glade, it stopped to graze upon the sweet grass, and refused obedience to its master's gentle exhortations to proceed. From exhortations the captain fell back upon deeds, and—concerning the immediate sequel, and how it happened, he had afterwards the most hazy notion. But, somehow or other, he came to himself lying at the base of a giant eucalyptus, bruised and sore, while the steed was following the example of the errant Stonewall. When at length he managed to rise, it was nowhere to be seen.

At first Captain Barkham scarcely realised his position; he was more anxious regarding the extent of his injuries. Then, all at once, some idea of the truth burst upon him.

'Let us see,' he said aloud. 'Horse gone—nigger gone —no food—adrift in foreign parts without bearings or compass—the night coming on—worse and worse, by the Lord Harry! But it can't be far to Hamilton Gap now, surely. Stop! What if I've missed it?—West by south, was it?—Anyway, it's plain I can't stay here. Horse or no horse, nigger or no nigger, I must go on—till I drop.'

He was bruised on the side and shoulder, but the fact was forgotten in the greatness of his peril. Much as he realised, however, he did not realise all. He had heard many and gruesome stories of like adventures, which to a sailor had seemed to smack of exaggeration and want of verisimilitude; and even now, as he set his face to his journey, he was only beginning to have some idea of that which lay before him. Meanwhile, there was but the one thought in his mind: to go on and on. In the end he must reach Hamilton—or somewhere. So on and on he went, heeding nothing but the fact that he was covering ground and, as he imagined, drawing nearer and nearer to his destination. For two hours this continued. After the first, he failed to glance at the sun to see if he were going in the right direction; after the second, to notice whether the scrub underfoot was thick or the opposite. Gradually the feeling of fatigue mastered him, but there was no sign yet of any habitation. At last he was compelled to halt. He looked around him: the scene seemed familiar. The little glade—the great gum-tree at the foot of which he had fallen—neither admitted of any doubt. In a word: he was following his own track in a circle, and had returned to the spot from which he had started an hour ago!

He was bushed.

For five minutes he stood as if spell-bound, trying to understand it; and then, with a groan of despair, he threw himself upon the grass. So this was the end of all his exertions! Plainly, it was useless to continue the unequal struggle. He was both hungry and dead tired; and, to make matters worse—as if they were not bad enough already—his bruises began to smart most painfully.

Bushed! Again he called to memory the tales he had heard of men who had wandered into the bush, never to come back; of others who had lost their way, and strayed for days and days, living on roots and berries; even of some who had got out in the end, but only with the loss of reason. And more than ever he regretted the cabin of the *Bird of Paradise*, the little schooner which lay at that moment in the harbour of Cooktown, unloading her cargo of shells and copra. Should he ever see her again? To his mind, the chances were against it; but if he did, he was ready to make a vow that this first parting from her on a long journey into the interior should be the last. But the chances were indeed against it. Even the parrots, mocking him from their posts in the tree-tops, could have told him that.

Thus one thought chased another through Captain Barkham's head as he lay, and all of them were black. It was while they were blackest that he heard a familiar sound, coming apparently from no great distance, and incontinently jumped to his feet with every sign of being mad save that he listened intently. Again it came—a gunshot, followed by a long, piercing cry which there was no mistaking.

'Coo—ey! Coo—oo.—ey!'

The captain, scarcely daring to credit his good fortune, drew his breath hard before he gave back the shout: 'Coo—ey! Coo—ey!'

There was an interval of a minute: it seemed an hour to the impatient listener. Then he was answered.

CHAPTER III.

THE HOMESTEAD OF HAMILTON GAP.

ON the morning of the same day, while Captain Barkham was following Stonewall into the bush, Frank Dennison was hammering at the door of his brother's room in the homestead of Hamilton Gap with all the impetuous eagerness of his fifteen years. His brown, handsome face was flushed with the exercise; there was a mischievous look in his eyes; and, being full of important news which he was burning to impart, he spared neither knuckles nor feet in the attempt to gain entry. But the door remained locked, and at length Frank was forced to use his voice.

'Walt!'

There was no answer.

'Walter!'

Still no answer.

'Open the door, Walter! I've a message for you.'

This drew forth a response. 'What is it? Out with it!'

'Open the door, first.' Persuasively: 'It's too important to be shouted through the keyhole—really it is. Honour bright, Walt!'

Walter took no notice: it was for the purpose of avoiding the intrusion of his brother that, having work to do, he had locked the door.   After a short interval the play of boot and knuckles began again.   He bore it for five minutes.

'You may as well go away, young 'un,' he said, losing patience at last.   'You needn't try to get in—I can't go out with you this morning.'

'It isn't that.   I met Brunton, and he says he has told Mr Maitland about last night.'

· 'If that's all'——

'It isn't.   Mr Maitland wants to see you.'

'Oh!'   There was a change in Walter's tone.   'Where is he?'

'In the veranda.'

'Tell him I'll be there in a minute.   And don't be afraid, Frank; it's only another row, I'll be bound.   Now be off, and let me get my work done.'

'How long will you be?   Jimmy says he saw an emu not an hour ago.'

Now, as it happened, the emu (or Australian ostrich) was rarely seen in the vicinity of Hamilton, and Walter had long wished to shoot one.   He perceived the pitfall, and avoided it.

'Can't be helped!'

'But you know you've always wanted to see one,' insisted Frank.

'It must wait.   Be off, or'——

He had no need to finish his sentence.   Frank knew —none better—the capacity of his brother's patience, and thought it wise to obey.   He went off whistling.

Walter leaned back in his chair to think.   In personal appearance he was very like Frank; he had the same tangle of hair, the same blue eyes, the same mischief-loving twinkle; but he was taller and more firmly knit, and at times—but only at times—he had a graver demeanour. Between the two, so near in age, and brought up side by side far from other companionship, there was the closest bond of union. As Mr Maitland was wont to put it, smiling in his quiet way, they were always in hot water together. It was of one of these scrapes that Walter was now thinking, not without perturbation. Brunton had seen Mr Maitland—he knew the meaning of that. Mr Maitland wished to see *him*—he could guess the meaning of that. At the utmost it meant a lecture; but a lecture from their guardian was perhaps that of all things most dreaded by the boys.

'Best to have it over as soon as possible,' he said to himself, philosophically. 'But first I must get these beastly sums done. Here goes!'

With that he bent over the accounts he was comparing for Mr Maitland, and in the course of twenty minutes had finished the work. Then, gathering up the papers, he went forth to meet his doom.

He found Mr Maitland in his usual place in the veranda. Every morning after breakfast the chair was wheeled thither, and there the settler received his subordinates, issued his orders, and exercised his rule over the whole station. A mighty change had taken place during the five years which have elapsed since the outbreak of the blacks and Mr Dennison's departure. The homestead, larger itself, was now surrounded on three sides by a garden, while the outhouses and sheep-pens had been removed beyond the fringe of trees, towards the base of the hills. There Brunton, the oversman, had his house. But it was on the low-lying ground on both banks of the river that there was the greatest change. Instead of pasturage, you now saw vast plantations of the sugar-cane; the site of the old homestead was occupied by the manufactory; and the place of the blackboy had been taken by the gentler and more industrious labourer from Polynesia. For Mr Maitland had been quick to recognise the suitability of the land for sugar-growing, and one of the first to take advantage of the importation of Kanaka labour. The conversion of his own run was now complete; but under Brunton the Dennison run, which had been extended into the hills, was still devoted to the raising of sheep and cattle.

All this, of course, had happened while the boys were too young to bear a share of the work. Notwithstanding, Mr Maitland had found time to educate them and little Ruth—and to educate them well, as they were to discover in after years. Only from books had they any idea of the great world on the other side of the equator; and Walter, alone of the three, gave a passing thought of wonder that a man like his tutor should bury himself so far from his fellows, with no companion except his Shakespeare, and no communication except an occasional business letter from Sydney or Cooktown.

This morning he was bending over his writing-table, which was littered with papers. He looked up as Walter approached. 'Are they all right?' he asked.

'I think so, sir.'

'Thanks.' He signed to the boy to sit down. 'And what is this complaint of you I hear from Brunton, Walter?' he went on.

Walter, feeling that his hour was come, plunged into his justification. 'I'm very sorry, sir, but really it was too good a chance'——

'What was?' inquired his guardian, interrupting. 'You forget that I don't know the story.'

'Oh! I thought Brunton had told you. Well, it was in this way. Frank and I were passing Brunton's house last night on the way home from the hills—we were getting those specimens you wanted, you remember—and chanced to look in. You know Brunton's hammock, sir? It hangs in the veranda, pretty low down. Well, Brunton was lying in it asleep, and near at hand was his bath-tub full of water.' He broke off, and looked into Mr Maitland's face. 'Now, what would you have done, sir?' he asked innocently.

Mr Maitland smiled. 'I can guess what *you* did, at any rate,' he said.

'We couldn't resist it, sir. And he had no business having the tub there if he didn't want people to use it. So we quietly drew it under the head of the hammock, and untied the head-ropes. Then we let the thing down gently till Brunton's head was within a foot of the water, when '—— He stopped again, as the memory of the prank proved too much for his gravity.

'Yes—when?'

'That was all. We let go, and hid ourselves under the veranda.'

'And what happened?'

'We heard a splash, and then Brunton got up and began to swear fearfully. Oh! it was an awful row, sir. This went on for a while, and after a bit we crept round to the corner of the house, and Frank shouted to him not to lose his temper. Then we bolted. But you would have laughed yourself to see him staring after us, with the water dripping from his beard, and not a word to say!—and,' he concluded, remembering his cue, 'I'm very sorry, sir.'

'Well, you must settle the matter with Brunton as best

you can,' said Mr Maitland; and, much to Walter's relief, he did not seem very angry. 'I've given him full powers, and advised him not to be sparing in the use of them. But really, Walter'—laying his hand affectionately on the boy's shoulder—'isn't it about time you were thinking of giving up these tricks? You're almost a man, remember.'

'I'll try, sir,' replied Walter, penitently. It was not the first time he had promised the same thing.

'And speak to Frank—I'm afraid he's as bad as you.— But it wasn't that I wanted to talk to you about, Walter,' continued Mr Maitland, with a change of tone. 'The fact is, I have a letter here which should interest you. I got it this morning.'

'A letter, sir?'

'Yes. Where did I put it? Ah! here it is. It is from Her Majesty's Commissioner in New Guinea, in answer to one I wrote him a month or two ago.'

'About—about my father?' Walter was serious enough now, for this was the one subject which was never long absent from his thoughts. Ever since they received Mr Dennison's last letter, three years before, there had been anxiety, and always anxiety, at Hamilton Gap in regard to him. Walter himself was too young to take other than a hopeful view; but as for his tutor, little as he cared to disturb the boy's peace of mind, he had not (latterly, at least) been altogether able to conceal his misgivings.

'About your father,' he answered gravely. 'You remember our last talk, when you proposed to go in search of him? Well, I wrote the very next day, for with you I thought it time that some inquiries were made. And this is the reply.'

Walter waited in suspense while he opened out and read the letter again.

'Is it good?' he could not refrain from asking.

'N-no. I can't say it is, Walter. Put shortly, it says that nothing whatever has been heard of your father—good or bad. One of·the Deputy-commissioners had lately been at the village he started from three years ago, but at that time nothing was known of him. Mr Douglas adds that probably he or the Deputy will pay a second visit to the place in the course of a few months, when he promises to make full inquiry and let me know. Until then, Walter,' he said, folding up the letter, 'I fear we can do nothing.'

'Is that all, sir?' asked Walter. 'May I see the letter?'

Mr Maitland hesitated for a moment, and then handed it to him. 'There is only an expression of the Commissioner's opinion,' he said. 'Perhaps, after all, you had better read it for yourself.'

Walter did so. His guardian had given him the sense of the contents—with the exception of the last sentence, in which the writer expressed the fear that, considering the duration of Mr Dennison's absence, and the want even of rumours regarding him, he had fallen a victim either to the climate or to the enmity of hostile tribes in the interior. Walter became thoughtful.

'Well?' inquired Mr Maitland.

'I don't believe it, sir!' he cried.

'And what grounds have you for putting up your opinion against Her Majesty's Commissioner's, pray?'

'Somehow, I feel he's not dead—he can't be! So many other things may have happened to him, you know.'

'For instance?'

'Oh! he may be a prisoner, or be lying wounded or ill

somewhere up country. Anyway, sir, I think we should try to make sure!'

Mr Maitland smiled at the boy's vehemence. 'That is, go in search of him, I suppose? And how do you propose to do it? New Guinea isn't one of the Fiji Islands, remember. In size it is almost a continent, and more unknown than the heart of Africa.'

'I know all that, sir. But where there's a will there's a way, and with your help,' he said, confidently, 'I'm sure we could find one.'

Here the conversation was interrupted by the sudden appearance in the paddock in front of the house of a horse at full gallop, bearing upon its back both Frank and Mr Maitland's little daughter. Her father did not fail to notice that Ruth, who was seated behind the boy, was holding him very securely by the waist, and to be somewhat amused thereat; nor could Walter, on his part, repress a start of amazement when presently he recognised the animal by head-mark.

'Surely there's a scarcity of horses somewhere,' remarked Mr Maitland, suspecting nothing, 'or perhaps it's only another of Master Frank's experiments.—As to what you say, Walter, I don't know that you're altogether wrong. But if you care to abide by my advice ——

'You know I will, sir!' cried Walter.

'In that case, I think we should wait until the Commissioner has made the inquiry he promises.'

'And then?'

'Then we can discuss the matter with some certainty. At present, we can't. But here are the scapegraces—no more just now. I leave you to tell Frank as much of this as you please.'

By this time the horse had been pulled up in front of the veranda, and Walter ran down to help Ruth to alight. That done, Frank rode off on the animal to the stables, while his companion kissed her father and nestled down beside his chair. She was a pretty, golden-haired, happy-faced little maid of fourteen, and to-day there was an unwontedly serious look in her blue eyes as she raised them to Mr Maitland's face.

'Well, what is it, Miss Mazeppa?' he demanded, pinching her ear. 'Eager for school-time, eh?'

'Not to-day, papa,' she replied.

'Indeed! And why not?'

'Frank wants a holiday—for Walter and him. You know Jimmy saw some emus in the bush this morning, and Frank has promised to get me some feathers.' Coaxingly: 'You'll let him off for to-day, won't you?'

'That's it, is it? And why can't Master Frank present his petitions in person?'

'Oh! 'cause he's afraid you would refuse. He's been doing something naughty again, he says, and so he didn't like to ask.'

'He didn't like? So! And what do *you* say to this audacious proposal, Walter?'

'I should like nothing better, sir.'

'Then I suppose I must give in. But here comes the timorous wrong-doer to plead his own cause'—this as Frank strolled up, trying to look unconcerned. To him: 'So you think, sir, you deserve a holiday?'

Frank shook his head rather doubtfully.

'No? Then why ask one, pray?'

'It's all those emus, sir,' answered the boy. 'We mayn't have another chance for months, and'—ingenuously—'it would be a pity if Ruth was cheated out of her feathers through no fault of hers, wouldn't it? Besides, it's such a long time since we had a holiday.'

'I daresay it is—not for a fortnight at least, I should say,' retorted Mr Maitland. 'However, we must not rob Ruth of her feathers. In return, perhaps she'll make up some lunch for you. There—no thanks! And one word, Walter. Be careful of the guns, and don't go too far. You'll take Jimmy, of course? Now, away with you all, and leave me to get my work done, so that Ruth and I may have a long afternoon's reading.'

The young people went off together, but before they separated—Walter to get the guns, Frank and Ruth to see about the lunch—something seemed to strike the former.

'By the bye, does anybody know where Jimmy is?' he asked. 'I haven't seen him to-day.'

'Oh! *I* know,' said Frank.

Walter, reassured, disappeared into the house.

Within ten minutes thereafter everything was ready; and the two, their guns in hand and their bags over their shoulders, set out on their expedition. As soon as they were beyond earshot of the veranda, Walter turned upon his brother with a sudden question.

'*Now*, young 'un, I should like to know where you got that horse of Brunton's?' he demanded.

Frank looked at him with an expression of some anxiety. 'I hope Mr Maitland didn't know the beast, Walt,' he said. 'I thought you would.'

'Of course he didn't, or we shouldn't be here. But what have you been up to?'

Frank began to laugh, and laughed uproariously until his

brother brought him to his senses by a punch in the ribs. Then he condescended to explain.

'It was Brunton's own fault. Why! you should have seen his face when I went off! I was down by the Long Plantation, and he was riding home for breakfast. After last night I didn't want to see him particularly, but he spotted me first, and headed me off before I had run fifty yards. Then I stopped—it was no use doing anything else—and said "Good-morning" quite politely. But I can tell you I was shaking, for I saw by his face that he meant mischief. Well, he got off the horse, and threw the reins over a stump. Says he, "You mayn't be aware, young man, that I have full powers from the boss?" I pretended not to understand, and asked as to what. "To settle accounts with you and the like o' you," he said, "and, what's more, I've one to settle now for last night!" Says I, "Oh! don't mention it, please; I only hoped you liked your bath!"'

'Which was cheeky,' remarked Walter.

'I couldn't help it, really. Then says he, "About as much as you'll like what you're about to get, young man," and I saw him hunting about along the edge of the plantation for something—a good stick, probably. Well, I had no fancy to be thrashed, and it was just then that the idea came into my head. I was nearer the horse than he was, and a second would do it. There was no time to think'——

'And of course you didn't?'

'No,' confessed Frank. 'Before he could stop me, I had the reins in my hand and was on the horse's back. He was about eight yards off, and I had just time to turn round, remind him that the account would have to be settled again, and say good-morning as politely as before. I left him staring—worse than last night, too. After that, I had the jolliest gallop down to the house, picking up Ruth by the way; and, thinking that it might be as well to be out of sight if Brunton took it into his head to follow on foot, I put her up to ask a holiday to go after the emus. I hadn't much fear.'

'All very well,' said Walter, grimly, 'but didn't it occur to you that it would be the worse in the long-run? Strikes me you're in a nice scrape, youngster.'

Frank admitted the truth of this, but seemed inclined to trust to his luck.

'And what about the horse?' Walter went on. 'Did you leave it in the stables?'

'I wasn't such a fool. I got hold of Jimmy, and sent him up to Brunton's with it and a message that I hoped he had liked his walk. I calculated that the blackboy would catch him at breakfast.'

'Worse and worse!' groaned the elder.

'As well be hanged for a sheep at once!' calmly answered the younger. 'As to Jimmy, I told him to meet us at the bridge—very likely he's there now. I was sure of the holiday, you see. But say, Walter,' he cried, laughing gleefully, 'didn't it serve old Brunton right? The beggar hates to walk!'

Walter laughed too; and then, remembering his guardian's words, he shook his head sadly. There might be some hope for him, but his brother was incorrigible.

CHAPTER IV.

JIMMY was at the rendezvous. As we know from Frank, the blackboy had been ordered to repair to the wooden bridge which Mr Maitland had lately thrown across the river to facilitate communication with the manufactory. The way thither lay through the plantations of sugar-cane, and here and there the boys passed a group of brown-skinned Kanakas, dreaming as they wrought of their homes in some isle of the New Hebrides, and hearing even in the heart of Australia the Pacific surf breaking upon the coral. For a moment they roused themselves to answer the cheerful salutations of the Dennison lads, who, on the strength of a few words of their language and the memory of an occasional kindness, were huge favourites of theirs—and this not the less because themselves were the only folks around Hamilton free from the boys' pranks.

From the broad grin on Jimmy's face, it was evident that he had a story to tell.

'Well, Jimmy, did Mr Brunton say anything?' asked Frank.

The grin broadened. 'Yohi, Missa Flank,' he made reply. 'Him at bleakfass, and fust he chuck plate. Head too much

hard—plate it breakum, and he swear.   Then Missa Bluntum
me call black scoun'rel, and he say, "Missa Flank him tell
look out—he catch it hot, no gammon!"   Me laugh, and
he chuck more plate.   That all.'

'But the plate didn't hit you, did it?'

Jimmy nodded.

'Oh! it did.   Does it hurt?'

'No hurt, missa, but plate it breakum,' proudly answered
the blackboy.

'In that case,' said Walter, laughing, 'you'd better take
the bags and let us get on after the emus.   How long should
we be in making up on them?'

Jimmy wasn't sure: they might not have strayed far,
or they might be twenty miles away by that time.   But
the latter was the more probable, and so the black shouldered
the lunch-bags with great good-will and set off, being fully
as eager for a holiday as his young masters.

Ten minutes' walk took them across the cultivated patch
to the border of the bush, and twenty minutes more to the
spot whence the emus had been sighted in the early morning.
For the next few hours they followed the track of the birds.
Frank, eager to learn the secrets of woodcraft, kept for the
most part by the side of the black, and the voluble chatter
between the two never ceased.   For, although each spoke
in his own dialect, Jimmy had apparently as little difficulty
in understanding the colloquialisms of the boy as the boy
had in understanding his broken English.   Walter held
behind, but his thoughts, engrossing as they were, were
not too engrossing to permit him to listen to the guide's
explanations of what a broken twig here, and a feather there,
might mean, or to admire the keen eyesight and unfailing
instinct of the bushman.   Jimmy in a state of nature

was a different man from Jimmy in the process of being civilised.

Thus for a time they proceeded, in the interest of the chase giving little heed to the heat of the day, and making light of the incidental obstacles in their path. Once or twice a good shot at a kangaroo offered, but the boys refrained from shooting. About two hours after noon, they reached a dell where there was a spring of fresh water: an ideal spot for luncheon. So Walter called a halt, notwithstanding the fact that, according to Jimmy, the emu-tracks were so fresh that the birds could not be far in advance; but it was not the first time he had said so. The boys had their cold mutton and damper; and for behoof of the blackboy, who disdained such luxuries, a parrot was shot, which he ate after a mere pretence of cooking it.

The repast over, Frank proposed to hurry on. Walter. however, had been thinking, and demurred.

'But, look here, we'll lose the emus if we don't,' his brother pointed out.

'Go you and Jimmy, then—I don't feel inclined,' answered Walter, in whose mind the emus had altogether given place to New Guinea. He wished to think out what Mr Maitland had told him, and, boylike, to think it out alone.

' You're not tired, are you?'

'No; but I don't feel inclined,' repeated Walter, in the same tone.

Frank did not press him further, aware from his knowledge of his elder brother's nature that it would be useless. 'I'm going, anyway,' he said. 'I must get those feathers for Ruth, you know.'

'Of course. And blaze the trees as you go along, mind.

I 'll either follow, or you can pick me up on your way back. Don't go too far, though.'

'No fear of that—eh, Jimmy?'

'No fear, my word! Emu plenty near now—me smellum close up, Missa Flank.   All righ?'

They disappeared, and Walter was left to his thoughts and day-dreams. He lay on his back by the water-side, looking at the patchwork of sky seen through the foliage of the trees, and wondered if his father were dead after all, or if his own belief were in truth the right one. He tried to conjure up a picture of a Papuan village in the mountains of the interior—the mud hovels, the savage, man-eating natives, and, above all, the white man living amongst them, held sacred as a god perhaps, or perhaps kept close prisoner because of his medical skill. Then he saw himself setting forth in search of him, and followed in his mind's eye the weary marches from village to village, the hairbreadth adventures, the disappointments and hopes until finally he was successful. For years Walter had read everything about New Guinea that he could find, and he was not without imagination; but not in his wildest flights of fancy did he dream of perils such as those he was to undergo before he was many months older, just as little as he dreamed that at that moment, within a few miles of him, was the man who would be the immediate cause of his dearest expectations being realised.

This for about an hour; and then Walter's attention strayed somewhat, and presently he bethought him of the emus. He remembered that he had always desired to shoot one, and was wilfully throwing away the chance. Even yet, if he walked fast, it might not be too late to be in at the finish. Refreshed by the rest, he pushed on at a goodly speed, and found no difficulty in following the track of his companions, marked out as it was by Jimmy's hatchet on the bark of the trees. But the afternoon was sultry, and when he had covered two or three miles he began to feel the weight of his gun a burden.

'Surely they can't be far now,' he said to himself, forgetting that they had an hour's start. 'I wonder if they're within earshot? Guess it can't do any harm to find out, any way.'

The signal of the boys, arranged in view of excursions like the present, was two shots fired at an interval of a minute, and then a long 'cooey.' Walter gave it, and waited for a response. It came, but sooner than he expected, and in a different manner. It was a single cry, distinct enough to show that it was from the near vicinity, and, strangest of all, in the voice neither of Frank nor of the blackboy. By the intonation, indeed, it was evidently from somebody not a bushman.

Walter was too much surprised to conjecture what it might mean, for promiscuous visitors to Hamilton Gap were quite unknown. One thing was plain : he must get to the bottom of the mystery.

He shouted again :

'Cooey ! Coo—ey ! Coo—oo—ey !'

Again the cry was repeated, and Walter took note of the direction. Then he went forward, calling loudly, and being guided by the answering shouts of the stranger. In five minutes he was at the verge of the glade, and the cries sounded quite near ; the next moment, breaking cover, he found himself in the strenuous embrace of Captain Barkham !

When at length the boy managed to free himself from the

grip of the overjoyed sailor, he saw before him a man rather beyond middle age, squat and square-shouldered, with a broad, honest countenance, burnt brown by the sun, and a pair of shrewd eyes. Just now there was a look of the utmost delight in them, as if their owner was congratulating himself on his escape from a great danger. His dress was a compromise between sea-garb and the conventional dress of cities; he wore heavy sea-boots; his broad-brimmed felt hat lay on the ground a short distance off; and there were not wanting indications that his journey through the bush had not been devoid of incident and mishap.

The two regarded each other for a minute without speaking, and then a shade of doubt flitted across the worthy skipper's face. He gripped Walter again.

'Here! You don't mean to say you're lost too, do you?' he demanded eagerly.

'Lost? Not likely!' replied Walter, with some contempt. 'Why, I know the bush round here like the palm of my hand!'

The captain breathed a sigh of relief. 'You belong to these parts, then?'

'Rather!' Tentatively: 'You're a stranger hereabouts?'

'I wish I wasn't!' cried Barkham, the memory of his sufferings being still fresh. 'It's the first time I've seen the place, and I'd give a lot if 'twas the last. I slept at Barouga last night, and left it this morning'——

'Not as you are, surely?' interrupted Walter. 'Not on foot, I mean.'

'Not exactly—I guess I had a nigger and a horse when I started. The nigger was the first to go, just about noon observation. Then the horse threw me off, and went too. Since then I've been wandering about on the look-out for a house called Hamilton Gap, and very glad I am,' he said, with another cordial handshake, 'to see somebody who's likely to know the road. How far might it happen to be, now?'

Walter gave a gasp. 'Hamilton Gap! Why, that's our house!' he exclaimed.

'Your house?   Then'——

He got no further, and for the next few minutes was left to his own reflections.   While he was speaking, Walter had heard a shot.   Now there was another and a 'cooey,' and the boy, rapidly reloading, replied to the signal.

'That's my brother Frank,' he explained to the captain. 'He must have heard the last signal as well as you. We're out after emus, you know.—Coo—ey!'

'Oh? that's it, is it?' said Barkham to himself, and a twinkle came into his eyes.

'He has a blackboy with him,' Walter went on, after some more shouting. 'I wonder if they've shot anything?— Coo—ey!—We might go and meet them, if you don't mind. It's on our way.'

The captain picked up his hat and followed, still nodding to himself as if well pleased. The responsive calls became louder and louder : the two parties were quickly approaching each other. When at last they came within sight, Walter was amazed to observe that his brother was riding a horse, while Jimmy—grinning as usual—brought up the rear. Walter, quite forgetting the stranger in his surprise, broke into a run.

'Hullo! where did you get the nag, Frank?' he cried, coming up.

'That's my emu—whoop!' replied Frank.

'Your emu?'

'All we got, anyway. We tracked 'em until Jimmy saw by their footmarks that they had made a big spurt, and it was no use going on. Something must have frightened them. Coming back, we sighted this animal grazing peacefully in our path, and easily caught him—saddle and bridle and all ! Wonder who he belongs to ?'

The captain stepped forward.

'The horse is mine, Mister Dennison !' he said. 'Thanks for catching him !'

'Yours ?' Frank looked at the stranger, and there was a world of unaffected amazement and perplexity expressed in the one word. Then he dismounted.

Walter was likewise perplexed. 'Say, how did you know our names ?' he demanded.

'Let me see—I shouldn't wonder if you were Mister Walter, now ?' said Barkham, ignoring the question.

Walter admitted it.

'And you—you 're Mister Frank, of course ?'

Frank nodded.

'As for this gentleman '—indicating Jimmy, who was still grinning—'I don't know *him*, but it strikes me he bears a remarkable family likeness to my runaway nigger.'

'Oh ! Jimmy's all right,' Walter hastened to assure him. 'He 's our confidential servant. But how '——

The captain, having enjoyed his laugh at the boys' surprise, was ready to explain. 'How ? Partly by guess-work,' he said—'partly from an old description of you. Besides, haven't I got a letter for you in my pouch ?'

Now the Dennison boys were not in the habit of receiving letters, and consequently they became more excited than ever.

'A letter !' cried Walter.

'For us!' cried Frank.

Both held out their hands for it.

'Slowly!' said Barkham. 'It's for you, right enough—I saw it written—but as it happens to be enclosed in one to Mr Maitland, I reckon you'll have to wait until we get to Hamilton Gap.'

Here a strange idea came into Walter's head.

'Is it—is it from New Guinea?' he asked, eager to know, yet half-hesitating to inquire.

'You've guessed it, boy! It *is* from New Guinea; straight from the land of the Golden Plume, as they call it. And that reminds me,' the captain went on, 'that I should have introduced myself long ago as James Barkham, master of the *Bird of Paradise*, at present lying in Cooktown harbour after a voyage to the Louisiade Islands and New Guinea. It was there, in New Guinea'—this in the most matter-of-fact tone—'that I ran across your father, and took up this commission. He's an old friend of mine, you know.—But what in the name o' creation's the matter?'

It was now the boys' turn to be demonstrative. To Walter, and in a less degree to his brother, the good news of their father's safety was so utterly unexpected that for a little they were speechless: they could only catch hold of the captain's hands—Frank the right, Walter the left—and shake them, as the former would have put it, for all they were worth. Barkham endured it with great good-humour for a minute or two, and then called a truce.

'Then he *is* alive?' said Walter. Having recovered his voice, he was eager for confirmation.

'As much alive as I am—more, maybe,' replied the captain, gently rubbing his bruised side. 'Or at least he was six weeks ago, when I saw him last.'

This was satisfactory, but when Frank had given utterance to a wild whoop of delight, Walter—who had still the Commissioner's letter on his mind—had another question to ask. He did it gravely :

' And well ?'

' And well—barring a slight limp, caused by putting his foot into a trap. I did the same myself once.'

' Why doesn't he come back, then ?' demanded Frank.

' If it isn't in the letter, I daresay I can give you a good reason for it, Mister Frank,' said Barkham. 'As it is, better wait for the letter. Which reminds me,' he went on, 'that I don't know yet how far it is to Hamilton Gap, and that I 'm getting peckish. We may as well tramp, I think.'

Needless to say, there was no opposition to the suggestion, for the boys were now as eager to reach Hamilton Gap as he was. They started at once, he on the horse, they on either side, and Jimmy as guide to strike out the nearest path. On the road he answered as best he could their numberless inquiries about Mr Dennison, or entertained them with a full and vivid account of his misadventures after leaving Baronga; and he had also a question or two to put by way of satisfying his own curiosity. For instance, with a glance at the guns :

' You are good at the shooting, I suppose ?' he surmised.

Walter admitted that they were pretty fair, while Frank seized advantage of the first opportunity to prove his ability by bringing down a bird on the wing. Said the captain, as he applauded the shot :

' And is your brother as good, Mister Frank ?'

' Better,' returned Frank, loyally : which was the case. Barkham seemed gratified.

In this way was the journey lightened; and by the time they issued from the bush, an hour or two before sundown, they were all the best of friends. Here Frank was sent forward to prepare his guardian. You may be sure he fulfilled the duty with breathless vehemence and with many gesticulations.

Mr Maitland was in his chair in the veranda when they arrived, ready to offer the new-comer a hearty greeting.

'You'll excuse me for not rising, sir,' he said. 'But you're welcome to Hamilton, and twice welcome that you bring good news. Now, not a word until you've had a wash and some dinner! It's a custom here.—Walter, take Mr Barkham to your room.'

CHAPTER V.

DINNER being over, the seniors lit their cigars, little Ruth squatted down in her favourite position beside her father's chair, and the boys set themselves to listen with all their ears to Captain Barkham's story.

'It was in this way that I met Mr Dennison first,' he began. 'Somewhere about three years ago I was chartered at Sydney by a man of the name of Lambert to run my schooner—the *Bird of Paradise* she's called—to run her to an out-of-the-way village at the head of the Gulf of Papua. I had never heard of the place myself, although I've sailed those seas for twenty years and more, but Lambert had the bearings, and seemed to know what he was about. He was very close about his plans, but they were plain enough, for he had any amount of exploring stuff and such like on board. Well, we arrived at the village in due course. Mr Dennison and another man—he's dead since, poor fellow—were waiting for Lambert there, keeping friendly with the natives. From what I saw I gathered that they were bound on a long trip into the interior in search of gold; and, as it happened, I saw a good deal of them, for we were detained for nearly a week by contrary winds. On the second or third day, I had a sort of an adventure. Somehow or other, I managed to put up the back of one of the savages—and it's easily enough done if you haven't the lay of their customs, and ain't careful—and as a consequence he came at me with his club. We had a bit of a tussle, and he got rather the best of it, not being hampered by clothes. Indeed, to tell the truth, he was just in the act of bringing down the club on my head when Dennison turned up and caught his arm—in the very nick of time. He cooled down then, and a paltry present squared him. But I was none the less grateful to Dennison, and then and there I made him a promise that I should look in at the place for news of him whenever I chanced to be in the latitude. That,' said the captain, 'was one point to him.'

His cigar had gone out, and he lit it afresh and continued:

'Well, I didn't forget my promise. Twice, at pretty long intervals, I called in; but he hadn't returned, and I could get no news of the party whatever. The visits had this good result, though—I did some trade with the natives, and so kept up the friendship for white men which they had had ever since Dennison's arrival. The third time I was more lucky. It was six or seven weeks ago, when, being on that coast, I thought that I would pay the place another visit. Not that I expected to find your friend, mark you—it was merely for curiosity's sake, and maybe to do a bit of trade. Well, judge of my surprise to see, the first thing after our anchor was down, a native boat put off with a white man in the stern! I must say I didn't recognise him at first, for his clothes were rather promiscuous, and he was bearded like an up-country digger. Then I heard a hail:

"Ahoy! Is that you, Barkham?"

"Not Dennison, bless my heart!" I cried, thinking I knew the voice.

'But it was Dennison—well and hearty, too, barring a sprained ankle. You may be sure we were delighted to see each other again. He had been there a month, having just missed one of the Commissioner-fellows by a week or two, and as he couldn't leave the place, my arrival was like a Godsend to him. Shortly told, his story was that for more than a couple of years he and his chums had been staying with a tribe up-country, who had such a high opinion of them that at first they wouldn't let them go at all, and afterwards not until they had promised to come back. More than that—but this was between ourselves—*they had struck gold*. Finally they got away on the promise aforesaid, which was just what they meant to do—of their own accord. On the road to the coast, however, they had managed to lose most of their things, and one of the three had died as well. As for the other man—Lambert—he was at that moment lying at death's door with swamp-fever, and Dennison was doubtful of pulling him through. And this was the pass he was in when I turned up; there were no means of leaving the country at that point, and even if there had been, he couldn't have done so because of Lambert. As to sending a letter to the Commissioner at Port Moresby, even putting out of sight the objection to that on the ground of policy, it would have been almost impossible to do it in the native boats. Not that he hadn't seriously thought of trying; indeed, the letter was written, enclosing one to be sent to you. By good luck, I arrived just in time to save him the trouble—one point to me. Of course, the first thing I did was to offer him a passage to Australia. But Lambert couldn't be moved; still less could he be left in the care of the natives; and as, owing to the nature of my cargo, I couldn't stay until there was a change for the better or the worse, there was nothing for it but to leave Dennison in Papua and be his messenger here. And this was his commission, Mr Maitland,' concluded the captain, producing from the depths of a capacious pocket a small but heavy parcel—'first, to bring this packet to you, which I 've done; second, to carry out certain instructions under your orders; and last, to get back to New Guinea with as much speed as might be.'

'And I'm sure you deserve our best thanks, Captain Barkham,' said Mr Maitland, as he took the packet and rapidly tore off the cover. The boys watched him with eager eyes. Inside were two letters and another little parcel. Of the former, one was addressed to himself, the other to Walter and Frank. The parcel, as being of minor importance, was put aside for future examination.

'Oh! not at all,' said Barkham, in answer to Mr Maitland. 'Why, bless my heart! I had a score to settle, and I 'd do the same again for a friend like Dennison—barring the trip through the bush,' he added. 'Next time I 'd take the road.'

The boys, meanwhile, were devouring their father's letter. It was short, and said little to the purpose of this narrative. For details of his adventures and further projects, they were referred to Mr Maitland.

He, happening to look up, noticed their look of anxious suspense, and had pity on them.

'Is there much in your letter, Walter?' he asked.

Walter handed it to him. 'Not much, sir, as you can see,' he said.

'In that case,' said Mr Maitland, when he had glanced over it, 'perhaps I had better read mine aloud, with Captain Barkham's permission.   So attend.'

The behest was superfluous, for never had reader an audience more eager to catch every word. The letter began with a reference to the trials and adventures of Mr Dennison and his companions on their journey into the interior, and went on to describe how they had fallen into the hands of a hostile tribe, amongst whom they had sojourned for more than two years. At first they were kept close prisoners, but it was not long before they acquired sufficient influence to gain a certain amount of freedom. Still it was impossible for them, owing, as Captain Barkham had hinted, to the natives' growing regard, to leave the mountain-valley which was the tribe's dwelling-place. They had this one consola-tion : they were plainly in a gold country, for their captors were the only Papuans they had encountered who wore ornaments of that metal. In the valley itself there was no trace of it; and it was Mr Dennison's chief object, after he had mastered the language, to discover whence it came. At last he succeeded. From one of the head-men he learned that the gold was got by barter from an adjacent and more powerful tribe, with whom it was plenti-ful; and he heard also the legend of a great idol made out of a single nugget, which was held in sacred veneration by its possessors. The head-man had never seen the idol, but a brother of his had; and if the tradition preserved in the tribe were to be believed, it was formed of the largest nugget of gold by far in the world !

Here the captain, who had been following the narrative with the most intense interest, interrupted with : 'Great life ! but that nugget would be worth having !'

'Just what Dennison thinks, unless I'm vastly mistaken,' said Mr Maitland quietly.

'Please go on, sir,' pleaded Walter, and his guardian did so.

As it happened (the letter continued) the two tribes were then at war—indeed, they were more often at war than at peace—and it would have been simple madness to try to penetrate into the enemy's country, more especially as Mr Dennison had no presents to offer them. From that moment he dreamed nightly of the holy nugget, while by day all his thoughts were given to plans for making it his. Honestly, there was but one way to do it—by purchase. Now this meant at least a journey to the coast and back, and thenceforth he wrought and schemed with the sole purpose of getting the natives' consent. Ultimately, as we know, it was given on the condition that he should return. The march to the coast was fruitful of mishap, but at length he and Lambert, with their Papuan companions, reached the friendly village at the head of the Gulf. Therefrom he now wrote to his old friend Maitland, asking him—if he received the letter— to raise a sum of money by the sale of the Dennison run or otherwise, and with it buy the articles mentioned in an enclosed list and ship them to him. It was the first time (he added) that Fortune had condescended to throw a cast with him, and on his part he meant to stake all.

This, with the customary greetings and inquiries, was the letter; but there was also a postscript of some importance, written after Captain Barkham's arrival. But for Lambert's danger, Mr Dennison said, he should have taken the opportunity to return to Australia and carry out the arrangements himself. As this was impossible, he enclosed—now that it was safe to do so—a specimen of native produce, which would both render the sale of the run unnecessary, and go to convince Mr Maitland that his proposed expedition was not altogether a wild-goose chase. One thing he begged : that secrecy, as far as possible, should be observed.

'And the "produce?"' asked Walter and Frank together.

'Is this, I suppose,' said their guardian, and took up the second packet.

While he was unwrapping the paper, the others, even to Barkham, could not restrain their curiosity, and left their chairs to gather round him. The 'produce' was enclosed in a square wooden box, the lid of which had to be broken open before the contents were visible. When this had been done, Mr Maitland uttered a quick exclamation.

'*Gold !*' he cried.

It was even so. In all there were some seven or eight small nuggets of the dull yellow metal—four of them in the rough, the others beaten rudely into the shape of armlets or neck ornaments. They were passed from hand to hand with many ejaculations of wonder, and finally Captain Barkham gave voice to the general desire for information.

'What might these little bits of gold be worth, now?' he asked.

'It's hard to guess off-hand,' replied Mr Maitland. 'Certainly more than a hundred pounds—probably two hundred.'

'In solid cash?'

'In solid cash.'

The captain whistled. 'Then all I have to say,' he remarked, 'is that they don't look it!' And the boys, to whom the sum named seemed an enormous one, were inclined to agree with him.

For a minute or two there was silence, while everybody had his own thoughts. But Walter and Frank exchanged a look full of meaning, and then, noticing that Ruth was watching them, blushed and dropped their eyes. She pretended not to have seen.

Barkham was again the first to speak.

'Well, sir, what do you intend to do, if I may ask?' he inquired.

'I don't know that we've any alternative, captain,' was the quiet answer. 'Dennison seems to have struck the right trail at last, and all we can do is to support him. If we didn't, he's just the man to go through with the adventure without us. The instructions are clear enough, anyhow. With this list,' he said, referring to the enumeration of articles mentioned in the letter, 'we can't go far wrong. As to money, that need not trouble us: these nuggets, with the run thrown in if necessary, are ample security.'

'You mean to sell them, of course?'

'I think not. It might make too much talk, and perhaps bring all the loafers in the colony up here in the belief that I had struck gold. No: my agent in Cooktown and I will manage the financial part of the business between us, and we'll keep the nuggets here in the meantime for Ruth to play with. One question, captain—when do you sail again for New Guinea?'

'It depends on this,' said Barkham, tapping the list with his finger. 'You see, we may have to send to Brisbane or even Sydney for some of these things. But not later than a month or six weeks hence; as soon as we possibly can, you may take my word.'

Here the boys whispered together. All this time they

had been unwontedly quiet, but now and again they had passed a furtive glance.

'Should we speak now?' asked Walter.

'This very minute!' returned Frank. Apparently the two had a thorough understanding.

'You or me?'

'You, of course. You're older.'

Walter nodded, and awaited his opportunity.

'Of course we're going to New Guinea, too, sir?' he said, when it came. From his matter-of-fact air you would have imagined that the thing was settled.

Mr Maitland turned sharply. 'What?' he cried. '*You?*'

'And me, sir,' said Frank.

'Preposterous! What put this silly idea into your heads, boys? Can't you see that it's impossible?'

'I don't know that it's silly or impossible, sir,' replied Walter, obstinately. 'Father's there, and he doesn't say anything in the letter about us not coming. If he hadn't expected us, he would. And if it's good enough for him, why, it's good enough for us.'

'Yes. Good enough for us!' echoed Frank.

Mr Maitland was about to answer, but he happened to catch Captain Barkham's eye and refrained. Instead, he wheeled his chair across the room, and the two consulted together in low tones.

'You were a bit too sharp, if you'll excuse me saying it,' began the captain. 'They're plucky lads, and I'm not sure that they're far wrong.'

'Then you have a message from Dennison about them?'

'Well, hardly a message,' said Barkham. 'But he was always speaking about them, and one day he says, "I shouldn't wonder, captain, if those lads of mine were to want to come across this trip. Of course I don't know how they have turned out, but they were sturdy little fellows five years ago." He was right, sir—it was their first thought, as you've heard. "What if they do?" I asked him. "It depends on them and on Maitland," he says; "though for my part, if they're strong and hardy, I believe it would do them good. Like to see them again? Of course I should! But keep your eyes open, captain, and at least you can give me your opinion of them when you return." "And if they *do* want to come?" says I again. "If they do—well, we must leave it to Maitland," he said. "He's the best judge." And that, sir,' said the captain, 'was all that passed between us.'

'And have you formed your opinion, captain?'

'I'm doing it. But one thing I'm certain of already— there's not much fear of either. I don't say this, mind you,' he explained, 'without having tried to find out what they can do in the way of shooting and otherwise.'

'In a word—the journey would do the boys no harm, you think.'

'Not a bit!' unhesitatingly replied the captain.

Mr Maitland became thoughtful. 'As to Dennison,' he said, presently, 'do you think he is really anxious for them?'

The captain had no doubt of it whatever.

'Then, if that be so,' Mr Maitland went on, 'it must be left to themselves, I'm afraid.' He turned to them, and pointed out the dangers and privations they would have to undergo if they were serious in their intention of accompanying their father in his journey—dangers from pestilence, from hostile natives, from a thousand causes which at present they were unable to realise. He pointed out also how different the life would be from that to which they were accustomed, and how heavy the odds were against them; and seriously and affectionately he asked them, speaking to them as he would have spoken to Mr Dennison himself, to consider the matter well before they decided—to do nothing in haste.

Walter had his answer ready.

'Haven't we considered it already, sir?' he said. 'You know we've often talked these matters over, and I think I understand about the risks and the dangers, and all that. Of course we'll be sorry to leave the Gap, and you and Ruth; but'—and here was the unanswerable argument—'my father's there, and I'm sure he expects us over to help him. It was different last time. We're old enough now.'

It was a shrewd guess to make, and on his part Mr Maitland could not deny it. He changed his ground.

'But surely one of you' - —

He got no further.

'I go with Walt!' cried Frank stoutly. Then: 'I beg your pardon, sir, but if Walter goes, I go. It wouldn't be fair to let him have all the danger to himself.'

'At any rate,' said Mr Maitland, 'there is no hurry. Sleep upon it, and to-morrow we'll discuss the matter soberly in full council—if Master Frank can wait until then.'

And the boys agreed, for they knew that they had carried their point: the battle was won.

Apparently another of the company, who had hitherto sat silent, thought otherwise, for little Ruth took an early opportunity to join the lads. Having listened intently to her father's address, she was in great tribulation.

'Walter—Frank—you won't go to that horrid place to be killed, will you?' she cried.

'Killed? Not if we can help it, you may be sure,' replied

Walter. 'We'll try our best not to be, Ruth. As to not going—why, of course we are.'

'But not you, Frank?'

'Tush! you're only a girl,' said Frank, with proper disdain. 'There! don't cry. Look here—if your father was in Brisbane, wouldn't you go to him?'

'Of course.'

'Then why shouldn't we go to New Guinea to ours?'

'But Brisbane isn't New Guinea. There aren't no savages in Brisbane.'

'Well, it's just like the difference between boys and girls,' said Frank, from the vantage-ground of his superiority. 'It wouldn't be half fun if there were no savages, and that's why we're going:' an answer, unsatisfactory as it was, with which Ruth had perforce to rest content, for just then there was a new-comer in the person of Brunton.

Frank's jaw dropped, and he felt inclined to seek protection behind the burly figure of Captain Barkham. The grim expression on the oversman's face boded him no good.

'Ah! is that you, Brunton?' cried Mr Maitland. 'Come in!—This is Captain Barkham, who has just brought us good news from New Guinea. You'll be glad to hear that Mr Dennison is safe and well, and seems on the track of luck at last.—Sit down, and help yourself.'

Brunton obeyed. 'Your health, sir!' he said, nodding to the captain. 'I *am* glad to hear the good news, Mr Maitland—and the more that it wasn't expected. Is he coming back, did you say?'

Now Frank was a lad of resource, and he judged from the relaxation of his old antagonist's countenance that here, with good fortune, lay a chance to escape his just deserts. So he hastened to take it upon himself to reply.

'No, Brunton—not just yet, at least—but Walter and I are maybe going over to New Guinea. You'll be glad to hear that too, I suppose?'

'Well, I don't know,' confessed Brunton, after he had tried (and failed) to assume a stern look. 'I won't deny that I came up here with a certain object—you can guess what, Master Frank; but after all boys will be boys, and—hang it ! I'm real sorry you're going ! For you'll be missed, both o' you—tricks and all.'

'And say, Brunton, we'll hold over our score for settlement until I come back, if you don't mind,' proposed Frank, in his glee.

'Oh ! all right,' said Brunton, laughing.

And Frank's answer was to declare him a trump, and to swear that he should go down to Cooktown with them when they went, and see them off.

CHAPTER VI.

THE VOYAGE.

HE council was duly held next morning after breakfast, but of course there could be but the one decision. Then came the preparations for the boys' departure. Captain Barkham had agreed to stay at Hamilton Gap for two or three days, and during that time there was not a moment of idleness. The outfits had to be got ready, rifles and revolvers chosen, plans and routes talked over, good advice given and received, and finally the partings taken. This proved to be the severest wrench of all; for everybody in the settlement, from Ruth and Brunton down to the Kanakas and the blackboys, showed so much genuine sorrow at the loss of the lads, that but for the prospect of meeting their father, and their dreams of the holy nugget, they might have been tempted to draw back even at the eleventh hour.

Poor Jimmy was inconsolable. First he begged hard for permission to follow them, and when that was gently refused, he vowed that he would never track another emu or circumvent another old-man kangaroo until they had returned to bear him company.

Meanwhile Captain Barkham, as was his habit, was making friends all round, and especially with Ruth and her father.

For the latter he had at once conceived a great admiration on account of his cheerful manner in misfortune, and his admiration was increased when he observed that the control exercised by Mr Maitland over the whole station was, notwithstanding his infirmity, a very real one. But one thing puzzled the worthy captain. Being himself a creature of simplicity, he could not understand why a man of his host's abilities and tastes (the latter as shown by his new library and range of reading) should care to hide his talents in the solitude of a desert. He brooded much over the problem, but a scruple of delicacy restrained him from seeking the solution. At last, while they were speaking one day of the boys, Mr Maitland let drop a hint.

'You are right, captain,' he said in reply to a remark of Barkham's; 'I shall miss them very much, and so will my little Ruth; she more than any of us, perhaps.'

The captain saw his chance. 'Especially when you're so lonely here,' he suggested, to give the other an opening.

Mr Maitland assented.

'I suppose you get used to it in time; but for myself,' Barkham went on, 'I don't think I'd like it much. It would be different, now, if you had neighbours within easy distance. But even that you haven't got, have you?'

'None nearer than twenty-five miles away—through the bush.

'At Baronga?'

'Exactly.'

'It's a good distance—especially through the bush. Now I wonder, if you'll excuse me saying it, that you haven't any womankind about the place,' for the captain in his wanderings, had not failed to take notice of their absence. 'They'd be a sort of comfort to you and the little girl, and there's many a thing they can do that a man can't. At least,' he said hastily, 'they're always home-like.'

A darker look had come into Mr Maitland's face at the mention of womankind, and he answered the captain with unusual bitterness of tone. 'Perhaps you would wonder less if you had my experience of them, sir,' he said, and then sat silent for a minute or two, lost in thoughts which seemingly were far from pleasant.

Barkham said nothing, and presently Mr Maitland went on :

'Do you know why I brought my little Ruth here, more than ten years ago? Simply that she, at any rate, should never be under the influence of women. It was a vow I made, and I've seen nothing since to cause me to change my mind. Never mind why, captain. It wouldn't interest you.'

'But surely they aren't all bad,' the captain ventured to remark.

'Perhaps not, but each of us must speak of them as he has found them.' There was another pause. 'But I daresay you're right,' he continued, with a laugh. 'As usual, I have been generalising a little too much. Let us speak of something else, captain. After all, you must admit that Hamilton Gap is hardly the place for ladies. Why, they would die of *ennui* in three months' time.'

And Captain Barkham, as became a man of sensibility, spared his host any further reference to the subject. But, thinking the matter over in private, he could not help drawing his own inference.

At length the day of parting arrived. Barkham and the boys, with Brunton to act as Mr Maitland's deputy at Cooktown and thence to bring back the horses, were ready; there was no excuse for lingering; and now the last words of fare-well were said on the veranda.

'You won't forget the old homestead, boys?' cried Mr Maitland, trying to smile.

They shook their heads.

'Then I need not tell you to be brave and enduring. I know you won't disgrace us. And—and God guard you both, and bring you back safe!' he concluded

Ruth held up her mouth to be kissed.

'What shall I fetch you from New Guinea, Ruth?' asked Walter.

'Let me see. Oh! you must bring me a big nugget like Captain Barkham's, and then I shall get a brooch made out of it. It's not too much, is it?'

Walter promised.

'And I, Ruth?' asked Frank.

'You? Why, you couldn't even get me those emu feathers the other day!'

'That's no answer. There are no emus in New Guinea—at least I don't think so.'

'But there's birds of Paradise.'

'And you shall have some bird of Paradise feathers—lots of them,' stoutly answered Frank; wherewith his tormentor was forced to declare herself satisfied.

So they took their leave, and at a brisk pace the little cavalcade crossed the bridge and the cultivated strip beyond the river. There, at the fringe of the bush, the boys turned to gain a last look at the homestead, and with heavy hearts waved their handkerchiefs in response to the farewell greetings of those on the veranda. Then they followed their companions. For a time nothing was said, on the boys' part because the separation was too recent, and on the elders' from a wise desire not to intrude upon their feelings. But it was not long before the influence of the fresh morning air, and the exhilaration at the thought that at last they had begun their great journey, had their natural effects upon their spirits. A few rough words of comfort from Barkham, and thenceforward all was laughter and gaiety. For the captain, now that he was in the charge of a capable guide, the bush had lost its terrors; and he recalled his former adventures only to make light of them. They dined at Baronga with the friendly lieutenant of the black police; slept that night at the house of a hospitable squatter fifteen miles farther on; and in due course arrived without mishap at Cooktown, to find to the captain's huge delight that in his absence no accident had befallen the *Bird of Paradise.*

It were needless to linger over the incidents of the fortnight that elapsed before the little schooner was ready to set sail for the great island of Papua. Those fourteen days in the township of Cooktown, with its wooden houses roofed with corrugated iron, were not days of idleness. Much had to be done—purchases made of the articles mentioned by Mr Dennison in his list, which included a tent and camp equipment, arms and ammunition, outfit for himself and Lambert, medicine chest, and a large parcel of cheap and showy presents and 'trade' tobacco* for native consumption. Cooktown itself is an uninteresting place, with no title to fame as yet, except the fact that the site of the town was visited in 1770 by Captain Cook, while on his first voyage round the world : whence its name. The great navigator was engaged in surveying the coast of Australia

---

* A coarse kind of tobacco, beloved of the natives, which is the currency in some parts of the island.

in the *Endeavour*, and his vessel having sprung a leak, he put into the stream afterwards called the Endeavour River, and beached her on the northern bank immediately opposite the site of the present harbour. There he achieved the necessary repairs in spite of the persistent hostility of the natives, and then sailed for New Guinea and Timor, and so home by way of Batavia, with the news of his strange voyagings and wonderful discoveries among the islands of the South Seas and around the great southern continent.

On the morning of the fifteenth day, the last package of the cargo having arrived and been safely stowed below, Brunton came aboard the *Bird of Paradise* as she lay at her moorings off the Pilot Jetty, ready to slip her cable and stand out for the Great Barrier Reef. There was a break in the honest fellow's voice as he said good-bye.

'Well, good-luck to you, boys!' he cried, squeezing their hands. 'And mind this bit of advice. Keep out of fighting if you can, and if you can't—why, keep cool and fire low. You especially, Master Frank—you're much too fond of fancy head work, which spells a miss. And'—he dropped his voice—'if gold's as plentiful over there as they say, you might put my name down for a spare claim if there's one going abegging. That's all, I think. Good-luck again! And be sure and remember me kindly to your father.'

With that he got into his boat; the head-sails were hoisted and the moorings cast off; and before long, with a favouring breeze, the *Bird of Paradise* had left the mouth of the Endeavour far behind her. The boys kept their eyes upon the land until only the summit of Mount Cook, rising behind the town, was visible.

A big form came between them, and a heavy hand fell upon Walter's shoulder.

'Off at last, lads!' cried the hearty voice of the captain in their ears. 'With every prospect of a good run, too! You're not sorry, are you?'

'Sorry?' replied Walter. 'No, captain! I only wish I was there!'

'And that you'll be in two or three days, if this wind holds good. Then for the cassowaries, and the birds of the Golden Plume, and the big nugget! I hope you haven't forgotten your gun, Master Frank?'

'Me? Ask Walter.'

'Oh! Frank's is all right,' said his brother. 'It has hardly been out of his hand for the last three weeks. I believe he takes it to bed with him.'

'Which isn't a bad idea,' said Barkham. 'It's what he'll have to do in Papua if the blacks are troublesome, anyhow. But there! I mustn't stand chattering here if we mean to get through the Barrier before sundown.'

To the captain and his merry men the voyage was un-eventful; to the boys it was far otherwise. Everything was fresh to them; the merest detail of seamanship, the surf breaking over a reef of coral, the eternal changing sea itself—all were interesting to up-country lads. Frank, light-hearted and irresponsible, had two happy, glorious days. When he was not aloft with the sailors, or alone, he was making the helmsman's life miserable by pathetic appeals to be permitted to steer—appeals which were laughingly but not the less firmly refused. Frank reclaimed to Barkham, confident of the result.

'Take the wheel, boy!' cried the captain, in amazement. 'You? Why, bless my heart, don't you know it's as much as the schooner's worth?'

'But it looks easy enough,' pleaded Frank.

Barkham smiled grimly. 'Does it? You've only to try it to find out your mistake, young man.'

'Just what I want to do!' Earnestly: 'Now, captain dear—only once!'

'And meanwhile you don't care if you play Harry with the vessel, eh? D'you see those reefs over there? Well, the chances are that you'll run her on one of them, and knock a hole in the bottom. No, my boy—better learn first. Ask Robertson to give you a lesson.'

This was enough; and the upshot was that Frank spent most of his day when Robertson, the mate, was at the helm, in learning the mysteries and overcoming the difficulties of the fine art of steersmanship. He was an apt pupil; so apt that before long he was raised to the seventh heaven by being allowed to have the schooner under his sole control for five short minutes at a time. Life seemed to have no greater delight in store for him.

Walter, although he shared in these excitements to some extent, was more often to be found in the captain's deck-chair aft, under the awning which the good Barkham had put up for the convenience of his passengers. And usually there was a map on his knees, a map dotted here and there with pins which marked out a certain imaginary course beginning at the coast. Is it difficult to guess whither it led?

So for two days, the breeze holding, they sped northward over that islet-studded, shallow sea, intricate with reefs and dangerous to careless navigators; and on the third morning the boys came on deck to a surprise. They were still among islets; around them were the sails of a pearl-fleet; but to starboard, and trending away in front of the bows, was a low, long streak of black—uninviting to the eye, but fascinating to them at least as being the coast-line of the land for which they were bound. They looked at it almost incredulously until Walter construed their feeling into words.

'Can *that* be New Guinea ?' he asked.

The captain hailed them from the wheel.

'Land at last, boys !' he shouted. 'Five hours more, and if the tide serves we're in !'

His good spirits were infectious. It was different from their expectations, but at anyrate it was New Guinea—the island of mystery and adventure, of which they had dreamed night and day for weeks. And in five hours they would step ashore upon it !

All forenoon, as the hours slipped past, they watched the advancing coast-line with ever greater interest. They were left entirely to themselves, everybody being too busy otherwise to listen to their questions and remarks. Even to Barkham they dared not speak, for his preternaturally grave face as he steered the vessel told them that the passage was a most difficult and hazardous one, and he never deserted the helm for a single moment. The appearance of the coast became more and more unattractive as they approached it. The coral reefs had been left behind, and with them the pretty schooners of the pearl-fishers; and now the *Bird of Paradise* ran on between vast mud-flats, formed by the soil carried down into the Gulf by innumerable rivers, and only broken here and there by a low-lying, mangrove-covered island. Indeed, until the flowing tide was nearly full, it was difficult to say where the mud-flats ended and the land began. Then, as they were gradually covered, the vessel had, so to speak, to feel its way inch by inch, while the captain's countenance grew quite stern and anxious. Thus they proceeded for half an hour, and at last ran between what seemed to be two islands, keeping close into the one to port. Next moment the skipper's face brightened; he gave the wheel into the hands of his mate, and with a chuckle of satisfaction walked forward to greet the boys. They, on their part, felt inclined to cheer when they saw that they had entered the estuary of a broad river.

'Have we arrived, captain?' demanded Walter, as Barkham joined them.

'Not quite, Mr Walter. But do you observe a red bluff to starboard, about half a mile up? Well, our village lies behind that. If you haven't patience to wait until we're there, you might get up your guns and give 'em a salute. I guess that'll bring your father aboard double-quick.'

'Just now?'

'Why, of course! He'll hear it right enough. Sound carries far in these latitudes.'

The boys needed no further incitement. Down they tumbled into the cabin, and up again with their rifles; and presently the swampy, tree-clad banks of the stream were echoing to the unusual sound of a volley of small-arms. Five minutes they waited in anxiety—ten minutes—but there was no response.

'Strange!' muttered Barkham to himself. Then: 'Give 'em another, boys! We're nearer now.'

They did give them another, but with precisely the same result. No boat appeared from behind the bluff, from which the boys' eyes never wandered.

The captain looked perplexed.

'Strange!' he repeated. 'It never happened before. I hope there's nothing wrong with your father. But that's impossible—we should have seen the natives.—Patience, lads! Another minute or two'll tell us the truth.'

It seemed an hour, so painful was their suspense, before the red bluff was on the stern of the *Bird of Paradise*, and the little village was before their eyes. In the middle of a clearing on a high bank of the river were a score or two of rude houses, surrounded by their patches of yams and bananas; and on the bank itself, drawn thither doubtless by the report of the shots, was grouped a crowd of native women and children, with a few old men—evidently the whole available population of the place. Not a youth or man of middle age was to be seen, nor was there a boat or canoe visible.

'It beats me!' confessed Captain Barkham. 'But we must sound it to the bottom at once. Here, men, let go the anchor and get out a boat: you, Tom, fetch up the guns and come with me. You too, boys. Mind! careful's the word. There's no saying what's in this.'

CHAPTER VII.

THE FIRST DAY IN PAPUA.

THE sailor Tom and Walter took the oars, Barkham and Frank seated themselves in the stern, and at the captain's word they put off from the ship's side. Ten yards from the bank, the order was given to mark time.

'Hold off for a minute,' cried Barkham. 'I must palaver with them a bit.'

Rising, he shouted something in the native dialect. There was a moment's hesitation, and then an old woman in the front row answered him at great length. Her reply seemed to satisfy the captain.

'That 's all right,' he said. 'Pull in, lads.'

Apparently their suspicions of the natives were groundless, for assuredly their reception lacked nothing in the way of heartiness. There was a shout of salutation as they landed, and a few of the women and old men, bolder than the rest, gathered round the skipper with words of greeting and inquiry. A gesture gained him silence. Speaking in tones lower than the boys were accustomed to hear from their bluff, boisterous friend, and addressing in particular the woman who had answered him in the boat, he 'palavered' for a little to the villagers. The woman replied; occasionally one or other of the elders chimed in; and there followed a brisk interchange of question and response, all, of course, quite unintelligible to the boys standing at attention by Barkham's side. But one thing was evident, to their joy: that, judging by his face, he was not extracting bad or indifferent news.

They, meanwhile, had leisure to look around them. There was much of deep interest to see: chief of all, the Papuans themselves, with whom they were for the first time at close quarters. Naturally enough, they had formed their conception of them from the blackboys of Queensland. They were agreeably surprised to find, relatively speaking, a higher type. The colour was lighter, the features—at least in the younger—better and more mobile, and the expression, as a rule, more intelligent. The old men were undistinguished, save for their great mop-like heads of hair; but some of the girls, in gay petticoats of woven grass, were graceful and far from ugly—which was more, however, than could truthfully be said of their elders. Then the children, clad in the garments of nature, shyly huddled in the background behind their dames and grand-dames, but not incapable of a sly glance at the strangers in their trim Norfolk suits, long leggings, and broad-brimmed sun-hats. Have you not the contrast between civilised and uncivilised here?

This, we have said, was interesting; but none the less there was still the uncertainty regarding their father to induce the boys to turn from it to watch the progress of the captain's palaver. He observed the anxiety in their faces, and broke off for a minute to reassure them.

'All's well so far, lads,' he said. 'Your father's at no great distance. From what I can gather, he's only putting the blacks up to a piece of strategy, bless him! The thing's simple enough. It seems that some strong tribe from the west has a habit of swooping down on this village once or twice a year, killing and burning, and carrying off a lot of women and children—for the cook-pot, as like as not. It's not the first time I've heard of the thing. Well, it never happened to strike the beggars here to oppose the enemy, far less try to circumvent 'em. But on this occasion your father was on the spot, and got 'em to try the dodge. When the news came a day or two ago that the cannibals weren't far off, he suggested to cross the river, prepare an ambuscade, and generally make it hot for the invaders. At first the idea was scouted—as being too bold, apparently—but in the end he had his way, and, in a word, that's where he is at this moment. I might have guessed it was something of the kind,' added Barkham. 'It's just Dennison's style: a scrimmage, if it's to help a friend, never comes amiss to him.'

'And the fight?' asked Walter eagerly. 'Is it going on just now, captain?'

'I daresay it is.'

'Then we must follow him at once!' cried the boy. 'Perhaps he needs our help. You said the other tribe was a strong one, you know.'

'Easily, my lad,' answered the captain. 'All in good time! We must find out first where the place is—which was what I was getting at in a roundabout way when I knocked off to report progress. A minute 'll do it.'

The dialogue with the old woman recommenced, and was varied as before by an occasional remark from the others. As the upshot the dame picked out a boy from the motley crowd behind her, gave him some instructions, and, not without reluctance on his part, pushed him forward towards the captain. At first the little fellow seemed very doubtful of the white man's intentions, but a kind word or two put him more at his ease, and when Barkham had closed the conference by distributing a few sticks of 'trade' tobacco, he accompanied him to the boat quite willingly.

'To the schooner first!' said the captain. 'I've to give Robertson his orders, and maybe we'd be the better of a six-shooter or two instead of these rifles. They're handier in a scrimmage. There, if our friend here knows the course, you won't be long in seeing your father. Give way!'

Both Walter and Tom, fired by the prospect of excitement, did so with a will, and no time was lost either in getting to the vessel's side or on board. Presently, Robertson having been instructed not to relax his watch until their return, the boat was being pulled up the river. Barkham had now an oar, while Walter was steering; the little pilot was in the bow, keeping a good look-out for the landing-place; and only Frank, seated beside his brother, had leisure to glance around him in search of novelties. But there was little worthy of attention in the dark, turgid waters of the stream, and less in the line of mangrove-trees on shore. The silence was unbroken even by the note of a bird, and for a little nobody cared to disturb it: least of all the two men, sweating at their oars in the still, hot, exhausting air. It was well for them that the tide was in their favour.

Thus they had progressed for about two miles, keeping well into the bank of the river opposite the village (the right bank), when an exclamation from the native boy caused Barkham to prick up his ears.

'He says he hears firing, as I understand his lingo,' he reported. 'Do you, lads?'

The boys listened, and soon, sure enough, they heard the report of a far-away shot.

'There it is!' cried Walter.

'Ah! that's where you have the pull over an old sailor,' said the captain. 'We can never quite manage to get the sound of the sea out of our ears. But here'——

'There it is again!' interrupted Frank. 'And louder! Oh! I hope we're in time, captain.'

The captain laughed. 'Don't bother yourself about *that*, Mr Frank,' he said. 'The fight won't be over before you get a chance of using your revolver, trust me! Anyway, we can't have far to go now.'

Nor had they. In less than five minutes, following their guide's instructions, they put into a little creek which here broke the line of mangroves. A hundred yards up, at a bend in the stream, they came upon a score or so of native boats moored securely to the bank, and from one of them were hailed by the Papuan on guard. He was easily satisfied. There was a short colloquy between him and the boy; the captain asked a question or two; and then, the boat having been given into the man's charge, they made their way on shore across the intervening craft. Before them, when they landed, a narrow path was to be seen winding back into the bush. In appearance it was not tempting. Underfoot the ground was marshy and treacherous; the trunks and lower branches of the trees were hidden by a slimy deposit; and the boughs, meeting above, shut out the sunshine and much of the light.

Little wonder that the boys looked at it, and then in each other's eyes, with considerable doubt. Without hesitation, however, they took their places behind Barkham, and in this order they started: the guide first, followed in single file by the captain, Walter, Frank, and the seaman. With the alternative before them, the Dennison boys would have dared any hazard. In this case, the worst in store for them was the unpleasantness of the route. Almost at every step, however careful they might be, they plunged ankle-deep in the moss, and more than once knee-deep; and they had also to avoid (not always with success) the jutting branches and affectionate tendrils of the parasite plants in their way. Luckily, the journey was short. Before long the sounds of firing were quite distinct; the ground began to rise slightly and the path to widen; and at length, less than a mile from the river-side, they arrived within view of the field of combat.

When the boys reached the side of Captain Barkham, who had halted to allow them to come up, this is the scene that lay before their eyes: the path had emerged into a long, sloping glade, carpeted with rough grass; and half-way down, where it narrowed a little, trees had been felled to make a rampart four feet high. Behind it cowered some fifty or sixty natives, armed with the primitive bow and spear, while others were posted in the branches of the trees around. At the foot of the glade there seemed to be a rivulet, and beyond, in the bush, the enemy had evidently their position —though, at the moment, not a brave was visible. Indeed, only one man was to be observed on the other side of the rampart, and he was equidistant between the two positions. It was on him, however, that the attention of the onlookers was intently fixed. His back was towards the new-comers, and all that could be seen of him was a naked form (naked but for a loin-cloth and armlets and necklet of some metal), surmounted by the huge mass of hair and a plume of cassowary feathers. He was shouting and flourishing his spear and shield in a most active manner; his movements were equally active; but his purpose did not strike the boys

—nor even, it may be, the captain—all at once. Frank, with his keen eyesight, was the first to suggest a reason.

'Look!' he cried. 'He's dodging the arrows from the other side. Well done!'

'Is that it?' asked Barkham. 'Ah! I see. He must be challenging 'em to come out and fight in the open. Ah! there he goes again! He's a plucky fellow for a Papuan, whoever he is.—But'—in a lower tone—'where's your father, boys? *I* can't spot him.'·

This was the question which Walter had been asking himself for the last minute or two. It was soon answered. Just then there was a report, and, following the sound, they saw a puff of white smoke arising from a clump of trees to the left of the rampart. Looking more closely, they made out several recumbent figures among the undergrowth.

'Yonder he is!' cried the impulsive Frank, who was inclined to walk by faith.

'Let us get on, then,' suggested his brother.

Barkham had no objection, but he hinted that it might be prudent to give Mr Dennison some warning of their approach. 'It's easily done,' he added, and forthwith emptied one of the chambers of his revolver into the air.

The effect was immediate. First their little guide took to his heels in unreasoning panic; the champion turned; while among the natives all was instantly wild commotion. But this the boys scarcely heeded: their eyes were glued to the clump of trees. Thence, as they advanced into the open, they beheld two men issue, one of them quickly and without precaution, the other more circumspectly. The former was certainly a white man, although his face was burned almost black by exposure to the sun; tall and spare, with a dark beard, streaked with gray; in his hand was a double-barrelled rifle; and his dress, notwithstanding much patching and divers ingenious devices to hide the ravages of time, was very considerably the worse of wear. Could this be their father? He, on his part, seemed to have no doubt of them. Dropping his gun, he broke into a run; and, before they had recovered from the first shock of surprise, he was shaking them and the captain heartily by the hand. His delight was not assumed.

'So you've brought them with you, Barkham?' he cried, and his voice dispelled the last remnant of uncertainty. 'They insisted on coming? Well, I had an idea they would!' Then he regarded them at arm's length, apparently with entire satisfaction. 'And how you've grown!' he exclaimed. 'I had no notion you would be so tall—either of you. Why, Frank, you were almost a baby when I left Hamilton Gap, weren't you?'

'And now I'm going to help you to lick those niggers, sir!' retorted Frank.

Here the other man came up, to be hailed by the captain as Lambert. Obviously he had not yet shaken off the effects of his fever, for his movements were languid, his clothes —such as they were—hung loosely about him, and his face was emaciated and cadaverous, in striking contrast to Mr Dennison's. Even his tone was lugubrious.

Dennison presented the boys with some pride. 'You've heard me speak of my sons, Lambert,' he said. 'Well, here they are—come over to take your place. This is Walter, and this Frank.'

He shook hands. 'They seem sturdy little fellows,' he admitted, 'but I guess they'll have enough of this blasted New Guinea before they're done with it. That's *my* belief. I've had enough, anyhow.'

'Come! you've had bad luck—that's all,' said Mr Dennison, with good humour. 'The fever isn't out of your bones yet, man. You only need a month with Barkham here to bring you back for another spell in "this blasted New Guinea."'

Lambert was inclined to demur, but Barkham thought it time to turn the conversation.

'How long have you been at this game?' he inquired.

'Since daybreak. The barricade was put up last night, and early this morning our scouts brought in the news that the enemy was advancing. You should have seen their consternation when they realised our move! Since then it has been a matter of skirmishing chiefly, for in spite of their numbers they have never ventured out of cover. Even Warupi'—indicating the native with the plume of cassowary feathers—'even he can't shame them into it on any pretext.'

'Eh! that's Warupi, is it?'

'Yes: my up-country friend. For three mortal hours he has been insulting them with the vilest abuse and the worst taunts in his vocabulary—only, it's doubtful if they understand his dialect—and yet they won't budge. Oh! he's in less danger than you might think. Lambert and I have covered him pretty well with our rifles, although I daresay we've frightened them rather than done actual damage.'

'And how many of the enemy are there?'

'Some two hundred, according to our scouts. We haven't half of that. But the others are a cowardly lot, and will probably retire at sundown—before which hour, however,' he added, 'we must manage to teach them such a lesson that they won't come back in a hurry. At present, you can see for yourself how we stand.'

'Then we're just in good time for the fighting?'

'As to that, I'm afraid there won't be much. All the same, we'll be the better of your help and your man's.' To the boys: 'You can shoot, I suppose?'

Before they could reply, a stop was put to further talk by loud cries from the natives behind the rampart. Mr Dennison turned sharply. Then it was observed that the enemy, taking advantage of the diversion caused by the strangers' arrival, had broken cover at last and set upon their intrepid tormentor, while he, disdaining to retreat, was holding his own nobly against them. One or two of the other natives were running to his aid: the rest, as if awaiting an order, held back in indecision.

It was not a moment for hesitation, and on Mr Dennison's side there was none.

'Quick! we have our chance at last!' cried he, picking up his rifle and loading it as he ran. 'I may depend upon you all? Boys, keep behind!'

Considering their father's speed, it was impossible for them—or, for that matter of it, the others—to do otherwise. In a second he was in the midst of the friendly Papuans, exhorting them by word and example to follow; the next, he was over the rampart, with Barkham, the boys, and (last of all) the natives close at his heels. For, as regards the latter, it needed only the good example to encourage them to gallantry. Then, with a shot or two into the group surrounding the unfallen Warupi, and a flight of spears, the fight began.

The few minutes which ensued left a very confused impression on the minds of the Dennison boys. All that they knew with certainty was that they emptied their revolvers; that at first there was much firing and spear-throwing; that they were swayed hither and thither by the opposing masses of savages among whom they found themselves; and that more than one around them fell. Early in the combat they were separated from their father, notwithstanding their strenuous efforts to keep near him; and only once did Walter catch a glimpse of him, wielding his rifle by the barrel-end. His own hands were full. In some dim way he remembers the dark, forbidding faces of the Papuans, and one in particular who loomed over him threateningly, club in air. In his endeavour to avoid the blow, he tripped; and the next thing he was conscious of was that he was on the ground, with the savage above him. There was a minute of agony, and then he was pulled from under his antagonist by the kind hands of Captain Barkham.

'Any damage done?' he asked.

'None, captain.'

'That's right. *He's* dead enough, anyway. But it was a narrow shave, young 'un. There! load your shooter and come on. We mustn't be left behind.'

Already the enemy was in full retreat. The fight had been a short and a sharp one; in that single minute it had been decided, and now the battle had become a rout. Even while Walter and the captain conversed, the last of their opponents and the first of their friends were crossing the little stream into the bush beyond, and the latter, heartened by victory, were pressing hot-foot upon their fleeing and disorganised assailants. Foremost amongst them the two could discern Frank and his father, and it was not without an effort that they reached Mr Dennison's side. For half a mile through the scrub the pursuit continued—until, weary of seeing men slain unresistingly, and assured that the lesson had been effectively taught, the leader called a halt.

'They've had enough, I think,' he said. 'They're thoroughly demoralised, and with twenty men under Warupi dogging their footsteps until nightfall, they won't dare to re-form. I'll give him his orders accordingly. As for us, the less of this sickening work the better.'

So Warupi was allowed to go on with a score of natives —regarding whom, Walter noticed that several, like the champion himself, wore golden ornaments—while the rest, somewhat unwillingly, retraced their steps with Mr Dennison. For the coast-men failed to see why they should not, now that they had the opportunity, wreak full vengeance upon their hereditary foes. The feeling was natural: they had many recollections of wrong and oppression to efface by the only method known to either civilised or uncivilised man. Being balked of further slaughter, they consoled themselves with decapitating the dead.

The whites turned away in disgust.

'It goes against the grain, I admit,' said Mr Dennison. 'But what would you have? We must remember they're savages, and for years past this tribe of cannibals has harried them—latterly completely terrorising them. Even the fighting wasn't a matter of choice. It was fight or be murdered. Thus it was a plain duty to put an end to the scourge, and to do it as thoroughly as possible. Well, we've done it; and having shown our friends how to lick the niggers, as Frank elegantly puts it, you may be sure they won't be harried again. These Papuans are eminently an imitative race. Perhaps, after all, the only thing to be regretted is the first taste we've given our young warriors here of native life. Let us hope it will be exceptionable.'

Did the boys echo the pious wish? A veracious historian, much as he would like to, dare not answer in the affirmative.

CHAPTER VIII.

MR DENNISON'S idea was to return to the village without ostentation, but in this he had reckoned without the natives. They, having apparently no wish to be left behind, swarmed after the white men as soon as they realised their intention; and the result was that what was meant for a quiet journey was soon changed into something of the nature of a triumphal procession. True that, being in the van, they succeeded in getting off first in the captain's boat. But the advantage was temporary. Before long they were overhauled and surrounded by the lighter craft of the Papuans, and thenceforward, until the village was reached, they had to endure with equanimity their part in the scene, and listen perforce to the low, monotonous cadences of the song with which their friends celebrated the defeat of the enemy. Only in the occasional lulls had Mr Dennison a chance of interposing a question to the boys about those at Hamilton Gap, or a remark to the captain regarding his future plans.

At the village it was worse. There they had a bad ten minutes among the grateful coast-folks, all of whom—women and children as well as men—seemed to be mad with elation. Indeed, to judge from their antics, the excitement had even spread to the dogs and pigs! But at last Mr Dennison managed by the judicious blending of flattery and authority to gain them a respite.

'It wasn't easy,' he said; 'in fact, they only agreed when I hinted that we were about to celebrate the victory with a feast, and threatened to retire to the vessel if we weren't allowed to feed here in peace. Instead, I got them to promise to send your men a boat-load of fruit.'

This the sailor Tom was told off to take on board, while the others walked through the village to Mr Dennison's hut, hampered no longer by the attentions of the natives. On the way thither Mr Dennison asked the captain if he noticed any change.

'That's what bothers me,' answered Barkham. 'There *is* a change, but what it is I'm shot if I can specify.'

His friend smiled. 'Try again,' he said.

'Well, I don't know,' said the captain, after an interval, 'unless maybe it is that things seem tidier and better kept, and there aren't so many pigs and wild dogs running about among your feet.'

'You've hit it! And it's all owing to the imitative nature of the people again. They saw that I didn't leave my dirt and refuse where it landed when it was thrown from the platform of the hut: in a few days they didn't either. That disposed of the pigs and the wild dogs. Then they saw that I kept my patch of plantation neat: they went and did likewise, or instructed their women accordingly. And wonderful patches they are!' cried Mr Dennison, waxing enthusiastic. 'There are few things they can't grow in them. Would you believe that I've found fifteen different varieties of yams here, ten of sweet potatoes, and as many as thirty of bananas? Indeed, the fertility of the place is marvellous.

We have mangoes, *taro*, melons, the sago-tree, and of course the palm. Even the sugar-cane isn't unknown, although they don't cultivate it.' He broke off. 'But here we are at my residence. You see, boys, they've honoured me with the biggest house in the village. Ah! never mind the skulls. I'd forgotten them.'

He referred to the most prominent feature in the decoration of the exterior of the hut—a collection of human skulls, of divers sizes and ages, with which the front was embellished. At first sight the lads had been a little startled, and hence the explanation. Curiosity succeeded surprise.

'What are they there for?' asked Frank.

'Partly as trophies of victory, but chiefly to keep away evil spirits. And the natives are so superstitious about these matters that it would mortally offend them if they were removed. That is why they are there now, not because I like them.'

The house itself (and they were all built much in the same style, varying only in size) consisted of a platform resting upon strong props driven into the ground, and bearing a light structure of wood thatched with pandanus leaves. The platform was some twelve feet from the ground, access to it being obtained by a rude ladder. Up this the party clambered, and were rewarded by a good view from the veranda—for that was practically the useful purpose it served —of the whole village and across the open space to the river. As to the house, it was spacious but almost unfurnished, save for the hammocks and other effects of Mr Dennison and Lambert; there was a doorway at each end, and owing to the total absence of windows the interior was always in twilight.

Presently they were all seated upon their haunches on the platform, doing full justice to such viands as Lambert could place before them at short notice. What though the plates were of earthenware or merely large slipper shells? The cold roast duck and native fruits were excellent, and the manner of their service but added the charm of novelty.

'Look there!' said Mr Dennison, pointing to the space between the village and the water, where various groups were busily engaged in piling firewood. 'They're making preparations for *their* feast, and after that we may see a native dance if we have luck. It's worth seeing, too.'

'Maybe, but I hope they don't expect us to join 'em,' remarked the captain, in assumed alarm. 'After roast duck, I, for one, don't feel equal to it.'

The boys laughed at the idea of the portly skipper gyrating round a huge bonfire, and even Lambert deigned to smile. Then the conversation took a more serious turn. They talked of many things—of Mr Maitland and the old homestead, of Captain Barkham's doings in Queensland, of past adventures and mishaps up country—before they came to matters more closely concerning this story. It was near sunset when at last they did; below them the fires had been lit, and the wind wafted a delicious odour of roast pig into their nostrils.

'Lambert and I have a good cargo ready for you, Barkham,' Mr Dennison said.

'Glad to hear it. What is it?'

'The usual trade. It mayn't be so valuable as pearl-shells or bêche-de-mer *—we're too far from the reefs here for those—but there's always a market for copra and yams, and

---

* Bêche-de-mer or trepang, a kind of sea-slug, highly valued by the Chinese for its nutritious qualities. It is found on the reefs in a few feet of water, cured by smoking or boiling, and when thoroughly dried is packed in sacks for shipment to Hong-kong, where it brings a good price.

we 've managed besides to get several loads of good skins and feathers. Over and above, you can have a passenger if you like.'

'A passenger!'

'Yes. Lambert here. In his state of health it would be madness for him to attempt another journey, and so we 've decided to ship him off for a sea-voyage. It only needs that to put him right.'

'I hope so,' interposed Lambert, but in a tone which showed that in reality he had very little hope. 'Any way, I guess I shall be glad to see the last of this island.'

'Not you!' replied Mr Dennison. 'In six or nine months you 'll be back looking us up, as free of fever as I am ! For that 's our plan,' he explained to the captain. 'I take charge of Lambert's interests in the interior, and in return he comes back here as soon as he 's better, and in nine months or so— a year at the latest—he starts in search of me if I 'm still absent. But by that time, if the luck holds, I should be waiting for him. It depends on a lot, of course.'

'That 's so, mate !' was Lambert's emphatic comment.

'Nobody is more alive to the fact than myself,' retorted Mr Dennison. 'All the same, I believe we 'll strike oil this trip, and—well, there 's the big nugget at the other end. It 's worth trying for. Even Lambert, fever and all, thinks the like in his heart of hearts.'

Lambert did not deny it. 'One thing,' he said—'you can reckon on me that my share in the bargain 's safe. We 've been pards too long to play cross, and, fever or not, I 'm bound to be on the spot as arranged. I mayn't like it—I don't say I do—but either you 've got to find me here or I 've got to find you in the hills ; and as to that,' said he, 'there ain't no chance of error.'

It was a long speech for him: more handsome in tone even than in words, when one considers his previous utterance; and his comrade answered it in one word.

'Shake!' he said.

And the two, who had been companions so long and were soon to part, shook hands with a grip in which there was much meaning.

Here there was like to be silence, for the darkness had—as the saying goes, and as the custom is in the tropics—come down with a run, and just then men do not care to talk much. Down below, also, all was momentarily quiet. Around the fires the natives were feasting, in view, perhaps, of the dance to follow; while on board the schooner the lamps had been lighted, and cast a pleasant reflection over the water.

It was then that Barkham, to keep the ball rolling, asked Mr Dennison when he purposed to start.

'As soon as I can—next week, if everything is ready. There's nothing to get by delay except fever. The lads will catch it sooner or later, of course; but I don't choose that they should while we're in the low country. In the hills they've twenty chances of a quick recovery to one that they have here.'

'Then I wish I had caught it there,' murmured Lambert.

'And your course?' continued the captain.

Mr Dennison went into details; but at this point it will suffice to mention that for six days he intended to ascend the river in native boats, and thereafter strike across a tract of country around which the stream, according to his observations, made a big detour. By this he calculated to avoid several cataracts which had proved troublesome to him on the way down, and save a day or two besides. As to natives, they had seen none thereabouts: the country seemed to be uninhabited. The river would be regained near its source, and their subsequent route would be straight into the heart of the mountains and so to their destination.

'And then?'

'Then,' said Mr Dennison, soberly, 'then comes the more difficult part. We must work by diplomacy, and slowly. I don't doubt of success: certainly we have wrought hard for it; ay, and suffered too, these five years past. Lambert can tell you that. But much, if not everything depends upon the natives, and above all on one native.'

'Warupi, namely?' suggested Barkham.

The boys looked up with a deeper interest, for somehow the cassowary-plumed bravo had caught their imagination.

Mr Dennison nodded. 'And if I'm sure of anything,' he went on, 'it is that I may depend upon Warupi to the death. You know the Papuans pretty well, Barkham, and you know how precious few of them can be trusted. I doubt if you've met one. But Warupi isn't an ordinary native; I think you've seen that to-day for yourself. He's a young man, and young men are usually without much influence in a tribe; but by sheer force of bravery and superior intelligence he and his brother are undisputed rulers of theirs. As to his bravery, it speaks for itself. His intelligence, however, is far above the average: I am bound to say that, barring his brother, I've never met another native with a tithe of it.' To the boys: 'For this is what I want you to fix firmly in your minds, lads, seeing that the success of our expedition may hang upon it: that he is in every way an exceptional native, and must be treated as such. Treat him well and honourably, and there is little fear. Treat him otherwise,

and I won't vouch for the consequences.   He has even, what
I have never met in one of his fellows, the makings of a
conscience in him, and a rude sense of honour.   I tell you
this in case anything may happen to me.   Warupi has the
deepest devotion to myself, beyond a doubt; so long as I'm
around there's little fear; and I think it only depends upon
yourselves to share it.   And remember that his devotion
carries with it the devotion, not only of the ten fine fellows
who are with him just now—they seem to have a good deal
of his spirit—but also of the whole tribe.   And that, mind
you, is worth getting.

'But from all this,' continued Mr Dennison, 'you
mustn't run away with the idea that he's a paragon of
virtues.   He has his faults like the rest of us, and when
all's said and done, he's a savage.   Sometimes he's not
too truthful, although that's a vice I don't despair of
curing him of.   He sees I don't like it, and already my
displeasure has worked an improvement.   Then he's vain
—that, being venial, is likely to remain.   Above all, he
is full of superstition: no better, no worse, than the most
degraded black down there; and it is precisely in this
respect that most care is needed.   I have studied him
pretty carefully, and I must confess I haven't sounded the
depths of his superstitious beliefs and fears.   For the comfort
and safety of the journey, I should advise you both to do
the same.'

The boys were quite willing, but the difficulty suggested
itself, how was it to be gone about?   Walter put the
question.

'By learning his language,' was the reply.   'That is the
first step, at any rate, and the one most absolutely necessary
in other respects.   So, as to that, we'll begin to-morrow.'

'And I thought we were done with lessons for good!' Frank whispered plaintively in his brother's ear.

The evening was far advanced before the natives began to tire of gorging themselves with pig's flesh and yams, and bethought themselves—doubtless with misgivings—of the dancing which was before them. Soon tokens of preparation were to be noticed—figures passing to and fro between the fires, here and there the flickering lights of torches, and over all a general hum of conversation. Presently, however, there was an interruption; amid shouts and excitement an exodus took place to the shore; and then, after a minute or two, the whole body of blacks swarmed through the village in the direction of Mr Dennison's hut.

'Hullo? what's up now?' cried the captain, feeling instinctively for the handle of his revolver.

His friend reassured him. 'It's only the return of Warupi and his men, I imagine,' he said. 'If they're coming here'——

'Which is pretty evident,' Barkham put in.

'Then we must go down and meet them in proper form. It's the etiquette of the place.'

Descending accordingly, just as the crowd drew up in front of the house, they saw, by the light of the torches carried by those of the coast-folks who had been feasting, that Warupi and his twenty followers were in the foreground. There was no need to inquire their purpose. The chief stepped forward at once and delivered himself, with many gestures, of his report regarding the chase and final dispersal of the enemy: this, of course, as Walter and his brother learned afterwards. Mr Dennison having replied in a sentence, a curious scene was enacted. One by one Warupi's men advanced, said a word to 'their white father,' and solemnly laid something at his feet. Captain Barkham and the boys leaned eagerly forward to discover what it was, and as quickly started back. For on the ground before him lay a ghastly heap of newly-severed human heads, looking more ghastly in the fitful light of the torches. Thus it was that the Papuans had fulfilled their instructions; and nothing in the day's experience could bring home more forcibly to the lads the fact that they were in a savage country.

Meanwhile Mr Dennison had awakened to the significance of the offering. Speaking less gently than was his custom to the natives, he demanded an explanation from Warupi, whereupon Warupi entered into a long harangue. Freely translated, it bore that the chief was very sorry if he had not pleased his father, but it had seemed good to him and his followers that the man to whom they owed the victory should get the trophies thereof; and that, moreover, he was certain to be tormented by the spirits of those he had killed unless he nailed their heads to the wall of his house. Therefore he begged his father to accept the offering of his children.

Mr Dennison seemed to hesitate; for, as we know, it was his policy in all matters of superstition to offend the susceptibilities of the natives as little as possible.

'What's to be done, I wonder?' he asked, half to himself.

'Done?' cried the captain. 'Why, chuck 'em at their heads and tell them to go hang!'

It was the only answer that could be given, but it had to be couched in more ambiguous language—and it was. Its effect was to make Warupi more anxious. The argument was prolonged, and did not end until Mr Dennison, losing patience, assured the chief that the spirits had no power over white men, and peremptorily requested him to have the heads removed. Warupi, with a significant shrug of the shoulders, gave in; the removal was quickly effected, but in a way which showed the savages' wonder at Mr Dennison's temerity and their fear of what might result —not unmingled, perhaps, with a feeling that after all it was no business of theirs. *They* had done their duty, and if misfortune overtook the scoffer it was upon his own head.

The colloquy between Mr Dennison and Warupi gave the boys an opportunity for a closer scrutiny of the latter than they had yet had. Earlier in the day they had noticed two things—that the skins of him and his followers were a shade darker than those of the coast-folks, and that physically they were much their superiors. Of this fact the men of the interior themselves seemed not unaware, for they held themselves aloof from their hosts in the evident consciousness of their aristocracy. It is always difficult to guess the exact age of savages, but these were all young: Warupi, youngest of the band, could not have been more than twenty-two or twenty-three, while the others were within a few years. The chief was a handsome fellow —muscular and well made; his bearing erect and fearless; his features aquiline, his eyes clear and straightforward, his mouth and chin good; with a countenance that in active play was far from unprepossessing. Here and there his chest and shoulders were tattooed, and—as did the rest— he wore several ornaments of gold. But that about him which best deserved attention was his headpiece. As to this, albeit his clothing otherwise was rather scanty, he had apparently spared no pains to make it elaborate and imposing. The huge mop of frizzed hair was kept back from the forehead by a band of shell, and decorated in front with bright-coloured feathers in such a way as to remind one irresistibly of the aureolas round the heads of saints in old pictures. Above all was the great plume of cassowary feathers.

Meanwhile, one ceremony being over, another took place. First, Mr Dennison spoke to the chief, and then he led his sons forward and presented them with due gravity. They, in ignorance of the language, could do nothing but look pleased, while he stared hard at them for a few moments.

'Good: alright!' he said at last, and offered them his hand. He had seen the white men do so, and copied their method (*his* was to rub noses) as a concession to foreign prejudice.

'They are his only words of English,' explained Mr Dennison. 'There! Shake hands with him, boys.'

And they did.

Thereafter the groups of torch-bearing natives melted gradually away; Warupi's men, who were lodged in a separate encampment, disappeared in search of food; and the chief himself, on the invitation of Mr Dennison, accompanied the whites to their platform to be regaled with fruit and the remains of the roast duck. The further proceedings of the evening were less interesting. There was the dance, indeed; but it was not of long duration, a fact excused by the captain on plausible grounds. One by one the coast-men appeared, dressed to represent some bird or fish—the cassowary, alligator, and pigeon being the favourites—and dressed, too, in a marvellously ingenious fashion. The dancing was disappointing. It was commenced to a slow, monotonous chant, but of active exercise there was little, and that chiefly of the arms, which were waved to and fro to the time of the music so called. As it never developed into anything approaching liveliness, nobody was sorry when at length it came to an end.

It was now late, and Captain Barkham sounded a blast on his whistle as a signal for a boat to take him on board the schooner.

'The boys go with me, I suppose?' he said.

'For to-night, at any rate,' returned Mr Dennison.

Only one incident disturbed their slumbers. Some time in the small hours they were awakened by a loud uproar on shore, and, alarmed by the unearthly howling and shrieking, were beginning to imagine all kinds of evil, when Barkham's head appeared in the doorway of the cabin.

'Asleep?' he asked.

'What is it, captain? What's wrong?' they demanded in one breath.

His reply was assuring. 'Nothing much, but I guessed you would be worriting, and looked in to tell you. The Bingis are trying to frighten the ghosts off, that's all. They call it evil spirits—*I* call it indigestion, brought on by a mixture of roast pig and dancing.'

CHAPTER IX.

'HULLO, sir!' cried Walter, as the boats came together for a moment at a bend of the river.

Mr Dennison looked up.

'Well?'

'Have we much more of this?'

'Not more than twenty miles. Getting tired of it? Well, with the same progress, we should be past the swamps and into a more open country before to-morrow night.'

'Thank goodness!' ejaculated Walter with fervour, and little wonder: for certainly the scene around was a most depressing one. The river ran between two ragged lines of mangroves which touched the water's edge; behind them, if the dank odour could be taken as proof, were tracks of swamp and alluvial ground; the air was that of a palm-house; and the doleful gloom of the place was not lessened by the heavy and persistent rain. The only signs of life, if we except the numerous alligators, were in the three native boats now pulling against the stream, each with a tiny Union Jack at the bow. In one were Mr Dennison and Frank, while of the others Walter and Warupi were the respective coxswains; for here, where the river was comparatively free from sandbanks and other obstructions, the leader had not scrupled to accede to his elder son's request for a responsible command.

They had started from the village that morning. Two days before, the *Bird of Paradise* had set sail for Cooktown with a good cargo, but not until arrangements had been made for periodical visits to New Guinea. Barkham had been loth to part with the boys, for whom he had a genuine affection; nor were they, on their side, less sorry to see the last of the kind-hearted captain. Lambert, who was to go on to Hamilton Gap to recruit his health, carried with him many messages and presents—including a first instalment from Frank to Ruth in the shape of a stuffed bird of Paradise and some feathers, for which he had 'traded' an old knife with one of the villagers. The next two days had been days of busy preparation. There were the boats to overhaul and get ready; the baggage and trade goods to be divided into loads; and—a delicate negotiation this—a dozen of the coast-men to choose to help Warupi's followers as rowers and afterwards as carriers. Of course Mr Dennison wanted the best, and after much palavering, and at the expense of many presents, he managed to get the pick of the tribe. Finally, with high hopes and stout hearts, they had begun their journey into the interior in the early morning hours.

At first, in face of dreary scenery and steady rain, they needed all their patience and good-humour. For some thirty-five miles from the sea the country is low and swampy, intersected by channels joining the various rivers, and shunned by both bird and beast. In a word, it is a dead-level of monotony. Their progress was good, considering the strong current against them—about fifteen miles before they were forced by the noon-tide heat to tie up the boats for several hours. Now they were going on in the cool of the evening.

After dinner, in an evil hour for himself, Frank had volunteered to take an oar, and his desire had been duly gratified. Bothered as he was by scrub-itch and sand-flies—mosquitoes he didn't mind so much, being used to them—he was already regretting it.

'Well, what do you think of the country now?' asked his father in banter.

'Not much!' was the emphatic reply. 'It's nothing but rivers and swamps and sand-flies, and not a shot to be got at anything.'

'Except alligators. But look at Warupi yonder—*he* seems quite cheerful.'

'Does he?' muttered Frank to himself. 'He wouldn't if he had wet clothes to wear, anyway.'

The chief, whose boat was close alongside, turned smilingly to Mr Dennison, and a brisk conversation ensued. Frank, who had picked up enough of the language to recognise a word here and there, became anxious to learn the cause of Warupi's light-heartedness, presumably that he might profit by it to ease his own discomfort.

'What is it?' he asked.

'Nothing very complimentary to our friends the villagers,' said his father, laughing. 'He says they are a tribe of thieves and dogs, that there is scarcely a man among them, that their magic men are fools and their spirits incapable of evil, and much more of the same kind which it's as well those of them with us don't understand. So his heart is glad because he has left them for ever, and is bound for his own country.'

'All very well for him,' commented Frank, 'but just set

him to an oar, and see what he's got to say then. I guess,' he added, 'he wouldn't be so jolly cheerful.'

'Which means that you're tired of *your* oar, I suppose?' Mr Dennison suggested.

But this Frank wasn't prepared to admit, and pluckily held on for half an hour longer before changing tasks. Mr Dennison was no believer in idleness. When either of the boys was not otherwise engaged, he gave them a turn at the two languages of the natives (for, it must not be forgotten, that spoken by Warupi was altogether different from that of the coast-folks), and this tuition, added to the constant practice and the comparative ease of the tongues, was soon to make them, and especially Walter, quite fluent in their use. Frank was more backward than his brother, perhaps because he had a strain of perversity in him, or perhaps because his attention was more readily distracted. Then there were also little bits of valuable advice to receive and store, and opportunities numberless to show their father that they were eager to gain wisdom through experience.

As examples of the advice :

'One thing you mustn't forget in dealing with natives is,' said Mr Dennison, 'never to hesitate. Learn to make up your mind swiftly, and when it is done, to carry out your plan firmly and steadily. Never hesitate between two plans —choose one and stick to it, or they will put it down to weakness. Remember that they are shrewd observers and keen critics, and that the white man's superiority over them is the result of his quick intelligence.'

'But if a better plan strikes you?'

'Stick to the first unless it means failure. You will soon learn to choose the best at the beginning.'

At another time :

'Always speak to a native in a low tone. They distrust shouting and blustering, which is associated in their minds with evil spirits. If it doesn't frighten them, it causes them to dislike you, and you will seldom gain your end by it.'

Or again :

'You have no idea the influence old women have in the tribes. I've always found it a good plan to propitiate them, and once or twice they've got me out of ugly scrapes in consequence. Once, in the hills—it was before I knew Warupi—they saved my life. How? In this way. The men of the place had agreed to kill us during the night, and we were warned of it by some ancient dames whom we had got round. So, when the murderers arrived, they received such a hot reception that they were glad to let us go in peace. But it was a bad ten minutes while it lasted.'

'And how is it done, sir ?' asked Frank.

'The squaring? How would you do it in Queensland, for instance ?'

Frank considered. 'By giving presents, I suppose,' he said.

'And that's exactly how it must be done here,' said Mr Dennison. 'Old women are the same the world over, with this difference in favour of Papua—they're not difficult to please. A string of beads or a stick of trade tobacco—no more is required.'

To return to our itinerary : it has to be related that just before sunset the boats reached a large island in mid-stream, on which it had been decided to camp for the night. It was a good spot for the purpose, for it stood higher out of the water than any land they had seen since leaving the village, and was covered with forest-trees instead of the objectionable mangrove. They did not arrive too soon. Indeed, they had only time to erect the tent before darkness was upon them, but in a few minutes, notwithstanding the dampness of the ground (the rain itself had stopped), two huge fires were throwing their light over the river. Around one crouched the coast-folk, around the other the men of the interior: they were too far apart in race and breeding to associate save in the face of a common danger.

Supper over, Mr Dennison and Warupi lay down to smoke a pipe and talk; while the boys, wearied with the exertions of the day, turned in at once. But it was not to sleep. Until one becomes accustomed to the ceaseless night sounds, there is always a feeling of strangeness in camping out; and in this case, what with mosquitoes and scrub-itch, our young adventurers lay long awake listening to the swish of the water against the banks, and watching through the open side of the tent the dusky figures around the fires. Frank was the first to fall asleep, and at last his brother dropped off also into a light, uneasy slumber. How long he lay there he knew not. But he dreamed that the camp was attacked by hordes of naked savages, that their own men fled to the boats without delivering a stroke, and that his father and Warupi were left to confront the enemy alone; and then he suddenly awoke, with the consciousness of a great uproar without, and of having really heard the noise of firing. Half-asleep as he was, it was quite enough for him; and, throwing off the mosquito-net, he seized his rifle and ran out into the open. There he halted for a moment in indecision. The fires were now burning with a red glare, and between them Mr Dennison and the natives stood in a group, doing—what?

Before Walter could decide, his father turned and observed him. He motioned him forward.

'Oh! is anything wrong, sir?' asked the boy.

'Nothing worse than evil spirits,' said Mr Dennison, smiling. 'Some of them got into the camp with designs against the men, and the foolish fellows asked me to fire off my gun to frighten them away. I've done it successfully, it seems.' More seriously: 'After all, Walter, I'm not sorry this happened. It's another of the lessons you must learn— to wake up with all your wits about you, and turn out promptly at the first signal of danger. Just now, as it happens, there was ample time to massacre us all between the first shot and your appearance. However,' he added, by way of encouragement, 'it's a thing that comes quite easily after a bit. Now off you go to bed again.'

'And you, sir?'

'I? Oh! I have two hours of this yet. It is my watch, you know.'

'And when is mine?' inquired Walter.

Mr Dennison laughed. 'Wait till we're tramping across country, my lad; there will be plenty of it then for us all. Just now, it's hardly worth while robbing you of your sleep.'

Walter returned thoughtfully to the tent, and there the first object that met his eyes was the unconscious Frank, who had slumbered peacefully through all the turmoil. Now it struck the elder as scarcely fair that he should have all the trouble and his brother reap the benefit; and, being impressed by his lesson, he deemed it his duty to impart it immediately. So, with a little trouble, he roused his sleeping junior.

'Hullo! what's the matter?' demanded Master Frank, not in the most grateful tones.

'Matter! Didn't you hear the row?'

'What row? You're dreaming! I don't hear anything.'

'Not now, I daresay,' returned Walter; 'but there was one, and we might all have been massacred the time you were sleeping there like a pig.'

'Fudge!' was the contemptuous retort. 'There are no natives hereabouts—I heard father say so in the afternoon. And if that was all you wakened me for, you might have left it till the morning. I call it a great shame.' And with a grunt of dissatisfaction he turned on his side and forthwith resumed the interrupted nap; while Walter, hurt by the base ingratitude, did not follow his example for at least ten minutes!

The second day differed from the first only in this: there were more frequent breaks in the monotony of the landscape, the banks of the river were better marked, and as the day advanced, game of divers kinds became more plentiful —or, rather, less scarce. One species which the river had never lacked, and now lacked less than ever, was the alligator. Speaking literally, the water swarmed with them, and many were the gruesome stories told by the natives—and for the boys' edification translated by Mr Dennison—of their ferocity and of narrow escapes from the jaws of the monsters. It was even said that they had been known to attack a canoe and drag a man into the stream; but this was dismissed as doubtful, particularly as they had hitherto made no attempt on either Walter or Frank.

It was not long, however, before the two had a nearer acquaintance with them than they relished. The boats had just been run aground upon a spit of sand, their occupants were leaving them in preparation for the mid-day rest, and the boys, having landed, were standing together by the water-side. Suddenly there was a cry from one of the natives, followed by a warning shout in their father's voice:

'An alligator!   Look out there, boys!'

Walter, glancing round, realised their danger.   The saurian was within ten feet, it was wobbling quickly towards them, and they were between it and the water—whither, having probably been roused from a noon-tide *siesta* by the din, it was retreating for safety.   He was aware that the reptiles seldom molest people on shore unless their way is barred, and instinctively he tried to get out of its path.   It was then that the accident happened, but whether as the result of his haste or of a stroke of the alligator's tail he could never say.   Somehow—so much is certain—he cannoned against Frank, precipitating him headlong into the river; and almost simultaneously there was another splash as the original cause of the mischief, its road clear, plunged likewise into its native element!

A moment of consternation—and no more.   While Walter stood aghast, the Papuans shrieked, and Mr Dennison ran forward.   They heard a third splash, and then Warupi triumphantly scrambled ashore with the unlucky Frank.   He was none the worse except for the wetting.

'What made you do it, Walt?' he asked reproachfully.

'You may thank your stars the alligator was as much frightened as yourself, and that it didn't strike the water at the same spot,' quietly said Mr Dennison.   'If it had, you wouldn't have been here.'

Frank was silent for a little.   Then: 'But what an ugly brute it was!' he exclaimed.   Thereafter, you may be sure, he had a wholesome aversion to alligators.

One effect which the adventure had was that, to Mr Dennison's gratification, it brought Warupi and the boys closer together.   Hitherto the result of which he had spoken at the village had not, in spite of his efforts, been attained.

The fault was Warupi's. Apparently it was due to shyness on the chief's part—assuredly it was due to no want of good-will on the boys'—and so, for good reasons of his own, the leader gave a warm welcome to anything tending to foster their friendship.

The journey up-stream was without further incidents of note. Before nightfall the region of swamps was left behind, and during the next four days they travelled through an undulating, well-wooded country, catching an occasional glimpse in the barer parts of hills in the background. Here there was game in plenty to shoot for the pot—ducks and geese, water-fowls, pigeons as big as turkeys (for the Goura pigeon, with its purple plumage and beautiful crest, weighs from five to seven pounds), kingfishers, and many others of the feathered family. Nor were they without variety of diet while the river was full of fish, and the natives had the skill to catch them. On the lower reaches a few villages were passed, and thereat, although the inhabitants knew Mr Dennison and were invariably friendly, certain ceremonies had to be gone through. Explanations of their purpose were demanded and given—to the inquirers' enlightenment, let it be hoped; a few presents, of little intrinsic value, were pressed upon the acceptance of the sorcerers and head-men; and the latter, in return, were never unwilling to supply the adventurers with fresh fruit. Finally, the *bow-wow* or great pipe was brought forth and gravely filled with the newly-acquired trade tobacco; and, having been lit, it was handed from man to man, each taking a few whiffs, until the contents were exhausted—all this in the most ceremonious manner, but with much talking. It was—as Frank, loyal to a favourite author, did not forget to mention—just like a scene out of Fenimore Cooper. And, when it was over, they resumed their voyage with the good wishes of the friendly savages.

But the villages, oddly enough, became less frequent as they advanced, until ultimately they ceased altogether. Mr Dennison had no explanation : game was quite as abundant, the country better, and the climate certainly no worse. Yet so it was; and for the last two days of their river-voyaging, which was now, owing to the narrowing channel and the increased speed of the stream, a matter of more difficulty and slower progress, they saw no signs of the aborigines whatever. I am not sure that they regretted it. If they did, the future had ample compensation in store for them.

CHAPTER X.

IT was in the forenoon of their sixth day since leaving the coast that Mr Dennison called the attention of the boys to a low, rumbling sound as of a distant cataract, and pointed out the small and ever-lessening headway the boats were making against the current.

'Is it the rapids?' asked Walter.

'Yes. They begin ten miles farther on, and from there to the mountains they are pretty numerous, as we found to our cost coming down. It was at the third cataract, about twenty miles up, that poor Jameson was lost.'

'And what shall we do now?'

'Another mile, and I'm afraid we must land,' replied Mr Dennison. 'Then for the hard work—how hard, depends on the nature of the country. According to my calculations, we have about fifty miles of it to cross before we strike the river again. How long should we take? Once more it depends. But if we start to-morrow morning—the preparations will occupy the rest of to-day—we should do it in three days at the outside, and probably in two. From what I saw of the country, it seemed to be fairly open, but here as elsewhere—only more so—appearances are apt to be deceptive. One thing: Frank will get game to his heart's content.'

'Even birds of Paradise?' inquired Frank.

'Most certainly.'

'And time, too,' remarked the boy. 'Except the one I sent to Ruth, I haven't seen any since we landed.'

Mr Dennison counselled patience. 'You may need it,' he said, 'for really it isn't an easy matter to bag the bird, especially when one has other things to do,' a fact which Frank was presently to learn for himself.

Just then, however, the subject had perforce to be dropped, for at that moment Mr Dennison espied a suitable spot for the disembarkation, and decided to battle no longer with the current. Accordingly, he gave the order to pull in. The camp was quickly formed; and thereafter the unloading of the boats, and, in view of to-morrow's march, the distribution of the various loads amongst the men, took up the best part of the afternoon. One measure of precaution remained to be performed—namely, to find a place of security wherein to hide the canoes in view of their return. This was left to Warupi, and duly done to the leader's satisfaction.

It was a motley band which started next morning. First went Warupi and two of his warriors to choose the path, or with their axes to clear one if necessary; then followed the score or so of naked bearers, loads upon head and spears in hand; while Mr Dennison and the boys, carrying their Winchesters and a revolver apiece, attended to the marshalling of the line and saw that there were no stragglers. Thus they struck out at right angles to the river, and plunged directly into the heart of the bush.

For the first few miles, travelling in the comparative cool

of morning, they made good progress in some comfort through a park-like country. The ground rose so slightly as hardly to be perceptible, and there was little undergrowth beneath the great forest-trees. To the boys every sight was full of interest. Now it was a clump of beautiful flowers of the hibiscus or croton families; again a no less beautiful creeper clinging to the trunk of a giant eucalyptus or evergreen oak; and next moment a flock of gaily-plumaged and chattering cockatoos, or an immense butterfly gorgeous in all the colours of the rainbow. For they were in a naturalist's paradise, and for an hour their language was one long exclamation of wonder.

Mr Dennison, who had been studying the lie of the ground, was less enthusiastic.

'Wait a little,' he said, in warning. 'We shall have a sharp climb presently, and when we begin to feel the heat of the sun '——

'It's bad enough already,' plaintively muttered Frank.

'Just wait for an hour!' repeated his father. 'It's nothing to what it will be then. So, if you take my advice, you'll reserve your strength. Believe me, you'll have little inclination to chase butterflies or spend five minutes in collecting crotons and orchids.'

He proved to be right. Before long the nature of the surface began to change. The ascent became steeper, and now their path had to be cut through the scrub of a dense thicket, in parts so impenetrable that even the carriers had to throw down their burdens and lend a hand. The work was hard in itself, and if the effect of the heat be added you may imagine the result. After five minutes of it, the lads felt as if they were being roasted alive; and the natives themselves to whom it could scarcely have been unwonted, commenced to hint vaguely that a rest and a smoke of 'tombaco' would not be undesirable. But Mr Dennison was obdurate : not until the summit was reached, or the usual hour of *siesta* arrived, should there be a halt, and to that they must make up their minds. It had to be, of course ; but it was not pleasant, more particularly when they disturbed a colony of red ants, and every leaf against which they brushed rained down its load upon their faces and necks. Now the red ant has a pair of nippers which meet in one's flesh with a potent smart, and when a legion of them are at the same game the mind is apt to wander back to ancient Egypt for a parallel. And it is small consolation, as Walter and Frank discovered, to be told that this is one of the least of Papuan plagues.

But even from ants and overpowering heat relief comes at last, and in due time, the ridge being crossed, they encamped beneath the shade of a dense grove of bananas. It was not too soon, for they were all more or less exhausted by the fatigues of the march. They had their recompense, however, in the prospect visible from their resting-place of a broad, swelling expanse of grassy country, only broken here and there by a clump of trees, and bounded some six or seven miles away by another bush-covered ridge.

Frank, contrary to his habit, was unusually silent during dinner ; and when the meal was over, and the bearers had gone to sleep as one man, he unburdened himself of the cause of his reflections.

'They're a queer lot, these natives,' he remarked sagely. 'Down at the coast, where the land isn't worth much, you'll find them in hundreds, and here, where there's any amount of game, you don't see one. I wonder why it is, now ? *I* can't understand it. Can you, Walter ?'

'Not I,' replied Walter.

'And there are others in the same position,' said their father. 'I've been puzzling my head over it all day, to no end. By all rules, the district should be densely populated. But it isn't—in fact, we haven't come across a single sign of any inhabitant. And, what makes it so annoying to a scientific mind like Frank's, there seems to be no reason whatever for it.'

'Maybe the country '——

'Oh! it's not that. Take it all round, in spite of bush ticks and red ants, it's a good country. It can't be the climate, there's no want of game, and the soil is marvellously fertile. Why, it only needs settlement and cultivation. And, Papuans or not,' he went on, 'that's what must come in time. True, it is lying in waste just now, but imagine the future it may have—almost certainly will have—when it is colonised by Englishmen. It may be a long time, for as yet our flag hasn't penetrated beyond the coast—has hardly made good its footing even there. But the future! For myself, I have no doubt that here there will be a plantation as rich as any in Ceylon or Java, for there's hardly a tropical crop that can't be grown in that soil. The only drawback is the want of labour, and as long as we can get coolies from India that needn't be insuperable.'

'Not counting the natives,' Walter put in.

'Who aren't quite numerous enough for the purpose— especially hereabouts,' said Mr Dennison. 'And that brings us back to the original question. After all, Frank, I'm afraid it must go unanswered, unless'—laughingly—'you ask the first one we happen to meet.'

'If he gives me the chance before sticking a spear through me,' returned Frank.

The march was resumed three hours later, and almost immediately their difficulties began afresh. Once more they had experience of the deceptiveness of Papuan appearances. For on the plain, so inviting from afar, the grass proved to be so high—never less than three feet, and in some places six—that it was well-nigh impassable. Nor was it ordinary grass, but the rough and flesh-piercing variety known as spear-grass, which sticks in one's clothing and soon changes one into the semblance of a great porcupine. Strange to say, it seemed to have no effect on the natives, who, bare-legged and barefoot as they were, wormed their way through it without scathe; while to the whites, protected by leggings and thick garments, it was the cause of such intense annoyance that Mr Dennison was forced to ask Warupi if there was no remedy.

The chief's reply was to the point.

'He says we have only one alternative—to burn the grass,' was the report, 'and as that would take a day or two it isn't to be thought of. We must go on. After all, boys, it's no more than six miles or so.'

'And six miles too much!' confided Frank in his brother's ear, as they panted in the wake of the carriers. 'Speak of travelling! I must say this isn't what I expected of New Guinea. And what about the adventures?'

'What!' exclaimed Walter; 'you don't mean that you're funking it already, young 'un?'

'I should think not!' The denial was given with proper indignation. 'All the same, I can't see the fun of this sort of thing. Can you?'

Walter ignored the question.

'Serves you right if you came to New Guinea for fun,' he said stoutly. 'If that was all you wanted, you should have stayed at home. Besides, it might be worse. How? Why, you should be jolly glad the grass isn't swarming with natives, for one thing. You'd get adventures *then*.—Hullo! what's that?'

The exclamation was caused by a sudden commotion in front as of the scurrying of many animals through the grass, and was followed by a shot from Mr Dennison. Running forward, they learned that the advance-guard had started a drove of wild pigs. The shot had missed, but before they went much farther they discovered, somewhat to the restoration of Frank's spirits, that the grass, if it did not swarm with natives, swarmed with pigs and kangaroos. Almost at every step they could be heard making off, and less frequently they gratified the travellers with a momentary glimpse of their tails. Some waste of ammunition was the result; until Mr Dennison forbade firing, on the ground that even if the animals were hit it would not be easy to retrieve them, while shooting for shooting's sake was an abomination.

Other and more unpleasant inhabitants were encountered as they worked their way inch by inch through the grass. Most numerous and dangerous were the huge carpet-snakes, as they are called in Australia, but with these the boys had been familiar from infancy, and knew how to avoid them. They were luckier than some of the bearers, too, in escaping the hornets which abounded. Twice was a nest of the insects disturbed, on both occasions to the proverbial cost of unfortunate natives. Notwithstanding these and other incidents, the journey became less and less to the taste of the adventurers. In two hours they covered hardly more than as many miles. Thereafter there was an improvement, or they grew more expert; and in the end (to shorten the story)

they succeeded in reaching the base of the ridge well before
sunset, there to rest in the comfortable knowledge of an
arduous task accomplished.

As far as the labour was concerned, the next day differed
but little from the first. The surface was hilly and more
broken, but on the other hand they had no such expanse
of grass to traverse, and towards nightfall their route was
through country which, after their recent experience, seemed
comparatively open. But the day was not to end without
its misadventure. In scrambling down the steep slope of
a hill-side Mr Dennison missed his footing and rolled to
the bottom, and when the boys gained the spot they found
him ruefully rubbing his left ankle.

'Are you hurt, sir?' asked Walter anxiously.

'I've twisted it badly, I'm afraid,' he returned. 'The
worst of it is that it's the foot which was hurt a month
or two ago, and which has been weak ever since. But if
I can walk'—— He took a few steps, and was forced by
the pain to desist. 'No! Then we must camp here, and
see what a night's rest will do. I daresay it will be all
right in the morning.'

So the tent was pitched by the side of a stream of clear
water in a beautiful little dell, bounded on two sides by
bush-clad ridges, and on another by a ring of high forest-
trees. But in the morning, although the pain was less,
the foot was still weak, and Mr Dennison deemed it prudent
rather to rest for another day than to risk disablement by
hurrying on. Needless to say, nobody objected—Master
Frank, for his own purposes, least of all.

'Say, Walter!' he whispered in a tone of mystery.

'Well, youngster?'

'Isn't it a good chance to shoot a bird of Paradise at

last? There must be lots in the bush over there. You might ask the pater.'

'What is it?' inquired Mr Dennison, looking up.

Walter proffered his brother's request.

'There's no reason why you shouldn't, if you can manage it without straying beyond earshot of the camp. That you mustn't do on any account. And if I were you I should take Warupi or another of the natives with me.'

But this, when they were ready to set forth, was found to be impracticable. Warupi and the pick of his men were nowhere to be seen, being engaged doubtless in a hunt on their own account; and as regards the rest of the natives, who were sleeping off a heavy meal of kangaroo flesh, the boys had little wish for their company.

It was a good morning for their purpose. Rain had fallen in the early hours, everything wore a look of freshness, and as yet the air was (for New Guinea) cool. They were in high spirits, therefore, as they made for the ring of trees, and presently were out of sight of the camp. Did not the excursion smack of adventure? For the first time, at least, they were alone in the Papuan bush. There was their father's injunction, indeed; and of course they had no desire to disobey it, especially as their interpretation of 'beyond earshot'—to wit, beyond sound of a rifle-shot—gave them considerable latitude. As things turned out, they could not help themselves. For although there was no scarcity of other birds and game in the stretch of park-like country which lay behind the line of trees—birds great and small, as well as wallabies, tree-climbing kangaroos, iguanas, and the rest—birds of Paradise were apparently to seek. But it was birds of Paradise they wanted, and meant to have; and as they wandered about on the outlook for them they refused in disdain many good shots which offered at lesser marks. At length they had their reward. Coming to an open part, Frank's keen eyes distinguished the brilliant plumage of their quarry in a distant tree-top.

'That's it, I'm sure!' he cried, in excitement. 'Quick, Walt! we must get nearer!'

This they proceeded to do with the wariness of experienced bushmen, creeping from cover to cover, and neglecting no precaution : only to discover when they arrived within gun-shot that, alas! their bird had flown. Again it (or another) was seen and followed—with the same result; and so the game went on until the boys had unwittingly strayed a good distance from camp, without getting even the chance of a shot at the coveted bird. Then they remembered their father's remark concerning the difficulty of bagging it, and for a little were discouraged. But they had perseverance, and beyond doubt they would have continued their efforts until success came to them, had it not been for an incident which was startling enough to put all thoughts save that of personal safety out of their heads.

They had just reached the summit of one of the low, bush-covered ridges so common thereabouts, which they had gradually been ascending for half an hour. Walter, who was first, gave a quick glance below him in search of their bird of Paradise, and as quickly threw himself upon the ground.

'What is it?' asked Frank, who had promptly followed his brother's example, and was now working himself forward to his side in the fashion of the serpent.

Walter waited until he was abreast, and then pointed below. 'Look!' he whispered.

Frank looked, and—

'*Natives!*' he cried, in great amazement.

It was even so. The lads were lying, as you know, on the ridge of the hill; below them was a steep and bare descent of perhaps two hundred feet; and at the foot, in a glade not dissimilar to that in which their own encampment was situated, this is what Frank had seen in his hurried survey. A collection of fragile, one-sided huts, about a score in number; several huge fires, around which a few naked savages were sleeping; and, scattered here and there about the dell in easy postures, numerous others. Altogether there could not have been less than a hundred of them visible.

Then, while the boys watched this scene as if fascinated, a sudden commotion seemed to arise in the natives' midst, loud cries were heard, and at once the outlying groups began to converge upon the fires.

Frank plucked his brother's sleeve. 'D' you think they've seen us, Walt?' he whispered.

'No'—emphatically.

'But what'——

'Hush!' said Walter. 'Watch!'

The natives with much gesticulation and waving of spears, gathered together in two large crowds, and a low hum as of talking arose to the boys. In five minutes the conference —if such it was—broke up, and Walter nudged his brother as a hint to go.

'Eh? what are you going to do?' asked Frank.

'Get back to camp like a shot,' was the reply. 'Quick! come on;' and, followed closely by the other, he backed cautiously out of his position. For a time, as long as they supposed themselves to be within earshot of the savages, they measured every footstep with the deliberation of red-skins, and their hearts jumped whenever a twig snapped under-foot. But nothing happened, and gradually they regained sufficient confidence to step out with more freedom. At last Walter halted, and listened with his ear to the ground.

'They're not after us, anyway,' he said, jumping up. 'Come on, Frank! We must make a run for it now.'

He set out at a goodly pace, Frank at his heels, and for six or seven minutes, notwithstanding the innumerable obstructions of the scrub, the speed was kept up. Then:

'Is it far yet, Walt?' inquired the younger, breathlessly.

'It can't be. Come on!'

Three minutes later still:

'Hey, Walter!'

'Come on!' reiterated the impatient Walter, over his shoulder.

'But I can't—I'm dead beat. Honour bright, Walt!'

The tone was so piteous that Walter was compelled to stop, and Frank took immediate advantage thereof to lie down.

'Just a minute to get my breath!' he pleaded.

The prayer was granted, and while he panted and sweated on the ground Walter tried to make out their bearings. He was sure he had not lost his direction, and yet the place seemed unfamiliar. Indeed, to his thinking, they should have reached the camp ere this, and that they had not done so he could only account for by the surmise that in the excitement of the chase they had gone farther than they imagined. Of anything worse he had no fear.

He was puzzling over this when his quick ear caught the sound of footsteps in front, evidently at no great distance. He hearkened: there could be no mistaking it. A hundred wild ideas darted through his head. Another moment, and one fact was certain: the foot was that of a native.

Was their retreat cut off?

CHAPTER XI.

THE FLIGHT TO THE RIVER.

ONLY a minute sufficed for the boys to conceal themselves amongst the undergrowth at the foot of a great evergreen oak, and there, with their guns ready, and the sickening dread of uncertainty in their hearts, to await the worst.

The patter of the light footfall sounded more and more distinct : in a second the new-comer would be abreast. Was he a friend or an enemy? In imagination Walter saw him peering suspiciously on all sides, and realised that he could scarcely miss their tracks. But before he had time to speculate on the issue, the man came into sight; there was an instant of hesitating scrutiny; and then, with a cry of relief to his brother, Walter rushed out of his hiding-place to greet him.

'Out, Frank! It's Warupi!'

The chief—for it was he—smiled with satisfaction on seeing first the one and then the other emerge from the scrub, but seemed somewhat taken aback by the warmth of their reception. Recovering, he told them in his own language—which Walter, and to a less degree Frank, now understood and spoke without difficulty—that he had been despatched to find them by their father, who had become anxious at

I

their long absence. Having found them, he proposed their immediate return.

'And the natives?' said Walter. 'Wouldn't it be as well to tell him, Frank?'

'*I* should.'

So, as well as he could, Walter related the story of their adventure, and by the gleam of intelligence in Warupi's eyes he was convinced that he was thoroughly understood. He heard him to the end without a word, and when the boy had finished he had but a single question to ask:

'How far?'

Walter tried to give him an idea of the distance.

The chief thought for a moment; and then, with a gesture which the boys interpreted to mean that they were to await him, he began to retrace their steps to the savages' camp. To a Papuan, who is invariably a good bushman, directions would have been superfluous: their trail was as obvious to Warupi as a turnpike road would be to an Englishman.

Frank watched him until he was lost to view.

'Looks as if he didn't believe us, somehow,' he remarked. 'Should we wait?'

'We 'd better, I think,' answered Walter.

The chief was back in less than half an hour, although to the boys it seemed an age. His countenance showed that he was in some perturbation of spirit, and his haste and laconism confirmed it.

'Come!' he said, quickly ; and no more.

Without a word they followed him as he strode in the direction of the camp, and not a syllable was uttered on the way. It was as if the shadow of a great evil was upon them all. Mr Dennison, leaning on his gun, was on the outlook at the belt of trees, and his face cleared when he saw that they were safe. For an hour he had been in suspense.

'Ah! you're there?' he cried, limping forward to meet them. 'Between you I've got a nice fright. Where have you been? What have you been doing?'

As shortly as possible, while they walked towards the encampment, Walter told him. His face became thoughtful again as he listened.

'Natives! Here?' he said. 'You're sure?'

'Ask Warupi, sir.'

He turned to the chief, who had hitherto taken no part in the conversation. Now he plunged into the narrative of what he had seen. His report, while it confirmed Walter's statement, added much to its seriousness, for the Papuan had noticed a meaning in many things that to the boy had no significance. Thus the slight, one-sided huts had told him that the camp was a temporary one, and the attire of the men and the absence of women that the party was out on a raiding expedition. Finally, Warupi had no doubt whatever of their grave danger. If they were discovered, they would be attacked, and if they were attacked—well, the chances were not in their favour.

Mr Dennison took a few steps up and down in front of the tent, pulling his beard thoughtfully.

'It's a serious matter, boys,' he said, at length. 'You've escaped a great danger—only to fall into another, perhaps. If we escape it also, let this be a lesson never in future to venture into the bush without Warupi or one of his men.— As to our present course'——

He broke off to consult with Warupi, and then he continued his walk. In two minutes he had resolved upon instant and decided action.

'Yes; it's our only course,' he said. 'We must break up camp at once, and go. I was calculating this morning that we had sixteen miles yet before striking the river at the point marked in my rough map. Well, if we make directly for it at its nearest point, it can't be more than ten or twelve. We shall have to cross lower down than I intended, but that doesn't matter a rap if we can manage it without the knowledge of the enemy. Once on the other side, I think we can laugh at them.'

'But your foot, sir?' said Walter.

'Oh! it's almost right again. The morning's rest has done it an immense deal of good. Now,' he continued, 'the sooner we're off, the better chance there is of eluding the natives. You've five minutes to get something to eat, boys; then, make sure that your firearms are loaded. You may need them.'

Meanwhile, Warupi had not been idle. First he had posted several of his warriors in the belt of trees to keep watch; and now, having roused the sleeping carriers, he spurred them on to work by word and example. Not that, as the news of the danger spread from man to man, much spurring was required. The tent was struck and the camp cleared with praiseworthy diligence, loads were adjusted and made up, and well within the time stated the procession was marshalled and ready to start. Mr Dennison, with Warupi and Frank, led the way; while Walter's heart was gladdened by the command of the rearguard, consisting of one of the chief's men and Amar, the head of the coast-natives. The leader's instructions were simple: to march together as far as the ground permitted, to be prepared to close up at the first signal, and, above all, to be always on the alert.

For a couple of miles the route was through the bush

which was familiar to the boys as the scene of the morning's ramble, and so far the progress made was excellent. Here every precaution was taken, but not a sign of the strangers was observable even to the hawk-eyed Warupi. Then, in the heat of the day, they had to cut a path through a stretch of thick scrub over a rough, hilly surface. This was their heaviest task, and that in which, in the event of an attack, there was the most danger; but fortunately it did not last long, and presently they were descending quickly through a more open country—towards the river, as Mr Dennison fondly hoped. Half the estimated distance had been covered, and yet there were no signs. Somewhat prematurely, he began to congratulate himself on the success of their flight.

The awakening was not long in coming. The vanguard had reached the bank of a stream, and suddenly Warupi stopped and pointed out a mark in the soft clay at the water-side. At once, of course, the whole procession was brought to a halt, and when Walter ran forward to ask the cause, he found his father and the chief minutely examining what was evidently the print of a naked foot. One discovery led to another. In a minute Warupi was able to show that they had struck a trail—and one, too, which had been much used. On the one side he followed it from the water to the point, twenty yards from it, at which it entered the bush, and on the other—it was plainer here—for a considerable distance down the opposite bank of the stream. One question remained, but it was the most important: was the trail new or old?

Mr Dennison put it to the chief.

'Has my white father forgotten this morning's rain?' returned Warupi; which, being interpreted by the whites, meant that the track had been used not later than a few hours previously. Even to them it was obvious that the impression in the clay had not been made *before* the rainfall.

Here the examination was interrupted in a startling manner by an inarticulate cry from Frank, followed instantly by the report of a shot from his rifle. The boy was standing with his back to the stream, facing the bush; and, turning swiftly, the others were just in time to catch a glimpse of a savage as he darted behind a tree. The whites stared, hardly knowing what to make of it; from the carriers arose a howl of disappointment and defiance, backed by a belated flight of spears.

'Missed!' cried Walter.

'Steady, Frank! What made you do that?' demanded Mr Dennison, sharply.

Frank's face fell. 'I—I don't know, sir,' he confessed. 'I saw the man come out of the bush, and somehow the gun seemed to go off of itself. I—I'm very sorry.'

'You should be, stupid,' said Walter in an undertone. 'It was an easy shot.'

Warupi said a word to Mr Dennison, who nodded; and the chief, throwing down his shield, followed the stranger quickly into the bush. The others, guessing his purpose, waited in expectancy not unmixed with fear. After all, it was only man against man.

Mr Dennison seized the opportunity to enforce a moral.

'Really, Frank, you must be more careful,' he said. 'For all we know, the man may have been friendly. Now, that unlucky shot of yours may bring the whole tribe down upon us, and where shall we be then? It was the surprise, of course, and I don't blame you. But you must learn to control yourself.'

'I'll try, sir,' answered Frank.

'And it won't be difficult to succeed, my lad. In this case, let us trust to Warupi that no harm's done.'

But Frank was not altogether satisfied, and he took the first chance of speaking to his brother apart.

'Look here,' he said—'what would you have done, Walt?'

'I don't know, but anyway I shouldn't have missed,' was the reply. 'Warupi's a good chap, but I prefer to do my work myself. He's doing yours now.'

Frank said no more, but in a few minutes he had the consolation of learning that Warupi had been as unsuccessful as himself. He had tracked the man as far as he dared, and had not overtaken him—had not, indeed, as much as come in sight of him. It was unpleasant news, for that the fugitive would alarm his tribe and lead them in their pursuit there could be little doubt. For them, their course was clear. If they could gain the river before the natives, and effect a crossing, they had still a chance of avoiding bloodshed—and its consequences.

Warupi had his suggestion. Water runs to water: why not follow the trail of the natives down the opposite bank of the stream? In his opinion it was the route they had traversed in marching from the river to their encampment in the bush, where the main body now was. True that they might encounter a detached party of them, but of that he had little fear, and at the best something must be risked. It seemed to him good: what said his white father?

'Lead on, Warupi,' answered Mr Dennison. 'It *is* good.'

Now all this, from the finding of the footprint until they went on again, had occupied not more than ten minutes. Thanks to those who had already passed that way, and to the eagerness of everybody to put his best foot forward, the time was easily recovered. For three miles they held by the side of the stream, which brawled along in a stony bed; the descent was gradual, and such difficulties as Nature had placed had been kindly cleared away by their predecessors. The path, albeit narrow, sufficed. The anxious part was that of those who brought up the rear, of whom Mr Dennison was now one. Knowing that the expected attack must fall upon them first, they had perforce to keep all their faculties on the stretch to anticipate it if it were possible, while all the time they had the uneasy feeling in their hearts that their efforts were futile against bushmen like the Papuans. When the blow came, it would come with the quickness of a lightning-flash.

'Of course your gun's loaded, Walter?' said his father.

'Yes—both barrels.'

'With small-shot?'

'One of them,' replied Walter. 'How stupid! Shall I make them both ball, sir?'

'Not if we can serve our purpose without. The shooting may frighten them off, and in that case there's nothing to be gained by killing a few; rather the opposite, for their desire for vengeance might soon overcome their fears.'

'And if we *are* attacked?'

'Try the small-shot first. Keep the other barrel until the fight really begins.'

'And then?'

'Then I'm afraid you won't have time to discriminate,' said Mr Dennison, quietly.

But three-fourths of the journey—presuming the estimate to be right—had been accomplished, and they had not been attacked. Was their luck to continue? Meanwhile, it was striking to observe the power of a touch of danger. In spite of the heat, the unusual speed, the weight of the loads, the anxiety—these combined—there were no pleas of fatigue and prayers for tobacco, no lingering, not even a grumble. The eager desire of all was to reach the river —that alone. At length they seemed to be approaching it. The stream on their right ceased its brawling and flowed smoothly, the character of the vegetation began to change, and there were other signs to the initiated that they were nearing swampy ground. 'On!' cried Mr Dennison. 'It can't be far now.'

Soon it was easier said than done. First the stream, which had been their guide so long, lost itself in the swamp; and then, a little farther on, Warupi passed the message back that the path had disappeared also, and that he was floundering in a bog. Would the commander call a halt while he searched for it?

Mr Dennison was too impatient.

'On! on!' he repeated. 'Tell him to get to the river —never mind the path.'

It was the beginning of difficulties compared with which those they had already surmounted were mere child's play. Every step plunged them deeper into the morass; and before long, instead of holding on by the branches as they felt their way, they were compelled to drag themselves laboriously through the great roots and along the gnarled trunks without touching the ground at all. This, indeed, was impossible; beneath was a black, slimy mud, into which an unfortunate bearer, missing his footing, would occasionally slip to the armpits. The same fate was like to be that of the whites more than once, for the trees were draped with moss to the height of twelve or fourteen feet—showing how high the water rose during flood-time—and as slippery as ice. That they escaped it, was due more to luck than to their caution. As to the headway made, it was miserably slow, and would have been slower still, or probably none, but for the wonderful entanglement of the roots and lower branches of the trees. In itself, the experience was in all conscience bad enough: with the momentary expectation of an attack added, it was almost unbearable.

More perhaps than the others, Mr Dennison felt this.

'God help us if we're surrounded here!' he said, half to himself, on one of the occasions when a stoppage was called to extract an unfortunate from the slime.

The attack, when it did come, came very suddenly. There was no warning of the enemy's approach, no signal: all that Walter and his father heard was a low cry from the coast-native Amar, and, turning together, they saw him clinging convulsively to a bough, with an arrow through the fleshy part of his shoulder.

'Ah!' said Mr Dennison.

'I see him!' excitedly cried Walter. 'There—in that big tree ahead. Shall I fire, sir?'

His father nodded. The two reports rang out simultaneously, a shriek followed, and then there was silence.

'Is he hit, sir?' asked the boy.

'It looks like it. Now, watch!'

While Walter reloaded, keeping an eye meantime on the tree, Mr Dennison climbed along to the wounded coast-man, pulled out the arrow, and roughly bandaged the shoulder with his handkerchief. That done, Amar resumed his journey to the front apparently little the worse. The others, who had stopped in consternation on hearing the shots, were ordered to do likewise; and only the two whites, with Warupi's man, waited for a minute in case of further aggression. But there was none; either the savage had been in advance of his fellows, or they had been frightened off; and so the rearguard crept on again —with many a fearful glance backward, you may be sure, and hearing many strange noises in the swamp around. The latter might have been imagination, but to Walter it seemed that they were surrounded, and with a shudder he recollected his father's words. The first blow had been given; his turn might come next. Looking down at the black mud, into which, the chances were, he would tumble if an arrow struck him, he wondered how it would feel to sink gradually and finally be smothered in the slime, or if he would feel anything.

And then there was a joyful hail from the front, telling of some happy discovery by Warupi or Frank, and with renewed hope the rearguard pressed forward. They had but one thought: that it was the river at last.

CHAPTER XII.

FRANK'S ILLNESS.

COMING up, they saw that the cause of the shout was not the sight of the river, but the discovery —or, rather, the recovery—of the path. It was hardly less welcome. No doubt it was narrow and tortuous, blocked here and there by fallen trees, and in places knee-deep in mud; still it was a path, with the evidence upon it of having been lately frequented, and in all probability it led direct to their destination. One consideration there was: what of the pursuers? Had they outflanked them and got to the river first, or were they still in the swamp?

'We shall know presently,' said the leader. 'Let us be thankful for present mercies, and get on.'

It was at this moment that Walter, who had hitherto been otherwise engaged, noticed his brother leaning wearily against a tree. He ran up to him.

'Hullo, Frank! Nothing wrong, is there?' he cried cheerily.

Frank raised his head. 'It's nothing much, thanks,' he began, making an effort to speak in his usual tones— and then, breaking down suddenly: 'Oh! I have such a splitting headache, Walt! I don't know '——

Frank is taken ill.

As he spoke he reeled against his brother, his gun slipped from his hand, and he would have fallen to the ground if Walter had not caught him. His cry brought up Mr Dennison, whose face became very grave when he observed what had happened. The poor boy had fainted.

'Is it serious, sir?' asked Walter, with some concern.

'Over-exertion—nothing worse, I hope,' answered his father. 'Nothing can be done here.—You, Dawan'—this to one of Warupi's warriors who had no load—'take his gun and carry him down to the river. Gently, now—that's right.— It can't be helped, Walter: we have the others to think of as well. And our post is here, where the danger is.'

So the procession went on, Mr Dennison counting the carriers as they passed him in single file. Not one was missing. When the last man was abreast, the whites turned to follow; but just as they did so Walter uttered a sudden exclamation, and pointed to the end of the hundred yards of the path visible from their standpoint. Looking behind, his father beheld several figures emerge quickly from cover, appear for an instant on the path, and as quickly disappear on the other side. It was the enemy, and at their backs.

Walter raised his rifle.

'Not yet, Walter!' cried Mr Dennison, interposing. 'We must lay a trap for them. This way—quick!'

With that he hurried after the procession of bearers, the tail of which was rounding a sharp curve of the path some ten yards down. Here he pulled up.

'This will do,' he said, crouching down in the shadow.

Walter did likewise, and presently they had the grati- fication of seeing first one native and then a crowd of others issue cautiously from their concealment, and with infinite care creep forward in the track of the invaders.

They were completely armed with spears and shield, club, and bow, and the naked form of the leading savage was daubed all over with alternate streaks of white and red paint. So much Walter had time to observe before his father gave the word to fire.

'Now!' he whispered. 'Small-shot again, Walter, and fire low. Ready?'

'Yes.'

Crack! crack! The rifles snapped together; and, when the smoke cleared away, they saw that the leader and two others were down, while the rest had stopped short and were huddled in a mass as if thunder-struck.

'Again!' cried Mr Dennison.

Before the echoes of the first volley had ceased reverberating among the trees, the second had completed the work. With one long howl of anguish or fear, the pursuers took to the bush, and in a moment the path was as free as if they had never been. Even the wounded men had disappeared.

'One thing's evident enough, and it's as well for us,' remarked Mr Dennison, as he rose—'that the beggars are quite unacquainted with firearms. Probably'—laughing—'they take us for devils. But at any rate our retreat's secure for the present, unless'—— He considered. 'No! it's not possible that they should get through the swamp and cut us off. Our experience is against it. To the river, then!'

He was right, as far at least as the securing of their retreat was concerned; for although the ruse above described was repeated more than once, the pursuers seemed too thoroughly frightened to show themselves, and did not do so until it was no longer necessary to hold the path. As it happened, the adventurers had not much farther to go. Soon they heard the welcome murmur of flowing water; and gradually the narrow track widened, ending finally in a broad stretch of sun-dried mudbank. They rushed forward. Beyond was the river—here a clear-running, shallow stream twenty yards wide. In their relief they felt like huzzahing, but the inclination passed as they realised from the attitude of their native companions, standing on the bank and gazing disconsolately across to the opposite shore, that all was not well. A single glance revealed the worst: a single word expressed it.

'Alligators!'

For so it was: the water was swarming with the hideous reptiles. Walter and his father stood for an instant staring in each other's face. To wade or swim across was manifestly out of the question—and to go back? Involuntarily the boy looked behind him: several figures were flitting about like phantoms among the trees on either side of the path from which the travellers had just issued. The dilemma was complete. Regard it as they might, there was apparently no escape from the conclusion that after all their efforts they were caught like rats in a trap.

Mr Dennison's eyes wandered from Frank, lying inert in Dawan's arms, to Walter.

'Foolish not to remember that the brutes were to be found as high as the last fall!' he muttered. 'And now? and now?—— Natives behind, alligators before, there's no blinking it—we're between the devil and the deep sea!'

But he had reckoned without Warupi. That astute savage, according to his wont, had been employing his time in scrutinising the marks by the water-side; and now, signalling to one of his warriors to follow, he betook himself along the verge in the direction of a clump of bush—with what intent, they were presently to know.

Mr Dennison, aware of the necessity for prompt action, gave the others no leisure to speculate. The pursuers were gathering in force at the exit of the path, and to his mind it could only be a question of minutes before they summoned up courage to hazard a rush, which of course it was imperatively needful to check midway. To this end Walter was ordered to fire at every native who showed the least disposition to advance, while a dozen of the carriers—and these the best—were relieved of their loads and formed up as a line of protection to their companions. Then, with due precaution, they awaited the onset.

For the space of a few minutes the two parties stood watching each other, and apparently not a motion was made on either side. But only apparently; for at length Walter discovered that the enemy was quietly attempting a flank movement in the direction of the clump of bush towards which Warupi had gone. His rifle rang out.

'Where is it?' demanded his father.

'There, sir—to the right! Don't you see? They're coming up from behind and dodging among the trees,' he returned. 'I fired at the first man.—Ah! they've stopped now.'

'Watch!' counselled Mr Dennison.

Here there was a shout from the bank of 'Warupi! Warupi!' and he turned—to get an explanation of the chief's absence in the welcome shape of two canoes, which he and his follower were poling up the river towards the mudbank. They were small, and evidently no more than the scooped-out trunks of trees, but with a continuance of good fortune—otherwise, the inactivity of the enemy—they were sufficient for the purpose. In his heart Mr Dennison blessed the name of Warupi.

Quickly he issued two orders—to the line of carriers to

remain alertly on guard, and to Walter not to spare his ammunition. Then he ran down to meet the boats. The chief's report was concise. His examination of the bank had convinced him that he should find craft of some kind in the vicinity; a swift survey of the river-side, that probably they were hidden in the clump of bush. In both guesses he was right. As to the number, he was sure there were but the two: the marks proved that.

Mr Dennison did not stop to draw deductions from the discovery of the canoes in such a spot. It was enough that they were there: it was now for him to use them. This he did with all speed. A survey of their capacity having shown him that two voyages must be made, he left it to Warupi to transport the non-combatant carriers, with Frank and the loads, to the other side in the first place, and return for him and the rest—they meanwhile keeping the enemy at bay. The first mentioned were at once divided into two parties and embarked; a couple of men in each boat—one at the bow, the other at the stern—took the long punting-poles, and at the word they pushed off into the stream.

'You will be quick?' said Mr Dennison to Warupi, and the chief nodded gravely.

The leader joined the small band of defenders not a moment too soon. Hitherto Walter's rifle, which had not been idle, had sufficed to hold the hostile savages in awe; but just then—angered perhaps by the escape of a moiety of their prey, or perhaps emboldened by the lessened numbers of their antagonists—they assumed for the first time an attitude of aggression. They began with a flight of arrows, followed it up by some spear-throwing, harmless by reason of the distance, and at last showed signs of closing up.

'They're preparing for a rush!' cried Walter.

'And our lives depend upon stopping it,' said his father. 'Don't waste a shot, Walter.'

Even while he spoke the rush was made, revealing at least that the enemy was in great strength ; and as the mass of naked Papuans came on, brandishing their spears and clubs and shouting wildly, the two whites fired straight into their midst, giving them both barrels. Three fell. The others hesitated ; and before they could muster heart to resume the charge, the guns had been reloaded and again fired. Then, as two more went down, a panic seemed to grip them : with one accord, without troubling about their fallen comrades, they wheeled and ran for shelter; and in an instant only five were to be seen where before there were scores, and these five the victims of the skirmish. They were followed into the bush by the jeers of the carriers, who had remained wonderfully steady throughout, and now clamoured for permission to chase the fugitives. But this Mr Dennison refused, knowing that it merely meant permission to decapitate the prostrate five.

'Now is our chance, before they return,' he said. 'If we had only the boats'—— Interrupting himself, he glanced over his shoulder, and saw that the two canoes had landed their passengers and were already on their way back. 'Ah ! here they are !' he cried. 'Now, down to the water— all together. Steady—don't hurry !'

One of the boats grounded just as they reached the water's edge, and as quickly as might be seven of the natives were told off and shipped on board. The other, with Warupi punting, came in a moment later.

There was a shot from Walter, who was on the lookout. 'The enemy's beginning to move again, sir,' he explained.

'Keep firing, then,' returned his father.

He did so, but in this case with less effect. Although every shot told, the savages still advanced—slowly at first, then more boldly as the distance between them and their opponents lessened. Not more than a hundred yards separated them when the first boatful put off, and the party left on the bank consisted, all told, of six natives and the two whites. With a howl of rage the enemy increased the pace, heedless now of Walter's magic.

'Quick, sir! I can't stop them!' cried the boy.

Mr Dennison took his place by Walter's side, while the remaining carriers scrambled into Warupi's boat. The intervening distance had shrunk to fifty yards.

'Now, Walter! In with you!'

Walter's last shot was answered by a flight of spears, which fell short by a few feet only. Turning, he jumped on board. One of Warupi's men had taken the stern-pole, while the chief himself stood in the bows, ready to push off.

'Right?' asked Mr Dennison, over his shoulder.

'Right! Be quick, sir!' replied Walter, in agony. The enemy was within twenty yards.

Mr Dennison halted on his heel long enough to bring down the foremost of the savages, and then coolly stepped into the boat. As he did so another report rang out, he was jerked suddenly off his feet, and a spear whizzed past the place where his head would have been. He rose to find that the craft was side-on to the stream, and that the two polesmen were punting vigorously to get her round; that in the water, within an inch or two of his coat-tails, was the ugly snout of an alligator; and that on shore the enemy had pulled up suddenly some forty feet from the verge, and were gathered round a warrior who lay prone on the ground.

Walter, who had evidently been using his revolver, said, 'I

think he must be a chief, for they stopped like a shot when he dropped. I saw him lift his spear to throw at you, and fired. But I was too late, and if you hadn't fallen when Warupi shoved off'——

'That alligator, who seems so disappointed, would have had me'—— His father finished the sentence for him.

Warupi uttered a sharp exclamation.

'Down!' cried Walter.

They ducked instinctively to avoid another volley of spears. Most of them, thanks to the chief's warning, passed harmlessly over the boat, one or two struck against the side or fell into it, and not one did the least damage. It was the last effort of the enemy. In a minute the canoe was into the centre of the stream; in another its nose had grounded on the opposite bank, and its occupants were landing amid the warm greetings of their companions.

Mr Dennison gave a great sigh of mingled relief and thankfulness as he leaped ashore.

'Safe!' he cried. 'It has been a tough fight, but we've pulled through at last, and,' he continued, laying his hand affectionately on his son's shoulder, 'the credit is Warupi's and yours, my boy. I don't know what I should have done without you.'

'And your own, sir,' said Walter. Then, pointing to the crowd of baffled natives gesticulating fiercely on the other side: '*Are* we safe?' he asked.

His father laughed. 'Leave that to the alligators,' he said.

'But are we sure they have no other means of crossing?'

'Not at this point—unless they make new boats, which can't be done under two or three days at the least. If they are really anxious to settle with us, as I have no doubt they are, their quickest way would be to follow the river upwards to the last fall, where they would be able to get across. But that again is a day's march from here, and they may consider well before pursuing "devils" who have two days' start. Besides, sufficient for the day—— No: all things considered, we haven't much to fear from *them.*'

'And in the meantime?'

'In the meantime, I shall leave you and Warupi to sink these boats, while I look at Frank.'

A hole was speedily knocked in the bottom of each canoe by Warupi and the boy, between whom the afternoon's perils had established a real bond of comradeship; and, when they were sunk in ten feet of water, the two walked together towards the tree under which Mr Dennison was bending over Frank. He rose and came to meet them.

'It's more serious than I imagined,' he said, in reply to Walter's mute interrogation. 'In fact, he's sickening from malarial fever. The only chance for him—for ourselves, indeed—is to get into the mountains as quickly as possible. Now he must be carried with some comfort, and how it's to be done'—— He broke off to think, with a look of grave uneasiness on his countenance. 'For even now we may be in a hostile country, and at any rate we shall have no security until we're among friendly tribes. To stop here is impossible, and to go on seems equally dangerous.—Poor Frank! If he could only be carried, we might manage it. I've given him some medicine, which may do some good, and at the worst the fever won't be at its height for a day or two. But he must have some sort of a litter, and litters take time to construct.'

'Perhaps Warupi'—— suggested Walter, who had much faith in the chief's resource.

In this instance it was not misplaced. Warupi, as soon

as he understood the difficulty, called to his aid several of his men; and, choosing two of the long punting-poles (preserved from the boats) for foundation, a strong and comfortable litter was quickly made out of a bread-bag, several coils of rattan rope, and the broad leaves of the pandanus. Then there was an adjustment of burdens; four of the natives went to the ends of the poles and shouldered the rude palanquin, Frank was laid therein asleep, and presently the travellers turned their backs upon the water with deep thankfulness, and again struck into the bush in due order. On the farther bank the savages were still howling and flourishing their arms.

From the river the country rose gradually and was fairly open, and for the three hours of daylight which remained the party journeyed onwards at a good speed without adventure or misadventure. At first they had a broad trail to follow, but by Warupi's advice they soon deserted it for a direction more to the west. There were two reasons for doing so: the first, that apparently it did not lead towards the mountains; the other, and more important, that it was indubitably the track of their late opponents, and must bring them sooner or later into their district.

'For there can be no doubt,' said Mr Dennison to Walter, 'that they belong to this side of the river, and are at present on one of their periodical raids. It explains many things— for example, the deserted state of the country we passed through. In all probability they have exterminated or driven back the inhabitants, until now it is no more than a hunting-ground for one small tribe.'

'And it seems to be much the same here,' remarked Walter, whose eyes had not been shut.

'I shouldn't wonder,' replied his father. 'Indeed, if this

isn't their own district, it is very likely. And all the better for us if it is so, too,' he added.

They gained the summit of the ascent not long before sundown, and were amply rewarded for their toil by the view which opened before them. The country dipped suddenly, and they looked across a broad valley to a range of low hills, backed in turn by mountains of a great altitude. Warupi's eyes rested at once on a triple-peaked summit in mid-distance. He drew Mr Dennison aside, and for a little the two spoke earnestly together. At last the leader gave the word to move on again.

'We must descend into the valley to camp,' he said. To Walter, in some excitement: 'The chief has got his bearings, lad—we're right now! Yonder safety lies. You see that peculiar triple peak? Well, he recognises it. On the lower slope there is a village so situated that, with the help of the inhabitants or without it, we may defy any number of assailants. But the natives are friendly, and if we can only reach it we shall have leisure to nurse Frank back to health. Thence it's plain sailing to Warupi's country, whatever may come after.'

'And how far is it?' inquired Walter.

'To the village? Probably three days' march, or even four.' He stopped for a moment. Then: 'How's Frank now?' he asked.

'Still asleep. I looked a minute ago.'

'It's a good sign, but the crisis is before us, and—the upshot is not in *our* hands, Walter. All the same, lad, we mustn't lose heart. There are many chances in our favour: it won't be my fault if we don't take them all.'

And in the gathering dusk the two, father and son, shook hands upon the compact.

CHAPTER XIII.

A VILLAGE IN THE MOUNTAINS.

PASSING over three days, we shall find our party of adventurers encamped on the afternoon of the third in a little glen in the heart of the mountains. For two they had been steadily climbing, and already they were more than a thousand feet above the sea-level. Here the air was drier and the heat more bearable, although not a breath of wind stirred the leaves of the trees which clothed the steep hill-sides to the top. For the purpose of the mid-day rest Mr Dennison had chosen a shady spot within view of a stream that leaped and tumbled in a series of cascades above them, and the sound of the falling water made a pleasant lullaby in the ears of the dozing bearers.

Mr Dennison himself was standing with his back to a tree, glancing alternately at a form which turned and tossed on a bed of dried ferns, and, more abstractedly, at the rush and swirl of the stream. To him entered Walter presently, and threw down a brace of scrub-fowl, the result of an after-dinner exploration in the direction of the cascades.

'Is Warupi not back yet?' asked the boy.

For they were now on the skirts of the country belonging to the friendly tribe mentioned in the last chapter, and that morning the chief, with an escort of his warriors, had been sent forward with presents to announce their coming and bespeak a good reception.

'Not yet,' replied Mr Dennison.

Walter bent over Frank, who was still tossing in high fever on his couch of ferns.

'How is he now?'

His father shook his head. 'I 'm afraid he'll be worse before he 's better,' he said. 'The delirium has gone off for the present, but otherwise the fever is still running its course. If we can only reach the village to-night, I don't despair. But that '——

'We can do it easily, can't we?'

'Who knows? Natives are unreliable at the best. It depends on how they've received Warupi, and I confess I 'm getting anxious about it. He should have been here by this time.'

'Oh, it'll be all right, sir—don't worry,' said Walter, cheerily. 'It 's sure to be!'

The three days which had passed, so trying to all, had been particularly arduous to Walter. After the fight with the savages, he felt himself entitled to claim a fuller share of the work and responsibility; for he knew that it was his duty to relieve his father's cares, already great enough, rather than augment them by showing himself incapable of either. Mr Dennison did not refuse, and, like a true Briton, Walter had not failed when thus put upon his mettle. He had shirked neither the work nor the responsibility. The first had been hard, but he had done his part with a readiness that went half-way to accomplish it, and an endurance that surprised even himself. Nothing had come amiss to his hands—the adjustment of the loads, helping

Warupi to clear the path, urging the carriers to further exertion by the force of example, keeping watch by night, or foraging for game for the pot. And all this with an infectious cheerfulness and a readiness to make light of obstacles which added much to the value of the effort. Warupi beamed approval; and albeit Mr Dennison's words of commendation were few, he paid the boy the higher compliment of consulting him at every step, and showing him more and more every day that it was not merely an empty form.

Over and above, there was Frank. At first, when the invalid was in the half-sane, half-delirious state common to those on whom the disease is gaining ground but slowly, he was inclined to be somewhat exacting, and on these occasions nothing soothed him like his brother's presence by the litter-side. So, hour after hour, over rough ground and smooth, Walter held on with his hand in his, comforting him when he was conscious enough to lament his condition and the trouble he gave; and when he was otherwise, listening sympathetically to his ravings about home and Ruth, the savages, birds of Paradise—a hundred things besides. But since the preceding day, the fever having increased, he had been unable to recognise Walter; and now his condition was such as to cause Mr Dennison grave alarm, and to make him eager to reach a place of comparative safety. Hence his impatience to learn the result of Warupi's embassy.

As it happened, they had not long to wait for the chief's return. Presently Walter descried him advancing up the glen alone.

'Here he is, sir,' he said.

With quick steps Mr Dennison went forward to meet him, leaving Walter to attend to the invalid. Sharing as he did his father's anxiety, the boy watched the two closely, and gathered from Warupi's demeanour and the other's exclamations of wonder that the report was of an unexpected nature. Apparently it was reassuring, however, for after a little Mr Dennison came back and at once ordered the march to be resumed.

'Then it's all right, sir?' Walter suggested, while the carriers were falling into line.

'That's just what I should like to be certain of,' doubtfully returned his father. 'The fact is, Warupi found the village deserted—and not the village only, but the country around as well. There were some signs of fighting, but they weren't recent. And what it means I cannot imagine, but anyhow we've no alternative but to go on with it.' This with a look at Frank, whom the natives were tenderly lifting into the litter.

'And Warupi's men?'

'Oh! he left them there, partly to get the place ready for us, partly as a precaution against surprise.'

Walter asked no more, and shortly thereafter they started under the chief's guidance upon the ten miles' march across a low spur of the hills to the deserted village. Laborious it was in the extreme: first up the steep slope of the mountain, cutting a path broad enough for the litter as they went, and then down again on the other side. The worst part was that of Frank's four bearers and of himself, and many a jerk and jostle the poor fellow must have got as they scrambled onwards, in spite of their utmost care. But at length they gained a track leading (so Warupi said) through a broad valley straight to their destination. Again they began to rise; soon the forest vegetation was varied with the sago and cocoa-nut palms; little neglected patches of yams and bananas were met with at intervals; and ultimately, after close upon four hours of strenuous exertion, they encountered one of Warupi's men, posted on guard at a spot where the path narrowed suddenly, and was lost to view as it ran zigzag up a mountain-side.

Mr Dennison called a halt.

'We haven't far to go now, but it's a stiffish climb,' he remarked. 'Shall we rest a bit, or go on?'

'Go on,' said Walter.

But here a difficulty cropped up. The path was obviously too narrow for the litter, and the thickness of the scrub seemed to render the task of widening it impossible—or at least too herculean to be attempted off-hand. What was to be done? Warupi solved the problem by volunteering to carry Frank in his arms; and Mr Dennison, not unaware of what was before them, had no hesitation in entrusting him with the boy. He knew that it was beyond his own powers, and probably beyond those of anybody save the sure-footed chief.

The scout led the way, followed in single file by Walter, his father, Warupi with Frank, and then the carriers. For several hundred feet the path wound through a dense undergrowth of bamboo, with here and there a great tree; always ascending, and as they rose becoming steeper and steeper until it came out on the bare hill-side. Much labour and ingenuity had gone to its construction. Every inequality of the ground had been used to full advantage, and at the more precipitous parts the climber had the aid of rude steps cut in the rock—notwithstanding which, the ascent was one to try the muscles and wind of the stoutest. Perhaps Warupi, burden and all, was the only man who did not feel it, and indeed he appeared to be surprised that the whites, unencumbered as they were, had to stop more than once for breath.

'You see how easy it would be to defend the place, Walter,' his father pointed out. 'Except for this path it is quite inaccessible, and there one native could defend against twenty others. Even with a company of soldiers I shouldn't care to attempt it.'

'And the place—where is it?' panted Walter.

'Look up!'

He looked up, and saw fifty feet above him a patch of green on the face of the precipice—or what seemed so. From this, as he looked, a shout was heard, which the scout answered.

'Another of Warupi's men,' said Mr Dennison. 'On, Walter!'

Some rough scrambling brought them to the verge of the vegetation, then the path took a turn, and suddenly they found themselves upon a broad platform or ledge, the warriors left by Warupi grinning welcome. Walter surveyed the scene with amazement. So little had been visible from beneath, that he was prepared to see a small, precarious eyrie; instead of which, he saw an uneven stretch of some extent (certainly not less than two acres, according to a computation afterwards made), and fairly well cultivated. A glance showed its suitability for defence. Above, the rock shelved gradually outwards, so that the place resembled nothing more than an immense shallow cave scooped out of the mountain-side; and all around, except at the spot where the path joined, it sheered straight down for a great distance, the edge being bordered by a protective fence of bamboo, in some parts broken. As to its general appearance, with its clumps of palms and gardens of indigenous fruit and vegetables, it might make themselves comfortable. When Walter left him, he was hastening the latter consummation by kicking the bones unceremoniously over the edge.

As the boy betook himself after his father, he noticed that the night was closing in, and that all over the platform the carriers went about their various duties with unusual quietness. The hut chosen by Warupi for the invalid's reception was conspicuous by its larger size; and, hardly knowing why, save that a strange fear was knocking at his heart, Walter hesitated for a little before climbing the ladder. From the doorway above him a shaft of light cut into the dusk, and as he lingered he heard a sound only too familiar to him. Then he ascended. By the light of the lamp which stood on a projection of the wall, he took in the whole scene. Mr Dennison was kneeling by the side of the patient, who was again calling out in delirium; and it needed not a second glance at either, and especially at the set face of the elder, to tell the onlooker the truth. His fear was justified.

Mr Dennison looked up at his entrance. ' You, Walter?' he cried. Then, quickly : 'He is worse, much worse. The crisis isn't far off. If he lasts the night'——

'Oh, sir! surely it isn't so bad as that?' interrupted the boy, with a catch in his voice.

'Listen !' said his father.

For a few minutes the silence was unbroken except by Frank's ravings and his uneasy tossing from side to side.

'Can I do anything, sir?' asked Walter.

'Nothing.' Mr Dennison shook his head, and straightway seemed to forget his presence in his anxiety to do all in his power to make the patient more comfortable. For an hour there was little apparent change, and all the time

Walter sat motionless, watching the painful restlessness of the one and the ceaseless efforts of the other to relieve it. It was a terrible hour. Afterwards he remembered as a dream the thoughts that were his, and the prayers that formed themselves in his heart for the safety of his brother. But for an answer he hardly dared to hope.

Outside it was now quite dark, and a cool, pleasant breeze was blowing across the valley to the mountain settlement. The two watchers smelt it through the open doorway.

'Ah! this is better,' said Mr Dennison, his face brightening a little. 'But you, Walter—you can do nothing here. Go down and get something to eat.'

Walter hesitated. 'And—and'——

'Never fear,' said his father. 'I will call for you if'——

He broke off suddenly, but Walter understood, for was not the dread of what was to ensue common to both of them? Sad at heart, he obeyed. Fires were flickering here and there among the brushwood, and the natives lay around them enjoying their supper or the evening smoke; but he had no appetite, and passed them all on his way to a large chair-shaped mass of rock which he had observed in his survey of the platform. On this, he saw as he approached, somebody was sitting by himself. He was about to turn back to seek a more solitary spot, when the figure rose and gave him greeting.

'Warupi!' he cried, recognising him.

The chief made room for him by his side, and he seated himself. At first neither spoke, Walter because he had his own thoughts, the savage because he had his pipe, and smoking to him was a more serious matter than talking. But the mere vicinity of his Papuan comrade was a comfort to the boy. The friendship between the two, having its have been a native plantation transplanted bodily from the low country to this giddy elevation. Evidently the soil was good, barring an occasional outcrop of rock; and the analogy held even to the narrow tracks running between the various patches. Following one of these, Walter reached a little spring of pure, cold water, which burst from the hill and fell into a hollow of the surface, thence dribbling over the ledge. It was the only thing necessary to make the place impregnable in the event of a siege.

Even the houses in this queer settlement had their peculiarity, for they were built, not upon the platform, but higher up in the branches of the trees which grew out from the face of the mountain. If it was for the sake of additional security, surely, thought Walter, the natives were a very timid folk; but perhaps—it was more likely—it was because all the ground beneath was required for cultivation. On investigation bent, he climbed into one of the huts by a primitive wooden ladder. The result did not repay him for the trouble: it was quite empty, and differed little from other native habitations. As he turned to descend, however, he was arrested by the magnificent prospect below and before him of mountain-range topping mountain-range to the horizon, the lower slopes tree-clad, the higher peaks ten or twelve thousand feet in altitude, and the whole softened by the blue haze of the quickly-approaching sunset.

He was recalled to earth by the sound of his father's voice. Warupi's men were pointing out to him the various discoveries they had made in their exploration of the village. They had entered every house, and found it as empty as its neighbour: even the family skulls had been removed from the exterior walls. Mr Dennison nodded in appreciation of the significance of this fact. Then they led him to the north end of the platform, and showed him a grisly heap of bones—all that the carrion-crows had left—lying near the edge, where the fence was broken, while round about the vegetation was trampled down. He nodded again.

'Has there been a fight, sir?' asked Walter.

'Certainly it looks like it,' he replied. 'If there has been, it may explain the disappearance of the villagers. Indeed, two things may have happened. Somehow an enemy may have captured the place, annihilated the natives, and then made off. That is the first theory, but several facts render it improbable. The other is more likely. Say there has been a dispute amongst themselves, ending in a free fight and the defeat of one of the parties—it is quite possible that the other, either in remorse or in fear of the spirits of those slain, should take a distaste for the village and depart. It seems foolish, but that is a circumstance which never strikes *them*. And how otherwise are we to account for the removal of the skulls and everything else? Not unless we disallow this evidence altogether '—indicating the bones—'and believe that, in the manner of their kind, they have simply migrated to another valley.—But this is mere talk,' he said, 'and wo 've something more serious to think about. I mustn't forget poor Frank. And here comes Warupi to remind me.'

The chief pointed out the hut into which the invalid had been carried, and Mr Dennison strode away. Walter held back for a moment to learn Warupi's opinion, and learned only that the practical-minded savage had a lofty contempt for theories. What did it matter where the villagers had gone, and how? It was sufficient that they *were* gone, and that their successors could now safely defy their pursuers, if the savages with whom they had fought at the river had been foolish enough to follow them, and in other ways beginning in the fight by the river, had been fostered since then by many things: chief of all by their lonely watches in the night, when a hundred sounds of the forest had seemed to them warnings of an enemy's coming and set their hearts beating. They had talked much together, and learned much from each other—the one of the strange country of the white man beyond the Gulf, the other of the customs and beliefs of the up-country races. And now their friendship was warmer than perhaps Walter himself realised. But, exclaims the gentle reader in amazement, it was a friendship between a white and a savage, between civilised and un-civilised! True; and true also that they were in the heart of New Guinea, where the fact had a different significance than it would have had in Sydney or Brisbane. In bravery, in resource, in bush-craft, in all that was necessary for the preservation of their lives in a hostile country, was the advantage on the side of the more civilised? For the rest, the English boy had the intelligence to appreciate the honour and rude virtues of his friend, and the courage to hail him by the name.

Presently the chief laid down his pipe and looked at him, waiting for him, according to his wont, to speak. But Walter's thoughts were still otherwhere.

'My brother is silent,' he hinted, at length.

Walter started. 'Let Warupi tell me of his people,' he said, in the Papuan's language. 'I am too weary to talk.'

Warupi touched him softly upon the shoulder. 'He is thinking of his sick brother?'

'Warupi is right.'

He considered for a moment. 'The white men have a Great Spirit, if I may speak of Him,' he went on, in the awe-stricken tones invariably used by natives in mentioning the Unseen Powers, 'and this Spirit watches over them and keeps them from harm. Therefore it is that the evil spirits of the country have no power over white men. My friend's father has told me this.'

'It is so, Warupi,' said Walter, who recognised in this form the fruits of his father's missionary teaching.

'Then, if it is so, why should my friend be afraid? His brother is very sick, but if he is in the hands of the Great Spirit, who is a good Spirit—ugh! he can come to no evil.' He rose. 'So let my friend make his mind easy, and fear not that his brother will die. To-morrow the fever will be gone.'

'Warupi is sure?'

'Warupi has seen it before,' he said quietly, and then disappeared into the darkness to visit the sentries whom he had posted to secure the safety of the settlement.

He left Walter to draw what solace he could from his assurance; and the latter, having no taste just then for theological discussion with an ignorant albeit intelligent savage, made no attempt to recall him. Besides, his conscience was not clear that he was altogether wrong. What if, just when he was inclined to stumble in his own faith, the words of this ignorant savage were meant for rebuke? He prayed that it was so. And thus thinking, he must have fallen into the dead sleep which is the reward of fatiguing exertions, for he knew no more until he was roused by somebody shaking him. Jumping up, he saw that the new-comer was his father, and at once anticipated the worst.

'Is it—is it all over, sir?' he asked. He could hardly find words for the question.

'All over? No, thank God!' fervently returned Mr Dennison. 'He has taken the turn; the rest is a matter of nursing, unless there is a relapse.   And that we can prevent '——

'And we shall!' cried Walter, in his great thankfulness.

'He is sleeping just now,' his father continued, 'and perhaps you had better follow his example.   Inside, I mean.' He took his arm, and thus they returned to the hut.   'I'll give you two hours, when you can have a spell of watching.'

It was the end of the ordeal.   When Frank awoke next morning, he was quite conscious, and the fever was gone. He was terribly weak, indeed, and the convalescence was likely to be slow, but what of that?   Remembering their fears, both Walter and his father were too grateful to grumble.

'You must think me an awful duffer to go like this just when the fun was beginning, Walter!' declared the patient that day, in his weak voice.

'As if you could help it, old man!'

'But *you* did!   Why, you're quite black, and ever so much bigger and stouter!   And me '——

'There! just wait till I'm down,' said Walter.   'It'll be your turn then.   And now shut up and go to sleep. You mustn't speak.   The pater's orders, you know.'

'I suppose it's because I spoke too much when I was ill,' conjectured Frank, and with that turned over and went off.   Just then his capacity for slumber was enormous.

CHAPTER XIV.

THE OATH OF THE BROTHER-IN-BLOOD.

They have looked each other between the eyes, and there they
    found no fault,
They have taken the oath of the Brother-in-blood on leavened
    bread and salt :
They have taken the oath of the Brother-in-blood on fire and
    fresh-cut sod,
On the hilt and the haft of the Khyber knife, and the Wondrous
    Names of God.

THERE is a strange rite which some of the New
Guinean natives practise in common with many
other savage and semi-savage races. How it
originated, and how it has survived where everything else has perished, is one of the mysteries of folklore;
but that its antiquity is respectable, and that it is carried out
to this day with much the same ceremonies by tribes widely
separated, related to each other by no tie of descent or
communion, so much is certain. It was known to the
ancients. In the Prose Edda and in various sagas we read
of it as having existed amongst our Norse progenitors.
To-day you will find it practised by people as much dissimilar
as the turbulent tribesmen on the Afghan frontier (as witness
the lines above quoted) and the Indians of the countries

behind the Andes. And this oath of blood-brotherhood, whether it be sworn by a Papuan savage or a Mussulman Afghan, has the same solemn significance. It is the highest honour that can be conferred upon a stranger or an old enemy, not a thing to be lightly undertaken; and when undertaken, not to be broken under the most active provocation. For by it the contracting parties bind themselves to be brothers in name and in truth; insults offered to one are to be avenged by the other as if offered to himself, and the followers of each are to be held at the other's service—all until the bond is broken by death. It can be broken by death alone.

To Mr Dennison, a student of these customs, not the least curious fact about the bond of blood-brotherhood was the extent of its distribution in New Guinea. About the coast it was quite unknown, and farther up-country he had found, for example, in two neighbouring tribes that the first practised it, while the second was ignorant even of its existence. It was not by any means general, indeed; but among those to whom it was a sort of religion were Warupi's people and Warupi himself.

Now it happened that, a day or two after their arrival at the little mountain village, the proposal came from the chief for the celebration of the rite between him and his friend Walter. He had considered the matter very carefully, as befitted its importance, and had not broached it to Mr Dennison without deliberation with the men of his tribe. And he begged his white father, if it seemed good to him, to lay it before Walter.

'At once, Warupi,' Mr Dennison promised.

He went in search of his son forthwith, and discovered him seated on the chair-shaped rock cleaning his gun.

'What do you think, Walter?' he said, sitting down beside him. 'I have just had a long conference with Warupi, who isn't content with your present relations, and wishes to make them closer still. So he proposes in due form that you and he should take the oath of blood-brotherhood.'

'What is that?' asked Walter.

'From his point of view, a very high honour,' answered his father, and told him the history and meaning of the rite as set down in the first paragraph of this chapter: with more of interest. 'There is another thing,' he continued. 'Merely as a matter of policy, the step would be a wise one. Not only would it bind Warupi himself more closely to our interest, but through you we should secure the devotion of his men also. What do you say to it? I leave it entirely to yourself. He is a savage, of course: there's that to be considered.'

'All the same, he's a good fellow,' said Walter; 'and if he's anxious for this, and it will do us any good—well, I don't mind pleasing him.'

'As a matter of policy, say?'

'And because I like him,' returned the boy.

Mr Dennison seemed to be gratified. 'Well, I think you're right,' he said, 'and I shouldn't advise it if I weren't prepared to do the same myself. Only, I didn't get the chance. By the bye,' he added, 'are you aware of the new name Warupi has given you? Kamara, or something like it. He says your own is too difficult to pronounce, and a name of some kind is necessary.'

'All the natives call me that,' replied Walter, laughing. 'It means "the jumper." Complimentary, isn't it?'

'Do you answer to it yet, Kamara?' asked his father, laughing too.

'Usually—when I don't forget.'

''Then be ready for the great ceremony. Now I must go and tell Warupi of your consent.'

The rite was celebrated later in the day, in the presence of Warupi's men, of the other natives (who watched it with much wonder), and of Mr Dennison and the shawl-wrapped Frank. It was of a simple character. First the two partook of a dish of meat and yams from the same platter, and thereafter they stood forth in the midst of a circle. A hole was dug in the earth, above which they joined their right hands; and with a formidable-looking bamboo knife Warupi's second in command, Dawan, cut them across the palms so as to draw blood. This ran into the hollow and was stirred up with the earth; and over the mould thus formed Warupi swore by the strength of his spear to be a brother unto Kamara until his life should end. Kamara, otherwise Walter, followed suit, and then the ceremony was brought to a close amid general handshaking and congratulations. That evening there was high feasting in the little cyric on the mountain-side.

'Now we are brothers indeed, Kamara!' cried Warupi; and as he appeared to be overjoyed by the fact, Walter strove to respond to his enthusiasm. For his own part he regarded it as little more than a break in the daily monotony, and little thought that before long he should have cause to bless it as perhaps the most important incident of his stay in New Guinea.

Frank had a conundrum to put to his brother.

'If Warupi is your brother now, and so am I, what relation am I to Warupi?' he asked.

Walter gave it up.

'A step-brother-in-blood,' suggested Mr Dennison : whereat

there was such mirth in the hut that Warupi rushed in to find out what was wrong.

The three weeks which followed, while the convalescent was slowly gathering strength, were spent very pleasantly in the haven of refuge among the mountains. To the carriers, especially after the labours of the retreat from the river, it seemed an ideal life. They had little to do, food was plentiful, and above all there was nothing to disturb their nightly and daily slumbers. For the villagers did not return, and of the enemy they saw not a sign—not a sign, in truth, of natives at all. And this although the brothers-in-blood made many excursions to the valley below them in search of game, of which there was no lack anywhere. The result was the fostering of a feeling of security and the consequent neglect of various precautions, and through these the way was paved for the misadventure which ended the sojourn at the village of two of the party, and to the others brought dismay and the pain of fearful suspense.

It came about thus. Cassowary feathers, as we know, were the distinctive head-decorations of Warupi and his warriors, and the cassowary was almost the only variety of game which was not to be found in the valley. But the great ostrich-like birds abounded in the lower country just beyond, and so the chief, having a natural desire to renew his plume, proposed that he and Walter, with one of the men, should await them at a chosen spot some ten or twelve miles distant, where he had lately observed their tracks. Then, as an afterthought, a midnight battue struck him as desirable, both because of its novelty and the better chance of making a good bag when the game ventured out to drink. Walter, eager for a new excitement, consented readily: his father with more reluctance. Even he, however, saw no occasion for more than a few words enjoining caution.

They started just before sunset, Mr Dennison and Frank (who was now, thanks to the invigorating air of the hills, on the road to a complete recovery of his strength) accompanying them to the foot of the path. As they parted, the latter bewailed his inability to go farther.

'Not that I don't feel fit, mind,' he added.

'Don't worry, Frank,' said his brother. 'Maybe the pater will allow you to come next time.'

'We'll see,' Mr Dennison said, and again pressed upon the chief and Walter to take care.

They promised.

The spot chosen was an open, bush-surrounded space by the side of a stream, and in due course they reached it without incident. In the soft light of the full moon, which by this time had risen, the tracks leading to the bank were easily read by Warupi and pronounced fresh. So far good: they disposed themselves under cover to await in patience the next visit of the cassowaries. It was dreary work. A small animal or two appeared, became alarmed, and hopped away across the clearing; but as to the cassowaries, either they were unusually wide-awake, or their thirst had ceased to trouble them. Finally, when an hour had passed and they came not, the chief declared for more active measures.

'But what can we do?' inquired Walter.

Warupi nodded his head wisely; and, not deigning to explain, he cautioned Walter to be on his guard for a sudden appearance of the game, and with his follower at heel disappeared into the bush. So quietly and carefully did they retreat that not a sound was heard by the listening boy.

Thus left to himself, he kept his senses, according to

orders, keenly on the alert. He did not trouble his brain with conjecture. Warupi was not the man to do a thing without sufficient reason: what more did he wish to learn? More than once, during the half-hour that ensued, his rifle was brought to shoulder by some night-call or other noise of the forest, but in each case the alarm was groundless. Then, as the moon rose higher in the sky, and the stretch of the stream became silvered for three-quarters of a mile down, his attention was attracted by a bright surface which reflected back the light. For a little he was in doubt whether it was a flat rock or merely an expansion of the water into a pool. The absence of ripples seemed to favour the former hypothesis, but he was still undecided (for might not his eyes be deceiving him?) when the problem was solved for him in an unexpected manner. He started up, his heart going pit-a-pat, as a long shadow was cast across the brilliant moon-lit surface—not motionless, like the shadow of a tree or inanimate object, but moving hither and thither in a most lively fashion. What on earth was it? The question was answered before it had quite formed itself in his mind. Suddenly the figure of a man emerged from the surrounding darkness, and for a moment stood still in the centre of the light. For a moment only; then he began to throw his arms about as if invoking Luna, and all at once Walter was at ease once more.

'Warupi! it must be Warupi!' he told himself, and indeed it never entered his head that it could possibly be anybody else. Then, as the man's gestures continued: 'But what can he mean?—Ah! I have it! It's a signal to join him down there!'

He did not stop to consider, but made his way as cautiously as he could across the clearing and through the low bush bordering the stream in the direction of the spot. Why was it that he had no presentiment to warn him of his danger? He had none; no suspicion, and not the least sense of dread: his only anxiety was to avoid such sounds as might alarm the game; and it was even with a feeling of relief that he finished his journey and came out upon a broad slab of rock. And then—— Warupi was not to be seen; the rock was unoccupied; the figure gone!

And, before he realised fully what this boded, there was a quick rush upon him from all sides, his gun was knocked from his hand, himself borne to the ground, and all was darkness.

CHAPTER XV.

PAPUAN HEAD-HUNTERS.

HEN Walter woke to consciousness it was full noon of the next day, and he was lying on his back staring into the branches of an evergreen oak high above him. At first he was sensible of nothing but a quick, throbbing pain in his head; he had no curiosity as to where he was and what had happened, and no wish except to sink back into the oblivion of stupefaction. For a little he lay thus with his eyes shut, trying to get rid of the frightful idea that somebody was battering in his skull. Then, as he rallied somewhat from his confusion, his mind began to take in the significance of the various sounds around him. Gradually, curiosity awakened. With some difficulty he managed to raise himself upon his elbow, and in a dazed sort of way saw that a strange native was squatted by his side spear in hand, while several others were standing around in divers attitudes. But in the new position the throbbing in his temples became unbearable, and again he was forced to fall back.

Presently the pain abated somewhat, and a dim recollection of the events of the preceding night returned to him. That he had been waylaid and knocked down, felled doubtless by a blow on the head, and was now a prisoner—so much he knew. As to Warupi and his warrior, he found himself wondering what their fate had been—whether like him they were captives, or had succeeded in eluding the enemy and effecting their escape. There was another supposition, indeed; but somehow, well as he knew how probable it was, he did not care to consider it. And his captors—who were they? The only guess he could make was that they were the savages who had been defeated at the river, and whose coming had been half-expected so long.

For a time he lay motionless, thinking in a vague, disconnected fashion of these and other matters, and listening to the footsteps and chatter of the natives. The latter he did not understand: the language was one with which he was quite unfamiliar. At last he mustered up sufficient inquisitiveness regarding the movements of his captors to turn on his side to watch them. Thereat the man beside him raised his spear threateningly, held it so for a moment, and then lowered it when he saw that his prisoner made no further effort.

Walter's first glance at the natives, three or four of whom were clustered around a fire a few yards away, disposed of his conjecture as to their identity. They differed entirely from the Papuans whom he had hitherto met. This was to be observed chiefly in the complete absence of decoration, for their bodies were neither painted nor tattooed, and their whole clothing consisted of a long girdle of woven grass or fibre. Ornaments they had none, and even their head-gear, usually the most elaborate portion of the native toilet, was merely a plain circlet of bone, in which were stuck some feathers and hibiscus blossoms. In a word, there was nothing to hide the fine, stalwart proportions of the men, and this simplicity, so much at variance with

the custom of the island, set the lad's wits a-puzzling once
more.

After a bit his attention was caught by the weapons,
and from these he got his first hint towards a solution.
Besides the customary variety of spears and clubs, bows
and arrows, and knives, each warrior had the ingenious
instrument known to Walter by repute as 'the man-catcher,'
which in shape is something like a butterfly net, with this
difference, that it has a sharp spike protruding from the
handle into the frame. Now the method of using the
man-catcher is as follows. Creeping up behind your unsuspecting victim, you slip the net adroitly over his head—
there is just room for it—and give the net a quick jerk;
as a consequence the spike penetrates the spine; and then,
without the least trouble or risk to yourself, another head
is added to the collection on the wall of your hut. Having
these advantages to recommend it, there can be no doubt of
its popularity with the young braves of Papua. But, as
Walter was aware, it is distinctively a war-weapon; while
in this case, seeing that the warriors were not painted for
the fray, it had evidently another use. A sudden suspicion
struck him. Then, as he turned round still further to gain
a better view of his captors, his eyes happened to fall
upon a pole which lay between him and the guardian
savage, and a cry unwittingly escaped from him when he
noticed that it was ornamented with two grinning heads.
Again the savage, looking at him curiously, raised his spear
as if to strike. But Walter saw him not, for he had closed
his eyes to shut out the ghastly sight.

When he opened them after a minute's interval it was
to examine the group around the fire more minutely than
before and learn the worst. There could be no mistake:

within reach of each man's hand was a pole similarly
embellished—most with two heads, at least one with
three.

In a flash the truth burst upon him : he was a prisoner
in the hands of a party of head-hunters.

So much he realised, but he did not realise the full
meaning of it at once. True, he had read of the doings
of these scourges in Borneo, and had heard that they were
equally feared in New Guinea; but not in his wildest
dreams had he imagined an encounter with them, far
less that he should find himself in their power. Little
by little he recalled all that his father had told him of
them : that in certain tribes they were a class apart,
regarded by their fellows as pursuing a profession almost
sacred; that their horrible occupation was the sole object
of their lives; that alike in war-time and peace no person
—man, woman, or child—was safe from their ravages; and
that, where their calling was concerned, the commonest
feelings of humanity were unknown to them. Their one
ambition was to get heads and more heads, how and where
mattered not. Thus for days they would lurk around the
villages of a neighbouring tribe in the hope of cutting
off a defenceless compatriot without endangering their own
skins. It might be an infirm patriarch or a child who
had strayed into the bush, it might be a woman with
her baby in her arms, it might even be—but this, by
reason of its risks, was rare—an unsuspicious warrior; but
whoever it was, the man-catcher was ready for its deadly
work, and presently the cowardly assassin was fleeing with
his trophy to his own country, there to be received with
congratulations on the latest proof of his prowess. As
to fair fighting, or anything remotely resembling it, they

Walter in the hands of the Head-hunters.

would have laughed the idea to scorn. Was not their method so much easier and safer?

Walter recalled all this, pointed by instances of their savagery drawn from the stores of his memory. And yet here he was in the clutch of the inhuman wretches, destined no doubt to share the fate of the other victims of the present raid. For what hope was there of mercy to him above others? He was not without nerve, but in his weak state the thought was too much for him, and again he relapsed into semi-insensibility.

The further events of that day were like a dream to him. His jailers brought him some food, which he swallowed mechanically; and then two of them, taking his arms, half-carried and half-dragged him through the bush at what seemed to him a prodigious speed. For a time he noted instinctively the nature and forms of the trees and the lie of the ground. He knew, likewise, that his head ached fearfully. Soon, however, he lost consciousness even of that. The next thing he remembered was a feeling of vast relief as he lay back on a bank of moss, gazing at the flickering shadows thrown by firelight across the scrub. He was free at last of the pain in his temples, and instead he felt a delightful coolness in the injured part. Putting up his hand, he discovered that it had been bandaged in some manner; and, a little reassured by this mark of kindness, he fell presently into a refreshing sleep.

He awoke next morning, the second after his capture, as if from a nightmare. His head was quite clear, and otherwise he was nearly himself again; but what were the horrible dreams he had had of man-catchers and ghastly, grinning heads? Alas! he had only to turn round to learn that they were sober reality. Two of the savages, one on

each side, guarded him closely, and on his slightest motion
a spear was lifted in menacing warning. Around the fire,
which had been fanned into a blaze for the preparation
of the morning meal, were three others; and before long
they were joined by a fourth, making altogether, if these
were all, a company of six. Walter's sensations of disgust
and apprehension returned with tenfold force when he
confirmed, in cold blood, his former observations concerning
the frightful occupation of the head-hunters, nor did a cooler
brain change his view of the hopelessness of his position.

This mood passed: he reflected that he was still alive,
and where there is life there is hope; and after all they
were but six to one. Many a man had escaped from
greater odds, and surely that which others had done was
not impossible to a Queenslander. At the worst, it was
better to die game than to be butchered like an ox. His
first step, accordingly, was to ascertain how he stood in
the matter of offence or defence. Of his rifle he perceived
no trace; probably it had been left by the savages as
useless. Then his hand wandered to his belt, and a great
thrill of joy shot through him as it encountered the holster
of his revolver with the weapon within. It had not been
removed by his captors, doubtless for the good reason that
they were unacquainted with the nature of firearms; and
the mere fact of its possession, with its assurance of protection and its power of self-defence, acted upon the boy
like magic. To some extent, at least, he was still master
of his fate.

He was impelled by this new knowledge of strength
to jump to his feet, heedless of the usual spear-flourishing
of his guardians. They rose too, picking up the trophies
of their raid as they did so; and the sight of the poles

gave birth in Walter's mind to a hideous doubt—a doubt whether on one or other of them he should not find the heads of Warupi and his man. It was a doubt that must be settled at once for good or bad.

'I *must* make sure,' he said to himself, and notwithstanding the repulsiveness of the quest and its probable difficulty, he set himself immediately to do it.

But here, contrary to his expectation, all was easy sailing. As soon as the savages comprehended his wish, they showed themselves, with the vanity of children, eager to gratify it, and as they proudly exhibited the heads, expatiated on them in a language of which Walter understood not a single word. More, they seemed to be immensely flattered by what they evidently considered the complimentary curiosity of their prisoner. He could not undeceive them, and so he nodded his head and tried to look pleasant—a feat which became easier when he found out that, as regarded the poles of his two guardians, his fears were not justified. But there were the others around the fire, and by signs he expressed a desire to examine them also. It was instantly done. The same exhibition and unmeaning explanations were gone through—again, to the boy's delight, with the same result. This he knew now for certain: that if these six formed the whole party of the head-hunters, neither Warupi nor his warrior had fallen a victim to their knives.

Walter tried to think out what it might imply. The chief was not the man to desert a comrade in need, especially when the comrade was his own blood-brother, and to a bushman like him the truth about the capture could not long remain hidden. And the conclusion? Either at that moment he was following close upon the head-hunters' tracks, awaiting his chance to effect a rescue, or he had returned to the mountain-village for help. In either case Walter's duty was plain.

'Whether it's Warupi himself, or him and the pater, I must be ready,' was the decision to which he came. 'They've had a day now, and they shouldn't take much longer to make up on us. Anyway, the only danger is getting a spear through me when the scrimmage begins, and I think'—handling his revolver-case fondly—'I can manage to prevent *that*.'

All these reflections made for comfort; and it was in capital spirits, therefore, that he sat down with his captors to the breakfast of roast iguana and wild yams. As the result of his interest in their trophies, they, for their part, appeared to regard him with more kindly eyes, and pressed upon him the more delicate portions of the animal, which to their taste were the entrails. Needless to say, Walter could not bring himself to deprive his kind hosts of them. And, in spite of their kindliness, they took good care to watch all his movements with the same alert suspicion as before.

Breakfast over, the march was immediately resumed. Walter had a half-formed plan to retard progress as far as he dared with impunity, so as to give his friends a better chance of overtaking him; but his guardians prevented such an attempt by seizing him again by the arms, and hurrying him along whether he would or not. The pace never slackened for an instant, proof of the head-hunters' familiarity with the ground. At first the way was through thin bush over a fairly level country, where there was nothing to remind one of the proximity of the mountains except numerous streams and water-channels; but as the day advanced the bush thickened, and before long not a few signs of habitation were to be noticed. These multiplied fast, and therewith, of course, the hope of rescue dwindled—until, for the present, it faded away altogether when the party halted about noon on the outskirts of a large village. For some reason the head-hunters did not enter it, but as compensation the whole population flocked out to greet them, bringing them offerings of food and milk; listening eagerly to the story of their exploits; admiring the heads; and generally treating them with the respect due to the aristocracy of the tribe. But the sensation of the hour was caused by Walter. Evidently the natives had never seen a white before, for they crowded round him with every appearance of wonder, touched the skin of his face and hands as if to make sure that it was really skin, and inspected his clothes with the utmost interest. He bore the ordeal with as much patience as he could command, but you may be sure he was not sorry when at last his captors seemed to tire of adulation, and gave the word to continue the journey. All afternoon they traversed a thickly-inhabited country, and at intervals the same thing happened. Thrice a stoppage was called just outside a village, but in no case was it for long: the head-hunters seemed anxious to hasten on.

But whither? Obviously they were amongst their own people, and it was inexplicable to Walter that their wanderings should show no token of coming to an end. Again he began to have misgivings. Now, too, they were for others besides himself, for if his father and Warupi were following him, as he doubted not, what result could there be in passing these villages save that they and those with them should be surrounded and cut to pieces? He had also a new and more terrible fear for himself, fostered by the manner in which the savages had handled him. He had heard of their taste for human flesh—and, contrary to their custom, his captors had taken him alive. The suspicion was enough. He seized the first opportunity to transfer the revolver unperceived from the holster into one of his jacket-pockets, where it lay more convenient to his hand.

Towards evening, leaving the populated belt behind, they struck through a rougher and more sterile district, and at nightfall encamped in the stony gully of a dry watercourse. It was not too soon for Walter. The incessant travelling and the excitement had been too much for his strength, and his head was again throbbing violently. Observing his condition, one of the savages who had remained by his side all day—Garougi, or by some such name, he was called by his companions—signed to him to lie down, and, while the others busied themselves in lighting the fire, searched about in the bush for various leaves. What these were he had no idea: all he cared to know was that when they were applied to his forehead he had instantly a feeling of immense relief. Presently, before supper was ready, he dropped off to sleep, and did not waken until he was roused ten hours later by the loud singing of the birds.

He sat up. Only four of the hunters were to be seen, three of them stretched out in slumber, and the fourth, Garougi, alternately keeping watch and regarding his brace of heads with proper admiration. His back being to Walter, the boy thought it not worth while to disturb him. But what was this? As his hand sought his pocket to discover if his precious revolver were safe, it came in contact with something sticking in his belt. He drew it out and looked at it, and his brain seemed to whirl as he noticed what it was. Then he looked a second time, pinching his arm to assure himself he was awake. There was no mistake : that which he held was beyond all doubt *a cassowary feather.*

He pulled himself together to think.

A cassowary feather sticking in his belt : it could mean but one thing. It was the badge of Warupi's tribe, and even although it had been worn by any of the head-hunters, which it was not, the significance was in the position. Warupi, then, was near at hand—he had stolen up during the night and left this message to bid him be of good heart—perhaps at that moment he was within sight of the camp! Walter felt himself armed with fresh courage in the knowledge that he was not alone.

Here Garougi showed symptoms of restlessness, and Walter had just time to conceal the feather before he turned round and greeted his prisoner with an affable smile. Nor did he raise any objection when the latter intimated, by signs, his desire to bathe his face in a pool of water in the bed of the gully, but very courteously accompanied him and witnessed the operation. Apparently it was rather new to him.

The next step of the savage, when his charge was back in his place freshened in body and blither of soul, was to rouse his comrades, and as the morning stir commenced one of the other men strolled in with the newly-killed carcass of a young kangaroo for breakfast. The meal was got ready and disposed of, but the sixth brave did not appear, plainly to the great perplexity of his fellows. At first Walter's own thoughts were too engrossing to permit him to notice this, but when half an hour had passed, and still the man was absent, his attention was caught by the fact. Was it a mere coincidence that his mind jumped at once to Warupi for cause ?

CHAPTER XVI.

ENTER WARUPI.

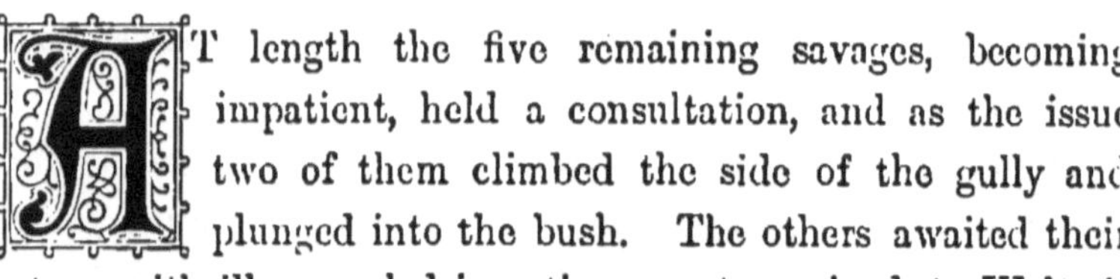

T length the five remaining savages, becoming impatient, held a consultation, and as the issue two of them climbed the side of the gully and plunged into the bush. The others awaited their return with ill-concealed impatience, not unmixed, to Walter's thinking, with uneasiness. The scouts were ten minutes away, and then came running back at their highest speed with every sign of astonishment on their countenances. As they gave in their report, their air of consternation—for so it appeared to the onlooker—spread to their companions; a short, heated conversation ensued; and in the end, with the haste of fear, weapons were caught up and the day's journey immediately begun. But that they were not by any means at ease was proved by the pains they took to keep closely together, by their pace, and, chiefly, by the apprehensive glances which they cast backward at every step.

Here was matter for infinite speculation to our hero. If it had been possible, he would have given much to learn what the scouts had discovered about their missing comrade, and in lieu of this knowledge he could only amuse himself with the vain imaginings of possibilities. One certainty and one feeling he had, however: the first that Warupi was behind, and therewith his instinct persisted in connecting the other event of the morning; the second, that the day would not pass without further incident of importance to him. It would not be his blame, he told himself, if it found him unready to play his part. Somehow, he had no fear of the result. As to the odds against him, they were but five to two now, instead of six to one.

His expectation of excitement was not falsified, although it was early in the afternoon before the startling occurrence now to be related happened. All forenoon they had been ascending once more into the mountainous region, across a tract of country without inhabitants and almost without game. Just before mid-day the route taken was over a high, rock-strewn plateau, and several times, as they toiled onwards over the rugged surface, Walter caught a glimpse of cloud-capped peaks far in front. Then he heard a low sound rumbling in the distance, which became louder and louder every moment until there could be no question what it was.

'A waterfall!' he thought.

Nearer and nearer they drew to it, and at last, an hour or so after noon, were pulled up on the edge of the plateau. Suddenly the rock sheered down precipitously for several hundred feet to a considerable stream, which roared and foamed in its narrow channel before disappearing in a cloud of foam as it threw itself headlong over a ledge. Where they stood, looking down upon the agitated water, they were five hundred yards above the fall; between them and a spur of rock that jutted out over it, several clumps of deodar cedars grew upon the cliff; and here, as may be guessed, the noise was deafening.

Walter would have liked to get a closer view of the great

cascade, say from the projection; but the head-hunters, to whom the sight was probably familiar, squatted down on their haunches and refused to understand his signs to that effect. So he had perforce to follow their example, and join in the demolition of the food which they had brought with them. That done, they lighted their pipes and composed themselves for a rest before going on, while he, with no reason save curiosity, again crept forward to the verge to watch the eddying water far below him. Presently a flock of birds rose screaming from the farthest of the clumps of deodars, and one of the savages, either out of bravado or because he forgot his fears for the minute, strolled carelessly towards it. His companions observed him with interest until he went out of sight behind the trees.

Walter, hardly knowing why, did the same.

It was then that the incident took place. Scarcely two minutes had passed, when all at once a loud shriek rang out above the din of the waterfall; there was another flight of scared birds; and with one accord the head-hunters and Walter jumped to their feet, startled and trembling. From the boy came a great cry of agony.

'Look! look!' he cried, forgetting that they were as ignorant of his tongue as he of theirs.

Already, however, their eyes had turned instinctively to the jutting point of rock overhanging the cascade. And this is what they saw: for one second a figure appeared upon it, spun round, as it were, on the edge, and then disappeared—disappeared into the water just where it took its great leap into the seething whirlpool beneath. No earthly power could have saved him—they knew it, and stood as if frozen to the ground. It was all over in a flash; the screaming birds settled down again amongst the branches;

and still the savages and their captive stood spell-bound, gazing at the scene of the tragedy. They had got only an instantaneous glimpse, but not for a second did Walter, nor, probably, any of the others, doubt who the man was and how he had met his fate.

This for a minute or two. Then the four Papuans turned, looked at each other, and without a word—without the least attempt at retaliation—seized their prisoner and hurried away from the spot with every appearance of deadly fear. Walter made no resistance. Indeed, he could make none; the horror of that which he had witnessed was heavy upon him; and not until long afterwards did he realise how good a chance he had missed of escaping while his guardians were stricken with dismay. But just then his mind was filled with the picture of the poor fellow spinning round in the air above the waterfall—with that and nothing else.

Soon, in concern for himself, he had, with an effort of will, to dismiss even that. The head-hunters, not without many a fearful look behind, struck up-stream along the brow of the cliff, and after half a mile the order of marching was changed to single file, Walter being placed second in the row. The reason appeared when they began to descend the escarpment towards the river by a precarious path. Down they went, at the imminent risk of their necks, to within fifty feet of the water, where the path ended in a narrow ledge running away up the gorge and so out of sight. The gorge itself was here some sixty feet across, and on each side the black walls of rock towered straight up to the arch of blue sky, in some places seeming almost to meet. Now the fugitives had passed from the strong glare of the sun—it was shining on the easterly precipice, half-way up its face—into a sort of twilight. It was like entering a prison-house, thought Walter, with a shuddering glance at the bare, forbidding sides of the cañon and the dangerous route in front.

Pausing not, the head-hunters pushed on along the ledge. Nowhere was it more than four feet wide, occasionally it was less than two, and seldom was it level for far. Now it rose high above the dark, foam-specked water, and again it fell until it was within a few feet of it, and was wet with a slippery slime. Every step had to be chosen with caution, for the least carelessness would certainly have resulted in an accident, and there an accident meant death. Danger they had always with them, yet on—still on—they hurried. Once or twice, indeed, a stoppage was called at the end of a long stretch. But it was not to rest : simply to discover if the unknown enemy were following upon their tracks. They saw nothing of him. Then, convinced that so far they had outrun him, on again for mile after mile of the same monotonous scene—the noisy stream below them, the black expanse of the gorge before, and above them the frowning walls, bare except where at rare intervals a hardy mountain shrub had secured foothold.

For a time Walter kept up the pace without conscious effort, but as the excitement died away he began to feel it, and felt it more and more as the afternoon wore on to nightfall and still the grim cañon stretched out in front. Apparently it was interminable.

'When is this to end ?' he asked himself.

It ended sooner than he had dared to expect. Ten minutes afterwards, they reached a spot where the ledge, which hitherto had never been wider than four feet at the utmost, broadened out to five or six yards, and extended so for some distance. Better still, vegetation was not altogether wanting, for, nestling under the cliff, were a clump or two of the wild plantain and a few bushes of rhododendrons, brilliant with red and white blossoms. The foremost man halted to wait for the others, and together they conferred for a minute. Then, to Walter's exceeding joy, the sign was given to camp. It was difficult to see what else could have been done. In the quickly gathering dusk it would have been impossible to advance much farther; here was a place better suited for the purpose than any they had passed since entering the cañon; and, besides, the boy had a shrewd idea that the day's exertions had told heavily even upon the wiry head-hunters, and that, amongst themselves, they were not sorry to have a decent pretext for resting until it was light enough to proceed in safety.

Camping was not complicated by elaborate arrangements: they had simply to choose the easiest positions and squat down. No fire was lit, for three good reasons, any one of which would have sufficed: there was no fuel, they had nothing to cook, and presumably they did not wish to inform a possible pursuer of their vicinity. The supper was equally primitive. It consisted of a few plantains and a drink of water from the river, enlivened on the part of the natives by a brisk discussion. Walter guessed the purport of it when, as the result, two of them took up their post just where the ledge commenced to broaden, and the remaining two lay down to snatch a few hours' slumber. They had decided, for precaution's sake, that one couple should watch while the other slept.

Walter was too tired not to do like the latter. The last thing he saw as he dropped off, with his back against the precipice, was the two sentries standing out like black statues against the less black darkness of the gorge.

Next moment, as it seemed to him, he was awakened and brought shivering to his feet by some indefinable cause—to find that the moon had risen high in the heavens and was shining straight into the cañon, flooding the ledge and the water below with a light scarcely less brilliant than that of day. And the cause? Whatever it was—perhaps a death-scream, perhaps the shout of a suddenly-roused sentry —it had also had its effect on the other sleepers, for now they were running forward to the point of guard, where one of the watchmen was to be seen bending over the prone form of his companion. Walter made to follow—then stopped as a howl of terror came from the two savages. One glance had shown them this: that there on the ground, in a pool of blood, lay the decapitated body of a comrade. Yet, though the moonlight illuminated the ledge for a hundred yards, not a trace of the assailant was visible.

Presently the first feeling of horror gave way to one of resentment towards the surviving sentry. Plainly he had been neglectful of his duty, and against this nothing—neither their fears nor the consciousness of the greater danger they would incur if they slew him—appeared to weigh with the two savages. With spears upraised to strike, they drove him back to the cliff, and there doubtless, in spite of his protests, they would have made short work of him had not their zeal been turned into another channel.

Their retreat had left the corpse of the slain head-hunter open to Walter's view, and he could not forbear a single glance. It was enough. He noticed one thing alone: that in the dead man's girdle was stuck a cassowary-feather. In his surprise an involuntary cry escaped from him.

The savages wheeled round. How it was that then, rather than upon the former occasions, they connected the boy with their mishaps, is a problem for your solution : perhaps they did not, and the action was prompted merely by the instinctive craving of blood for blood. At all events, they turned fiercely upon him, the lately threatened sentry fiercest of all. Walter felt that the critical moment had arrived : that, one against three, he must now fight them for his life; and, as he jumped quickly back, his hand sought his revolver. Then, with his back to the wall, he awaited their onset.

It never came. Of the three there was one man, and he Garougi, who had already shown Walter some kindness; and now, the first blind impulse past, his voice was to be heard raised on the boy's behalf. Alternately, as could be learned from his tones, he entreated and commanded. And not without effect. The others listened sulkily—hesitated— finally lowered their spears. For the moment the danger was averted, and Garougi beckoned the boy forward to take his place in the line.

It was now Walter's turn to hesitate. He saw that, in their panic, his captors meant to continue their retreat by moonlight, and at once. For himself, he would have done much to escape a continuance of the ordeal, even to the extent of fighting and having it over; and indeed, in the tension of his nerves, he would almost have welcomed the savages' rush. But it was one thing to shoot down men in self-defence, and another to assume the aggressive. He could not do it, he felt, and blamed himself next instant for weakness; and, in a word, he fell at last into line, but not before assuring himself that the native behind him was Garougi. He had no desire to be treacherously speared in the back.

So, with not another look at the headless trunk of their

late companion, they crossed the platform and hastily resumed their march along the ledge, which was again narrow and precarious. For two hours they sped forward hot-foot, and as long as the moon lit up the gorge they had little difficulty in picking their footsteps; no more, at least, than they had had during the day. But before long the soft light, deserting the path, began to climb the walls of rock; and still, though they could scarcely see the ground at their feet, and with every minute the darkness deepened, their terror impelled them to stumble on and on. Now, however, it was more slowly, for they had each to grope his way with hand on rock, and feel every step before it was taken. Even then the chances of a fall were great, and more than once the heart of one or other leaped into his mouth as he caught himself halting on the very brink. Yet still they drove on. With the black fear on their souls, it was to them the alternative of the certainty of death and the chance, however small, of life; and Walter realised that nothing but an accident, which must come sooner or later, would stop their mad flight. It came soon. Suddenly the leading savage slipped, and by the merest miracle saved himself from tumbling headlong into the stream; and, although there was actually no damage done, he was so thoroughly frightened that he declined to advance another inch. Evidently he preferred a death by cold steel to one by water.

'What will they do now?' Walter wondered, as the other two closed up to consult with him.

In view of the leader's flat refusal to move, they had no choice. The last man protested strongly, but as he was the surviving sentry, posted in the rear as a punishment, his appeals were disregarded; and in the end the four, captors and captive, seated themselves on the ledge to await in

misery the coming of the dawn. And the savages, to do
them justice, accepted the inevitable with at least a simu-
lation of stoicism.

Then began perhaps the most terrible experience of
Walter's life. To this day he remembers with a shiver
every incident and every thought of that night: the minutes
that seemed hours, the hours that seemed days; the dreary
vigil in the shadow of the precipice, the river glinting below,
and far overhead the starlit arch of sky; the only sound the
swish-swish of the water and the heavy breathing of his
black companions; and above all the nameless horror that
oppressed his spirit and could not be shaken off. A hundred
mad impulses chased each other through his brain. First
it was an inclination—and here his hand fondled the revolver
in his pocket—to try the effect of a shot upon the nerves of
the Papuans, and he laughed softly to himself in the con-
templation of their consternation. Then he speculated upon
Warupi's whereabouts, and what would ensue if he shouted
out his name, and in fancy listened to it as it echoed down
the cañon, summoning the chief to his side. But the worst
impulse of all was that which came as the slow hours
lengthened out, when he felt an attraction almost irresistible
towards the swirling water at his feet, and with closed hands
and clenched teeth had to beat down the insane desire to
throw himself into it. It passed; and thereafter he must
have fallen into a merciful doze, for of the rest of the watch
he remembers but the sudden awakening to the darkness
and the full terror of the spot. As to the miserable head-
hunters, who can tell *their* thoughts and fears? But if the
night was terrible to Walter, sure it is that it must have
been trebly so to them.

You may imagine, then, with what hope they looked

forward to the blessed dawn—the natives, that their awful suspense might cease; Walter, because expectation was rising high in his breast of some sign from Warupi. At last it broke, and in the first faint light of the incoming day the weary-eyed travellers gazed behind them—and saw nothing. No further time was lost. On the one part with alacrity, on the other with deep disappointment, they pursued their journey. There is no need to describe it in detail: the itinerary differed from that already set down only in the facts that the cañon gradually narrowed, and that the ledge ascended by slow gradients until it was about forty feet above the water. For three hours they followed it, the savages halting often to glance suspiciously behind them. Then, all at once, the leader broke into a run. Ten yards up, a natural bridge of rock spanned the gorge to a platform upon the other side, and there Walter made out a black opening as to a cave in the mountain-side. Was it the end of their wanderings at last?

One by one they crossed the bridge and entered the cavern. The boy had just time to observe that it extended back for a considerable distance, and in the dim light to see that the walls were ornamented with scores of human skulls, when a shadow fell across the opening.

He looked round.

'Warupi!' he cried.

CHAPTER XVII.

WARUPI TELLS HIS STORY.

T was indeed the chief who had thus opportunely appeared.

He stalked across the bridge as coolly as if he were approaching his own house, halted at the entrance to the cave, and there stood framed in the opening calmly scrutinising its occupants. Even in the first flush of surprise, Walter did not fail to notice that a rifle, doubtless the lad's own, was slung over his shoulder, that in his right hand was his club, and that in his left he carried one of the head-hunters' poles—not with two or three heads upon it, but at the least with half a dozen. Walter recognised two of them.

For a full minute Warupi looked at the amazed and fear-stricken natives; and then, with an exclamation of contemptuous insult, he cast the pole at their feet and turned to his blood-brother with a cheerful greeting.

'Hoi, Kamara!' he shouted.

It was like a signal to the boy. Pulling out his revolver, he darted forward to the chief's side.

The movement was made not an instant too soon for his safety. The sight of the heads and the cry, taken together, had served to recall the savages' scattered wits: apparently they realised that there was but one thing to be done; and so, uttering a yell which sounded bravely enough, they rushed with uplifted spears at their antagonists.

There was a hurried warning from Warupi.

'Quick, Kamara! He in the middle!'

Walter saw the centre man raising his arm as if to throw the spear, and fired. Not two feet separated them: the savage fell dead, shot through the brain. And, before the report had ceased to reverberate through the cavern, Warupi had disposed of another by seizing the opportunity of his momentary consternation to knock aside his weapon, and bring down his heavy club with full force upon his skull. It cracked like an egg.

The third man was Garougi; and he, watching his chance, essayed a sudden dash for the open air. Walter could have stopped him, and indeed he had his revolver raised to fire. But all at once, as he caught sight of his terrified countenance, a recollection swept over him of the fellow's kindness to himself, and he refrained. Garougi rushed past: so close that, if he had pleased, he could have plucked him by the girdle. Acting upon impulse, with no thought of the consequence, he let him go.

It was otherwise with Warupi. He, when he had assured himself of the efficacy of his stroke, was just in time to behold the fugitive darting across the bridge.

'Fire, Kamara!' he shouted, himself running forward. 'He will raise the tribe! Fire!'

Now this was a contingency which had never struck Walter, but he could not gainsay its probability. So, reluctantly enough, he took aim at the fleeing figure. As the shot rang out, the savage, who had now reached the opposite ledge, leaped two feet into the air, and then fell forward on his face. In a moment, however, he was on his legs again, continuing his headlong flight down the gorge.

'Missed!' cried Walter. He was not sure that he was altogether sorry.

'Again! Fire again!'

He did so, but with no greater effect; and, before he could shoot a third time, Garougi had disappeared behind a projection of the cliff. At first Warupi seemed inclined to pursue him, and started to do so. Then, thinking better of it, he returned to the cave-mouth, and clasped Walter's hand in his.

'It matters little, Kamara,' he said. 'He is only a dog— all his tribe are dogs. Have we not two days' start of them? It is enough.'

Walter tried to thank him for his devotion, but he would not listen: evidently he was quite unconscious of having done anything particularly meriting gratitude.

'Am I not Kamara's brother?' he asked simply.

With that he turned to examine the bodies of the two victims of the fight, calling them, in the manner of savages, by many insulting names, and spurning them with his foot. He was proceeding to worse—in a word, he had his knife out to add their heads to his other trophies—when Walter interfered, and begged him to desist. Although he agreed willingly enough, it was not without a look which said very plainly that the scruples of white men were beyond *his* comprehension; and as he threw the bodies unceremoniously into the water, he warned the spirits of the deceased head-hunters that they need not, in spite of his brother's folly, come back to haunt him, because they would find it useless.

'Let them,' said he, 'return to their own people, who were

cowardly dogs, and more easily frightened than such warriors as Kamara and he.'

The next step was to explore the cavern. Just beyond the entrance it was about twelve feet high and as many in ·width, but as it ran back it broadened to more than thirty at the farther extremity. On either side, as Walter had already remarked, the walls were decorated at the height of a man's shoulders with triple rows of grinning skulls, affixed to points chiselled out of the hard rock. The end wall was similarly embellished—only more so, for, except in the middle, it was almost completely covered with the ghastly emblems of murder, and these in all stages of decomposition. In the middle, however, was a more startling object. Here a shaft of light struck down transversely from a narrow crevice, and illuminated the most hideous presentment of the human face that Walter had ever seen. It was at least four times life size, and rudely hewn ; and yet the artist—whether he were present-day Papuan or had lived in an age long past—had succeeded in giving it an expression of relentless, diabolical fiendishness hard to describe in words, but eminently suited to the grim array of heads surrounding it. Walter gazed at it with a kind of fascination until Warupi touched him on the arm.

'Look !' he said, pointing down.

He looked. At his feet, and directly beneath the idol, was a flat-surfaced slab raised a few inches from the ground, with nothing noteworthy about it save a small, curiously-shaped depression at the upper end.

'Is it ?'——

'So !' answered the chief, and thereupon went through a realistic pantomime of a victim being laid on the slab, with his head in the cavity, and duly decapitated in sacrifice to the

Evil Spirit depicted above. And afterwards? Walter did not care to inquire further. And this was the fate destined for himself! He knew now why he had been saved alive: he was intended as a nobler tribute to the god of the tribe, propitiated thus by means of human lives to withhold his hand from evil.

He turned away half-sickened.

'And the devil?' asked Warupi, with an expressive glance over his shoulder.

'Well?'

'He must have his offering,' explained the chief. Then: 'Ah! let him have these,' he said; and, picking up the various head-embellished poles which were lying about where they had been dropped by himself and the hunters, he again approached the idol. Walter, standing in the opening, could hear him speaking to it with many endearing words, while one by one he affixed the heads.

Presently he joined the boy on the ledge, bringing with him the weapons of the dead savages. These he threw down, and then unslung the rifle.

'It is yours, Kamara,' he said, handing it to him.

Walter wished to ask him how it had come into his hands, and a hundred questions more, for he was burning for enlightenment on as many points. Instead, noticing the chief surveying the ledge as if for the easiest spot, he contented himself with one:

'What now, Warupi?'

Warupi made his choice and lay down. 'Sleep!' was his laconic reply.

'Sleep!'

'And wherefore not, Kamara?' he asked. 'My eyes are heavy: I have slept none for three nights.'

'For three nights!' repeated Walter in wonder. 'And you did it for me, Warupi!' Not until then, perhaps, had he realised to the full the strength of his blood-brother's devotion. 'There! you must go to sleep at once. I will keep guard.'

'Good!' said the chief; and, turning over, he was immediately lost in deep slumber.

Walter leaned on his newly-recovered rifle and watched him for a little, thinking gratefully of all that this naked Papuan had done for him in the name of friendship. Somehow, after the events of the past few hours, the world seemed a better and fairer place to the boy. The prison-like walls of the cañon were still there, below was the quick-running river, the sacrificial cavern and its protecting deity, in hard rock, were behind; but now the gloom had fled, and the air had quite a different smell in his nostrils. Also, he was very hungry. His first move, then, was to explore the ledge and around it in search of something to eat, and he was lucky enough to discover in a hollow of the cliff a patch of melons and a few more plantain-trees. Not very satisfying food, you say; but in the absence of better they had to suffice, and Walter was too happy to grumble over-much at scanty fare.

It was late in the afternoon before Warupi awoke, stretched himself, and without a word set himself to demolish the pile of fruit which Walter had got ready for him. Having succeeded, he looked up into his companion's expectant countenance.

'And now, Kamara?'

'And now—your story, Warupi.'

Warupi glanced at the height of the sun, assumed the most comfortable attitude, and forthwith began. Like most natives, he prided himself on his story-telling powers, and really not without cause; but unfortunately it is impossible to translate his imagery and queer turns of fancy into sober English prose. Concisely put, his narrative was as follows. He and his warrior returned to the spot where they had left Walter, just in time to witness the struggle in the distance, and with all speed they made their way to the scene of it, bent upon rescue. The head-hunters, warned by the noise of their approach, were prepared to receive them; they were two against seven; and as the result they were forced to beat a hasty retreat, Warupi's man badly wounded, but not before the chief had reduced the number of the enemy by one. In the night watches he decided upon his plan of campaign. The wounded warrior he sent back to the mountain-village, with a message to Mr Dennison telling him what had befallen, and begging him not to be alarmed. If he came back with Walter within a few days, well and good; if not, the leader was to betake himself as soon as he was ready to the chief's country, where doubtless he would find him and his son awaiting him. To Dawan, his second in command, he sent the same instructions, with orders enjoining strict obedience to Mr Dennison's commands.

Here Walter interrupted him with an ejaculation of surprise.

'It was thus, Kamara,' he explained. 'I was but one against six, and I knew not whither the chase might lead me—perhaps to the borders of my own country, and assuredly through the country of the head-hunters. Return might be difficult, and so it was that I sent the message that our white father should not be anxious. For I was determined to follow them wherever they went, until you were free or not one of them remained alive.'

'But the dangers! Were you not afraid, Warupi?'

Warupi laughed scornfully. 'And wherefore? Surely it

would be a strange thing if a chief were afraid of dogs like these—yea! and all their tribe!' he cried; and enlarged upon the theme to the verge of boastfulness.

'Go on,' Walter begged.

At dawn, continued the chief, he repaired with great caution to the camping-place of the head-hunters, only to discover that they had already flown. On the ground were Walter's gun and the weapons of the man whom he had slain. Of these he took possession of the gun and the 'man-catcher,' and then followed hard upon the track. During the first two days he could do nothing. On the first, indeed, he never came in sight of the enemy until near sundown, and all that night they kept guard only too well. The second day was even worse. Twenty times, while passing through the inhabited belt, he was in peril of being espied, and each time escaped by the skin of his teeth: on more than one occasion vastly to his own surprise—whence, perhaps, his low opinion of the tribe. But his opportunity arrived that evening. Misled probably by their vicinity to the villages, the head-hunters kept but indifferent watch, and he had no difficulty in creeping forward to leave Walter the token of the cassowary-feather. Then, in the early morning hours, one of the savages, for his sins, happened to stroll in the direction of his hiding-place, and fell by means of his late comrade's man-catcher—fell before he could utter a word to warn the others. We know how they went in quest of him: Warupi, hidden in the branches of a tree nigh at hand, saw how they found his decapitated body and fled in dismay. He laughed loud at the recollection.

'Ugh! what dogs they were,' he repeated for the tenth time.

'Go on,' said Walter again, impatient of digressions.

Thereafter, by reason of the enemy's terror, the pursuit was easy. Crossing the plateau, he had taken a parallel line to theirs, and thus reached the waterfall almost as soon. The first flight of birds marked his arrival at the clump of trees : the second the moment when, the unfortunate scout having ventured too near the edge, he had sent him spinning into mid-air. Concerning this incident, his only regret was that he had failed to secure the man's head. He had anticipated reprisals, and, the odds being now reduced to two against one, would not have hesitated to bring the adventure to an issue there and then. However, it was not to be just yet ; again the retreat was continued ; and of his experience in the cañon he had little to relate that you have not already guessed. But all afternoon he had kept at no great distance behind, always taking the precaution at a turn to assure himself of the stretch in front being clear. And at dark he closed up, and both sentries were asleep. As for the rest, he had approached within a few yards during the second halt, falling back once more with daylight ; and when the cave was gained, he had judged it expedient to end the matter—with what result you know.

Walter, having complimented him on his prowess, had one question to ask.

'And how about food, Warupi ?'

'Food ?' The chief seemed surprised. 'For two days were there not birds and beasts and fruit in plenty ? And then'—— Well, he rubbed his stomach reflectively and said no more.

Next Walter told *his* story, more shortly and much less dramatically, and the way was clear for the discussion of plans for the future. Ten minutes served. They could not stay where they were, and in view of the fact, as put by Warupi,

that Garougi would certainly rouse his tribe and so make a
return extremely dangerous, they dared not go back. What
remained? They must go forward, and trust to the instinct
of the chief to lead them across the mountains to his country.
He, for his part, had no doubt of his ability, and Walter was
fain, having no alternative, to stifle his scruples concerning
that and his father's anxiety and leave the upshot to Provi-
dence. As to pursuit, Warupi laughed at the idea: the
cowardly dogs might secure the mouth of the gorge, but they
would not venture along it even in their utmost strength.
And, it being by this time within an hour of sunset, the start
was fixed for the morrow.

As the enterprise appeared likely to be a risky one, Walter
took stock of his ammunition, while Warupi completed his
equipment with the best of the head-hunters' spears and
bows and arrows.

The night sped without incident, and as soon as the sun
rose they made a frugal breakfast of fruit and set out on
their journey, turning their backs for ever upon the cavern
and its grisly contents. For a mile or two the ledge
remained at the same height above the stream, and still the
walls of rock on either side sheered up precipitously to a great
altitude. Thereafter, however, there was a change. Gradually the gorge broadened out, and at the same time became
more and more shallow; and here and there, as the cliffs
receded, they were clothed with straggling masses of vegetation. Soon the ledge itself began to lose its distinctive
character, and now the travellers had more difficulty in
making good progress along the mountain-side. Plainly
they were nearing the head of the cañon.

Early in the forenoon, while they were picking their way
through the skirt of an undergrowth of bamboo, Walter

managed to bring down a brace of large birds of a species unknown to him, but somewhat resembling the pheasant. Luckily, they fell into the scrub, and so were easily recovered. Warupi pronounced them good to eat.

'Raw?' inquired Walter laughing.

The chief, without wasting words in reply, proceeded at once to gather materials for a fire. Walter watched him with interest, wondering how he intended to light it. His method was simplicity itself. First he made a split in a fragment of dry wood, inserting a peg to keep it agape; and into this split he put loosely a piece of tinder plucked from his girdle. Next he cut a short length from the coil of rattan rope which, like most of his fellows, he wore hanging behind, laid it on a flat, smooth rock, and over it placed the tinder in the cleft stick. Then, with his knee on the end of the stick, he drew the rattan rapidly to and fro under it until the tinder ignited, and, by blowing gently through the split, the spark was quickly fanned into a flame. The whole thing was done in a few minutes, the fire lit, and the game frizzling merrily above it. And, after their long fast from solid food, be sure that the two did full justice to the meal.

Four hours later, they reached a point where it was possible to climb the precipice, and, doing so, they saw on all sides of them a vast jumble of peaks and ravines, apparently impassable, and with scarcely a sign of life in all the wide expanse. Warupi pointed in a north-easterly direction.

Across there, Kamara, lies the country of my tribe,' he said.

Walter looked: in that direction the range shot up to its greatest height, and seemed, so to speak, even more impassable than elsewhere.

'I suppose there's a way through,' he thought, 'but—it won't be easy to find it.' And he was right: it was not.

CHAPTER XVIII.

A LEAP FOR LIFE.

BUT it is not my purpose to describe in detail the vicissitudes that befell our travellers in their passage of the mountain-range. Only a word can be spared for the events of the first few days, for I must hurry on to the more remarkable adventures that were soon to happen.

During their week's wandering amongst the mighty peaks and ravines of central Papua, every experience which can fall to the lot of travellers was theirs. Now they were scrambling along the summit of a tree-clad cliff, seven thousand feet above the sea-level; again their route lay through a gloomy gorge in the heart of the hills, or across a brawling torrent; at other times the path wound along the face of a precipice, where a single false step meant inevitable and immediate destruction; and more than once they had to climb the steep walls of rock on hands and knees, helped upwards by roots and jutting inequalities. Twenty times a day they were in danger of their lives, until peril itself became a matter of habit and passed un-heeded. Nothing daunted them: if one route was blocked, they turned back and tried another; and so on they went with unflinching courage, keeping always, to the best of their ability, in the right direction. Early in the journey they made acquaintance with hunger, but for the most part game was plentiful enough, and at the worst there was fruit to be had for the searching. Minor discomforts—alternations of heat and cold, heavy rains, insect bites, and the like— were not wanting; these are the commonplaces of travel, and as such held unworthy of notice. Of them, therefore, no more in this place.

In truth it was a weary and toilsome journey—to Walter in particular, upheld only by the hope of the meeting with his father and brother, and to some extent by the bond of comradeship between him and Warupi. Daily his debt of gratitude to the chief increased; and daily, in the knowledge of difficulties surmounted together and dangers shared, the tie between them grew closer and more tender.

What with detours and returns, they had no means of computing their actual progress, but assuredly—and, in view of the stupendous obstacles, the blame was not theirs—it was not phenomenal. Not until the fourth day, indeed, were they certain that they had crossed the watershed and were gradually descending on the other side. And on the sixth occurred the adventure which I have now to record.

That morning they had made their way down into a ravine that seemed not only to lead in their direction, but to offer an easier passage than had latterly been their portion. At first it was comparatively open; the gradient was gentle and the undergrowth scanty; and as they wended their course by the right bank of the stream flowing through it, they congratulated themselves, somewhat prematurely, on their good fortune. Then, as they advanced, they noticed with misgiving that the cliffs on each side were closing in, while the valley itself was quickly assuming a more stony and sterile appearance. Only too well did they know the signs.

Suddenly Walter stopped.

'What is it, Kamara?' asked his companion.

'Listen!'

Warupi did so, and his face fell as he heard the low, familiar rumbling of a distant cascade.

'Come!' he said simply.

Eager to learn the worst, they hurried on. Remorselessly the sides of the gorge closed in, until at last there was barely room for the stream and a few feet on either bank. A little farther, and their fears were realised. Before them was the end of the valley : here the walls were no more than twelve feet apart; and between them the river found its outlet and flung itself over a ledge into the ravine beneath, filling the whole passage with its swirling, foam-crested current. Beyond, as if to add to their annoyance, they caught just a glimpse of a more open country.

Walter turned away in keen disappointment.

'The usual luck!' he said lugubriously. 'There's nothing for it but to go back, I suppose?'

But Warupi had been scrutinising the cliffs, and now he pointed out on the opposite side a narrow shelf some fifty feet above the water, that with care might, said he, serve their purpose. Seemingly it ran right round the face of the rock.

'What!' cried Walter, looking at it doubtfully. 'You don't mean us to try *that*, Warupi?'

'If Kamara pleases,' was the quiet answer.

'And how are we to get to it?'

The chief retraced his steps for a few yards to a spot where the stream was split into two by an outcrop of rock.

It made two long jumps necessary, and these none of the safest, but with an effort it might be done.

'And then?' asked Walter.

'We must climb,' replied Warupi.

But how? The opposite cliff appeared to be a smooth, perpendicular wall of granite, accessible only to a monkey. Walter had sufficient faith in his comrade, however, to follow his lead even in this; and after all there was the comforting reflection that anything was better than to go back. The chief was ready: taking a short run, he leaped over and landed safe on the rock in mid-stream; and Walter, coming hard upon his heels, was caught by him and prevented in the impetus of the jump from falling headlong into the water on the far side. They stood for a moment, looking at the more difficult part that was still before them. For here the leap was fully longer, while of course they had no run; and the current, too, was swifter.

Warupi drew himself together for the attempt.

'Come!' he repeated.

Then he jumped again, and again landed safe, and from the contracted strip of dry ground between the river and the cliff beckoned upon Walter to follow. It had to be done; and with but one glance at the rushing stream to measure the distance, the boy threw himself forward with all his strength. Next instant his companion had seized him just as his toes touched the verge, and he was standing secure on firm earth.

Now came the formidable task of scaling the fifty feet of sheer cliff. They lost no time—stopping only to adjust the weapons slung upon their backs—in searching out the most promising place at which to make the trial, and, finding it, Warupi essayed the seemingly impossible ascent at once.

The chief, thanks to his bare feet and native agility, could climb like a cat, and slowly but surely he drew himself up with the aid of such unevennesses—and they were neither many nor prominent—as the surface afforded. Time after time did Walter, watching him from below with painful eagerness, expect him to fall, and the anxiety grew as he scrambled higher and higher. But somehow he kept his footing, and at last a shout told the excited onlooker that he had gained the ledge in safety.

It was now Walter's turn. Thrice he slipped back before he had clambered a dozen feet, and with bleeding hands and shaken nerves had to start anew. The fourth attempt was more successful. Directed from above, he succeeded with infinite trouble and caution in reaching to within ten feet of his comrade's position. There, however, he stuck. He could not advance a step, for he saw no foothold and nothing which *he* could grasp; and as for returning—well, it could only be by falling. For a second he hung there, not daring to look down. Then something dropped gently between his head and the rock; and, glancing up, he made out that Warupi had unwound and lowered his girdle, and was leaning over the ledge with one hand gripping a projection of the precipice. He signed to him to seize hold.

Walter hesitated. Considering the chief's position, his power to draw him up seemed anything but sure, and for himself he must unloose both hands to catch the girdle. It was like abandoning his last hope.

Apparently, however, this was not Warupi's opinion. 'Quick, Kamara!' he said, impatiently.

Once more the habit of trust served the boy in good stead. Very gingerly he loosened first one hand, seized the girdle, and then followed suit with the other. The rest was the

work of Warupi.   Walter had a confused, momentary feeling
of swaying to and fro in mid-air; then, somehow or other,
he was pulled upon the ledge on his knees, and at last,
with his companion's assistance, stood breathless upon the
narrow foothold with his face to the cliff. There, with his
forehead pressed against the rock and his eyes shut, he had
to halt for a minute to steady himself. When finally he
ventured to look down, he realised to the full the peril of
their undertaking, and shuddered at the prospect.   The
ledge was not more than eight or nine inches in width;
above it the cliff bulged slightly outward; and between his
heels the lad could see, apparently right below, the rushing
current of the stream and the waterfall beyond—that and
no more.   He grew giddy as he looked : it seemed to summon
him down, and between him and it there was nothing but
the inadequate and dangerous strip which wound round the
precipice and over the cascade, broadening not, as far it
was visible, to the extent of a single inch.

He withdrew his eyes, understanding that he must not
look again if he wished to keep his nerve, and just then
Warupi shouted into his ear above the din of the fall :

'Courage, Kamara !   Only five minutes more, and we
are safe on the other side.'

'I am ready, Warupi,' he answered.

For now the feeling of weakness had passed, and in his
heart was a stout determination, come what might, to conquer
the difficulty.   So, moving one foot at a time, and hugging
the rock closely, he moved along inch by inch in the wake
of the chief. It was slow work, and painfully laborious.
He had to edge sideways; the arching cliff seemed to press
him outwards; and beneath him, as he glanced down to
choose his steps, there was ever the swirling water waiting.

The distance between him and his barefoot comrade, more agile than he, increased every minute; and as on he went, a cold sweat broke out upon him and a mist came before his eyes. But he fought down the weakness, as he had fought it down before, and in due course—although to him it appeared an eternity—stood at length in the gut of the pass, where, fifty feet below him, the river forced its way between the walls of rock at their narrowest, and flung itself into the broader vale beyond.

It was then that he heard a sudden shout from Warupi, who was a few yards in front; and, half-turning his head, was just in time to see him take, as he thought, a mad leap into mid-air.

The same glance revealed the new terror. At this point some four or five feet of the ledge had crumbled away right to the base, and by that distance he was separated from the chance of safety. It was a long jump to attempt standing: in his condition, perhaps impossible. And the fall was directly below.

He closed his eyes and cowered against the precipice, battling with the overmastering idea that it was all over. He could not think. Then he opened them again when he heard a second shout from Warupi, to perceive the chief on hands and knees on the other side of the gap—safe. The sense of his utterance was lost in the noise of the cataract, but Walter could guess what it was. His instinct said the same.

He too must jump.

He did not stop long to consider. To do so—and he knew it—was to court disaster. Slowly he edged along the shelf until he reached the break, and paused there for a moment while he steeled himself for the effort. It needed all his courage, for he must turn to face the chasm before adventuring the leap. But, muttering a prayer, he did it; although never had he expected to stare death so nearly in the eyes.

Then, bending his knees and fixing his gaze on the wished-for destination, he sprang forth.

He gained the opposite bank, but his feet slipped on the narrow pathway, and, losing his balance, he toppled backwards. Warupi, who had retreated a little to give him room to land, tried to prevent the inevitable. Down he slid into the abyss yawning to receive him, his hands clutching in vain at the smooth rock; and then, after a second—before he had time to realise that in all human probability he was lost—he found himself clinging with desperation to the branches of a shrub which grew out from a cleft in the precipice about fifteen feet below the ledge. It, and it alone, had saved him from immediate death.

It was well that in this new and more terrible peril the boy's presence of mind did not desert him. Instead, he looked the situation in the face with more calmness—even were it the calmness of desperation—than had been his since the beginning of that eventful day. To climb was clearly impracticable, and what remained? To hang there helpless until his strength failed him, or the branch gave way, and thereafter drop like a stone into the broken, foam-crested water. The shrub, indeed, seemed to be firmly rooted, but a mere postponement of the end was little consolation. And that was all he dared to expect. It was a question of minutes, for the full weight of his body was upon his arms, and already he felt his strength going.

He had abandoned hope—for what hope was there?—when suddenly he was hailed from below. Glancing down, he beheld, to his great joy, another ledge beneath him, only a few feet to the right. On this Warupi was standing; having in some manner discovered it from above and managed to descend. The lad had but to reach it to be in safety, but how to do so was the problem. All at once the idea struck him that by swaying his body to and fro he might easily give the branch impetus enough to be able to swing himself into the arms of his comrade. Two jerks, and the thing was done; and, next moment, he had been caught by the chief's outstretched hands and pulled upon the ledge.

With not a word Warupi set out at once; for although the worst was over, the passage was not yet accomplished. Notwithstanding his growing faintness, Walter had perforce to follow. A yard or two brought them to the turn; thereafter the cliff began to fall away; and presently they saw their course clear for a descent into the broader valley which they had dared so much to gain. It was a rough scramble, albeit comparatively easy after their recent experience. Warupi, going first, had no difficulty; but even here, with the end of his troubles in view, the boy's bad fortune pursued him. He was within twenty feet of the ground, when suddenly the reaction told, his brain reeled, and he clutched wildly at a projection of the rock. It was in vain. For an instant he clung; then, losing his hold, he tumbled headlong to the bottom and fell at Warupi's feet.

.   .   .   .   .   .

Four days slipped past before Walter struggled back to consciousness, and then he emerged as from an ugly dream to find himself lying in darkness. He felt no pain, only a sensation of utter weakness; and when he tried to move his limbs, he found that he could not. That at first, and with it a strong desire to know where he was. But he dropped asleep before he had speculated much, and did not awaken again until the dawn of the fifth day was breaking. A familiar figure was bending over him in the gray light.

'Warupi!' he cried out, and was surprised at the feebleness of his voice.

The chief raised him gently with one arm, and held a cup, formed of the half of a cocoa-nut shell, to his lips. It contained a broth of some sort, and he drank it with eagerness.

'I have been ill, Warupi?' he remarked, after a little.

'Very ill, Kamara.'

'How long?'

Warupi told him.

'Four days!' To himself: 'And poor Frank wasn't here after all!' He wondered vaguely what had become of his father and brother: it was like a century since he had parted from them. Gradually the memory of all that had occurred returned to him—his captivity among the head-hunters, the incident of the cavern, the passage of the mountains, down to his terrible leap for life above the waterfall. Since then— what? He looked up into the chief's face. 'Where are we now, Warupi? what has happened?' he asked.

'Afterwards: my brother must sleep,' replied Warupi, with an air copied from Mr Dennison.

'But I can't. I'm all right now.'

And the chief complied. His story was short. His first step after Walter's fall was to examine him, and finding that no bones were broken he had carried him to the water- side. All his endeavours to revive him were fruitless; where- upon he set himself with praiseworthy promptitude to rig up a rude hut for the boy's protection. The valley turned out to be quite a fertile oasis; branches were plentiful, and to a native the rest was easy. By evening the shelter was erected, and by evening Walter was also in a high fever. It had run its course, and, thanks to his constitution, he had pulled through without scathe. Warupi could do little but watch the patient and attend to his comfort, and these he had done with single-hearted devotedness. Of sleep he could not have had much, for there was likewise food to provide—although in this respect they were lucky in their habitation—and he had not even neglected to make a survey of the valley, discovering no sign whatever of savages—no sign, indeed, that the foot of man had ever before trodden its surface.

When the chief had finished, Walter pressed his hand in silence. If he had been an Englishman, he would probably have summed up his gratitude in one sentence—he was a 'brick;' but he could not tell him in his own language how greatly he appreciated this new proof of his attachment. Perhaps Warupi understood.

Presently Walter remembered his comrade's superstitious fears, and in all seriousness asked him : 'And the evil spirits, Warupi?'

'Warupi has heard them not,' he said, simply. 'Was not the good Spirit of my white brother here?'

The boy could not doubt it.

That day he spent mostly in slumber, but next morning he awoke feeling so much stronger that, Warupi being absent, he ventured into the open air. He was still weak, and one leg and arm—those on which he had fallen—were very stiff; but surely, he thought, the sunshine had never been so brilliant, the foliage of the trees so beautiful, and the songs of the birds so sweet in his ears. For a little he stood at the hut-door, and tasted once more the joy of living, taking deep breaths of the hot air, and watching with a fresh interest the gaily-coloured insects which flitted amongst the boughs. Then he moved slowly towards the river-side. Here the valley was more open, and he could obtain a better view of his surroundings. The great cascade was a quarter of a mile above, and the water was still broken and white-crested; and Walter could not look at the terrible fall, and think how narrowly he had escaped being engulfed in its roaring current, without a shuddering sense of dread—not unmingled, let us hope, with deep thankfulness.

From this he turned gladly to the valley itself. On all sides the mountains rose up to a great height, but save for them there was little to remind him of the country through which he had lately passed. Everywhere was a tropical luxuriance of verdure—giant trees, tangled undergrowth, lovely flowering shrubs, and with them an abundance of animal life. To the boy it seemed a corner of Paradise.

He heard a footstep behind him, and glanced round to greet Warupi.

'How now, Kamara?' inquired the chief.

'Ready to start again—almost,' was the quick reply.

Warupi laughed. 'My brother must be content,' he said. 'What is before us? We know not. Perhaps it is danger like that'—and he pointed grimly to the waterfall. '*Then* we shall need all our strength again. So,' he added, 'let Kamara rest content until he gains his. It will not be long.'

'As you will, Warupi,' said Walter.

For ten days he rested content accordingly, but not in idleness. As his health returned, the chief taught him much of his lore—how to use the native weapons, the snaring of birds and animals, the secrets of woodcraft, and the like— and so apt a pupil was he that before long he won his master's approbation, and was in a fair way to become an adept. On his part, he could only, as far as the scarcity of ammunition permitted, teach Warupi to handle the rifle; a matter of no great difficulty, when he had succeeded in breaking down his comrade's superstitious awe of the weapon.

And at length, a fortnight having elapsed since their arrival in the valley, he deemed it time to reopen the question of going on. He would never, he told himself, be more fit.

'Let it be soon, Warupi,' he said.

'To-morrow?'

'To-morrow be it! And the course?'

'We must follow the river,' replied the chief. 'We cannot be far from my tribe, and yet this country is unknown to me. There will be danger? Perhaps. In two days I may speak, but not now. And,' he said, 'let my brother pray to the Spirit of his race.'

CHAPTER XIX.

THE VALLEY OF GOLD.

SO they started down-stream at daybreak on the morrow, and before noon had left the fertile valley behind them and were once more amidst broken and rocky scenery. Again the mountains closed in and contracted the river-valley to the dimension of a ravine, and their journey that day and the next was simply a repetition of their former wanderings. Here and there they passed isolated patches of vegetation, but for the most part the district was bare and sterile.

As they proceeded, Warupi began to evince symptoms of uneasiness. It was plain that he was unacquainted with the route, but all the same he would not admit the probability of having made a mistake in the beginning.

'My country is *yonder*,' he held with steadfast assurance, 'and we must reach it soon, Kamara. Let us go on.'

'We can do nothing else,' said Walter, and tried to believe that it was all right.

But he could not: not even when, towards the evening of the second day, the valley broadened a little and the face of Nature became more kindly.

That evening they camped as usual by the water-side. Next morning the chief went off to forage for breakfast, and Walter, having first replenished the fire, bethought himself of the desirability of a bathe in the river. A suitable pool was not far to seek; and, quickly undressing, he plunged into the cool water. For a minute or two he splashed about in thorough enjoyment, all unconscious of pending misfortune; and then, happening to look up, he saw on the opposite bank a sight that struck him with utter paralysis.

For there, watching him from the shadow of a clump of bush, stood a group of perhaps half-a-dozen savages, apparently not less thunder-struck than himself. So silently had they taken up their position, that not a sound had fallen upon the boy's ears to warn him of their vicinity. Now an exclamation escaped from one of them, he raised his arm as if to throw a spear, and doubtless would have done so had not a more humane, or more curious, companion interfered.

The action recalled Walter's mind to his danger. Recovering instantly, he scrambled out of the water and, not troubling to dry himself, commenced to dress with all speed, keeping his eyes at the same time on the natives on the other side. Presently they were joined by several more, and, after some hesitation, advanced with the evident intention of crossing the stream. To do so they had to ascend a few hundred yards, and this gave Walter the opportunity both to clothe himself and to examine them more at his leisure. In appearance and dress they resembled Warupi very closely, except that their heads were adorned with the feathers of the bird of Paradise instead of the cassowary; their weapons were much the same; and they had even similar ornaments of gold upon their necks and arms. And, judging from their demeanour, he was the first white whom they had ever seen.

For him the question was: in what way was he to receive them—as friends or as enemies? He longed eagerly for the return of his comrade.

After all, there seemed but the one course. The strangers had as yet manifested no disposition towards hostility; over and above, they were ten or twelve to one; and he had not even his rifle, which Warupi had insisted on carrying for him since his illness. Discretion, in this case, was obviously the better part.

He had just come to this decision, and was drawing on his jacket, when the first of the savages forded the stream and halted to await his followers. He was a man somewhat older than the others, with an expression of countenance not unpleasant, and he it was who had prevented the throwing of the spear. At once Walter made up his mind what to do. Hastily buckling his belt, and taking the precaution to keep his hand on his revolver, he went forward and gave him greeting in the language of Warupi.

The result was disappointing. The savage only stared at him, and so did his companions as they issued from the water and gathered round: stared and did or said nothing. It was certainly embarrassing, but not so much so as to dismay the boy.

Venturing a little nearer, and assuming his most benevolent smile, he repeated the salutation.

Greatly to his surprise, he was understood.

'Greeting!' answered the eldest native—pronouncing the word, however, with a different accent from that of Warupi's people. Then suddenly, with the air of one making a bold experiment, he stepped forward and laid his hand on the boy's shoulder. Perhaps he expected him to melt away or to assume another shape; and when he did neither, but stood smiling into his face, he proceeded, with more confidence to turn up the sleeve of his jacket for a closer examination of the white skin. The other natives, emboldened by their leader's example, crowded round to look and touch likewise, with many ejaculations of amazement and childlike wonder.

Walter suffered them to have their way, and tried to appear happy under the infliction. Meanwhile, his brain was not idle. His first thought was that they belonged to his comrade's tribe, but this, for obvious reasons, he was forced to dismiss as improbable, and he was confirmed in the doubt when the leader addressed him again, as he did presently. For although he spoke in a language which had much in common with that of Warupi, the dialect was evidently entirely different. Indeed, Walter could only recognise a word here and there, and had to guess the rest.

At last the savage had decided that he was human, and with natural curiosity wished to know whence he came.

'From beyond the mountains,' he answered, speaking slowly and distinctly.

The natives looked at each other and laughed: whether at the strangeness of his accent or in disbelief of his statement, he had no idea. But plainly they comprehended, which was gratifying in itself, and he deemed it wise policy to chime in. They laughed more vehemently than ever.

'The mountains?' repeated the leader.

Walter's arm was raised to point out the direction, when all at once he perceived something that caused it to drop limp to his side and him to utter a quick cry. Just at that moment, not a hundred yards above, Warupi had emerged from the cover of the bush and appeared in sight, carrying two brace of birds. The chief saw the new-comers, and stopped dead. Apparently, from his action, he did not like the situation. But he had no time to hide; they, too, had espied him; and now they hailed his arrival with a belligerent shout, while spears were grasped threateningly. Thus they stood regarding each other for a second. Then, at a word from the leader, three of the natives separated from the company and rushed towards him; and he, waiting only to wave his hand to Walter, threw down the birds and darted into the bush.

Involuntarily Walter made to follow him. But the leader's grip was still on his shoulder, and, by design or accident, the others had closed round in such a manner as to prevent his flight. An instant's reflection told him that to struggle would be worse than useless, for even if he got free he was between two fires, and already pursuers and pursued were alike out of view. So, resuming his former attitude of indifference, he awaited in some anxiety the issue of the new development. It could scarcely fail, he thought, to have an adverse effect upon his fortunes.

As to this, however, he had at first no means of judging. Without another word to him, the leader gave several commands; the savages drew round the fire; Warupi's birds were picked up, plucked, and roasted; and presently they were all breakfasting off them as if nothing had happened, Walter getting his due share. It was a silent meal, interrupted only by the report of a far-away shot. To the natives it seemed to have no meaning, for they did not even lift their heads; but to Walter it had a double significance, telling him for one thing that his captors were ignorant of firearms, and for the other that his blood-brother had used his rifle to rid himself of one of his pursuers—successfully, he could not help hoping.

After breakfast, there was much discussion among the savages, and although they talked too fast to permit the boy to follow them, he did not doubt what their subject was. It was himself; and perhaps his fate depended upon the result of the debate. At last the leader ended it by turning to him with a question.

'The stranger will come with us?' he asked.

'It is my wish,' answered Walter, readily. Having no alternative, he thought it wise to comply with a good grace.

A start was made at once. Two men were left at the camp, probably to await those who were in chase of Warupi; and the rest, half a dozen or so in number, placed Walter in their midst, crossed the river, and struck into the bush in the direction of the mountains. All forenoon they skirted their base in an easterly direction.

Walter tried to review the position judicially. No doubt his chief anxiety should have been for Warupi, but somehow he had sufficient faith in his friend's prowess to believe that he was quite safe. There were but three enemies against him—perhaps only two—and after the affair of the head-hunters the boy had no fear of the upshot.

And himself? Well, he saw no reason as yet for being down-hearted. Except that he was closely surrounded, his captors exercised no restraint whatever upon his movements; they had left him his knife and revolver; and in more ways than one, as the day sped, they showed themselves kindly disposed towards him. He would have liked to find out, indeed, whither he was being carried. But the leader strode on by his side without speaking a syllable, and he did not care to take the initiative. At the blackest, all things considered, he was no worse off than he had been when he was formerly in the hands of natives; he had still his revolver, Warupi was free as before, and, above all, he had confidence in his good luck.

Having thus set his mind at ease, he began to look about him with more interest. The country through which they were now passing struck him as differing in some respects from the usual. It was bare and rocky, strewn with great boulders, and intersected with innumerable small streams, and the soil was of a peculiar colour. He remembered having seen the like somewhere, but not in New Guinea. At length he recollected where. Two or three years before, he had accompanied Brunton to the gold-fields of the Palmer district of Queensland; and, but for the absence of all signs of industry, he could almost have imagined himself to be there at that moment. The inference set his heart beating. In old days he had often listened to the 'prospecting' stories of his father, and to the talk between him and Mr Maitland concerning the search for the precious metal; and, like all Queenslanders, his interest in the subject was more than academic. Thus it was not altogether in ignorance that he proceeded to think out the probabilities of his idea.

He glanced at the ornaments of his companions. They were of gold, sure enough; and now he noticed for the first time that their weapons were also rudely embellished with the same metal—both the shafts of the spears and the tips of the bows. Then he recalled what he had learned from Warupi on the subject: that his tribe got the gold used by them from a neighbouring and more powerful one, in whose country it was found. It might, of course, be the same with Walter's captors. On the other hand, there was a possibility which staggered him—namely, what if these natives belonged to the powerful tribe in question? It would explain much—among other things, the similarity of dialect and his comrade's sudden flight.

He was still speculating on the supposition and all that it meant, if it were to prove well founded, when a halt was called for the mid-day rest by the side of one of the little streams. Then the auriferous nature of the country was placed beyond all doubt, and one of the questions solved.

It was in this way. While two of the savages disappeared in quest of game, the others, except the leader, amused themselves by damming the water and overturning the stones in the shallow bed of the stream. Their purpose did not strike Walter at once—not until, indeed, one of them uttered a shout and came towards him with something displayed in the palm of his hand. One look, and he comprehended.

The object was a nugget of gold!

The savage, showing his two rows of white teeth in a broad smile, offered it to Walter, but the boy was so much surprised by the unexpected act that he could only stare at the man, standing there with outstretched hand.

'Take it!' he said, with another comprehensive grin.

Walter glanced towards the leader, doubtful whether to accept or refuse. He signed to him to accept.

'There are plenty more in the stream,' he understood him to say.

So Walter took it, and without waiting for thanks the finder went off to resume his search. The nugget weighed perhaps ten ounces, being about the size of a marble, and in shape not unlike it. The boy turned it over and over again, but his thoughts were elsewhere. By the merest accident he had stumbled upon a spot such as his father had undergone so many hardships to reach, and had failed to reach after all: a spot where nuggets were, literally speaking, to be picked up for the seeking, and where the natives had so little idea of their value, or valued them so little, that they presented them off-hand to a chance acquaintance! He had to pinch himself to make sure that he wasn't dreaming.

The nugget, at any rate, was real enough.

'It will do for Ruth's present—if I ever get back,' he said to himself, dropping it gently into his pocket.

No more were discovered, and the men soon grew tired of the diversion; and, their companions having now returned with some game, luncheon was quickly prepared and eaten. Half an hour later, the journey was continued. Before long, leaving the auriferous track behind, they trended south and ascended a low spur of the hills. The summit was gained early in the afternoon, and thence Walter got a magnificent view across an extensive, mountain-encircled valley to a broad lake some ten miles distant. He turned inquiringly to the leader.

'It is the country of my tribe,' said the savage, proudly.

The descent was speedily accomplished, and thereafter the natives pushed on through a rich and fertile district with the speed of men bent on an important mission. In two hours the bank of a river was struck; perhaps that which they had left in the morning augmented by tributary streams. For other two hours they followed it downward by a well-defined track, and every minute the signs of habitation became plainer and more frequent, until ultimately they entered a good-sized village. But it was not to stop, even to satisfy the curiosity of the villagers; and when the latter, by thronging round, threatened to block the path, the escort did not hesitate to use their spears to clear it. Not to be outdone, the villagers—men and women alike—formed up behind to follow. The rest of the march was through a thickly-populated area, cultivated like a garden. Large villages and clusters of huts were numerous, and at each—in default of information from the escort, who pursued their course heedless both of entreaties and curses—the procession was swelled by scores of gaping Papuans. By the time the lake-side was reached, they must have had three or four hundred followers.

They skirted the lake for half a mile from the point at which the river entered it, and then at length Walter saw whither he was being taken. A spur of rock jutted into the water and broadened at the farther extremity, having from a distance the appearance of an island joined to land by a narrow causeway; and on the promontory was situated a village—that, beyond doubt, to which they were bound. Its position made it easy of defence against native methods of warfare, and almost impregnable to assault.

Coming in a few minutes to the beginning of the neck, the boy noticed that it was further defended in the middle, where the isthmus was narrowest, by a stockade of logs. There was a single opening, at which they were challenged by a couple of warriors. They passed through; then the leader gave the men an order, and as the result they stood in the gap and prevented the crowd from pushing in. Notwithstanding the uncertainty of his own fate, Walter could not help smiling at the woe-begone aspect of the disappointed ones.

The village itself was like no other that he had seen in New Guinea. It occupied three or four acres of ground, and all the huts were built in two rows on the lake's edge—all save one, which stood by itself at the extremity of the promontory, and was much larger than the rest. Between the rows was an ample space, broken only by a few clumps of trees.

Near one of these the leader halted his men, and went forward to a mound of earth on which an old man was dozing. Gently awakening him, he said a few words in his ear. The patriarch started up, glanced quickly towards Walter, and then engaged in a low conversation with the other. From the gestures of the latter, Walter guessed that he was relating the story of his capture; from his attitude of respect, that the old man was a person of distinction, perhaps the chief himself.

As, meanwhile, each hut was pouring forth its complement of staring women and children—of men there were not many visible—he was not sorry when at last his captor beckoned him to approach.

He did so with his bravest air.

CHAPTER XX.

AGAIN A CAPTIVE.

'GOURI, this is he,' said Walter's captor, presenting him with due form.

The old fellow, who could not have seen less than seventy years, scrutinised the boy with eyes that were undimmed by age. He, on his part did the same. His first impression of the chief was not too favourable. He seemed to have been long a stranger to water, plentiful as it was around; his bent and emaciated body was daubed all over with a hideous, whitey-gray paint; even his head-dress was neglected; and as for the robe of kangaroo skin flung over his shoulders, the best that can be said of it was that it was tattered and very ancient. Only through his countenance, which was still keen and alert, did he reveal his share—and apparently it was no small share—of the wisdom of the serpent.

He motioned Walter to draw nearer, and with nervous fingers rubbed the skin of his wrist as if to assure himself that the colour was natural. Walter bore the ordeal stoically: he was becoming used to it. Then, evidently satisfied, Gouri opened the conversation by demanding his name.

'Kamara,' he answered, simply.

Next he understood him to ask where his country lay—for,

as in the case of the leader, he had partly to guess the questioner's meaning. It was a difficulty, however, that disappeared with a little practice.

Now, this struck Walter as a more difficult matter to explain, especially as he was rather doubtful of his ability to make himself comprehended, but he made a gallant attempt to do it. He came, he said, from a country many days' journey distant, where all the people were white like himself: a statement which caused his two auditors to look at each other and at him in obvious disbelief. As to his purpose, it was to see the land and become friendly with its inhabitants; and he finished by claiming from Gouri, a chief whose fame was not confined to his own valley—which, thought he, was likely enough—the rights of hospitality and welcome due to a stranger.

The chief appeared to follow him, for he listened gravely, but as long as he was speaking he gave no sign of being pleased or otherwise. Then, when he was done, he inquired cunningly: 'And what offering has Kamara brought to Gouri from this distant country?'

Walter, taken quite by surprise, had no answer for a moment. The question was repeated: all at once, the boy saw his opportunity; and, drawing his knife from his belt, he handed it to the astute old beggar.

'This, Gouri,' he said.

The chief's eyes lighted up as he examined it carefully, and without more ado tried it on the tree-trunk. The result was satisfactory: it was a weapon such as even a superannuated brave could appreciate, and appreciate it he did. He beamed upon Walter with more kindliness than he had hitherto shown, and Walter began to congratulate himself on the happy effect of his idea.

The feeling was premature. Presently the younger savage whispered something to his superior, who nodded wisely and turned again to the boy.

'Kamara was not alone when he met my people?' he suggested. 'There was a warrior with him?'

'Gouri is right,' answered Walter, dropping naturally into the other's habit of speech.

'Of this country?' He admitted it.

'And his name was'——

'Warupi,' said he, thoughtlessly.

The instant the word was uttered he perceived his mistake, and that he had good cause to blame himself was quickly evident. The attitude of the savages changed at once: Gouri's to one of sudden anger. Plainly the name of Warupi was not unknown—and was not popular.

'The stranger has lied!' cried the chief, handling his new weapon as if he would dearly like it to make acquaintance with its former owner's inside. 'Speak not of dogs! Perhaps Warupi comes from a distant country too?'

Walter, keeping cool with an effort, retorted upon him in his own fashion.

'Perhaps they have such knives as that in Warupi's country?' he said, pointing to it. 'Kamara knows not, for he has never seen Warupi's country.'

They stared at him incredulously.

'Perhaps Warupi has been in the stranger's, then?' hinted Gouri, sarcastically.

'Perhaps. Has Gouri heard of him these many moons back?'

It was a bold stroke to play, but it was successful. Somewhat staggered by Walter's assurance, the chief glanced at his companion.

Walter retorted upon him in his own fashion.

'It is true,' said the latter, speaking aloud for the first time. 'There has been war, and yet our young men have not seen him. Perhaps Kamara is right. They said he had gone on a long journey.'

Suddenly Gouri jumped to his feet in excitement, only to fall back exhausted by the effort.

'The white men!' he cried. 'Was there not a report, long ago, of three magic-men with white faces, whom Marik saw in Warupi's valley? I said it was a lie, and Marik was slain, but perhaps it was true.' He thought for a little, while Walter watched him anxiously. 'And this Warupi,' he went on, addressing the boy—'my young men will bring in his head to-morrow, and then we shall see him. For you, Kamara'—— He stopped again, his strength seeming to fail him.

Walter's heart beat faster.

'Yoshida!'

The other native stood at attention.

'Take Kamara to your hut, and give him food and milk. I will speak more with him to-morrow.'

So saying, he sank back and shut his eyes; and Yoshida, motioning Walter to follow him, strode across the promontory to one of the huts on the lake's verge. There was a rush of the villagers—who had hitherto kept in the background, doubtless from motives of prudence—towards the two; but the warrior took no more notice of them than he had done of their compatriots in the afternoon, and halted presently in front of his house. It was raised by a few steps from the ground, and was a large building for Papua. Here he was received by a woman, whom he greeted affectionately, and by a little boy of nine or ten. The latter he presented to his guest by catching him by the ear and pulling him forward.

'It is my son, Pari,' he said.

Walter offered to clap the lad's head, whereupon he broke from Yoshida and, much to the warrior's amusement, hid himself behind his mother. From this point of vantage he gazed with wide-open eyes at the stranger.

The hut was divided by a thin partition of bamboo into two rooms, and to the inner of these Walter was conducted, food placed before him, and his bed of mats indicated. Then, it being now past sundown, Yoshida left him to himself. For hours he lay tossing in the darkness, unable to sleep for the thought of his situation. One thing was now put beyond all question: that he was in truth in the hands of Warupi's hereditary enemies, the 'neighbouring and more powerful tribe' which had possession of the Valley of Gold and the great nugget. The country of his blood-brother could not be far away, and perhaps, at that moment, his father and Frank were awaiting him there. His own danger—and he could not hide from himself that he was in danger—troubled him less than his anxiety regarding his relatives. He might not be able to escape; he realised clearly enough the risk of attempting it; but nevertheless he resolved, if he got the chance, to make a brave effort to elude his captors. Whether they held him as a prisoner or as a guest, he could not learn until the morrow.

After breakfast, then, he proceeded to settle the point. Yoshida was absent, and his wife and son did not stop him, but only stared, as he passed through the outer room and into the open air. He strolled carelessly towards the stockade, unheeding the curious glances of the few people who were about. As before, the opening was guarded by two warriors, and upon his approach they jumped up and lifted their spears in menace. He had his answer: in that direction, at least, there was no retreat.

Turning, he noticed that one of his captors of yesterday was close at his heels. The man answered his salutation very affably, but continued to dog his footsteps, and suddenly the truth struck him—not only was his retreat cut off by land, but he was being watched in case he should escape by water!

He was a prisoner.

As he went back to his hut more slowly, thinking of these things, he happened to run against his host. Yoshida gave him greeting. He tackled him at once.

'What is the meaning of this, Yoshida?' he asked, pointing to the man behind.

'It is the chief's command,' was the answer. 'Kamara may go where he pleases within the village, but Gouri forbids him to leave. He wishes no evil to befall him outside. Here he is safe.'

'He is very kind,' said Walter to himself; but all the same he determined, if it were at all possible, to frustrate the benevolent designs of the old fox.

To this end he kept his eyes open during the day. Barring some annoyance caused by the persistent curiosity of the villagers, he found much to interest and amuse him. The men of the place, except a few, seemed to be absent on an expedition, and so the work of agriculture, as is commonly the case in Papua, fell entirely to the women. Their patches were on the mainland, and all day long they passed between them and the village, now carrying an armful of fruit, and again stopping for a little to attend to their household duties. Both they and the few males wore heavy ornaments of gold, and even some of the children did the same. As for Gouri, he did not show himself: 'He was sick,' said Yoshida. Walter, if truth were told, was not sorry.

P

The afternoon was spent most agreeably in overcoming the shyness of Pari, his host's son : for a purpose other than amusement. He was a lively, merry-faced little fellow, very dear to his father, and before evening he and the stranger were the best of friends—so good, that he offered to teach him the gentle art of fishing as practised in the valley. Walter accepted, of course : he had an inquiry or two to make, and he might gain much information from the boy's innocent prattling.

So next morning found them seated together by the lake-side, the guardian warrior just beyond earshot. Pari had little to teach, and Walter less to learn. The tackle was primitive, consisting merely of a line of fibre and a small piece of bone, and on this occasion the fishing was not very successful. But it gave Walter the opportunity he wanted.

'Tell me, Pari,' he said, in a tone of assumed indifference : 'you have heard of Warupi?'

Pari's answer was prompt. 'Both of him and his brother Kerepuna, and I mean to kill them when I am a man ! They are great warriors,' he added.

'Their country is not far away, then?'

Pari laughed. 'Not far,' he said, and pointed westward across the lake to the high range of mountains which bounded the valley, five or six miles distant. 'It is over there, beyond the mountains. A bird could soon fly to it.'

'And a man?'

'Not so quickly. *He* must go by the pass, and that is two days' journey. I have heard my father say it.' Then he glanced up appealingly into his new friend's face, as an alarming suspicion occurred to him. 'But Kamara is not going, surely? They are very fierce men, and would eat him.

Let him stay here and become a warrior, and fight Warupi and Kerepuna.'

Walter comforted the boy. 'Kamara does not wish to be eaten, little one,' he assured him.

Thus relieved, Pari went on to tell him much more of interest concerning Warupi's tribe—how they were continually at war with his, and how sometimes the one side lost men and sometimes the other. Their fate he left to Walter's imagination.

He, meanwhile, having learned all that he wanted to know on one point, was anxious for enlightenment upon another. This was the use of the large hut built at the extremity of the promontory, about which his curiosity had been roused by several facts. For one thing, closely as he had watched it on the preceding day, he had observed not a soul entering or indeed approaching it. You will remember that it stood by itself midway between the two rows of houses. There appeared to be no door or other opening into it; the façade was quite covered, in the mode of the country, by sun-bleached skulls; and in front, extending to about seventy feet, was a space marked out by a low palisade, within which the grass was scorched in several spots as if by fire. Now the facts which seemed curious to Walter were these. First, it was obviously uninhabited; and second, it was so sedulously avoided by the natives that if they had to cross the promontory they made a wide detour, and even then scurried past with averted faces. It was, in short, a mystery which puzzled him much, and he looked to Pari for its solution with some interest. But, luckily for his peace of mind, the solution was not to be his just yet. For, when he broached the subject, the little savage gave signs of the most lively fear, and absolutely refused to discuss it.

'Hush, Kamara!' he said, quickly.   'It must not be spoken of.   Hush!'

He demanded why.

'Hush!' he repeated, in such a tone of agony that Walter was compelled, in pity for him, to say no more.   But he did not think the less about it, albeit never to much purpose; and perhaps it was well that he had no suspicion of the connection which he was soon to have with the mystery in his own person.

Not at once, however.   A week passed away without incident; and, after the first feeling of novelty had worn off, it was very monotonous to the prisoner.   With Yoshida and his family he was on the best of terms, and the villagers in general were as kindly as he could expect.   Even the old chief, on the rare occasions when he ventured out to sun himself on his favourite seat under the trees, showed a liking for his company, and listened intently, but with evident incredulity, to his descriptions of his people.   But all the time he could not forget how precarious his position was: he had always the carking dread in his heart.

Then gradually there came a change.   It began with the return of the men of the village, who brought with them a round dozen of miserable-looking captives.   At first Walter was half-afraid to examine them, lest they should prove to be of Warupi's tribe, but a glance at their head-dresses disposed of the doubt.   Not only did they wear no cassowary feathers, but in hue they were a shade lighter than his friends.   A less welcome discovery followed: that among the escort were the two warriors who had been left behind on the day of his own capture.   He could not explain why, but somehow their appearance seemed to him to bode no good.

He was wondering if it would be wise to accost them for

news of the other three—those who had chased Warupi—when he was hailed by his host.

'Come!' he said. 'It is Gouri's command.'

As he approached the chief's seat, he noticed that there were two strangers with him—one a very tall man, the other a youth. Both were in full war-costume.

'Who are they?' he asked of Yoshida.

'Vali, the son of Gouri,' answered Yoshida, in a low tone, 'and *his* son, Koura. Vali is a great magic-man.'

He was also a splendid man physically, and Walter could not help admiring him as he bent over his old father in earnest talk. His admiration was somewhat damped, however, when he heard the word 'Warupi' repeated more than once; and it disappeared altogether when Vali turned and Walter saw his countenance. A more cruel and brutish face the boy thought he had never beheld, even among the blackboys of Queensland. Now it scowled upon him, and instinctively he felt that here was an implacable enemy.

The savage eyed him for a minute before speaking.

'*He* may tell us,' he said at last, addressing Gouri. Then, to Walter: 'Speak, stranger! You know the dog whom they call Warupi?'

Walter returned his look fearlessly. 'I know Warupi.'

'Then tell me—was he alone with you when Yoshida saw him eight days ago?'

'He was alone.'

'It cannot be!' the man burst out. 'Three against one! Yet the warriors have not returned with his head. If he has slain them and escaped'—— Breaking off, he turned again to Walter. 'But perhaps the stranger can tell us what has happened?' he sneeringly suggested. 'They say he is very wise.'

Walter had a shrewd suspicion, but he deemed it better to reveal his reputed wisdom by keeping it to himself and pleading ignorance.   He did so.

'Is it so?' asked Vali, still with a sneer.   'It is well for the stranger—for the present.   But if the young men return not, let him beware!'   He touched his spear significantly. 'Blood demands blood.   And,' he added, 'Koura here is ready to ask the price of his kinsmen's heads.'

'And *now!*' said Koura, stepping forward with alacrity. He seemed a year or two older than Walter, and was taller; and, judging from his physiognomy and the pleasure which he showed at the prospect of shedding the stranger's blood, he was a credit to his amiable parent's teaching.

But the old chief interposed.

'Wait, Koura!' he said.

'Ay, wait—until the moon is full,' echoed Vali, and turned carelessly away.

CHAPTER XXI.

WHEN THE MOON WAS FULL.

'WAIT—*until the moon is full.*'

The phrase struck Walter as significant when he heard it from Vali's lips, and it became more significant by repetition during the next ten days. That it had a meaning deeper than that upon its face he did not doubt. To him it was a threat, to the savages something more: a reminder, perhaps, of an event important in their annals. But even from Yoshida he could glean no information concerning it, and had perforce to possess his soul in patience. One answer only could he get: that he would know all soon enough. It was scant comfort.

As regards himself, things went from bad to worse in those ten days. Vali was plainly a man of supreme influence in the tribe—to all intents, its chief. He bore the boy no good-will; and the villagers, taking their cue from him, soon changed from an attitude of kindly indifference to one of scarcely-veiled hostility. His greetings were not returned; black looks succeeded friendliness; and, save for his host and little Pari, he had not a single well-wisher on whom he could rely. Even they, for their own sakes, were compelled in public to assume a bearing expressive of disgust and aversion. His freedom was not restricted, indeed; but probably that was merely because there was so little of it to restrict. Had there been the slightest chance of his escape, doubtless it would have been.

In a hundred other ways, however, he was made to realise his position. Vali's way was to scowl upon him without speaking—he seldom spoke to him—and to tap his spear or club meaningly; that of his hopeful son was to remind him of the progress of the moon, and demand insultingly if he had yet heard from his friend Warupi.

'And if not, Kamara'—— A gesture copied from his father said the rest.

Half-a-dozen times a day was the young savage wont to annoy the captive thus, and to find the liveliest amusement in doing it—an amusement that, although Walter ignored him consistently, seemed never to pall. All the same, our prisoner would have given much for the opportunity of having Koura to himself for five minutes in a quiet spot, without the risk of getting a vagrant spear through his back.

The reason of it all was not far to seek. Apparently, in connection with the tribe's warfare, a tide of bad luck had set in. Thrice during the ten days did a party of warriors return from the field without prisoners and otherwise the worse of their excursion; and after each occasion the villagers' murmuring increased in volume and their ill-will towards Walter was manifested more openly. How he was concerned in their misfortune he could not imagine, until Pari revealed the secret.

'They wish to kill you, Kamara,' said the boy, one day.

'Why, little one?'

'Because you turn their hearts to water, and they cannot

fight. Vali tells them so. There will be few prisoners to offer to Koa-punu this year, he says, and if Koa-punu is angry'——

'But this Koa-punu—who is he?'

The boy's eyes dilated with fear. 'Does Kamara not know him?' he asked in a whisper, solemnly. 'He sends the thunder and the rain, and he lives—*yonder*.' He jerked his finger in the direction of the skull-covered, solitary hut, and then drew it back timorously. 'And if he is angry'——

'Yes?' Walter was thoroughly interested: at last it looked as if he was to discover something.

'Oh! he may eat up the whole village, or cause it to fall into the water. Vali says so, and he is a great magic-man. And,' he went on, hastily, 'the people would have killed you at once, for they were angry. But Vali stopped them. "*Wait*," he said. "*When the moon is full*"'—— He broke off. 'It is only five days now, Kamara,' he said.

'And then?' impatiently asked Walter.

'Then, who knows?' said Pari. 'Not you—not my father. Is it not with the good Koa-punu?' And more, notwithstanding Walter's coaxing, he would not disclose.

He, if he had not learned as much as he should have liked, had learned enough to confirm him in his worst fears. The plan of the astute magic-man was easy to read. That he would succeed was certain—lacking a miracle. And himself? He had five days yet, and thereafter ——

But he was still to have one faint gleam of hope, and that, strangely enough, at the hands of Vali. It came the next day. In the afternoon he was summoned to the presence of him and Gouri, and with them he found a strange warrior, bedraggled and travel-stained as from a long journey. All three eyed him curiously, the stranger particularly so. Vali gave him an ironical salutation; and then the new-comer bent towards the magic-man and whispered something in his ear.

'Repeat your story, Timar,' said he. To Walter: 'Listen, Kamara! Perhaps Timar has good news for you.'

Both obeyed. Shortly put, Timar's narrative was that he had accompanied a party of warriors upon an expedition of surprise into a neighbouring valley; that at the pass they had unexpectedly been confronted by the enemy, who were on the watch for them; and that for two days they had fought without success—had indeed (Timar didn't say so, but Walter guessed it) been beaten ignominiously back. Then, in a tone of wonder, he mentioned the interesting fact which sent Walter's blood tingling through his veins. It was this: that among the enemy, held by them in high honour, were two strangers with white skins all covered up—'like him,' added the man, pointing to Walter. At Vali's behest he described them: one as a man whose face was hidden by black hair, and spoke much to Kerepuna; the other as a boy.

'Like Kamara,' he repeated, again pointing to Walter, 'but younger and not so tall. At first I thought they were the same.'

Vali glanced at his captive's flushed and eager countenance, and laughed maliciously. But Walter did not hear him: he had his own thoughts. So his father and Frank were safe—more, they were among Warupi's tribesmen, only two days' journey distant! The description and the mention of his comrade's brother left no room for doubt. It was good to know so much, and for the moment the one feeling in his heart was that of joy.

He was roused by another question from Vali to Timar.

'And these strangers—did *they* fight?' he asked.

The answer was that they did not, although the younger seemed anxious : they kept in the background, and consulted much with Kerepuna. Walter told himself that there had been no need for their assistance.

Now Gouri spoke for the first time.

'Kamara knows these white-faces?' he hinted. 'Doubtless they are his kindred?'

Walter admitted that it might be so.

'And yet they are in Warupi's country, which Kamara has never seen!' This he said in a tone of triumph, as if he had convicted the boy out of his own mouth of an ingenious lie, and was proud of the feat.

Before Walter could explain, Vali broke in impatiently.

'What matters it?' he demanded scornfully. 'Is not Kamara a liar? Are not his kinsmen cowards, who are afraid to fight for their friends? Timar has told us so.'

'Does Vali speak of cowards?' retorted Walter, losing his temper under the insult, and therewith all sense of his imprudence. 'He comes of a brave tribe, surely! Three of his young men set out to capture Warupi, and is Warupi captured? Let the young men say. His warriors have fought against Warupi's tribe : where are their prisoners? Let Timar say. Oh! I know'—this as the magic-man raised his spear angrily—'I know that Vali, like a brave chief, wants to kill me. To what end? He may kill me, but does he think that these white men will not hear of it? Let him listen. If he kills me, be sure that, as certainly as night follows day, these white men will fall upon his tribe; they will kill all his people; they will burn the villages and leave not a hut in the valley. These are not idle words. What is his magic to theirs? . . . Does Vali wish to hear more? I am not done.'

'Speak on, boaster!'

'Then I tell him this, further—that before ho can kill me he will be food for the crows himself.'

Having once begun, he had spoken out fearlessly—in exaggerated language, it might be, but that only because no other would have had its effect—and now he awaited the consequences, with one hand in pocket grasping his revolver. His defiance, he believed, could have but one result. But he was resolved not to go under until he had shown that his threat was not an empty boast. If die he must, he would die 'game'—and Vali would go first. So he watched for the first movement of the magic-man's spear-arm as a signal to draw.

For a little it seemed as if only the chief's rage stood between him and the beginning of hostilities. His face was working horribly—his hands were clenched in a convulsive grip—he was momentarily incapable of action. It was the same with the aged chief and Timar: they also were too much astounded to speak or move. Vali was the first to recover. He glared upon Walter with all the hatred of his nature expressed in his eyes, hesitating, no doubt, whether to spear the presumptuous boy on the spot or to hoard up his hate for a sweeter revenge in the future. Finally the promptings of his low cunning made him choose the latter course, and with an evil laugh he addressed himself to his prisoner.

'Kamara uses bold words,' he said, 'and doubt not that the chance will be his to prove them. But not to-day: the moon is not yet full. He speaks of his friends. Let them come: there will be a welcome for them from Vali —and from Koa-punu. Now go!'

He was glad to obey, for at the least it was a respite—

for four days. And his father was near. If he could only get a message sent!

For the rest of the day he deemed it wise to keep indoors. Yoshida was on the mainland, and he awaited his return in the evening with some expectancy. When he came, he saw at once from his grave demeanour that he had heard the news.

'The village is full of it,' he said, answering his question. 'Vali was not your friend before, Kamara; he is now your enemy, and it is not good to be Vali's enemy.'

'Then there is no hope for me, Yoshida?'

Yoshida bent his head. 'Who knows?' he asked, with an assumption of cheerfulness. '*Until the moon is full*'——

Again the sinister phrase!

—— 'Kamara is safe, and before then much may happen.' But his tone belied his optimism.

'*Until the moon is full*.' Walter repeated the words. 'They say something will happen *then*, Yoshida. Tell me what it is. Surely it is well that I should know?'

The savage considered, Walter waiting in suspense.

'It may not be spoken of,' he said at last. 'And yet'—— He looked round him apprehensively, and then suddenly went on: 'Yes, I will tell Kamara. Know that it is then only that we see the face of the god Koa-punu, and bring him our yearly offerings of food and men. For it is a great festival. Our prisoners are slain as a sacrifice to him, and those who have offended against the laws of the tribe—they are eaten to give us new courage in warfare; and for three nights Koa-punu smiles upon his servants. So it has been from the time of our fathers, who have left this word—that a stranger may not look upon the face of the god and live. One only has done it—Kerepuna, the brother of Warupi—and there can be no peace between his tribe and mine until his head has been offered to Koa-punu. And now Kamara knows all,' he said quickly, as if he were glad to have an unpleasant and dangerous task done.

'Three nights!' repeated Walter. 'And on which of them shall I be slain as a sacrifice to Koa-punu?' asked he, eager to learn the worst.

'When Vali wills it,' was the answer.

'And afterwards?'

'Afterwards! It will matter not to Kamara. Vali's arm is strong and his spear sharp.'

So this was the worst: to become the victim of the cannibalistic orgies of a tribe of savages. The scales dropped from his eyes. He could hope for no mercy from his captors, and he realised that the chance of a rescue was equally hopeless. For an instant, indeed, he had a wild idea of appealing to Yoshida to carry or send a message to his father, and then he saw the impracticability of the scheme. His host dared not leave the village, nor was there another man or a woman to whom he could entrust it. No: think of it as he might, he could see no way of escape from the terrible fate which awaited him. And he had four days of torturing suspense before him—four days, if you please, in which to prepare himself. Just then, in his misery, he was inclined to wish that the end had followed upon his defiance of Vali, lest his nerve should fail him at the last, and he should die in a manner unworthy of his race.

The four days passed somehow.

At length it was the morning of the eventful day, and its coming was almost welcome to Walter, notwithstanding that within fourteen hours—about nine that night—the moon would be full and the great festival begun. At breakfast Yoshida warned him against venturing out of doors: he would be safer within, he said. But his restlessness was greater than his prudence, and before long he was standing with Pari in the middle of the village, an interested spectator of the preparations for the evening's ceremony.

The first of these was the departure of the females. Many had already gone, and by noon not a single woman or girl was to be perceived in or near the village. He turned to his companion for an explanation.

'Such sights are not for women,' replied Pari, with the inborn contempt of the savage for the sex.

To take their place, men poured in all morning from the surrounding district, bringing with them offerings of fruit and other food to lay before Koa-punu. It was deposited within the enclosure around the shrine of the god, who still remained hidden; and Walter had the curiosity to ask what he did with it, or what became of it.

'He gives it to Gouri and the magic-men,' was the simple answer of Pari, who saw nothing strange in such an action. To Walter it explained their liking for the festival.

For an hour or two he was allowed to watch the scene unmolested. Vali was not to be seen, and everybody else was either too busy to notice him or had no interest in objecting to his presence. Then the magic-man appeared, noticed him, and at once gave Yoshida an order. The latter came towards him, accompanied by the boy Koura.

'Kamara must go indoors,' said his host, peremptorily. 'It is Vali's command.'

'But it will not be for long, Kamara,' Koura supplemented, with a loud laugh. 'To-night the moon will be full. Is Kamara afraid? For then'——

Walter turned his back upon him, not seeking to hide his contempt, and without further ado returned to his hut. Koura's jeers followed him to the doorway.

All day he lay on his bed listening to the turmoil outside, and cudgelling his brains for some plan whereby he might hope to escape the fate designed for him. One occurred to him at last: one in which the expedient was dangerous to a degree and the chance of success the smallest; and by the time he was called to attend the ceremony he had strung himself up, come the worst, to hazard the attempt. The odds, he knew, were a hundred to one against its accomplishment, but surely anything was better than to give in without a struggle.

Yoshida arrived for him an hour or so after sundown.

'Is Kamara ready?' he asked. 'Gouri has sent for him.'

'I am ready, Yoshida,' he replied, and at once followed his host into the open air, where they were received by two guards with lighted torches. They placed themselves one on each side of the boy, Yoshida bringing up the rear.

The moon had not yet risen, but the sky was luminous and clear, and objects were very distinct in the peaceful half-light of the evening. The middle of the village, right up to the palisade in front of the shrine, was occupied by a dense mass of warriors, of whom there could not have been less than seven or eight hundred in all. Beyond, broad circles of light were cast by several great fires and by numerous torches in the hands of the tribesmen.

Two facts struck Walter as noteworthy, as his escort cleared a path to the enclosure: the first, that in the crowd of savages outside the palisade—within, it was different—not one was armed; and the second, the complete silence which prevailed. Then, entering the enclosure itself, he found other

things at which to wonder. Here four huge bonfires lit up
the space between the palisade and the hut, and threw their
glare upon a line of some fifty people, among whom he
recognised the prisoners brought in by Vali ten days before.
Behind each a villager stood motionless, holding a torch
in his left hand and a club in his right. The dejected
and hopeless attitude of those in the first row left the boy
in no doubt as to their identity: they were the victims-
designate of the festival—and they knew it. Was *his* place
likewise in the ranks of the doomed? A minute would
settle it.

Stationed more in the shadow was another group of natives,
armed also, but without torches. All these were near the
palisade; and in the remainder of the enclosure two figures
only were visible, and they between the fires and the hut.
Towards them Walter was led by his guards. Of the pair,
one squatting on the ground was easily distinguished as
the old chief; the other, who stood by his side, was his
grandson Koura. Walter was surprised to see no sign of
Vali.

Gouri said something to Yoshida, and altogether ignored
the captive. It was otherwise with Koura. *He* could not
resist the opportunity—it might be the last—of airing his
favourite jibe.

'Does Kamara watch the sky?' he asked. 'Look! the
fires are burning well, and Koa-punu is hungry. The moon
is nearly full, yet Kamara's white kinsmen are not here.
There will be need for his magic soon.'

Yoshida interrupted him.

'Come, Kamara!' he said.

Turning, they retraced their steps to the palisade, and
there Walter was posted at the right extremity of the line of

prisoners, with Yoshida by his side, and the two torch-bearing warriors behind. Doubtless it was as a tribute to his importance that he had one more guard than the others.

Now, for the first time, he had leisure to examine the face of the god Koa-punu. He was directly opposite to it. The skull-covered façade of the hut had been removed bodily; the fire-light shone full upon the great idol; and as he watched the gleams playing over its glittering surface, a conjecture that for long had been in his mind became a certainty. The idol stood upon a platform or mound, decked out at present with flowers—orchids, the crimson blossoms of the hibiscus, the purple blossoms of the croton, and many more—and was itself fashioned in the shape of a man's head, perhaps one and a half times life-size. As a work of art it had little to commend it: the human features were there, indeed, but chiselled in the rudest and most elementary way, and of expression there was none whatever. But it was neither the design nor the execution which held Walter spell-bound: it was the substance out of which the idol was formed. And that, if the colour did not mislead him, was gold. He could not doubt his eyes: before him, beyond all question, was the Holy Nugget of which he had first heard in the dining-room at Hamilton Gap—the Holy Nugget which was the primary cause of his father's expedition—the Holy Nugget, too, which now awaited its sacrifice.

He gazed at it—oblivious of everything else, both of the offerings of food heaped up by the side of the shrine and the changing demeanour of the people—until he was roused by a low murmur from those around. Looking up, he saw that the rim of the moon had appeared above the lake. Now a feeling of expectancy seemed to be general, and the eyes of the savages were turned eagerly towards the isthmus which joined the promontory to the mainland. Then, after a few minutes' deep silence, a whisper ran through the crowd:

'The magic-men! the magic-men!'

Suddenly a number of strange figures darted across the narrow point and entered the village; the savages fell back on either side; and, dancing through them, the new-comers rushed pell-mell into the enclosure. In all there were a dozen of them, got up in the most extraordinary manner. From the neck downwards they were clothed in long, loose robes, made of the leaves of the draconœna; their faces and heads were quite hidden by large masks of cuscus skin, elaborately ornamented with bird of Paradise feathers and boars' tusks; and for arms each man carried a spear and a club. One only did Walter recognise, and that because there was no mistaking his huge form—to wit, Vali.

Threading their way between the fires, they prostrated themselves before the idol, and remained thus for a full minute. Then they rose; Gouri, doing the same, gave them welcome in his croaking voice; and immediately, resuming the dance-like movement, they advanced towards the line of prisoners. To Walter's mind the critical moment had come. He was mistaken: it was not to be just yet. For, led by Vali, the magic-men passed up the line without halting or speaking —all save the last, who stumbled against the boy. As he made to draw back, he felt something soft pressed into his hand; the man recovered himself and followed his companions; and, when he had done so, Walter glanced at that which he had given him—half-indifferently at first, then with eager interest.

It was a cassowary feather!

CHAPTER XXII.

THE FESTIVAL OF KOA-PUNU.

THE whole thing had been done so quickly that, when Walter raised his eyes, the last magic-man was not more than half-way up the line. Very anxiously did he scrutinise his figure. For although on the face of it the message could bear no other meaning than that his comrade had, somehow or other, succeeded in coming to his rescue, he dared scarcely believe in such good luck. The feat seemed an impossible one, even for Warupi. To accomplish this he must have deluded Vali, and undergone a hundred risks which would have proved fatal to a man of less resource. The figure told Walter nothing. It might have been Warupi's, and certainly the height corresponded; but on the other hand it might be that of any other savage, and with its trappings it had no outstanding feature to guide the searcher after truth.

For a moment Walter was inclined to treat the incident as a dream, and, if it were possible, to dismiss it from his mind. But the feather was still in his hand : it at least was tangible enough, and assuredly it had arrived there by no accident. The inference could not be burked, and the question arose, what *he* should do in view of this new development.

Nothing, as an instant's thought showed him, for the

simple reason that he could do nothing. He must await events. It was for him, more now than ever, to be alert and watchful.

First he glanced at Yoshida, fearful that he had observed anything or had been rendered suspicious by his excitement. But his host's attention was elsewhere, and he gave no sign. For safety's sake, however, Walter slipped the feather into his pocket; and then, somewhat reassured, he turned to watch the movements of the magic-men. They had again drawn together in the middle of the enclosure, and were gyrating between the fires in a curious kind of dance—each man executing a step of his own, and occasionally wheeling towards Koa-punu as if in obeisance. Presently a low monotonous chant was struck up; the people, who had hitherto remained silent as statues, joined in; and as the tune rose in volume, the dancers skipped forward towards the row of prisoners, halted half-way, retreated, and advanced again. This went on for perhaps half-a-dozen times, and momentarily the motion became faster and the chant swelled to a higher pitch. Then, when it was at its highest, Vali darted suddenly forth and plunged his spear into the breast of one of the captives. The chant stopped, while the crowd behind the barricade craned eagerly forward; from the wretch came a faint cry, which was checked in his throat by a stunning blow on the head from the club of the warrior behind him; and at the same moment the man extinguished his torch and stepped aside. In a second the magic-men had surrounded the body, it was dragged with scant ceremony to the foot of the idol, and there the savage deed was completed still more savagely.

A shudder ran along the line of unfortunate prisoners at this horrible object-lesson of the fate in store for them all. It was shared to the full by Walter, although the victim had been separated from him by two-score others; for all he knew, he might be the next one chosen; and instinctively his hand sought his revolver and he prepared himself for the worst. In a minute it might be his part to put into execution the plan which he had formed. It was this: to shoot down the magic-man as soon as he had made his rush forward, and then dash past the others and try to reach the lake-side. If he escaped the clubs of his guards, he trusted to the confusion and to his luck to manage the rest. The critical portion of the adventure would follow—the swimming of the lake in the moonlight, and the inevitable pursuit. Even if he gained the mainland, what chance had he of ultimate escape? Little, as he was well aware. For it was two days' journey to Warupi's country; he was ignorant of the direction; and, as a matter of course, he must soon be overtaken by the infuriated natives. Yet, with the madness of desperation, he was ready to attempt the impossible if need were.

He had one doubt: would his nerve last?

He found sufficient to test it as the ceremony went on. Twice was the murder of a prisoner repeated in the same way down to the minutest detail—save one, that in each case the executioner was a different magic-man. Dreadful as was the sight, he could not take his eyes off it. The eerie dancing, the chant, the moment of suspense before the fateful leap forward, the subsequent horrors—all combined to hold him fascinated. And on each occasion the position in the line of the victim chosen was nearer to his. Something seemed to whisper that he would be the next.

Meanwhile, one crumb of hope was vouchsafed to him. Warupi, if it were he, retained his post at the left wing of

the magic-men—the post, that is, directly opposite to him.
There was comfort in the thought that it was not altogether
by inadvertence—until the dancers advanced for the fourth
time, and then a curious dilemma flashed upon him. What
if *he*, of all the others, were to select him? It might
be Warupi, and in that case his plan of escape was futile.
But, on the other hand, what if he had made a mistake after
all, and the man was not his blood-brother?

He had little time in which to decide. The chant waxed
louder, the dance quickened, and to his imagination the
warriors behind him drew themselves up in preparation for
the *coup-de-grâce*. Then, just as he had feared, the left-wing
man—were it Warupi or another—darted forth, straight
towards him. It was an agonising second. His revolver
was in his hand, but he dared not fire. He shut his eyes,
awaiting the spear-thrust, and tried to pray. But the stroke
never came. Amid a medley of sounds the song died away ;
as from a distance he heard—or thought he heard—an
inarticulate cry from Yoshida ; there was the thud of a
falling body ; and, opening his eyes, he saw that in his stead
had been chosen the captive to his immediate left. Already
the guardian warrior's torch was extinguished, and the magic-
men were thronging vulture-like round the spot.

A sob of relief escaped from him.

'Courage, Kamara !' whispered Yoshida in his ear.

He required it all. For half an hour longer the suspense
continued, but it is unnecessary to describe it more fully. It
was merely a repetition of that which had already passed :
horror heaped upon horror without the least variance, until
some sixteen corpses lay before the shrine of Koa-punu.
And then at last the magic-men appeared to tire of the
slaughter.

'Courage, Kamara!' said Yoshida again.   'You are safe—for to-night.'

He scarcely heard him: he was absorbed in watching the second act of the evening's drama.   The magic-men, exhausted by their efforts, had thrown themselves on the ground beside the old chief, and it was the turn of the group of warriors who had hitherto remained inactive in the background.   Coming forward, they produced from a corner of the enclosure several great vessels filled with water, which were set upon the fires; and, that done, they laid down a number of mats of plaited fibre, and upon each placed one of the bodies.   Only when they took their next step was their horrible purpose guessed by Walter.

Yoshida confirmed the supposition.

'Look, Kamara!' he said: 'they are making the preparations for the great feast.'

    .   .   .   .   .   .

What ensued cannot be described here, and in truth the sickening details are better left untold.   Fortunately Walter was spared the full horror of the spectacle.   The preliminary cutting-up was enough for him—that, combined with the reaction from the feverish excitement of the previous events —and before the thing had well begun he fainted away in Yoshida's arms.

    .   .   .   .   .   .

He was brought to himself somewhat of the suddenest by a sharp prick in the arm from the spear of Koura.   Yoshida was still supporting him, although a considerable time must have gone since his lapse into unconsciousness, for the moon was now high in the heavens, and in her radiance everything was as clearly discernible as at noontide.   The whole scene was one not readily to be forgotten: the mingled lights of the moon and the great fires, the dark mass of savages behind the palisade, the groups dotted here and there within the enclosure, and beyond all the impassive front of the god and the stretch of silvery water.

As his wits returned to him, he found that confronting him were Koura and the leader of the magic-men. The latter, who was not to be mistaken in spite of his disguise, offered him something wrapped in a large leaf.

'It is a gift from Koa-punu,' he explained. 'Take it, Kamara.'

Walter glanced at it. Then he drew back with utter loathing.

'Take it!' repeated Vali, more peremptorily.

The boy made no sign.

'Take it, Kamara!' whispered Yoshida. 'It may be that Koa-punu will relent. And it is good.'

Vali stood in an attitude of expectation, while his son played carelessly with his spear and grinned in Walter's face. He looked round him for the giver of the cassowary feather, with some half-formed hope that he would come to his aid, but could not distinguish the man in the throng of savages. There seemed to be no alternative; and, beating down his disgust, he put forth his hand and took the proffered mess.

'Kamara is wise,' remarked Vali.

Then he waited—he, and his son, and Yoshida—and all with ill-concealed curiosity. Evidently more was expected of the boy. Surely it could not be——

'Quick! Kamara must eat it!' Yoshida put in.

It was the last straw. He felt that death would be preferable; and, acting upon the impulse of the moment, forgetful of everything except this last outrage against all civilised teaching, he threw the gift back into Vali's face. He did not

see how it was taken, for at the same moment Koura came at
him with his spear, and he just managed to thrust it aside
with one hand, and with the other to knock down the young
savage.   Now the fat was in the fire with a vengeance.   But
he was cool enough in the face of an actual danger—almost
eager, indeed, for the onset of his captors.   For a little they
hesitated; then a sullen, angry murmur began to rise from the
crowd behind the barricade; those around closed in; while
others, smelling a commotion, were to be perceived running
up from every direction.   And amongst them Walter saw his
friend of the feather at last.   If he was Warupi, would he be
in time to share in the struggle—and the sequel?

Yet again, however, did Vali belie just expectation.   At
first he had been too thunder-stricken by the unexpected revolt
to be able to do anything; but now, as the other natives drew
round the boy in menace, he interposed.   His son had arisen
from the ground with a bloody nose and an intention of
murder, and he waved him authoritatively aside.   Koura
obeyed not too willingly.

'Stop!' cried the magic-man.

An immediate silence befell.

'It is not thus that the matter must be settled,' he went on,
speaking gravely, but, to Walter's surprise, with not a trace
of anger in his tones.   'The stranger has refused the gift of
Koa-punu, and the insult is to Koa-punu alone.   He it is,
then, who must deal with the stranger.'

A hum of approval came from the bystanders, while Walter
wondered what was to follow.

'But not to-night,' continued Vali.   'Is not the sacrifice
over?   Doubt not, however, that Koa-punu will punish him
in his own good time: the festival ends not with the rising of
to-morrow's sun.   There are yet two nights, and,' he added,

significantly, 'Koa-punu never forgets.—For you, stranger,' he said, turning to Walter, 'it would be wise to prepare for the death of those who look upon Koa-punu's face and are not of Koa-punu's tribe. The way is with him, and it may not be pleasant to Kamara. For the present, Yoshida's door is open. Go!'

Walter did not obey at once. This respite was not what he had anticipated, and in his state of mind he was not sure that he preferred it to the speedier settlement for which he was prepared. At the best it was other two days of intolerable suspense.

'Come, Kamara!' said Yoshida.

Just at this moment, while he was undecided, his eyes caught the form of Warupi—somehow, his doubt regarding his identity had vanished—and it seemed to him that the man inclined his head very slightly. Whether he did so, or it were mere imagination, he accepted it as an omen.

'Come!' reiterated Yoshida, losing patience.

Without a word he went with his host, the two guards placing themselves on either side as before, and not a word was said as they passed through the crowd and across the promontory to the hut. He entered; Yoshida gave an order to the warriors, who took up their position at the door; and then, with a nod of farewell, he left the boy to his meditations. Doubtless he was eager to be amid the excitement once more.

For hours the din of the festival, becoming louder as the night advanced, kept Walter from sleeping—that and his own thoughts. But towards daybreak he fell into a broken, uneasy slumber, and when he awoke it was an hour or two after sunrise. Little Pari was weeping by his bed-side.

'What is it, little one?' he asked, sitting up.

'What has Kamara done?' he replied. 'Koa-punu is angry with him, and he is to be slain to-morrow night. Koura told me so. It will be a great sight, he says.'

'The young brute!' was Walter's mental comment, and his determination to astonish him and his worthy father by a display of 'white magic' was not lessened. As to the time of his sacrifice, it was of little consequence. The next night meant the last night of the festival—well, perhaps it was comforting to know for certain. Of one thing he had no doubt: it would not be later.

Presently Yoshida himself walked in, looking none the worse of his want of sleep, and confirmation was forthcoming.

'Kamara is honoured above others,' he said, 'for the magic-men have decided that he shall be the last sacrifice to Koa-punu—that he shall be sacrificed alone, with special ceremonies. To-day he is to stay indoors.'

He had little wish to do otherwise; but, for curiosity's sake, he ventured during the forenoon as far as the open doorway. Outside were two guards. He had expected it, of course; his only hope of escape—and it of the faintest—was not by his own exertions or strategy, but by those of—Warupi.

CHAPTER XXIII.

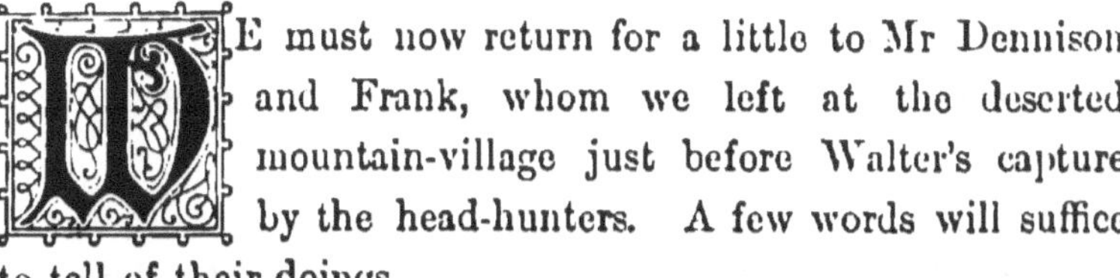

E must now return for a little to Mr Dennison and Frank, whom we left at the deserted mountain-village just before Walter's capture by the head-hunters. A few words will suffice to tell of their doings.

Several anxious days followed the arrival of the wounded warrior with the news of the misadventure and Warupi's message. Neither he nor Walter came back, as you know; and when a week had passed, and still there was no sign of them, Mr Dennison resolved, not without misgiving, to obey the chief's recommendation. By that time Frank had completely recovered his strength; there was nothing to delay the start; and so, under Dawan's guidance, they set out for Warupi's country at once—rather less cheerfully, perhaps, than they might have done if Walter had not been missing. A big detour was made to avoid the head-hunters' tribe, and fortunately they succeeded in this. Such natives as they happened to meet were friendly; the route was not over-arduous; and as for the incidents, they were merely the common experiences of the traveller, and none of them striking enough to merit particular mention. Frank's heart, however, was gladdened by the shooting of several birds of

Paradise. He, to do him justice, spared no effort to fill the place of his brother, and only the limits of human capacity, not to speak of experience, prevented him trying to fill Warupi's shoes likewise.

So in due time they reached their destination, and were received with open arms by Warupi's brother Kerepuna and all the tribe. Their own joy was somewhat marred by the intelligence that nothing had been heard of the missing men, but Kerepuna consoled them by refusing to believe in the ability of any number of common savages to outwit or overpower his brother. Let them, he said, have patience, and meanwhile enjoy themselves, for the wanderers would, certainly appear before long.

Mr Dennison tried to do as he was bidden, and was indifferently successful. Frank, less responsible, found a keener zest in life. He was only grave when he remembered to be so; like Kerepuna, he had infinite faith in the resources both of Warupi and of Walter, and little doubt concerning the upshot of the adventure; and, other things being thoroughly to his taste, he had no scruple in enjoying himself to the utmost.

Kerepuna's chief village was a strongly fortified place on the brow of a steep hill, overlooking the whole valley—itself a fertile, well-watered glen lying amongst high mountains. It was inhabited by nearly a thousand people, over whom Kerepuna played the part of the wise autocrat, and played it so well that he was loyally obeyed by the men and worshipped by the women. They seemed happy and contented, and not without reason. They wanted for nothing; and as for the attack of enemies, their situation made it a matter of difficulty, even leaving out of account the valour of the warriors. Much was due, of course, to the two chiefs.

In no other part of New Guinea known to Mr Dennison
was the system of tribal chieftainship better developed or
happier in its result.   Kerepuna himself resembled Warupi
very strongly, alike in appearance and in character.   Although his word was law, power had not blunted an inborn
sense of justice, and few had cause to complain of his actions
—except perhaps the surrounding tribes.   In a word, he
had only one rival in the affections of his followers—his
brother Warupi.   It was cause for rejoicing that the two
were excellent friends.

Even in his anxiety about Walter—an anxiety which not
.all the chief's assurances could allay, and which increased
as the days slipped past and he came not—Mr Dennison
did not forget the principal object of the expedition.   His
first step was to learn all that could be learned of the
neighbouring tribe, the possessors of the great Nugget.
During his previous stay in the valley both the brethren
had been strangely reticent, Kerepuna particularly so.   Now,
however, he regarded the visitors almost as tribesmen, and
was quite willing to lend them every assistance.   The two
races were at war at present, he told them; the pass between
the valleys was held by his young men; and at that moment,
indeed, fighting was probably going on there.   It was not
au unusual occurrence by any means, but just then the
enemy had good reasons for making a more determined effort
than ordinary, and therefore, foreseeing this, it had been
Kerepuna's object to defeat the invasion.

'And I have done it,' he said proudly.   'They may send
out their warriors very quietly, hoping to get through the
mountains and capture a few old men and boys, but what
good if we hold the pass?   They forget that Kerepuna's
memory is long.'

He had mentioned the enemy's reasons: Mr Dennison begged to know what they were.

'They are these,' said the chief, and went on to tell him much that is already familiar to you—of the approach of his neighbours' great festival, the sacrifices which they made to their god, and their yearly forays in search of prisoners. 'Once or twice they surprised us, but it was long ago. This year they must go elsewhere for their victims, or slay some of themselves. Why not? Dogs are plentiful enough in the tribe.'

'And this festival—have you seen it, Kerepuna?' asked Mr Dennison, deeply interested.

'Once.' He smiled at the recollection. 'They say I am the only stranger who has ever beheld the face of the god and lived, and so I must be sacrificed before there is peace between our tribes. It was in this way. At that time there *was* peace, and old Gouri invited me to visit his village on the lake. It may have been a trap, but I went. And while I was there the festival began. In the midst of it Vali, old Gouri's son—he bears me no love—demanded that the tradition of the tribe should be carried out, and the stranger slain. What could Gouri do? It was the custom—he dared not refuse, and he ordered that the sacrifice should be offered on the second or third night. It was then the first. For me, I was surrounded by warriors, and could do nothing. But that night the old chief sent this message to my hut by a trusty man, one Yoshida—to be off at once, for the sacrifice was fixed for the next evening. So I cut a hole in the wall, swam the lake, and made off. One dog tried to stop me, but *he* was easily slain. Perhaps they chased me. I know not: I saw none of them, and reached my own valley in safety. Thence I sent a messenger to

Vali, telling him that if he wished my head as an offering to his god, to come for it—I was ready. He has never come. Some day I shall go to him and kill him; but not Gouri and Yoshida, for the service that they did me in my great need.'

'You saw the god, then?'

'Koa-punu? Surely!'

'Tell me of it, Kerepuna.'

Kerepuna described it with the contempt which a savage feels for all other idols than his own, but faithfully enough to show Mr Dennison that its value had not been exaggerated. 'Would my white father like to possess it?' he asked. 'Some day, when Warupi returns, we may visit Vali, and perhaps'—he laughed—'the god will take a liking to the stranger, and go with him to his country beyond the mountains. Will my friend come?'

'Perhaps,' answered Mr Dennison.

Next day the chief asked his guests to accompany him to the pass, whither he was bound with reinforcements: the beginning of the enemy's festival being now near, and their activity likely to be greater in consequence. Not that he feared them, he explained; but, like a wise leader, he preferred to leave nothing to chance. Mr Dennison was only too glad to accept. The pass was a good day's journey distant, and at the point occupied by Kerepuna's forces was a narrow, easily-held gorge. Sure enough, fighting was going on—it was that of which Timar had brought the unwelcome news to Vali—but it was never more serious than skirmishing, and at no time were the defenders hard pressed. Walter, in fact, had guessed rightly.

'Is there no other pass between the valleys?' inquired Mr Dennison that evening.

'None,' said Kerepuna—'else it might go hard with my tribe, for Gouri has three warriors to my one.' Then he recollected himself. 'Yet am I wrong. There *is* another way—hardly a pass, for it is very dangerous, and never used. It is known to few, although the distance by it is little more than half. Let not my white friend think of it,' he urged, sinking his voice. 'An evil spirit dwells there, and every year he claims the soul of the bravest man who passes through it. It has always been so.'

'And this pass—where is it?'

'Far from here, at the upper end of the valley,' was the reply, and as the chief seemed reluctant to talk about it Mr Dennison said no more. He did not guess how soon he was to make acquaintance with it.

The enemy withdrew on the second day, but Kerepuna held his position until there was no further danger to be feared—until, that is, the day on which the festival of Koa-punu began in the adjacent country. Then, leaving a small guard behind for precaution's sake, he returned with his guests to the village.

The Englishmen had now been for more than a fortnight in the valley, and Mr Dennison thought it time to recur to the subject of the missing Warupi and Walter. Hitherto he had kept his misgivings pretty much to himself, at least after the chief's assurance. But at length his anxiety would not permit of a longer silence; and, while they sat in the moonlight on the next evening, he brought the conversation round to the desired point. Was it not possible, he asked, to attempt in some way to discover the truth?

'I have done so,' quietly answered Kerepuna. 'Scouts have been sent out in every direction, and have come back without news. But let not my friend be anxious. His son is safe with Warupi, and doubtless we shall see them before many days are past.'

Mr Dennison was not convinced, and pointed out that it was a month since their disappearance. They *might* be safe, but was the reverse not quite as likely? His own judgment said more so.

'They *are* safe,' repeated Kerepuna.

'I suppose nothing more can be done?' said the other, despairing of changing his opinion—not wishing to, it may be.

'Nothing.'

Mr Dennison smoked on in silence, and assuredly his thoughts led to no pleasant conclusion. What if Walter were really dead? The expedition might succeed in its ostensible purpose, but he felt that not all the riches of Papua were worth the sacrifice of the boy. And, most bitter pill to swallow, he could acquit himself of no iota of the blame.

His reflections were interrupted by a sudden commotion at the entrance to the village. A challenge rang out, there was a clamour of tongues, dogs began to bark, and then a voice of command was heard above the din.

Frank jumped excitedly to his feet.

'Warupi!' he cried. 'I know his voice!—There! It *is* Warupi.—Hurrah!'

Next moment he and his father and Kerepuna were running to meet the crowd of natives advancing quickly through the village—a crowd that was augmented at every step by fresh groups of eager-faced men and women. And Frank was right, for out of the throng darted a figure which there was no mistaking. It *was* Warupi's. The dogs barked louder as their contribution to the welcome; the new-comer greeted his brother and his white friends most affectionately; the people around clamoured to know whence he came, and for a little all was confusion and a babel of tongues.

At last Warupi made himself heard.

'Food!' he said laconically, and immediately a score of kind-hearted folks rushed off to prepare it.

Meanwhile, Mr Dennison had eyes only for that which the chief carried in his hand—to wit, Walter's rifle. He grasped the chief's arm.

'Tell me, what of Walter—Kamara?' he demanded. 'Where is he? Is—is he alive?'

' He is alive '——

'Thank God!' cried Mr Dennison.

'But he is in the hands of Gouri, and he will be slain to-morrow night as an offering to Koa-punu if we do not save him before then. That is why I am here.—And now, give me food. I cannot speak until I have eaten.'

He stuck to his resolve, and not another word did he utter until he had satisfied his hunger. Mr Dennison and Frank, dying to hear more, thought he would never finish. But at length he did; and, sitting in the midst of the circle of elders and magic-men, began his story.

We know already how he tracked the head-hunters and saved Walter from their clutches, how the pair crossed the mountains, and how Walter fell again into the power of hostile natives. Warupi had recognised the captors at once as a party of his hereditary enemies, and had deemed it wiser to flee, leaving the boy's rescue for a more convenient opportunity. He had disposed of his three pursuers without difficulty, two by means of the rifle and the other hand-to-hand; and then, evading the men left on guard at the camp, he had followed the track right to the lake-side. There, however, he was baffled. Day after day he had ventured out of his hiding-place in the bush in the hope of finding some chance of communicating with the prisoner, and day after day had failed. His own position was extremely precarious, the risk of discovery being great and continual. More than once, indeed, he had given himself up for lost. The enemy kept a good watch, he admitted—so good, that although he had seen Walter several times from the other side of the water, he had never dared, nor had it been possible, to penetrate into the village.

So things had gone on for a few days. He was almost in despair, and seriously considering the project of returning to his valley for armed assistance, when he had happened to notice various curious incidents, and all at once remembered about the festival of Koa-punu. It decided him to await events where he was. And, that evening, the bush around his retreat was invaded by a warrior, who set himself to build a rude hut. He had recognised the fellow as one of the magic-men of the tribe, and knowing something of the procedure of these gentry on the occasion of a great ceremony, had watched him closely and with much interest. During daylight the man was an ordinary villager, occupied like the others; but at night he repaired to the hut, and there got himself ready for his part in the coming festival— Warupi marking every step through an interstice in the wall, and meanwhile thinking out a daring plan to achieve his purpose.

When the all-important evening arrived he was ready. The magic-man had entered the hut at the usual time, and proceeded to rig himself out in his peculiar costume; and, choosing his opportunity, Warupi had stalked in, surprised and overpowered him. Then, with his spear at his throat,

he had extracted from him all the information he required—
the time and meeting-place of the magic-men, his position
in the line—by good luck it was the last—and the order of
business. Thereafter it had been an easy matter to get
himself up for the part he intended to play—for they were
much of a height and build—to bind and gag the fellow,
and finally to assume his character for the night. The disguise had succeeded: he had joined the others safely, and
without suspicion had taken his share in the ceremony.
Once within the enclosure, it only remained to warn Walter
of his vicinity and to devise a method of escape. The
cassowary feather had sufficed for the first, but the other
was more difficult. All through the evening his attention
had been evenly divided between his own rôle and his
supervision of the boy's safety. You know how Walter
himself brought the thing to a head. During the dispute
Warupi had been prepared to try a diversion in his favour
if need were, but in order to gain time he had advised
submission for the present. In the early morning hours
the council of magic-men had been held to decree the fate
of the sacrilegious captive. It was a foregone conclusion,
of course: he must be sacrificed—the only question was
when, and that Vali decided by proposing the third night
of the festival, and by suggesting divers additions of refined
torture as a peace-offering to Koa-punu. Warupi promised
himself pleasure in checkmating him most effectually.

The rest was soon told. The council over—for good
reasons he had been a silent member of it—he had quickly
made up his mind as to his course. Returning to the hut
and changing his garb, he had started at once for his own
valley. The way he had taken was by the nearer but more
dangerous pass described by Kerepuna in his conversation

with Mr Dennison as haunted; he had encountered no
obstacles except that of delay, caused by nightfall and the
consequent stoppage until the moon rose; and there he was
in safety, none the worse of his exertions, and ready to lead
his friends by the same path to his blood-brother's rescue.

This, shortly put, was his story; and I need not say with
what absorbing interest his hearers listened to it, and with
what gratitude two of them thanked him for all that he had
done and suffered in their service.

'Then you think Kamara can be saved, Warupi?' eagerly
demanded Mr Dennison.

'He *will* be saved,' was the confident answer. 'It is thus.
Kerepuna will choose a hundred of our best warriors; we
shall start at daybreak, and before nightfall we shall be at
the mouth of the pass and in Gouri's country. There we
shall wait until it is dark, and before the moon rises we
shall reach the lake. The rest will be easy.' He yawned
portentously. 'And now I must sleep until dawn. Sleep
is better than talk.'

He rose to retire, but Frank had still a question to ask
him.

'You have forgotten to tell us what became of the magic-
man whose dress you stole,' he suggested.

Warupi laughed rather grimly.

'Fear not, little warrior,' he said. 'He lies safely at the
bottom of the lake.'

CHAPTER XXIV.

TO THE RESCUE.

KEREPUNA did not belie Mr Dennison's estimate of his character. Although the enterprise was likely to prove a hazardous one, he did not hesitate for a moment to give effect to his brother's suggestions. The best men of the village were chosen on the spot, and couriers despatched at once to bring up others from outlying parts of the valley. It said much for him and for them that, in spite of the sinister reputation of the pass, not a word was to be heard in disfavour of the plan, nor a doubt of its success. On the other hand, everybody seemed to realise the gravity of the situation, and to be determined to do his utmost to carry it through. Mr Dennison's opinion of the natives rose several degrees.

When all was done that could be done that night, the chief counselled his guests to follow Warupi's example, and take several hours' slumber. They would need it, he said. The advice being good, they retired to their hut forthwith, but it is problematical if either slept much : their excitement was too great.

In the gray of the early morning, the party assembled outside the village. The hundred men were the pick of the tribe, all young and renowned warriors, in full war-dress, and eager for the adventure. Both chiefs were of the company, but at first there was some question whether Frank should go or be left behind in the charge of Dawan. Mr Dennison inclined to the latter view, having a fear that his strength might not be equal to his will.

Frank protested.

'It's really too bad,' he averred. 'I'm all right now, and as for what I can do—why, another revolver is worth half-a-dozen natives. Ask Warupi.'

So the point was referred to the chief, who gave his decision in the boy's favour on the very ground stated.

'And perhaps he will slay Vali: who knows?' he added, patting him on the shoulder.

'You're a brick, Warupi!' cried the delighted Frank.

Mr Dennison made no further demur, but armed his son with the same weapons as he carried himself—a light repeating rifle and a revolver. Then they set out.

An hour's march brought them to the base of the mountains at the point at which they must ascend, and for the next five their work was the arduous climbing of a slope five thousand feet or so in height, now scaling a cliff with scarce foothold for a goat, and again creeping carefully in single line along a ridge on hands and knees. Path there was none, and Mr Dennison wondered no longer at the myth which had arisen to prevent the path being used. Pass, indeed, it could only be termed by extreme courtesy; certainly it was one which no man in his sober senses would choose except, as in this case, in the direst need. Up, and still up, they clambered towards the summit of the mountain, their difficulties increasing as they rose. The day was excessively hot, the fatigue proportionately great. Even Warupi, who led, felt it at length, and consented, unwillingly enough, to a halt demanded by the state of the others. Then up again, overcoming new obstacles as they had overcome those behind them, until, with a sigh of relief, they gained the highest point.

The route was now across a bare, uneven plateau which connected two peaks, and for a little the travelling was easy—at least in comparison with what they had already undergone. Mr Dennison and Frank seized the opportunity to walk alongside Warupi, and learn from him more about his adventures, and about the valley for which they were bound, and its inhabitants. Incidentally, the former mentioned his wonder that his friends took no precautions to guard the pass.

'Why so?' asked the chief.

'In case of a surprise from Vali and his warriors. They know about this route, I suppose?'

'Some of them—not all. Few people have gone by it. They dare not, for fear of the evil spirit who dwells here. *He* is guard enough against a surprise.'

'And to-day?'

'Perhaps he is asleep. If he is not, be sure that he will claim his toll before long.' .

And he seemed to believe so firmly in the legend, that Mr Dennison, in fear of the consequence if he dwelt too much upon it, hastened to recall him to a more profitable subject of conversation. All the same, it shed a strong light on the overpowering influence of superstition upon the savage mind.

Presently their difficulties began afresh. The plateau ended in a sheer precipice of nearly a thousand feet, down which at first sight it appeared impossible to scramble. But their guide knew what he was doing. He pointed out a spot at one of the sides where it was less precipitous than elsewhere, and where there was a break such as might have been worn by the channel of a watercourse. It did not seem inviting: a false step meant death, or at the best a broken limb; but there was no other way, and, he assured them, it was perfectly safe—with care. Only, they must descend it singly.

Mr Dennison inspected it carefully.

'Go on, Warupi,' he said.

The chief disappeared over the edge, and in a little a shout from below told them that he had reached the bottom. Then the Englishmen followed one by one, Mr Dennison first, Frank close in his wake. It was the most perilous part of the undertaking; the footing was of the insecurest, the necessity for caution imperative; twenty times, as slowly and painfully they lowered themselves, they were in imminent danger of their lives; but at last, by great good luck, they accomplished the task, and stood beside Warupi at the foot of the precipice. Looking up to watch the descent of the savage who came next, they wondered how they had done it at all.

'So far good!' cried Mr Dennison. 'But how on earth are we to get up again on our return, Warupi?'

'As I did last night,' he replied, and went on to assure them that it was easier to climb than to descend.

They were glad to accept his word for it.

While the others were scrambling down, they had plenty of time to examine their position. They stood upon another plateau, much smaller than that above; on three sides were steep cliffs, those to right and left being much higher than that down which they had just come; while the foreground was almost entirely occupied by an immense mass of rock, with scarcely room on either side for three men to pass abreast. Going forward, they saw that the rock was a perfect miracle of exquisite balance. For, although it was at least a hundred feet in height, and must have weighed thousands of tons, it rested upon a pillar not more than four feet in diameter. As Frank put it, it looked as if a good push would knock it over.

Warupi, to judge from his demeanour, shared his opinion.

'Let not my white friends venture too near it,' he said, and himself kept at a respectful distance.

But they did, and a closer inspection added to their wonder in this—that the great mass rose on the extreme verge of a slope, beyond which the sides of rock contracted gradually, until, a hundred yards farther on, they were hardly more than a dozen feet apart.

'What if the thing *were* to go over?' inquired Frank when he had gazed at it awe-struck for a few minutes.

'The result would be anything but pleasant to us, I'm afraid,' said his father. 'It would roll down the slope, stick in that narrow gut, and most effectually block the pass.'

'For ever,' supplemented Warupi, quietly.

Even the possibility of such a thing was not agreeable to contemplate, and so they joined the others on the plateau. About a third of the company was now assembled below, and the residue were fast falling in; and Kerepuna, observing that they had covered half the distance, and had got the worst of the journey over, proposed an hour's rest for dinner. There were no objections. Each man had brought food sufficient for three meals with him, and after recent exertions was ready to lessen the weight of his load.

Starting again after this interval, they crept past the great rock—somewhat timidly, doubtless, and with a feeling of tightness about their hearts—and did not breathe freely until they were through the gut and beyond the chance of a mishap. The remainder of the journey may be dismissed in a word or two. If there were no stupendous obstacles to surmount, it was toilsome to a degree—a weary march along a gorge between high cliffs, or, latterly, down the rough face of a mountain. Frank was the one who might be supposed to feel it most, but, knowing that he had his selection to justify, he bore up as bravely as the best, and assuredly was never the first to lag behind or to call a halt. The monotony of the afternoon was varied by an accident to one of the warriors, who slipped his foot as he was descending a steep place, and was unlucky enough to break his left arm. Mr Dennison, having set it—rather primitively, as was unavoidable—proposed that he should be left behind to await their return, but the man refused point-blank to stay, and there was nothing for it but to let him have his will. Warupi and Kerepuna refused to interfere : it was at his own risk, they said, and he had always the use of his right arm. Apparently the fellow preferred taking his chance to a night in the company of the evil spirit.

It was still two hours from sundown when they arrived at the mouth of the pass, and beheld before them the whole stretch of the valley and the lake in its midst. Warupi, leaving them to admire the view or to rest themselves, went off to reconnoitre. He came back in an hour with the report that all was well : the coast was clear for their attempt ; and he thought they might even venture forth at once.

‘What ! In daylight ?’ asked Mr Dennison.

‘There is no danger,’ said the chief ; ‘and if we can get through the bush and into a track before darkness comes, wherefore not ? I have seen no sign of people.’

The argument could not be gainsaid, and Mr Dennison had too much faith in his friend to try.

'I leave it to you, Warupi,' he said.

He had reason to congratulate himself that he did so, for the penetration of the belt of bush proved to be a tough piece of work for daylight, and what it would have been after nightfall the Englishman did not care to imagine. As it was, they were not too soon. The darkness—fortunately it was not very dense—came down just as they struck a narrow path. Thereafter all was plain sailing. Now, however, they were in an inhabited country, and it behoved them to advance with care and to neglect no precaution. Nor did they; but, although they passed several collections of huts and patches of cultivated land, they saw not the smallest trace of any native—man, woman, or child.

'Why is this, Warupi?' Mr Dennison asked.

'Because the warriors are all at the festival, and the women and children have gone farther up the valley for safety. Perhaps they were wise,' he added, laughingly.

'And these warriors—how many shall we find against us in the fight?'

'Eight hundred—or nine.'

'Eight hundred!' Mr Dennison could hardly believe his ears. 'Tell me, what chance have we against such a number?'

Warupi laughed again. 'Surely my white father is not afraid?' he said. 'He need not be, for they are not armed—not more than a hundred, or it may be sixty of them. Koapunu likes not to see his servants in their war-dress. Why, I know not.' *

---

* The reason may be a desire on the part of the magic-men to prevent tumult and bloodshed—a contingency not unlikely to arise at a cannibalistic feast.

The company was again stopped within a mile of the lake to allow Warupi to reconnoitre. Then, all being well, they pushed on to the point at which the river emptied itself. Here it was spanned by a rude bridge of wood; and crossing this, they concealed themselves in the thick bush by the water-side, within sight of the promontory and the isthmus. In the village all was yet dark; the backs of the huts stood out black above the lake, and not a sound came across the intervening space.

'We are in good time,' whispered Warupi, and once more went off as scout.

The others waited and watched patiently. Before they had been long in their hiding-place, lights began to show here and there among the huts, and presently a vivid reflection told them that the bonfires had been lit. Now, too, they heard the hum of many voices, and could even discern figures passing to and fro upon the promontory. Mr Dennison's anxiety, already intense, grew almost unbearable as a new idea struck him. What if Warupi's absence on the previous evening had awakened Vali's suspicions, and he had made the matter sure by sacrificing Walter then? It was at least possible.

He hinted his fear to Kerepuna.

'It cannot be!' cried the chief. 'But if it is so, let my white friend content himself, for we shall slay every warrior in the tribe, even to Gouri and Yoshida, and leave not a house in the village. Kerepuna swears it.'

It was an assurance that did credit to him, but it is to be doubted if it had the effect intended. Mr Dennison much preferred to content himself with the safety of his son.

Suddenly they were startled by the appearance of a warrior clad in a long robe and a mask of cuscus skin, who stalked into their midst as if he had a right there. As half-a-dozen natives jumped up to seize him, he pulled off the head-piece, and then they realised that it was only Warupi masquerading in the garb of the deceased magic-man. He smiled at their amazement.

'But surely you don't intend to wear it, Warupi?' said Mr Dennison.

'Why not?' he asked. 'It is a good jest, and it may please Koa-punu. But look!' he cried. 'The moon is rising, and it is almost time for the attack.'

The last dispositions were quickly made, the men marshalled, and their instructions given to them. Then just as these preparations had been made, the guide called their attention to a procession of figures dancing across the isthmus and out of view behind the huts.

'They are the magic-men,' he said, 'and now there is nothing to keep us here. Are my white friends ready?'

'Ready!' replied Mr Dennison.

The word was given, and they crept forward to the end of the isthmus. There Warupi broke away from them, and walked boldly to the palisade: his purpose being to discover if it was guarded—it had not been on the first evening, but, of course, anything might have happened since—and, if so, to engage the sentinels. In the one case, the sound of a struggle was to be the signal for the rush; in the other, he was to imitate the bark of a dog twice in rapid succession. The latter was the signal given: the opening was undefended. In a moment the Englishmen and Kerepuna were beside him, the rest close behind. Standing there in the concealment of the palisade, they saw before them the whole scene—the two rows of houses, the crowd of men, and beyond those the moving figures in the glare of the fire and the torches.

Seemingly not a soul was looking in their direction, or had been alarmed by the barking.

Warupi pointed out the deep shadow cast by one of the lines of houses, and in a whisper proposed a modification of their plans. He would take ten men, and get nearer to the palisade; the surprise would be the more complete if the assault came from two points instead of one.

Mr Dennison assented.

'And the signal?'

'Give me a pistol,' he replied. 'And forget not to leave other ten warriors to hold the gate.'

He chose the men, and one by one they glided through the opening and into the shadow. The rest waited. Hitherto the silence all over the promontory had been so profound that one might almost have heard the beating of their hearts, but now it was suddenly broken by a burst of singing from the nugget-worshippers, low at first, but gradually rising to a higher and yet higher pitch. It was the chant which immediately preceded the sacrifice.

And then, above the noise of the voices, a pistol-shot rang out.

CHAPTER XXV.

THE THIRD EVENING OF THE FESTIVAL.

IT is said that custom will reconcile a man to any situation, however equivocal or unpleasant. Walter did not find it so as he took his place that evening at the end of the row of captives, now reduced in number to fifteen besides himself. Hope had entirely deserted him. In all human probability—and he realised it fully—it was his last night upon earth : nothing remained to him but to try the final expedient of despair, and at the best that was only a choice of two evils—death after a fight for life, instead of an unresisting acquiescence in his fate. But, if his recent experiences had had no other effect, they had strengthened his determination to die in his own way, and before he went, to fulfil his threat towards Vali to the letter.

To appearance things were as they had been on the first night of the festival. Outside the barricade, there was the same throng of eager spectators ; inside, the rank of dejected prisoners, except that it had diminished two-thirds in length, their guards behind, the huge fires, Gouri and his grandson sitting in solitary state, the idol in the background—all were as before. Also, the same method was pursued down to the smallest detail in the arrival of the magic-men—the

expectant hush, the sudden entrance, the obeisance before Koa-punu, and finally the starting of the chant. How familiar it all seemed to the boy !

As the ceremony began, he noticed that Vali had changed his position from the right wing of the line to the extreme left. The fact struck him as ominous of what was coming, and not to him alone. For they were now opposite to each other, and so more convenient for the magic-man's purpose— and more convenient also, although Vali guessed it not, for that of Walter.

He was thinking of this alone, unsuspecting the aid which was near at hand—the chant was rising in volume and the dancing becoming faster and faster—when, without warning, the blow fell. The savages heard a strange sound ringing out above the din, a sound hitherto unknown to them; Walter, the report of a pistol-shot, with all that it signified. One of the magic-men dropped. Then the shot was followed by a great shout; the singing stopped; the people stood dumfounded—all except one, and he Vali. With a hoarse cry he rushed straight at Walter, and the boy had just time to draw his revolver and fire. To miss was impossible : the man was not ten paces from him. He fell dead.

A minute of confusion ensued. There was more firing, a sudden rush of warriors into the enclosure ; the stupefied villagers, magic-men and others, were swept back, some into the fires ; and then, out of the press, a man in the festival garb darted forward and plunged his spear time after time into the body of Vali. Walter doubted no longer.

'Warupi !' he cried.

The chief turned to greet him, but just then there was another report at the boy's ear, and at the same instant he heard a familiar voice.

'Frank !'

'And just in time, Walt! This beggar was going to stick you in the back—and would have done it, too, if I hadn't come up and put a bullet into him.'

Walter glanced down at the recumbent form. It was that of Koura.

'And we've licked 'em !' continued Frank. 'See! here's father and Kerepuna.'

A firm hand-grip was all that passed between father and son, meeting in such strange circumstances, and, on the one part, after hope had been abandoned. But it was not the moment for demonstration while half of the work remained to do. The surprise of the enemy was complete, indeed; the resistance had been of the slightest, and now they were scattered in mortal terror; but they might rally at any minute, and there was yet the retreat to secure.

'Quick ! we must get back to the entrance at once !' said Mr Dennison.

Warupi gave the order, and his warriors formed up, ready to cut their way to the mainland through any opposition. But Walter interposed.

'The prisoners !' he cried. 'We can't leave them to be killed, sir.'

'You're right, Walter.' In the native dialect: 'Tell them to come, Warupi—and quickly, unless they wish to be left behind and eaten.'

Warupi seemed scarcely to understand such interest in people whom they had never seen before, but nevertheless he did as he was asked. The wretches, huddled together in a corner of the enclosure, made no response at first; and it was not until the chief bade them hurry in his sharpest tones that they obeyed. Even then, it was unwillingly:

perhaps they feared the exchange of one fate for another equally undesirable.

The retreat to the isthmus was effected without striking a blow, the crowd of unarmed and panic-stricken tribesmen opening up and making haste to get out of their way. Then, the entrance being gained, the question arose what to do next. For the present they were safe enough, but there was always the probability that the enemy would pluck up courage the moment they were gone, and take advantage of a better knowledge of the valley to pursue them in overwhelming numbers. And they had done so well already that Mr Dennison—he at least—had no desire for further bloodshed.

Warupi settled the point in his downright manner.

'The danger lies in the presence of my white friends, he said, frankly, 'for their steps are slower, and they are strangers to the bush. This is my plan, then. With Kerepuna and fifty of the warriors they will retire to the pass and await me, while I and the other fifty will keep the gate here until they are in safety. It may be,' he admitted, 'that there will be a little fighting, but what then? Gouri's men are cowards, and they are penned in like pigs: they cannot reach their arms unless by swimming the lake, and that may be prevented if my father will lend me his gun. In two hours we shall follow you, and they will be fleet in foot if they overtake us. Tell me, is the plan good?'

Mr Dennison did not like the idea of leaving him to bear the brunt of battle, and said so. But both Warupi and his brother overruled the objection, and he had perforce to agree. Next the chief turned to the batch of ex-prisoners, and advised them to make off while they had the opportunity, for, he said, it would not be long before the magic-men were on their track. They went with alacrity, looking as if they could hardly believe in their good fortune. Let us hope that they reached their country safely, there to be received by their people as those risen from the dead.

In a few minutes the whites and their escort followed their example; and, as they started, they saw that within the village all was still silent, that the tribesmen were standing where they had left them, utterly confounded by the extraordinary events of the night.

Walter himself, trudging along between his father and Frank, did not find it easy to realise that he was saved.

'I had given myself up, you see,' he said, when they had heard an outline of his story, 'although when Warupi didn't appear last night, I thought for a second that he might have gone for help. Then I remembered what Pari had told me —that it was two days' journey to his valley—and I lost heart again. I couldn't imagine what had become of him unless he had been discovered by Vali and killed.'

'And what did you intend to do if the worst came?' asked Mr Dennison.

Walter detailed his project. 'I know I couldn't have got off,' he concluded, 'but all the same I meant to have a shot at it. Besides, I had my score to settle with Vali.'

'Which you did,' Frank put in.

So the conversation went on in the intervals of forcing their way through the bush, and was interrupted only by their arrival at the mouth of the pass. Scarcely had they squatted down to await Warupi's coming in comfort, when Kerepuna brought them to their feet again in excitement by pointing out that to the east, in the direction of the lake, the sky was lit up by a lurid glare. The chief appeared to be hugely elated by the sight.

'What is it?' asked Mr Dennison.

'It is Warupi's signal to us,' was the answer. 'Doubtless he has fired the village, and will soon be here with the news.'

They watched the reflection for an hour and a half, trying to imagine what had happened; and then, sure enough, the rearguard rejoined them. Warupi was full of his exploit. After their departure the villagers had made one attempt to escape, but had easily been beaten back; and several efforts on the part of foolhardy warriors to swim the lake had been frustrated still more easily by means of the rifle. For a little their tedium had been relieved by the lamentations of a crowd of women assembled by the water-side, but they too had been frightened away by the shots. At length, when it was time to go, Warupi had observed the warriors forming up for another rush, and, desirous of pressing the lesson home, he had charged once more into the village, scattered the enemy, rounded off the work satisfactorily by setting fire to the houses, and finally retired in good order. His loss was trifling: one man slain, and three others wounded more or less seriously. He said nothing about the loss of the other side.

'And that is not all,' he continued, proudly disclosing something which he carried under his arm. 'Look !'

'Not Koa-punu !' cried Walter.

'The great Nugget !' cried his father.

'Even so,' he replied, laughing. 'I thought that Kamara might like to see him again, and brought him away. Perhaps he was ashamed of his servants, for he came without a word.'

The three Englishmen thronged round him to examine the idol, but Kerepuna recalled them to their senses by suggesting that it could wait, and meanwhile they might make the most of the moonlight to continue their retreat. The enemy might not follow them, but it was as well to trust nothing to chance. So they started again, leaving one of the swiftest runners behind to watch for the first sign of pursuit, and for three hours toiled on in the cool air— until the moonlight failed them, and they were forced to camp for the few hours that were left of the night.

They were astir with daybreak; the remainder of the food was eaten; and without waste of time the homeward march was resumed, Warupi carrying the god Koa-punu with the care due to his importance. They had one good reason for haste to begin with: the sky was overcast by threatening clouds, boding a storm, and the chiefs had no wish to be caught by it within the pass. They had another before they had covered two miles, for then the scout overtook them with the intelligence that the enemy was following hard upon their heels.

‘ How many ?’ asked Warupi.

‘ The whole tribe.

‘ But surely they cannot make up our start ?’ said Mr Dennison.

‘ They have good reason to try,’ answered the chief. ‘ Have we not taken their god captive ? Doubt not that they will not spare themselves as long as they have a chance to recover him.’

They pushed on with all speed, then; but the route lay up-hill, and naturally they were not so fresh as they had been on the previous day; and when they reached the narrow gut below the huge mass of balanced rock, the cry arose from the rear that the enemy was in sight. It was scarcely credible, for their own exertions had been great, and to gain upon them so quickly their pursuers' must have been immense. But so it was; and, to add to the gravity of the position, there was still the precipice to climb—a matter in itself requiring considerable time, for it could only be ascended in single file. A fight seemed inevitable.

Warupi drew up in the gut.

'We must hold this while the others are climbing,' said he. 'Ten men can do it.'

'With us,' said Mr Dennison. 'Our guns, as Frank would put it, will be of more use than other ten.'

'As you will.'

The orders were given, and those chosen took their places in the gorge at its narrowest point, from which they could see a long distance down the pass. Presently the advance-guard of the enemy, in their mad rush forward, came within range; Mr Dennison gave the word, and the reports of two shots echoed down the gut. The foremost of the assailants pulled up.

'Take the first man who moves, Frank!' cried his father. 'Probably they're only waiting until the rest join them.— Ah!'

The exclamation was caused by a sudden, vivid flash of lightning; then the cliffs resounded with peal upon peal of thunder; and, next moment, the storm broke in all the fury peculiar to the tropics, the rain fell in a solid sheet, and in the narrow pass the darkness was like that of night. There may have been grandeur in the scene—the lightning playing along the face of the cliffs amid the deluge of water, with the thunder reverberating overhead—but our adventurers had other thoughts. Frank gave them voice in two words:

'The rock!'

The same fear had occurred to Mr Dennison: he could

not feel at ease while they were on the wrong side of the fearsome-looking mass in such a storm. He turned to Warupi.

'We shall be safer on the other side of it,' he said, 'and the pass will be defended as easily.'

'Come!' said the chief. He, too, had his misgivings.

In a minute they were standing among the others on the little platform between the rock and the precipice. Already a stream of water was tumbling down the channel by which they had descended the cliff, and in that direction, for the present, their retreat was cut off also. Mr Dennison and Warupi looked at each other, then at the rock.

'Can it be done?' asked the former.

Warupi considered, and—

'Let us try,' said he.

For this is the expedient which had struck them both— to stop the pursuit at once and effectually by the overthrow of the great rock. The whole strength of the party was immediately set upon the herculean attempt.

And, just then, the enemy appeared in the gut below them. First amongst them Walter recognised Yoshida.

'Go back!' shouted Warupi, showing himself in the space between the rock and the right-hand cliff, and holding the idol high above his head. 'Koa-punu commands it. Go back!' While they yet hesitated, there was a flash more vivid than before and a loud peal; the warriors behind the rock started back; and then—whether it was caused by the lightning or by their efforts will never be known—the great mass moved from its base, and with a noise which sounded above the elements rolled down the slope and crashed into the gut.

     .   .   .   .   .   .

For a full minute they stared at the vacant spot.

'Let us go down,' suggested Warupi, at last.

The two chiefs and Mr Dennison descended to where the fallen block was wedged into the gorge, and a very cursory inspection served to convince them that they need fear no more from their pursuers. The pass was closed as effectually as if it had been hermetically sealed—and, in Warupi's words, for ever.

'It is so,' said the chief. 'And Kamara may take heart, for his head is in danger no longer.'

'The credit is yours, Warupi,' returned Mr Dennison, with some emotion. 'You have saved his life, not once or twice, but many times. I cannot thank you'——

'Speak not of thanks,' said he, turning away. 'Is he not my blood-brother?'

The storm, severe while it lasted, soon passed away; the channel was dry again, and possible of ascent, before the afternoon was far gone; and before nightfall the victorious warriors had accomplished the remainder of the journey, and arrived safely in their own valley, to be welcomed back with rejoicings and congratulations which were recompense sufficient for all that they had undergone. And for the first time Walter and Frank learned what it was to be popular heroes.

CHAPTER XXVI.

THE REDEMPTION OF KOA-PUNU; AND THE END.

HE little that remains to be told is concerned chiefly with the great Nugget. Next day it was formally presented by Warupi to his blood-brother—for, as he said, *he* had no need for it, and in the years to come it might serve to remind Kamara of his adventures in the Land of the Golden Plume.

'And of Warupi's kindness and bravery most of all, surely,' said Walter, taking his friend's hand.

The exchange of compliments was interrupted by Frank, who had made an interesting discovery while handling the idol.

'Here! feel the weight of the thing!' he cried. 'Why, it's quite light!'

'And no wonder!' said Mr Dennison, after a moment's examination. 'It's hollow in the inside—in a word, not a nugget at all, but literally a hollow sham.'

'Hollow!' repeated Frank, in a tone of disappointment.

'Hollow!' echoed Walter.

'Beyond a doubt,' said their father. 'See for yourselves!'

Doing so, they perceived that in truth there was no mistake. To outward seeming the idol was formed of a solid mass of gold—for it was gold, right enough, such of it as there was—but they had only to turn it over to discover the deception. The strangest thing about it was that there was no trace of welding: apparently it was one piece, with the interior scooped out, and sides no thicker than the eighth of an inch. How it had been done was a mystery, but there it was—of some value, doubtless, but of a value far less than that of the largest nugget in the world. All at once the day-dreams which the boys had founded upon its possession crumbled into nothing.

In spite of the keenness of his own disappointment, Mr Dennison smiled at their crestfallen demeanour.

'Come, cheer up!' he said. 'We must take it as we find it, and at any rate it's a curiosity. But to think of Koa-punu playing us such a trick !'

The opinion of Frank, who was also inclined to suspect a trick, although he was not quite certain on whose part, was characteristic.

'Koa-punu's a fraud !' he exclaimed, sententiously.

Walter agreed. 'All the same, I wonder if the natives knew ?' he said.

To judge from the surprise of Warupi and his tribesmen at their guests' chagrin, it meant little whether they did or not. For themselves, they could not understand what it mattered. To them gold represented nothing except a useful metal for ornamental purposes, and in this respect the fact of the idol's hollowness was rather in its favour than otherwise. But, of course, they were not civilised.

The discovery annoyed the whites for a few days; it seemed as if, after all their trouble, they were not a whit nearer the accomplishment of their object; but, as events turned out, the misfortune proved to be no misfortune after all. It befell thus. One morning, about a week after the rescue, a messenger came in from the pass with the report that Yoshida had appeared on the preceding day, and begged an interview with the chiefs and their white friends. He was now head of the tribe, he bade the warrior tell them— Vali and Koura having been slain by the stranger's magic, and old Gouri trampled to death in Warupi's last rush; and, being by nature a kindly man, he was desirous of peace between the two valleys. Therefore, would the chiefs deign to enter into talk with him on that and other points?

'Yoshida's words are soft,' said Warupi, grinning. 'He wishes something.'

'But you will go?' asked Mr Dennison.

'There will be no harm, and it may be.well to find out his purpose. Besides, is he not Kamara's friend?'

'And mine,' said Kerepuna.

So they set out for the pass at once, not neglecting to take a strong escort; and, next morning, the confabulation was duly held at a spot midway between the two forces. Yoshida, it must be said, did not appear to be cast down by the recent reverse and by the death of his leaders. Indeed, he greeted Walter very cheerfully, albeit with the respect due to a superior being.

'Kamara's words were true,' he said—'he did not lie about the wonderful magic of the white men. Have I not seen it with my own eyes?'

Upon this theme he enlarged for a little, paying Walter and his friends many compliments on their prowess; admitted that his tribe had been badly beaten; said that perhaps they deserved it; and then, at a hint from Warupi, came to the point. It was this: he wished the return of the stolen idol. His followers were clamouring for it, believing that no good luck would be theirs until the god was in safe and respectful custody once more; and, realising the futility, as things were, of trying to regain it by force of arms, they had deputed him to negotiate for its exchange.

'For what?' demanded Warupi.

'Whatever the valley has,' was the prompt answer.

'Even all the yellow metal which Yoshida's people possess?' asked the chief, who knew Mr Dennison's desire.

The three whites awaited Yoshida's reply with some eagerness, hardly daring to believe in the possibility of his consent. He made a show of deliberation, and then assented readily enough; and, unless his expression belied him, he congratulated himself on driving a good bargain. Frank felt disposed to cheer.

'It rests with my white father,' said Warupi, turning to Mr Dennison.

'And what do *you* think, Warupi?'

He shrugged his shoulders. 'I care not,' he said. 'Koa-punu belongs to Kamara.'

'And you, Walter? It is certainly a good offer—for us.'

'Take it, of course. The gold is of no use to them, and if they miss it they can get plenty more.'

'Very well, then,' he said, 'but first we have several preliminaries to settle. For one thing, we have to frighten him out of his cannibalism.'—Addressing Yoshida: 'Let it be as Warupi proposes, but on this condition—that no more prisoners are sacrificed to Koa-punu. Does Yoshida hesitate? If Koa-punu is a god, has he not shown already that he wishes none? Otherwise, does Yoshida think that he would have allowed his captive to escape and his enemies to slay his servants, burn down his village, and carry him off? Speak!'

Plainly Yoshida was deeply impressed. 'It shall be as the stranger commands,' he returned.

'See that it is,' Mr Dennison went on, speaking more sternly. 'For if not, be sure that punishment worse than they have suffered already shall fall upon the tribe. Yoshida has seen a little of a magic greater than Koa-punu. Let him heed the warning, unless he wishes to see much of it. It will not be pleasant.'

The chief looked as if he thoroughly believed it, and earnestly repeated that he would obey the stipulation to the letter. He was evidently sincere, and Mr Dennison said no more just then: he had gained his object in thoroughly frightening the man. For him, however, this was more than balanced by the successful issue of the negotiation, and he departed in glee to inform his tribesmen, promising to be back in three days with the gold.

'Koa-punu will be ready?' were his last words.

'Be in no fear,' laughingly retorted Warupi. 'Here his lodging is among the pigs, and he is anxious to return.'

The exchange was effected at the time stated, and Mr Dennison had no reason to complain of niggardly dealing; for apparently every piece of gold in the valley, from newly-dug nuggets to the women's ornaments, had been scraped together to redeem the idol. It was an imposing heap, but even then Yoshida had doubts of its sufficiency.

'If it is not enough,' he said, 'my young men will search for more, and bring it to the white strangers.'

'I am satisfied, Yoshida,' said Mr Dennison.

And he had good cause to be.

So the idol was transferred to the reverent hands of its former possessors, and there the transaction seemed at an end. But Yoshida had yet a strange request to proffer. It was nothing less than that the strangers, or any of them, should take up their abode in his valley, and teach the inhabitants their ways and magic! He promised them every consideration and attention.

Mr Dennison thanked him. 'It cannot be, Yoshida,' he answered: 'the time is near when we must return to our own country; but some day, perhaps, other white men will come and take our places, and teach you about a Spirit greater than Koa-punu. Until then, it is for you to be a good chief over your people, and to remember your compact to bring no offerings of prisoners to Koa-punu. More than that,' he continued, 'I hope there will be peace between you and my friends here. Many have looked upon Koa-punu's face whom you cannot slay for it, and so the need for war is past. Is it to be peace?'

'Let Kerepuna and Warupi say,' replied Yoshida.

They were quite willing; and so, for the present at least, the hostile tribes agreed to live in amity. Mr Dennison did not flatter himself that the arrangement would be permanent. Among savages it was perhaps impossible; but still it was something to have laid the foundation of a good understanding, and there was no saying what the result of it might be.

Then they parted the best of friends, Yoshida carrying away with him—besides the precious idol—many greetings and presents from Walter to little Pari, and our adventurers returning to the village much richer than they had gone forth.

'Are you sorry I didn't accept Yoshida's offer, boys?' asked their father on the way back. 'Just imagine the wealth we might have amassed in that valley of gold! To some people it would have been a temptation, I suppose; but for us—

well, we have quite enough to carry to the coast, and more than ever I hoped to get. As for Yoshida, perhaps the day will come—although I hope not—when instead of praying white men to stay with him, he will wish that he had never seen them. For it isn't difficult to guess what the effect would be if the valley were turned into a mining-camp, as doubtless it will be sooner or later. But one thing I'm determined upon—it won't be through me. I have gained the object for which I have been working for the last seventeen years, since my poor father died and left me his solemn injunction to get back the old house and the lands which had been ours for generations, until his misfortunes forced him to sell them. It was a promise, or perhaps my heart would have failed me long ago. It has been a weary quest, boys. Now it is over; and, please God, we shall all be under our roof-tree in Old England before many months are past. Let us be thankful, and leave the future of this country to others.'

·   ·   ·   ·   ·   ·

They had now no reason to postpone their departure except a possible objection on the part of the chiefs. Mr Dennison broached the subject that night with some diffidence, for he was eager to be off, and yet half-afraid to run his head against a wall of obstinate opposition.

Somewhat to his surprise, it was well received.

'We have talked about this, Kerepuna and I,' said Warupi, 'and have agreed that it must be. Every man longs for his own valley. At first,' he went on, 'I had a mind to go with my friends, and see the wonders of which Kamara has told me. But it is impossible. A chief's place is with his own tribe—to lead them in the fight, to choose a wife of his people, and be a father to them in peace and war. Here I am a chief : in my friend's country, where the men are wiser and greater, who knows what I should be? Go, then, although the parting will make our hearts sad. But not all of you!' he added, as if by an afterthought. 'You will leave Kamara with us to speak in my white father's voice, and recall his face to us when he is gone. Is it good?'

'Warupi has spoken well,' Kerepuna chimed in.

'Listen!' the chief cried, when Mr Dennison would have answered. 'He will become a chief of the tribe—Kerepuna and I have said so—and when my white father returns, he will find him a great warrior, with many heads upon his hut, and perhaps a wife.'

What could Mr Dennison say? The thing was clearly impracticable, and as gently as might be he pointed out the objections. His son was honoured by the offer; he could never forget the gratitude he owed to Warupi; but for the present he must go back to his own land to learn its wisdom. When he was a man——

'He will return?' eagerly asked the chief.

'It is for himself to speak.'

'And I will!' cried Walter. 'You may depend upon me, Warupi.'

'I will look for my brother every day until he comes,' said Warupi, simply.

Thus was it settled, and it only remained to arrange for the transportation of the gold—a matter beyond the capacity of the dozen coast-natives in their service. Again Warupi came to their aid by offering to accompany them as far as the point at which they had left the boats, with warriors sufficient both for carriage and defence. For more reasons than one, they accepted gladly.

Four days later, they said farewell to their host, and amid

the general lamentation of the tribe began their homeward
march. All that need be said of it here is that it was not
barren of incident; that in due course they passed the
mountains and gained the river, which was crossed some ten
miles above the spot of their first encounter with the
Papuans; and that this time no misadventure happened in
their journey over the plains. It was just before sundown
one evening when they struck the river again, and to their
joy found the canoes safe and in good condition. Much of
the night was spent in talk about the approaching separation
between them and Warupi, and they retired at last in a
sadder mood than befitted the occasion.

And, when they rose in the morning, the chief and his
warriors were gone.

It was practically the end of their wanderings: the voyage
down-stream, rowing with the current, was rapid and pleasant,
and in three days they arrived at the coast-village, there to
learn that Captain Barkham had not yet called in. A weary
wait of nearly a month followed; and then, one fine day, the
Bird of Paradise sailed up the river, with the captain and
Lambert on board. I need not tell you of the handshakings
and rejoicings that ensued: how the captain listened open-
mouthed to Walter's story, and declared with an emphatic
slap of his thigh that Warupi was a trump; how Lambert
admitted that after all there might be some good in New
Guinea; how they rewarded Amar and his faithful men;
how the gold was divided into four portions, one for each of
the whites who had taken part in that or the previous
expedition; and how, finally, they repaired on board the
schooner and set sail for Australia. Were they sorry to see
the last of the island? They scarcely knew.

Nor need I describe the scene at Hamilton Gap a fortnight

or so afterwards, when the three bronzed and tattered adventurers rode up to the house on borrowed horses, and Jimmy raised a yell of welcome which must have been audible at Baronga, and Ruth came running down the veranda steps, and Mr Maitland's cheery voice was heard in congratulation, and all round the station the rumour sped from blackboy to Kanaka that the young masters were back. But in the evening, the Odyssey of their adventures having been told and retold, Ruth drew the boys aside to thank them for their presents, Frank for his bundle of Paradise feathers, Walter for the nugget which he had brought to her from the valley of gold.

'And to think that you kept it all the time you were among those horrid savages, Walter!' she cried, 'and even when you were nearly killed!'

'And eaten!' added Frank.

The two elders and Brunton were sitting by the fireside, and a sentence or two of their conversation drifted across the room.

'When do you leave for the old country?' asked Brunton.

'Sometime next month.—No, I don't think I shall have any difficulty. The man who bought the place is an old friend, and I fancy he'll be ready enough to sell at a good price.—Walter will go to Oxford, of course—Frank too, if he wants. But I imagine he'd rather prefer Sandhurst. He had always a hankering after soldiering, and his Papuan experiences haven't cured him.'

Ruth looked ruefully at the boys. 'Oh! you're not going away again, surely?' she demanded.

They could not deny it.

'Never to come back, I suppose?

'Rubbish!' said Frank. 'You and Mr Maitland are to

come to England whenever we 're settled, for I heard the
pater say so, and your father's to consult the London doctors
about his paralysis.   And if you don't—why, Walter and I
have promised to go back to see Warupi some day, and we 'll
call in here on the way.   For we mean to go : don't we,
Walt ?'

'Of course,' returned Walter.

THE END.

Edinburgh :
Printed by W. & R. Chambers, Limited.

BOOKS

SUITABLE FOR PRIZES AND PRESENTATION.

Price 5s.

OLIVIA: the New Story for Girls. By Mrs MOLESWORTH. With eight Illustrations by Robert Barnes. **5/**

A tale of good society in English provincial life, told with all the charm and brightness of this favourite authoress. A strong contrast is drawn between the home of Olivia and her sister Pussy in the quiet vicarage, and the more fashionable world of Greylands, the scene of a mischievous freak on the part of the heroine, leading to her suffering and repentance, as well as to the greatest happiness of her life.

BETTY: a School Girl. By L. T. MEADE. With eight Illustrations by Everard Hopkins. **5/**

A very realistic story of school-girl life, told in a skilful and entertaining manner, while good principles are inculcated. It gives the lights and shadows in the life of Betty, a motherless girl between eleven and twelve, when suddenly removed from the old home in London, and plunged into boarding-school life near Dorchester. Betty gets into trouble with silly companions and a French governess, but though tempted, comes off victorious.

BLANCHE: a Story for Girls. By Mrs MOLESWORTH, author of *Robin Redbreast, The Next-Door House,* &c. With eight Illustrations by Robert Barnes. **5/**

'A story for girls, full of literary grace, and of sustained interest.' —*Glasgow Herald.*

'Eminently healthy ... pretty and interesting, free from sentimentality.'—*Queen.*

W. & R. Chambers, Limited, London and Edinburgh.

DIAMOND DYKE, or the Lone Farm on the Veldt: a Story of South African Adventure. By GEORGE MANVILLE FENN, author of *Rajah of Dah, Dingo Boys,* &c. With eight Illustrations by W. Boucher.   **5/**

One of Mr Fenn's popular stories of adventure. Vandyke Emson and his half-brother Joseph are engaged in ostrich-farming in South Africa, to little profit, when the story opens; the free, wild, adventurous life of the two brothers being given with great realism. There are hunting scenes, adventures with lions, swollen rivers to cross, wagon journeys; and a long period of illness and disaster on the part of Joseph, when he is nursed by Dyke, who proves himself a genuine hero. Thanks to a good-hearted colonist, and to a remarkable discovery of diamonds, the tide turns in their favour.

REAL GOLD: a Story of Adventure. By GEORGE MANVILLE FENN. With eight Illustrations by W. S. Stacey.   **5/**

'In the author's best style, and brimful of life and adventure. . . . Equal to any of the tales of adventure Mr Fenn has yet written.'— *Standard.*

'Mr Fenn has scored another triumph in this remarkable story.'— *European Mail.*

'One of the best of this prolific author's numberless tales of adventure.'—*World.*

'The very model of a book for a boy.'—*Journal of Education.*

POMONA. By the author of *Laddie, Rose and Lavender, Zoe, Baby John,* &c. With eight Illustrations by Robert Barnes.   **5/**

'A brightly written tale, full of good descriptive writing, and with frequent touches of both humour and pathos. The aim of the story is to illustrate the bitter fruit of selfishness.'—*Methodist Times.*

'Really first-rate, quite one of the best tales of this Christmas. . . . The writing is bright with the unusual charm of style that distinguishes this author.'—*Guardian.*

'A pretty story, prettily told, and it makes very good reading for girls, big girls, who like love-stories that are neither mawkish, foolish, nor sentimental.'—*Queen.*

'A bright, healthy story for girls.'—*Bookseller.*

W. & R. Chambers, Limited, London and Edinburgh.

From OLIVIA, *by Mrs Molesworth; price 5s.*

WESTERN STORIES. By WILLIAM ATKINSON. With Frontispiece.   **5/**

> 'These stories touch a very high point of excellence. They are natural, vivid, and thoroughly interesting, with a freshness and breeziness quite delightful to the jaded reader of "Society" fiction.'—*Speaker.*

DOMESTIC ANNALS OF SCOTLAND, from the Reformation to the Rebellion of 1745. By ROBERT CHAMBERS, LL.D. Abridged from the original octavo edition in three volumes.   **5/**

ALL ROUND THE YEAR. A Monthly Garland by THOMAS MILLER, author of *English Country Life,* &c. And Key to the Calendar. With Twelve Allegorical Designs by John Leighton, F.S.A., and other Illustrations.   **5/**

Price 3s. 6d.

THE REBEL COMMODORE (Paul Jones); being Memoirs of the Earlier Adventures of Sir Ascott Dalrymple. By D. LAWSON JOHNSTONE.   With six Illustrations by W. Boucher.   **3/6**

> A story of Galloway a hundred years ago, which opens with a description of some of the lawless doings of the smugglers or 'free traders.' The hero is taken prisoner by Paul Jones, but makes a remarkable escape in the Firth of Forth, and afterwards aids the escape of other prisoners in the Low Countries. History has been followed in the main in the narrative of Paul Jones's descent upon the British coast, and his doings in Holland. While to some extent a story of the same country-side, and treating the same theme as the *Raiders,* the period is half a century later, and the tale was written before the issue of Mr Crockett's book.

ROBIN REDBREAST: a Story for Girls. By Mrs MOLESWORTH, author of *Imogen, Next-Door House, The Cuckoo Clock,* &c. With six original Illustrations by Robert Barnes.   **3/6**

> 'It is a long time since we read a story for girls more simple, natural, or interesting.'—*Publishers' Circular.*
>
> 'Equal to anything she has written. . . . Can be heartily recommended for girls' reading.'—*Standard.*

W. & R. Chambers, Limited, London and Edinburgh.

From POMONA, *by the Author of 'Laddie,' &c. ; price 5s.*

THE WHITE KAID OF THE ATLAS. By J. MACLAREN COBBAN. With six Illustrations by W. S. Stacey.   **3/6**

A story crowded with healthy incident and adventure. Tom Malleson, a fine, well-formed youth, whose heart is not in business, turns his back upon his father's counting-house in London, and is sent to Mogador as assistant to the agent of the house of Malleson. His cousin supplants and plays him false; with the result of his being taken to the interior as prisoner of the Kaid El Madani. He rises in favour, trains the native soldiers, performs prodigies of valour, and gains the title of the White Kaid. Eventually he grows so useful, and is so much at home, that he settles in Morocco.

THE YELLOW GOD: a Tale of some Strange Adventures. By REGINALD HORSLEY. With six Illustrations by W. S. Stacey. **3/6**

A lively and humorous tale, in which Jack Brook and Michael O'Brien, instead of reaching their destination in a merchant's office at Valparaiso, are shipwrecked in the Pacific, picked up from a raft, and landed in Sydney, where further adventures await them. Accompanied by an 'old hand' and a native, they go inland, and, through a happy accident, make one of the first great gold discoveries, which enriches all concerned. They have a terrific attack from bushrangers, in which Daisy Revel and an Indian knife play an important part.

PRISONER AMONG PIRATES. By DAVID KER, author of *Cossack and Czar, The Wild Horseman of the Pampas,* &c. With six Illustrations by W. S. Stacey.   **3/6**

'A singularly good story, calculated to encourage what is noble and manly in boys.'—*Athenæum.*

'There is no writer of boys' books that can spin a yarn better than Mr David Ker, and this is an unusually good example of his skill. . . . Told with unflagging spirit, and in admirable style, this is the best boys' book we have read for many a day.'—*Daily Chronicle.*

'In point of variety of incident it would be hard to find a book which surpasses it.—*Educational Times.*

JOSIAH MASON: A BIOGRAPHY. With Sketches of the History of the Steel Pen and Electroplating Trades. By JOHN THACKRAY BUNCE. Portrait and Illustrations.   **3/6**

W. & R. Chambers, Limited, London and Edinburgh.

From THE REBEL COMMODORE (Paul Jones), *by D. Lawson Johnstone;*
price 3s. 6d.

IN THE LAND OF THE GOLDEN PLUME: a Tale of Adventure. By David Lawson Johnstone, author of *The Paradise of the North, The Mountain Kingdom*, &c. With six Illustrations by W. S. Stacey. 3/6

> 'Most thrilling, and excellently worked out.'—*Graphic.*
>
> 'A genuine old-fashioned boys' book of the Kingston-Ballantyne stamp. It merits a place on the same shelf with the *Coral Island* and *King Solomon's Mines.*'—*School Monthly.*

FOUR ON AN ISLAND: a Story of Adventure. By L. T. Meade, author of *Daddy's Boy, Scamp and I, Wilton Chase*, &c. With six original Illustrations by W. Rainey. 3/6

> 'Crusoe stories have a charm about them which is not readily worn out—what child has not fancied himself a Crusoe at some time or another?—and in the hands of so practised a writer as Mrs Meade are sure to have a success. *Four on an Island* is a favourable specimen of its class.'—*Spectator.*
>
> 'This is a very bright description of modern Crusoes.'—*Graphic.*

THE DINGO BOYS, or the Squatters of Wallaby Range. By George Manville Fenn, author of *The Rajah of Dah, In the King's Name*, &c. With six original Illustrations by W. S. Stacey. 3/6

> 'The many stirring incidents, and the light, fluent, conversational style in which it is written, will make the book a favourite among boy readers. The action is bright and vivid, and the outward features of the book are remarkably attractive.'—*Birmingham Gazette.*

THE CHILDREN OF WILTON CHASE. By L. T. Meade, author of *Four on an Island, Scamp and I*, &c. With six Illustrations by Everard Hopkins. 3/6

> 'Both entertaining and instructive.'—*Spectator.*
>
> 'A first-rate story, well told.'—*Board Teacher.*
>
> 'A charmingly written story.'—*Liverpool Daily Post.*
>
> 'Great skill is shown in the narration; the authoress hits off in the happiest manner characteristics of child life.'—*Leeds Mercury.*

From THE WHITE KAID OF THE ATLAS, *by J. Maclaren Cobban;*
price 3s. 6d.

THE PARADISE OF THE NORTH: a Story of Discovery and Adventure around the Pole. By D. LAWSON JOHNSTONE, author of *Richard Tregellas, The Mountain Kingdom,* &c. With fifteen Illustrations by W. Boucher.   **3/6**

> 'A lively story of adventure, and a decided addition to Polar literature.'—*Spectator.*
>
> 'Marked by a Verne-like fertility of fancy.'—*Saturday Review.*

THE RAJAH OF DAH. By GEORGE MANVILLE FENN, author of *In the King's Name,* &c. With six Illustrations by W. S. Stacey.   **3/6**

> 'One of Mr Fenn's most successful efforts to cater for the young.'—*Athenæum.*
>
> 'Will be found thoroughly satisfactory as a prize.'—*Journal of Education.*
>
> 'A story of rapid and lively interest, every page being informed with that light-hearted cheerfulness which so happily distinguishes Mr Fenn's work.'—*School Board Chronicle.*

Price 2s. 6d.

ELOCUTION, a Book for Reciters and Readers. Edited by R. C. H. MORISON.   **2/6**

> 'No elocutionist's library can be said to be complete without this neatly bound volume of 500 pages. . . . An introduction on the art of elocution is a gem of conciseness and intellectual teaching.'—*Era.*
>
> 'One of the best books of its kind in the English language.'—*Glasgow Citizen.*

THISTLE AND ROSE: a Story for Girls. By AMY WALTON. Illustrated by Robert Barnes.   **2/6**

> The story of a London girl transported to unaccustomed sights and sounds in the country, and in her new surroundings called upon to make a choice between what is right and what is easiest and most pleasing to herself. How she made her choice, suffered, and repented, is here told with easy grace and simplicity.

W. & R. Chambers, Limited, London and Edinburgh.

From THE YELLOW GOD, *by Reginald Horsley; price 3s. 6d.*

VANISHED, or the Strange Adventures of Arthur Hawkesleigh. By DAVID KER.   Illustrated by W. Boucher.   **2/6**

A tale in David Ker's best manner, the scene of which is laid in the South of England, in India, and Tibet, where the author is on familiar ground.   Viscount Culverstone, the ward of his uncle, suddenly disappears in a way that arouses strong suspicion against his guardian, John Hawkesleigh.   How the uncle searches for the lost youth at home and abroad, finds him after incredible hardships, and clears his character triumphantly, is fully related in the interesting narrative.

ADVENTURE AND ADVENTURERS; being True Tales of Daring, Peril, and Heroism.   With Illustrations.   **2/6**

These true tales of daring and heroism include stories of hunting, pioneering, and exploring; there are two lion hunts related by Thomas Pringle; some of the African adventures of F. C. Selous, of Captain Lugard, and the pioneers in Mashonaland and Matabeleland.   Under mountain-climbing, the exploits of Edward Whymper and W. M. Conway are described.   Other adventurers are Robert MacGregor of the 'Rob Roy' canoe, Herman Melville, George Borrow, Paul Jones, Sir William Phips, &c.

BLACK, WHITE, AND GRAY: a Story of Three Homes.   By AMY WALTON, author of *White Lilac, A Pair of Clogs,* &c.   With four Illustrations by Robert Barnes.   **2/6**

'Told with all the simple charm that Miss Walton knows so well how to use.   There are few more capable writers for the young than the authoress of this handsome book.'—*Schoolmaster.*

OUT OF REACH: a Story.   By ESMÈ STUART, author of *Through the Flood, A Little Brown Girl,* &c.   With four Illustrations by Robert Barnes.   **2/6**

'The story is a very good one, and the book can be recommended for girls' reading.'—*Standard.*

IMOGEN, or Only Eighteen.   By Mrs MOLESWORTH.   With four Illustrations by H. A. Bone.   **2/6**

'The book is an extremely clever one.'—*Daily Chronicle.*

'A readable and very pretty story.'—*Black and White.*

W. & R. Chambers, Limited, London and Edinburgh.

From VANISHED, *by David Ker ; price* 2s. 6d.

THE LOST TRADER, or the Mystery of the *Lombardy.* By HENRY FRITH, author of *The Cruise of the ' Wasp,' The Log of the ' Bombastes,'* &c. With four Illustrations by W. Boucher.   **2/6**

'An excellent story by one of the best writers of sea-stories for boys.'—*Standard.*

'Mr Frith writes good sea-stories, and this is the best of them that we have read.'—*Academy.*

THE NEXT-DOOR HOUSE. By Mrs MOLESWORTH. With six Illustrations by W. Hatherell.   **2/6**

'This is a children's story, about children and for children, and will be welcome in many nursery libraries.'—*Glasgow Herald.*

'I venture to predict for it as loving a welcome as that received by the inimitable *Carrots.'*—*Manchester Courier.*

COSSACK AND CZAR. By DAVID KER, author of *The Boy Slave in Bokhara, The Wild Horseman of the Pampas,* &c. With original Illustrations by W. S. Stacey.   **2/6**

'A good dramatic style, bold incidents, and realistic characters, stamp the book as one of the best of its kind.'—*Publishers' Circular.*

'There is not an uninteresting and scarcely a careless line in it.'—*Spectator.*

'With his own personal knowledge of Cossack life in the Steppes, and so brisk a theme as the struggle between Peter and Charles XII. of Sweden, no wonder that Mr Ker's volume is exciting.'—*Graphic.*

THROUGH THE FLOOD, the Story of an Out-of-the-Way Place. By ESMÉ STUART. With Illustrations.   **2/6**

'A bright story of two girls, and shows how goodness rather than beauty in a face can heal old strifes.'—*Friendly Leaves.*

WHEN WE WERE YOUNG. By Mrs O'REILLY, author of *Joan and Jerry, Phœbe's Fortunes,* &c. With four Illustrations by H. A. Bone.   **2/6**

'A very interesting story suitable for either boys or girls.'—*Standard.*

'A delightfully natural and attractive story.'—*Journal of Education.*

W. & R. Chambers, Limited, London and Edinburgh.

From THE LOST TRADER, *by Henry Frith ; price 2s. 6d.*

ROSE AND LAVENDER. By the author of *Laddie, Miss Toosey's Mission*, &c. With four original Illustrations by Herbert A. Bone. **2/6**

> 'This book teaches more than one valuable lesson, and we can thoroughly recommend it as a suitable present for young women.' —*School Guardian.*

> 'A brightly-written tale, the characters in which, taken from humble life, are sketched with life-like naturalness.'—*Manchester Examiner.*

BASIL WOOLLCOMBE, MIDSHIPMAN. By ARTHUR LEE KNIGHT, author of *The Adventures of a Midshipmite*, &c. With Frontispiece by W. S. Stacey, and other Illustrations. **2/6**

> 'A delightful book. Adventures both by sea and land does the youthful hero encounter, and hardship and peril. . . . Basil is a fine, manly fellow, and his character is well portrayed.'—*Dundee Advertiser.*

JOAN AND JERRY. By Mrs O'REILLY, author of *Sussex Stories*, &c. With four original Illustrations by Herbert A. Bone. **2/6**

> 'An unusually satisfactory story for girls.'—*Manchester Guardian.*

> 'Written with all the charm which so many of this lady's works possess.'—*Daily Chronicle.*

> 'There is a deal of brightness and sprightliness in *Joan and Jerry.*'—*Times.*

> 'Mrs O'Reilly always tells her stories well. A fine taste keeps her from exaggeration in the drawing of character, and she can interest her readers without startling incidents or surprises. . . . We can recommend *Joan and Jerry* highly.'—*Spectator.*

THE YOUNG RANCHMEN, or Perils of Pioneering in the Wild West. By CHARLES R. KENYON. With four original Illustrations by W. S. Stacey, and other Illustrations. **2/6**

> 'A stirring story of prairie life, with plenty of buffalo-hunting, adventures with Indians, and other stirring incidents.'—*Glasgow Herald.*

> 'Calculated to afford boundless delight to boy readers, brimful as it is of excitement and adventure. Girls, too, will find it most interesting, for Connie and her handsome lover are outstanding figures.'—*Dundee Advertiser.*

W. & R. Chambers, Limited, London and Edinburgh.

From THROUGH STORM AND STRESS, *by J. S. Fletcher; price 2s.*

MEMOIR OF WILLIAM AND ROBERT CHAMBERS. With Autobiographic Reminiscences of William Chambers, and Supplemental Chapter. 14th edition. With Portraits and Illustrations.   **2/6**

> 'What would be the story of popular education in this island if the names of William and Robert Chambers, and of all that they did, could be cut out? . . . As a matter of social history the book is indispensable; for who can be said to possess a knowledge of the England and the Scotland of the nineteenth century who is not familiar with the story of the brothers Chambers?'— *School Board Chronicle.*

POPULAR RHYMES OF SCOTLAND. By ROBERT CHAMBERS. **2/6**

> A collection of the traditionary verse of Scotland, in which the author has gathered together a multitude of rhymes and short snatches of verse applicable to places, families, natural objects, games, &c., wherewith the cottage fireside was amused in days gone past.

TRADITIONS OF EDINBURGH. By ROBERT CHAMBERS. *New Edition.* With Illustrations.   **2/6**

> 'The work is too well known to need any description here. It is an accepted storehouse of the legendary history of this city. The new edition is well printed, handy in form, cheap in price, and will doubtless be widely sought for.'—*Scotsman.*

HISTORY OF THE REBELLION OF 1745-6. By ROBERT CHAMBERS. *New Edition,* with Index and Illustrations.   **2/6**

> 'A book which will delight all young folks with any vein of romance or love of adventure.'—*New York Critic.*
>
> 'There is not to be found anywhere a better account of the events of '45 than that given here.'—*Newcastle Chronicle.*

GOOD AND GREAT WOMEN: a Book for Girls. Comprises brief lives of Queen Victoria, Florence Nightingale, Baroness Burdett-Coutts, Mrs Beecher-Stowe, Jenny Lind, Charlotte Brontë, Mrs Hemans, Dorothy Pattison. Numerous Illustrations.   **2/6**

> 'A brightly written volume, full to the brim of interesting and instructive matter; and either as reader, reward, or library book, is equally suitable.'—*Teachers' Aid.*

From FIVE VICTIMS, *by M. Bramston; price 2s.*

LIVES OF LEADING NATURALISTS. By H. ALLEYNE NICHOL-
SON, Professor of Natural History in the University of Aberdeen.
Illustrated.   **2/6**

> 'Popular and interesting by the skilful manner in which notices
> of the lives of distinguished naturalists, from John Ray and Francis
> Willoughby to Charles Darwin, are interwoven with the methodical
> exposition of the progress of the science to which they are devoted.'
> —*Scotsman.*

BENEFICENT AND USEFUL LIVES. Comprising Lord Shaftes-
bury, George Peabody, Andrew Carnegie, Walter Besant, Samuel
Morley, Sir James Y. Simpson, Dr Arnold of Rugby, &c. By
R. COCHRANE. Numerous Illustrations.   **2/6**

> 'Highly interesting and exceedingly attractive. It is a really
> *good* book in every particular, and deserves to be widely used as a
> reward.'—*Teachers' Aid.*

> 'Nothing could be better than the author's selection of facts
> setting forth the beneficent lives of those generous men in the
> narrow compass which the capacity of the volume allows.'—*School
> Board Chronicle.*

GREAT THINKERS AND WORKERS; being the Lives of Thomas
Carlyle, Lord Armstrong, Lord Tennyson, Charles Dickens, Sir
Titus Salt, W. M. Thackeray, Sir Henry Bessemer, John Ruskin,
James Nasmyth, Charles Kingsley, Builders of the Forth
Bridge, &c. With numerous Illustrations.   **2/6**

> 'One of the most fitting presents for a thoughtful boy that we have
> come across.'—*Review of Reviews.*

> . 'The volume is worthy of a place in every boy's library in the
> kingdom, and has our warmest commendation.'—*Practical Teacher.*

> 'Within the limits assigned to them, his sketches could scarcely be
> improved upon. The striking features of each career are ably brought
> out, and indeed nothing seems to have been omitted that could help
> to give a good general idea of the character and life-work of these
> thinkers and workers.'—*Glasgow Herald.*

GREAT HISTORIC EVENTS. The Conquest of India, Indian
Mutiny, French Revolution, the Crusades, the Conquest of
Mexico, Napoleon's Russian Campaign. Illustrated.   **2/6**

From ELIZABETH, *by Henley I. Arden ; price 2s.*

RECENT TRAVEL AND ADVENTURE. Comprising Stanley and the Congo, Lieutenant Greely, Joseph Thomson, Livingstone, Lady Brassey, Vambéry, Burton, &c. Illustrated. Cloth. **2/6**

> ‘It is wonderful how much that is of absorbing interest has been packed into this small volume.’—*Scotsman.*
>
> ‘The narratives are clearly and tersely written.’—*School Newspaper.*
>
> ‘A first-rate book for a reward—indeed, we know of none better.’ —*Teachers' Aid.*

SONGS OF SCOTLAND prior to Burns, with the Tunes, edited by ROBERT CHAMBERS, LL.D. With Illustrations. **2/6**

> This volume embodies the whole of the pre-Burnsian songs of Scotland that possess merit and are presentable, along with the music; each accompanied by its own history.

LITERARY CELEBRITIES. **2/6**

> Being brief biographies of Wordsworth, Campbell, Moore, Jeffrey, and Macaulay. Illustrated.

HISTORICAL CELEBRITIES. Comprising lives of Oliver Cromwell, Washington, Napoleon Bonaparte, Duke of Wellington. Illustrated. **2/6**

> ‘The story of their life-work is told in such a way as to teach important historical, as well as personal, lessons bearing upon the political history of this country.’—*Schoolmaster.*

STORIES OF REMARKABLE PERSONS. The Herschels, Mary Somerville, Sir Walter Scott, A. T. Stewart, &c. By WILLIAM CHAMBERS, LL.D. **2/6**

> Embraces about two dozen lives, and the biographical sketches are freely interspersed with anecdotes, so as to make it popular and stimulating reading for both young and old.

YOUTH'S COMPANION AND COUNSELLOR. By WILLIAM CHAMBERS, LL.D. **2/6**

> This is a new and enlarged edition of the first issue of 1857, which met with a gratifying degree of approval. The book offers friendly counsel to the young on everyday matters which concern their welfare; the hints, advices, and suggestions therein offered being the result of observation and experience drawn from the long and busy life of the writer.

From BEGUMBAGH, *by George Manville Fenn; price 1s. 6d.*

TALES FOR TRAVELLERS. Selected from Chambers's *Papers for the People.* 2 volumes.   **2/6**

> Containing twelve tales by the author of *John Halifax, Gentleman,* George Cupples, and other well-known writers.

STORIES OF OLD FAMILIES. By W. Chambers, LL.D.   **2/6**

> The Setons—Lady Jean Gordon—Countess of Nithsdale—Lady Grisell Baillie—Grisell Cochrane—the Keiths—Lady Grange—Lady Jane Douglas—Story of Wedderburn—Story of Erskine—Countess of Eglintoun—Lady Forbes—the Dalrymples—Montrose—Buccleuch Family—Argyll Family, &c.

Price 2s.

GREAT WARRIORS ; Nelson, Wellington, Napoleon.   **2/**

HEROIC LIVES ; Livingstone, Stanley, General Gordon, Lord Dundonald.   **2/**

THE REMARKABLE ADVENTURES OF WALTER TRELAWNEY, Parish 'Prentice of Plymouth, in the year of the Great Armada. Re-told by J. S. Fletcher, author of *Through Storm and Stress,* &c. With Frontispiece by W. S. Stacey.   **2/**

> 'A first-rate story.'—*Daily Chronicle.*
>
> 'A wonderfully vivid story of the year of the Great Armada ; far more effective than the unwholesome trash which so often does duty for boys' books nowadays.'—*Idler.*

THROUGH STORM AND STRESS. By J. S. Fletcher. With Frontispiece by W. S. Stacey.   **2/**

> 'Full of excitement and incident.'—*Dundee Advertiser.*

FIVE VICTIMS : a School-room Story. By M. Bramston, author of *Boys and Girls, Uncle Ivan,* &c. With Frontispiece by H. A. Bone.   **2/**

> 'A delightful book for children. Miss Bramston has told her simple story extremely well.'—*Associates' Journal.*

W. & R. Chambers, Limited, London and Edinburgh.

From THE LITTLE KNIGHT, *by Edith C. Kenyon ; price 1s.*

SOME BRAVE BOYS AND GIRLS.   By EDITH C. KENYON, author
of *The Little Knight, Wilfrid Clifford,* &c.   2/

   'A capital book : will be read with delight by both boys and
girls.'—*Manchester Examiner.*

ELIZABETH, or Cloud and Sunshine.   By HENLEY I. ARDEN,
author of *Leather Mill Farm, Aunt Bell,* &c.   With Frontispiece by Herbert A. Bone.   2/

   'A brave, rustic heroine, capitally sketched by H. I. Arden.'—
Graphic.

   'This is a charming story, and in every way suitable as a gift-
book or prize for girls.'—*Schoolmaster.*

   'An attractive little story which carries the reader cheerfully along
to its happy ending.'—*Pall Mall Gazette.*

HEROES OF ROMANTIC ADVENTURE, being Biographical Sketches
of Lord Clive, founder of British supremacy in India; Captain
John Smith, founder of the colony of Virginia; the Good Knight
Bayard; and Garibaldi, the Italian patriot.   Illustrated.   2/

OUR ANIMAL FRIENDS—the Dog, Cat, Horse, and Elephant.
With numerous Illustrations.   2/

   A popular account, freely interspersed with anecdotes showing the
personal attachment, fidelity, and sagacity of the dog ; the affection,
courage, and memory of the cat ; the courage, revenge, and docility
of the horse ; and the various characteristics of the elephant,
including the famous Jumbo.

FAMOUS MEN.   Illustrated.   2/

   Comprising Biographical Sketches of Lord Dundonald, George
Stephenson, Lord Nelson, Louis Napoleon, Captain Cook, George
Washington, Sir Walter Scott, Peter the Great, Christopher
Columbus, John Howard, William Hutton, William Penn, James
Watt, Alexander Selkirk, Sir William Jones, Dr Leyden, Dr Murray,
Alexander Wilson, J. F. Oberlin.

LIFE OF BENJAMIN FRANKLIN.   Illustrated.   2/

   'A fine example of attractive biographical writing, and the dogged
perseverance, untiring energy, and ultimate success of the hero are
found to leave an influence for good on the mind of the youthful
reader.   A short address, "The Way to Wealth," should be read by
every young man in the kingdom.'—*Teachers' Aid.*

W. & R. Chambers, Limited, London and Edinburgh.

From THE BEWITCHED LAMP, *by Mrs Molesworth; price 1s.*

EMINENT WOMEN, and Tales for Girls.   Illustrated.   **2/**

'The lives include those of Grace Darling, Joan of Arc, Flora Macdonald, Helen Gray, Madame Roland, and others; while the stories, which are mainly of a domestic character, embrace such favourites as Passion and Principle, Love is Power, Three Ways of Living, Annals of the Poor, Sister of Rembrandt, and others equally entertaining and good.'—*Teachers' Aid.*

TALES FROM CHAMBERS'S JOURNAL.   4 vols. each   **2/**

Comprise interesting short stories by James Payn, Hugh Conway, D. Christie Murray, Walter Thornbury, G. Manville Fenn, Dutton Cook, J. B. Harwood, and other popular writers.

BIOGRAPHY, EXEMPLARY AND INSTRUCTIVE.   Edited by W. CHAMBERS, LL.D.   **2/**

The Editor gives in this volume a selection of biographies of those who, while exemplary in their private lives, became the benefactors of their species by the still more exemplary efforts of their intellect.

AILIE GILROY.   By W. CHAMBERS, LL.D.   **2/**

'The life of a poor Scotch lassie . . . a book that will be highly esteemed for its goodness as well as for its attractiveness.'—*Teachers' Aid.*

ESSAYS, FAMILIAR AND HUMOROUS.   By ROBERT CHAMBERS, LL.D.   2 vols.   **2/**

Comprises some of the finest essays, tales, and social sketches of the author of *Traditions of Edinburgh*, reprinted from *Chambers's Journal.*

MARITIME DISCOVERY AND ADVENTURE.   Illustrated.   **2/**

Columbus—Balboa—Richard Falconer—North-east Passage—South Sea Marauders—Alexander Selkirk—Crossing the Line—Genuine Crusoes—Castaway—Scene with a Pirate, &c.

SHIPWRECKS AND TALES OF THE SEA.   Illustrated.   **2/**

'A collection of narratives of many famous shipwrecks, with other tales of the sea. . . . The tales of fortitude under difficulties, and in times of extreme peril, as well as the records of adherence to duty, contained in this volume, cannot but be of service.'—*Practical Teacher.*

W. & R. Chambers, Limited, London and Edinburgh.

From THE GREEN CASKET, *&c., by Mrs Molesworth ; price 1s.*

SKETCHES, LIGHT AND DESCRIPTIVE. By W. Chambers, LL.D.
2/

A selection from contributions to *Chambers's Journal*, ranging over a period of thirty years.

MISCELLANY OF INSTRUCTIVE AND ENTERTAINING TRACTS. 2/

These Tracts comprise Tales, Poetry, Ballads, Remarkable Episodes in History, Papers on Social Economy, Domestic Management, Science, Travel, &c. The articles contain wholesome and attractive reading for Mechanics', Parish, School, and Cottage Libraries.

	s.	d.		s.	d.
20 Vols. cloth	20	0	10 Vols. half-calf	45	0
10 Vols. cloth	20	0	160 Nos. ...... each	0	1
10 Vols. cloth, gilt edges	25	0	Which may be had separately.		

Price 1s. 6d.

With Illustrations.

RAILWAYS AND RAILWAY MEN.   1/6

'A readable and entertaining book.'—*Manchester Guardian.*

'As reliable as it is interesting.'—*Glasgow Herald.*

'In a clear, readable, and interesting style, we are told in brief space all that the intelligent general reader need care to know about the functional duties of each official on the railway.'—*Aberdeen Free Press.*

SKETCHES OF ANIMAL LIFE AND HABITS.   By Andrew Wilson, Ph.D., &c.   1/6

A popular natural history text-book, and a guide to the use of the observing powers. Compiled with a view of affording the young and the general reader trustworthy ideas of the animal world.

EXPERIENCES OF A BARRISTER.   1/6

Eleven tales embracing experiences of a barrister and attorney.

BEGUMBAGH, a Tale of the Indian Mutiny.   1/6

A thrilling tale by George Manville Fenn.

THE BUFFALO HUNTERS, and other Tales.   1/6

Fourteen short stories reprinted from *Chambers's Journal.*

TALES OF THE COASTGUARD, and other Stories.   1/6

Fifteen interesting stories from *Chambers's Journal.*

W. & R. Chambers, Limited, London and Edinburgh.

THE CONSCRIPT, and other Tales. - **1/6**
Twenty-two short stories specially adapted for perusal by the young.

THE DETECTIVE OFFICER, by 'WATERS;' and other Tales.   **1/6**
Nine entertaining detective stories, with three others.

FIRESIDE TALES AND SKETCHES.   **1/6**
Contains eighteen tales and sketches by R. Chambers, LL.D., and others by P. B. St John, A. M. Sargeant, &c.

THE GOLD-SEEKERS, and other Tales.   **1/6**
Seventeen interesting tales from *Chambers's Journal.*

THE HOPE OF LEASCOMBE, and other Stories.   **1/6**
The principal tale inculcates the lesson that we cannot have everything our own way, and that passion and impulse are not reliable counsellors.

THE ITALIAN'S CHILD, and other Tales.   **1/6**
Fifteen short stories from *Chambers's Journal.*

JURY-ROOM TALES.   **1/6**
Entertaining stories by James Payn, G. M. Fenn, and others.

KINDNESS TO ANIMALS.   By W. CHAMBERS, LL.D.   **1/6**
'Illustrates, by means of a series of anecdotes, the intelligence, gentleness, and docility of the brute creation. It proves abundantly that kindness will obtain more from animals than cruelty. The anecdotes are striking, and in many cases novel, and the book may be warmly commended.'—*Sunday Times.*

THE MIDNIGHT JOURNEY.   By LEITCH RITCHIE; and other Tales.   **1/6**
Sixteen short stories from *Chambers's Journal.*

OLDEN STORIES.   **1/6**
Sixteen short stories from *Chambers's Journal.*

THE RIVAL CLERKS, and other Tales.   **1/6**
The first tale shows how dishonesty and roguery are punished, and virtue triumphs in the end.

ROBINSON CRUSOE.   By DANIEL DEFOE.   **1/6**
A handy edition, profusely illustrated.

PARLOUR TALES AND STORIES.   1/6

> Seventeen short tales from the old series of *Chambers's Journal*, by Anna Maria Sargeant, Mrs Crowe, Percy B. St John, Leitch Ritchie, &c.

THE SQUIRE'S DAUGHTER, and other Tales.   1/6

> Fifteen short stories from *Chambers's Journal.*

TALES FOR HOME READING.   1/6

> Sixteen short stories from the old series of *Chambers's Journal*, by A. M. Sargeant, Frances Brown, Percy B. St John, Mrs Crowe, and others.

TALES FOR YOUNG AND OLD.   1/6

> Fourteen short stories from *Chambers's Journal*, by Mrs Crowe, Miss Sargeant, Percy B. St John, &c.

TALES OF ADVENTURE.   1/6

> Twenty-one tales, comprising wonderful escapes from wolves and bears, American Indians, and pirates; life on a desert island; extraordinary swimming adventures, &c.

TALES OF THE SEA.   1/6

> Five thrilling sea tales, by G. Manville Fenn, J. B. Harwood, and others.

TALES AND STORIES TO SHORTEN THE WAY.   1/6

> Fifteen interesting tales from *Chambers's Journal.*

TALES FOR TOWN AND COUNTRY.   1/6

> Twenty-two tales and sketches, by R. Chambers, LL.D., and other writers.

HOME-NURSING. By RACHEL A. NEUMAN.   1/6

> A work intended to help the inexperienced and those who in a sudden emergency are called upon to do the work of home-nursing.

Price 1s.

COOKERY FOR YOUNG HOUSEWIVES. By ANNIE M. GRIGGS. 1/

> A book of practical utility, showing how tasteful and nutritious dishes may be prepared at little expense.

W. & R. Chambers, Limited, London and Edinburgh.

NEW SERIES OF CHAMBERS'S LIBRARY FOR YOUNG PEOPLE.

Illustrated.

Price 1s.

QUEEN VICTORIA; the Story of her Life and Reign. 1/

GENERAL GORDON AND LORD DUNDONALD; the Story of Two Heroic Lives. 1/

LIVINGSTONE AND STANLEY; the Story of the opening up of the Dark Continent. 1/

COLUMBUS AND COOK; the Story of their Lives, Voyages, and Discoveries. 1/

THE STORY OF THE LIFE OF SIR WALTER SCOTT. By ROBERT CHAMBERS, LL.D. Revised with additions, including the AUTO-BIOGRAPHY. 1/

Besides the AUTOBIOGRAPHY, many interesting and characteristic anecdotes of the boyhood of Scott, which challenge the attention of the young reader, have been added; while the whole has been revised and brought up to date.

THE STORY OF HOWARD AND OBERLIN. 1/

The book is equally divided between the lives of Howard the prison reformer, and Oberlin the pastor and philanthropist, who worked such a wonderful reformation amongst the dwellers in a valley of the Vosges Mountains.

THE STORY OF NAPOLEON BONAPARTE. 1/

A brief and graphic life of the first Napoleon, set in a history of his own times: the battle of Waterloo, as of special interest to English readers, being pretty fully narrated.

W. & R. Chambers, Limited, London and Edinburgh.

BABY JOHN. By the author of *Laddie, Tip Cat, Rose and Lavender*, &c.   With Frontispiece by H. A. Bone.   1/

> 'Told with quite an unusual amount of pathos.'—*Spectator.*
>
> 'A beautifully pathetic and touching story, full of human nature and genuine feeling.'—*School Board Chronicle.*

THE GREEN CASKET; LEO'S POST-OFFICE; BRAVE LITTLE DENIS. By Mrs MOLESWORTH.   1/

> Three charming stories by the author of the *Cuckoo Clock*, each teaching an important moral lesson.

THE STORY OF WATT AND STEPHENSON.   1/

> 'As a gift-book for boys this is simply first-rate.'—*Schoolmaster.*
>
> 'A concise and well-written account of the labours of these inventors.'—*Glasgow Herald.*
>
> 'An excellent book to put into the hands of a boy.'—*Spectator.*

THE STORY OF NELSON AND WELLINGTON.   1/

> 'This book is cheap, artistic, and instructive. It should be in the library of every home and school.'—*Schoolmaster.*

JOHN'S ADVENTURES: a Tale of Old England. By THOMAS MILLER, author of *Boy's Country Book*, &c.   1/

THE BEWITCHED LAMP. By Mrs MOLESWORTH.   With Frontispiece by Robert Barnes.   1/

> 'Mrs Molesworth has written many charming stories for children, but nothing better, we think, than the above little volume.'—*Newcastle Chronicle.*

ERNEST'S GOLDEN THREAD.   1/

> 'The story of a very little boy who tries to do right under trying circumstances. . . . The moral of the tale is excellent, and little boys and girls will follow Ernest's trials and struggles with interest.'—*School Guardian.*

LITTLE MARY, and other Stories.   By L. T. MEADE.   1/

THE LITTLE KNIGHT. By EDITH C. KENYON.   1/

> 'Has an admirable moral. . . . Natural, amusing, pathetic.'—*Manchester Guardian.*

W. & R. Chambers, Limited, London and Edinburgh.

WILFRID CLIFFORD, or The Little Knight Again.   By Edith C. Kenyon.   With Frontispiece by W. S. Stacey.   1/
> 'The author has certainly written nothing sprightlier or healthier.
> . . . Some of the incidents are exceptionally well told.'—*Spectator.*

ZOE.   By the author of *Tip Cat, Laddie,* &c.   1/
> 'A charming and touching study of child life.'—*Scotsman.*

UNCLE SAM'S MONEY-BOX.   By Mrs S. C. Hall.   1/

THEIR HAPPIEST CHRISTMAS.   By Edna Lyall, author of *Donovan,* &c.   1/
> 'It is said that the Queen thinks *Donovan* the best novel she ever read, and children will have good reason for saying that this little story of the way in which a brother and sister, whose mother was ill, spent a certain Christmas Day, is very delightful.'—*Western Morning News.*
> 'A delightful story for children, simple, interesting, and conveying a useful lesson.'—*School Board Chronicle.*

FIRESIDE AMUSEMENTS; a Book of Indoor Games.   1/
> 'A thoroughly useful work, which should be welcomed by all who have the organisation of children's parties.'—*Review of Reviews.*

THE STEADFAST GABRIEL; a Tale of Wichnor Wood.   By Mary Howitt.   1/

GRANDMAMMA'S POCKETS.   By Mrs S. C. Hall.   1/

THE SWAN'S EGG.   By Mrs S. C. Hall.   1/

MUTINY OF THE BOUNTY, AND LIFE OF A SAILOR BOY.   1/

PERSEVERANCE AND SUCCESS; the Life of William Hutton.   1/

DUTY AND AFFECTION, or the Drummer-boy.   1/
> A thrilling narrative of the wars of the first Napoleon.

STORY OF A LONG AND BUSY LIFE.   By W. Chambers, LL.D.   1/

W. & R. Chambers, Limited, London and Edinburgh.

POPULAR BIOGRAPHIES, 1s. each.

'Not less interesting than fiction.'—*School Board Chronicle.*

'Excellent popular biographies.'—*British Weekly.*

'Admirably written biographies.'—*Review of Reviews.*

'Present concisely and in a graphic manner the life-story of the celebrities mentioned. Much praise is due to the publishers for this very handy and useful series.'—*Bookseller.*

QUEEN VICTORIA; the Story of her Life and Reign.

GENERAL GORDON AND LORD DUNDONALD; the Story of Two Heroic Lives.

LIVINGSTONE AND STANLEY; the Story of the opening up of the Dark Continent.

COLUMBUS AND COOK; the Story of their Lives, Voyages, and Discoveries.

SIR WALTER SCOTT. By R. Chambers. Including Scott's Autobiography.

NAPOLEON BONAPARTE. **WATT AND STEPHENSON.**

HOWARD AND OBERLIN. **NELSON AND WELLINGTON.**

Price 9d.

Cloth, Illustrated.

CLEVER BOYS.

THE LITTLE ROBINSON.

MIDSUMMER HOLIDAY.

MY BIRTHDAY BOOK.

ALICE ERROL, and other Tales.

THE WHISPERER. By Mrs S. C. Hall.

TRUE HEROISM, and other Stories.

PICCIOLA, and other Tales.

W. & R. Chambers, Limited, London and Edinburgh.

Price 6d.

Cloth, with Illustrations.

'For good literature at a cheap rate, commend us to a little series published by W. & R. Chambers, which consists of a number of readable stories by good writers.'—*Review of Reviews.*

'One contains three little stories from the pen of Mrs Molesworth, one of the most charming of writers for the little ones; and the name of L. T. Meade is a guarantee of good reading of a kind which children are sure to enjoy.'—*School Board Chronicle.*

GERALD AND DOT. By Mrs FAIRBAIRN.

KITTY AND HARRY. By EMMA GELLIBRAND, author of *J. Cole.*

DICKORY DOCK. By L. T. MEADE, author of *Scamp and I,* &c.

FRED STAMFORD'S START IN LIFE. By Mrs FAIRBAIRN.

NESTA; or Fragments of a Little Life. By Mrs MOLESWORTH, author of *Tell me a Story, Carrots,* &c.

NIGHT-HAWKS. By the Hon. EVA KNATCHBULL-HUGESSEN.

A FARTHINGFUL. By L. T. MEADE.

POOR MISS CAROLINA. By L. T. MEADE.

THE GOLDEN LADY. By L. T. MEADE.

MALCOLM AND DORIS; or, Learning to Help. By DAVINA WATERSON.

WILLIE NICHOLLS; or, False Shame and True Shame.

SELF-DENIAL. By Miss EDGEWORTH.

W. & R. Chambers, Limited, London and Edinburgh.

PICTORIAL BIBLE. With Numerous Notes by JOHN KITTO, D.D., F.S.A. It also contains Notes regarding the Discoveries of Mr Layard and others. Illustrated with Steel Engravings, Wood-cuts, and Maps.

4 Volumes, royal 8vo, cloth	£1 10	0
" " half-calf, antique	2 5	0
" " morocco, gilt edges	3 6	0

BOOK OF DAYS: A Repertory of Popular Antiquities, Folklore, Anniversary Days of Notable Events, Curious Fugitive and Inedited Pieces, and other Curiosities of Literature. Elaborately illustrated with Engravings. Edited by ROBERT CHAMBERS, LL.D.

2 Volumes, imperial 8vo, cloth	£1 1	0
" " half-calf	1 10	0

CYCLOPÆDIA OF ENGLISH LITERATURE: being a History, Critical and Biographical, of British Authors, from the Earliest. to the Present Times; with Specimens of their Writings. Edited by ROBERT CHAMBERS, LL.D. Fourth Edition, revised by ROBERT CARRUTHERS, LL.D. Illustrated with Portraits.

2 Volumes, royal 8vo, cloth	£1 0	0
" " half-calf	1 7	0
17 Parts, at 1s. each	0 17	0

INFORMATION FOR THE PEOPLE. Containing Treatises on Science, Philosophy, History, Geography, Literature, and all the more important departments of general knowledge. Illustrated by Wood-engravings.

2 Volumes, royal 8vo, cloth	£0 16	0
" " half-calf	1 3	0
104 Nos. at 1½d. each	0 13	0

SHAKESPEARE'S WORKS—CHAMBERS'S HOUSEHOLD EDITION. Purged of impurities and objectionable phrases; with Introductions and Notes.

10 Volumes, post 8vo, cloth	£1 10	0

LIFE AND WORKS OF BURNS. Edited by ROBERT CHAMBERS, LL.D. New and cheaper edition in 2 vols., demy 8vo. **10/6**

'Has a value of its own which nothing can supersede, and must ever retain its place among standard books on the life and works of our national poet. In this issue the original four volumes are bound in two. They are handsome and in every respect admirably got up.' .—*Scotsman.*

ST GILES', EDINBURGH: CHURCH, COLLEGE, AND CATHEDRAL. By J. CAMERON LEES, D.D., LL.D., Minister of St Giles'. In One Volume, demy quarto, Roxburghe binding. **25/**

With three original Drawings by GEORGE REID, R.S.A., etched and printed by AMAND-DURAND, Paris; steel plate of the exterior of the Church in 1790; plans of the interior at various periods; an engraving from a Drawing by Sir W. FETTES-DOUGLAS, P.R.S.A.; and another by Sir NOEL PATON, R.S.A., specially designed for this work; and numerous other Illustrations.

PAPERS FOR THE PEOPLE. This series embraces History, Archæology, Biography, Science, the Industrial and Fine Arts, the leading topics in Social Economy, together with Criticism, Fiction, Personal Narrative, and other branches of Literature— each number containing a distinct subject.

 12 Volumes, crown 8vo, boards...18/ •
  6 "   "   cloth...18/
 96 Nos..each 1½d.

ETYMOLOGICAL DICTIONARY of the English Language, containing Etymology, Pronunciation, and Meanings: Etymology of Names of Places; Words and Phrases from the Latin, the Greek, and Modern Foreign Languages; Abbreviations; List of Mythological and Classical Names. 1 vol. crown 8vo, cloth. **3/6**

 Roan, 4/; half-calf, 5/6; half-morocco, 6/.

W. & R. Chambers, Limited, London and Edinburgh.

In Crown 8vo, Cloth, price 6s.

CHAMBERS'S
CONCISE GAZETTEER

OF

THE WORLD.

TOPOGRAPHICAL, STATISTICAL, HISTORICAL.

With **pronunciation** of the more difficult Names of Places, numerous Etymologies, and information regarding the Derivations of Names.

1832—1894.

CHAMBERS'S JOURNAL,

THE PIONEER OF CHEAP LITERATURE,

Has long been recognised as the Best Family Magazine.

Each Monthly Part contains an interesting story of some length, complete; several short stories and papers by eminent writers, with articles on modern travel, popular science, and other topics of current interest.

Price 7d. or 8d. Monthly.
Annual Subscription, 7s. 5d., or by Post, 9s. 1d.

Edinburgh:
Printed by W. & R. Chambers, Limited.